THE FAE KINGS' BARGAIN

WILLOW MCCAIN

Copyright © 2022 by Bethany Adams

ISBN 978-1-953171-11-5

All rights reserved.

No part of this book may be reproduced in any form or by any electronic or mechanical means, including information storage and retrieval systems, without written permission from the author, except for the use of brief quotations in a book review.

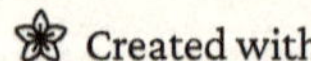 Created with Vellum

AUTHOR'S NOTE

The Fae Kings' Bargain was born as a serial published on Amazon's new Vella platform. This compilation isn't vastly different, only cleaning up a few typos and such. But I am excited to finally bring it all together here.

The sequel is currently in progress on Vella as a season 2, but this is a complete book with its own ending. Don't worry, though. Season 2 will make its way here as an ebook when the season is done.

For any updates, be sure to follow me on Facebook @authorwillowmccain. I also post under my main pen name, Bethany Adams (@writerbethany), but I try to keep the two separate.

CHAPTER 1

THE SUMMONS

Ria paused outside the workroom and sucked in a few deep breaths. Her father's terse shout boded ill, but she didn't dare spend time pondering how she'd angered him again. He could be upset about literally anything. So instead of scouring her memories for any possible misdeed, she shoved her shoulders back, lifted her chin, and pushed through the door.

The large, open workroom was much as she'd left it. One wall held shelves crammed full of rolls of fabric and baskets of adornments, and a few ready-made dresses stood on their displays along the other side. But the center...that was controlled chaos. Long tables held fabric in various stages of cutting and piecing, and dress forms full of partially completed projects were scattered around the center.

Her father, of course, still sat at his table on the far end.

Weaving her way around a dress form draped in fabric worth more than her life and then between a series of carts holding yet more cloth, Ria reached the spot where her father created his sought-after patterns—or something resembling. They wouldn't be complete until she added her own touch.

Not that he would admit it.

Ria stopped again and cast her gaze down so she wouldn't accidentally catch her father's eyes when he glanced up.

His cold, hard voice washed over her. "You are late."

"Please forgive me," Ria said, careful to keep her tone pitched low. "I did not realize I had taken overlong with my luncheon."

"It is just as well." Cloth rustled, and her father's wooden stool scraped against the floor. "I doubt you were fit to be seen by the kings' messenger."

Her eyes widened. "The kings?"

"I did not misspeak." Her father's hand cracked loudly against the table, and she flinched. "Pay attention. High King Toren and King Mehl have commissioned a new set of clothing in anticipation of their coming breeding alliance."

Ria almost opened her mouth to ask what breeding alliance, but she wouldn't escape a blow if she made the mistake of questioning him again. Even if it was a valid point. Kings Toren and Mehl had wed decades ago, but they would still need to produce an heir—and soon. Rumor had it that High King Toren's brother intended to challenge him to the throne within the next couple of years if he didn't. There'd also been talk of them searching for a woman to bear them a child, but no announcement had occurred.

Perhaps it was a secret?

"Although I dislike the thought of allowing you near such important clients, your gift works best if you see the people who will wear the designs. That means you'll need to make yourself presentable enough to accompany me to the palace."

Sick dread twisted in her stomach. If she'd thought her father was beastly in the workshop on an average day, he would be endlessly worse if she made a mistake in such an important setting. But what choice did she have? If she openly set out on her own, he would only drag her back, and if he couldn't, he'd see her killed. He would never let the world know how much he relied upon her gift.

"Of course, Father."

She swallowed down her fear. Kings or no, this would be just another job to complete. Ria almost had enough money hidden to pay for a true escape, and she couldn't let herself be distracted from that goal. Once her death had been faked, she would be free. Maybe someday, she would even have a child her father couldn't threaten to take.

A few more commissions, and she was done.

TOREN GLARED out at the city spread below, although his ire had no true focus. Not an external one, in any case. This fury was borne of tradition. Of helplessness. Of feeling bound. If not for the threat of his brother, he could have solved the latter two by shucking the first. Unfortunately, Toren didn't have it in him to resign his people to misery for his own comfort.

Their people had cheered at Toren's and Mehl's wedding nearly a century before, and they had ruled well together since. Why did tradition demand an heir from the reigning monarchs within that first century? Toren had ascended the throne young, and he and his husband would rule for millennia more.

Barring war or assassination, of course. Not even fae lives were guaranteed.

Arms wrapped around his waist and tugged, and Toren let himself lean on Mehl's strength for a moment. The tradition was unfair—enough so that it had largely been ignored for generations. His own parents hadn't had him until three hundred years after their marriage, yet his uncle hadn't thought to demand the throne based on an ancient ideal.

Mehl's breath whispered across his ear a moment before he nipped. "Stop worrying."

"I cannot abide this," Toren grumbled.

"You bedded women before we committed. We've even done so together a time or two." Mehl shifted impatiently against his back. "Surely, we can manage now."

Toren tugged himself free and spun to face his husband. "Before we swore at our wedding to stay true."

"I didn't think about that." Mehl frowned. "But considering the wording… If we find a woman we can agree on, we have broken no trust between us. The laws do not require you to marry her. So long as she does not expect commitment…"

"A foreign princess or local noblewoman certainly would." Toren ground his teeth together at the thought of all the women he'd considered over the past month. "I cannot believe my brother is insisting on upholding this. We only have a handful of years."

And therein lay the reason for next week's announcement. Toren hadn't quietly found someone willing to enter a breeding alliance—not anyone he would trust, at any rate—so he would begin to search beyond the courtiers and nobility. It was foolhardy to throw that intention out there, but his brother's missive made action imperative. Ber would return within the year to issue a formal challenge.

The bastard couldn't even wait for the full century to pass.

"Have faith, my love," Mehl said softly, taking hold of his hand. "We'll find someone."

Dread curled through Toren all the same.

RIA TRAILED her father through the marketplace lining the main road up to the palace. Here, the wealthy nobles sent their servants to buy luxury goods, but she and her father were well known among the cloth and dye vendors, too. Where else would they acquire what they needed to outfit the elite clients her father sought?

When they neared the outer stall in front of the dye merchant's shop, Enry caught sight of her and waved her over. Ria's breath hitched. Had he finally found it? She sped up until she walked near her father's left hand, though she was careful not to get ahead.

"Pardon me, Father," Ria said, careful to stifle any hint of excitement. "But I believe Enry wishes to speak to you."

Her father scowled. "We are needed at the palace."

Drat. If he refused to stop, she would have to find a way to sneak back by, and then her father might think she'd found a new lover. That would never do. He grew even more obsessive about her if he believed she might bear a child he could abuse.

"Of course, you are correct. I only wondered if he'd found that royal green dye you wanted. If so, I'm certain he would hold it for you until later."

"That would be a benefit for this appointment," her father mused softly. Then his ill-humor dropped, replaced by the fake affability he used in public to mask his perfidy. "Come, now, Ria. We may take a moment's pause."

His loud, cheerful announcement wasn't intended for her, and they both knew it. But far too many of those around them had no clue. "As you say."

Any observers might have thought she'd been trying to talk him out of the stop, but she had long ago learned that others' perceptions made no difference to her life. They saw what they wanted, and what they never *wanted* to do was help. Even if they'd noticed how cruel her father could be, they never would have confronted him on her behalf. They were too busy convincing themselves that they must be mistaken.

What wealth didn't hide, it suppressed or erased.

Ria was taking enough of a chance trusting Enry, and even he didn't know the full extent of it. Thankfully, the glance he gave her held no hint of the mission he'd undertaken. He greeted her father normally and did his best not to give her special attention.

"We've been summoned to the palace, boy," her father said, his voice ringing proudly around them. "So I must keep this brief. Did you find what I requested?"

Enry inclined his head. "I did, Sir."

"Good. Give the parcel to my daughter, then, and send the bill to my workshop."

Normally, she would have paid upon receipt for such a costly dye, but Enry ducked into the shop to retrieve the packet without argument. Was it because of the mission? Gods, she hoped so. It would be magnificent if he delivered her freedom right in front of her father without him realizing.

Enry rushed back through the door, every inch the earnest apprentice. Her father called him a boy, but Enry was twenty-five, only a year older than she was. It wouldn't be long before he'd learned enough to set out on his own or at least manage a different shop beneath his mother's supervision.

"Here you are, Ria," Enry said politely as he handed over a small waxed-paper bundle. "There should be ample for your needs."

Her heart slammed in her chest. That was the code they'd developed between them. He'd truly done it.

"Thank you," she answered. Ria tucked the bundle into her basket and hoped her father didn't notice how her hands trembled. "Your service is well-timed."

"You are welcome."

Enry gave her the briefest smile before turning away. Almost as soon as he had, her father grabbed her elbow in a firm grip just short of painful and directed her back to the path. His pleasant expression didn't slip, but when he spoke, his voice was low and brutal.

"I warned you I would not allow you to wed. Do not think to defy me with Enry. Lovers only, and not with customers or clients."

"I have no romantic feelings or intentions toward Enry," Ria said. Quiet earnestly, since it was the truth. Her defiance had nothing to do with marriage. "I promise. A hint of familiarity earns us more dye for our coin, but I would never give him cause to consider courting."

His hold loosened. "Just remember that you and any children you might bear belong to me. It is the least I deserve after marrying your mother for your sake."

"Naturally."

Ria's throat constricted until she knew she wouldn't be able to get another word out, but her father was done talking anyway. He wouldn't risk being overheard as they eased into the wealthier crowd heading up toward the inner palace. If they knew she had human blood from her mother's side, her father could lose business.

Not that the fae nobles were as pure as they claimed. Human lovers were more likely to produce offspring, so no small number of desperate lords or ladies sought out mixed children from amongst the minor nobility or wealthier merchant classes. The sin wasn't in the doing—it was in the revealing. Even high-placed nobles who *knew* they had human blood would refuse to do business with someone open about it.

Her basket grew heavy on her arm as they passed through two sets of gates and around to the keep's secondary entrance.

Though her father stiffened at being directed through here instead of the main doors, he didn't dare argue. He hadn't been sent to the servants' entrance, so he had to know better than to claim a slight.

He would no doubt save his temper for her later.

That thought weighed down her feet as they passed through elaborate hallways and up finely carved stairs. A few times, her steps began to slow, but she was fairly certain she caught herself before her father noticed. He'd already criticized the fine dress she'd donned and the simple braid of her long brown hair. No need to give him anything else.

Finally, a guard led them to a carved and embossed door, and the import of who she was about to meet truly hit her. The kings of the realm. High King Toren and his husband, King Mehl. She'd created clothing for a few amongst the nobility, but never royalty. Either of these men could send her to the dungeon with the slightest gesture.

Stop it, Ria. Do not *think of that.*

Before she had time to agree or argue with her mental admonishment, the door opened, and a servant gestured them inside. Ria drew the basket tight against her belly and followed her father across the threshold. Magic tingled around her, and the servant stiffened to attention beside her.

Then she could see nothing but the two men standing tall in the center of a massive sitting room. Gods above. She'd had cause to wave at the kings as they'd paraded by during festivals, but she had never been close. From afar, they hadn't seemed as handsome as legend claimed, but not even the ballads were near the truth. Not even close.

One had lustrous, silver-white hair that curled lovingly around a sculpted form draped in nothing but a dressing robe. Ria didn't dare look long enough to discern the color of his eyes, but his high cheekbones and firm jaw must have been created by the gods. Same for the man beside him, though his hair was as black as obsidian dye, and his shoulders were wider, more like a soldier's.

Ria must have curtsied when her father bowed, but she honestly couldn't have said. She was too busy trying to figure out the proper place to rest her eyes. One king's robe had parted enough that she could count the ridges of muscles leading down to—

A sudden, painful pinch on her shoulder interrupted her thoughts, and before she could process what was happening, someone shoved her to her knees. And it wasn't her father. He was still in front of her, just now turning to see the source of the commotion—which was apparently her.

"We have an assassin, Your Majesties."

Ria peered up at the servant pinching her shoulder, the same man who'd welcomed them at the door. "An assassin?"

The servant didn't even look down.

"Explain, Feref," one of the kings snapped.

"Forgive me, Your Majesty, but the spell detected poison," Feref said, his fingers digging harder into her flesh. "And this woman carries it."

CHAPTER 2

AT THE KINGS' FEET

Mehl locked his gaze on the woman trembling at Feref's feet. In appearance, she looked nothing like an assassin—which was, of course, the point. She wore a fine gown in a fabric and style favored by the more prosperous merchant class, and her light brown hair was deftly braided into a simple but acceptable style. The type of basket she carried could be seen all through the castle and surrounding villages. Furthermore, she had spoken to Feref in apparent surprise.

Also typical of assassin and innocent both.

But Mehl had protected Toren long before they'd fallen in love, and he had seen more than a few ill-intentioned people over the last couple of centuries. He would swear she wasn't one of them. It was in the way that awareness had crept across her face after Feref had shoved her down, a shift from neutral, to shock, and finally to a fear that was difficult to feign.

Belak, the tailor she'd accompanied, had spun to stare at her, and no small part of the woman's terror seemed directed at him as much as Feref, the guards, or even Mehl and Toren. Was she the man's wife? Mehl narrowed his gaze on her face. No, he didn't think so. She shared Belak's coloring, and there was a similarity around their eyes that suggested a familial connection.

"Explain yourself, Ria," Belak demanded.

Toren's arm stiffened against Mehl's. "Do not forget your place. It is for I or King Mehl to question here."

Mehl almost smiled, both at Toren's adherence to formality while standing in his dressing robe and Belak's splotchy, stricken face as he turned to bow to his kings. The man's eyes, though. There was calculation there. He might appear contrite, but he would exert control as soon as he could.

"Address my servant's claim," Toren said, and the woman flinched as though he'd hit her.

That reaction erased Mehl's humor. Never in their reign had he or Toren struck one of their subjects, barring self-defense. Was their reputation more wretched than they knew, or did she have something to hide?

"Your Majesty, I don't..." Her eyes went wide. "The dye! Our supplier gave us a bundle of royal green on the way here, and that could be to blame. Some of the herbs used are no doubt caustic. Perhaps the spell detected that?"

The woman's hands trembled as she opened the lid of the basket, and Mehl itched to grab the sword he no longer carried. As it was, he couldn't stop himself from stepping in front of Toren, who huffed out an impatient breath and pushed at his lower back. But only when the guards had rushed forward did he allow himself to return to Toren's side.

Toren shot him a telling look—*You are not my bodyguard*—and Mehl gave a quick, unrepentant grin in answer.

In the center of the room, the woman withdrew a bundle of

waxed paper, and only then did she take in the guards who had advanced with swords drawn. She froze, her hand wavering like a water-drenched leaf beneath her burden.

"I'm sorry," she said carefully. "I suppose I should have had your servant take this from the basket."

"Open the bundle," Toren ordered.

She bit her lower lip, and Mehl's body gave an unexpected twinge of interest. Frowning, he shoved the reaction down deep and focused on the paper in her hand. She was beautiful, but she might be deadly. He knew all too well the cost of distraction.

Finally, the woman gathered the courage to unwrap the bundle, and the lump of greenish-black seemed to confirm her claim. At least as far as Mehl knew. He'd never had cause to use any kind of dye, so his knowledge here was terribly lacking. Toren's probably was, too, if his frustrated sigh was anything to go by.

"Feref," Mehl said, drawing the attention that had mostly been reserved for Toren. "Are you familiar with such things?"

Feref inclined his head. "A little, Your Majesty."

"Is that dye as she claims?"

"It appears to be so," the servant answered. "But I would need to examine it more closely. I can at least see if this is what triggered the warning spell."

As usual, Toren took charge once more. "Do so. And have her walk through without it."

Mehl held back a sigh. A simple request for clothing had turned into a farce. He'd told Toren this extra step was unnecessary, but of course, his husband had wanted to make a statement. As if a new bit of fabric would prove their intent. Now poor Feref carried the paper bundle through with his arm extended, no doubt worried about what it contained.

What a mess.

~

TOREN KEPT his eyes trained on the woman as a guard nudged her through the door behind Feref. At first, he'd been furious at her deception, but deliberation had soon taken over. Nothing about her spoke of treachery. Fear and honest pride, perhaps, but not deceit. And he'd be willing to bet Mehl had come to the same conclusion, or he never would have stepped aside when she'd drawn out her bundle.

They'd been married nearly a century, but Mehl still guarded him the same.

He leaned close to Mehl. "Thoughts?"

"Innocent," Mehl answered, his voice too low for the others to hear. "Though something about the tailor..."

Toren had to agree. If he'd known anything about Belak beyond the quality of his designs, he never would have commissioned the man. Belak tried hard to hide his fury, but the knuckles of his clenched hands were white, and the looks he darted toward the doorway were far from concerned. Curious, since rumor had it the woman was his daughter.

Ria. That was what he'd called her. There was something curious about Ria, too, and it wasn't her current situation. She was beautiful in a way that stole his breath, and the way her father had snapped out her name had sparked Toren's own anger. It made no sense, but it was different enough that he might risk unfurling a piece of his magic to test her. That had been hard enough on Mehl, a warrior. What might it do to a young tailor's apprentice?

His curiosity would have to remain unappeased.

"You're frowning," Mehl murmured.

"A common enough complaint."

Mehl snickered, but the woman reentered before either could speak again. Toren wasn't attuned to the spell on the door—his gift would overwhelm it—but Mehl showed no reaction, at least not until Feref entered with the bundle. And the castle healer.

"She is clear of poison, but this isn't," Feref announced. "Forgive me for taking the liberty, Your Majesties, but I thought you might want this analyzed quickly and so summoned the healer."

For the sake of efficiency, Toren bit down on his irritation at the breach in protocol. "Very well."

"Pardon me." Belak took a tiny step forward, bowing as though that would excuse his presumption. "Might I speak with my daughter, Your Majesties? I would like to see to her health during this shock."

Hah. It was more than obvious that the tailor cared little for his daughter's well-being, but Toren could think of no good reason to deny the request. Besides, observing the interaction could be...enlightening.

"You may do so while the healer works," Toren granted.

The man bowed and spun away, but it wasn't relief in his eyes.

It was calculation.

RIA FROZE at the king's words, and her attention locked on her father as he strode her way. His lips were pinched in a thin line, and his piercing gaze would have incinerated her on the spot if he'd been capable. Oh, she was going to hurt later. He wouldn't kill her, of course, but she would wish he had. If she were lucky, the kings wouldn't cancel their commission over this, since her father would need her skill for the task. That might save her some agony.

Belak gripped her upper arm and tugged her to the side of the room, as far from anyone else as he could get under the circumstances. He leaned close, his hand still on her arm as though offering comfort. But with his back to the others, he gave his fury free reign across the landscape of his face.

"What have you done?" he demanded in a low, terrible voice.

"Nothing," Ria answered, although she knew that was partly a lie. "You've been with me the whole time."

Belak's nostrils flared. "I knew there was something strange about your interaction with Enry. You planned this, didn't you?"

Her heart pounded hard in her ears, and her hands went cold. "No."

She had, of course, but not in the way he likely thought—which he confirmed with his next words.

"You let him bed you," her father snarled. "He was far too familiar with you. But if you think to see me imprisoned so you can be together, then I promise you will pay. And if he got you with child, they'll pay, too. You'll both be mine until you've repaid me the indignity of having a human-blooded child."

Ria sagged in his hold. How had her plan gone so awry? She hadn't considered a spell that could detect such small amounts of dangerous herbs when she'd taken the bundle from Enry. She should have risked a second trip. Now, all would be lost. At any moment, the healer would identify the herb Enry had included beneath the dye.

"I've found a small amount of *elek terin*, Your Majesties," the healer said, just in time to seal her doom. "It is not usually included with royal green dye, and there is not enough to cause death. Unconsciousness near to death, perhaps."

Her breath expelled in a rush, but the sound was buried beneath her father's harsh curse. "Was that for you or me?"

"I would never harm you or anyone," Ria said, well aware her words weren't a true answer.

"When we return home—"

"Silence."

The king didn't shout, but the word was delivered with such authority that even her father complied. Belak spun around to face the kings, his fingers digging into her arm until tears gathered in her eyes. Now, she could see High King Toren's hard expression as he pinned them both with a glare, and any hint of hope died.

Then again, if they didn't believe in her innocence, at least she would be imprisoned away from her father. Being stuck in an iron-barred cell sounded like a blessing compared to the beating she would receive at home. Even death would be better than centuries more of that.

Toren had heard every word of the foul man's diatribe, and it was all he could do to keep his power leashed. He wanted to rip Belak away from Ria with one quick flex of magic, but he resisted. This had to be handled the right way. No good would come of being hasty.

"I will give each of you permission to plead your case," Toren said, struggling to keep his tone even. "And I warn you not to offer me falsehoods."

Belak swung his daughter around until she was nearly in front of him, almost as though he meant to use her as a physical shield. "I believe Ria intended to use that herb to harm or kill me so she could leave with her lover."

Toren lifted an eyebrow. "There was not enough of the substance to kill. Do you have other evidence of this plot?"

"She and the dye merchant exchanged heated glances when the package was handed over, and their words were overly familiar." Belak's hold tightened, and the woman winced, prodding Toren's fury to new heights. "She would love nothing more than to ruin me."

"Need I remind you," Toren began smoothly, "That no one is required to serve another in this kingdom? Your daughter may take any lover she wishes, and she has no need of poison to leave if she so desires."

Belak hesitated, no doubt searching for some new lie to weave. Or perhaps he realized how much he had revealed— and to whom. "She owes me a debt that must be repaid."

At Toren's side, Mehl stirred. "Physical service to satisfy a debt is not allowed."

"She is willing." Belak turned a strange, angry-but-pleading look upon his daughter. "It is our tradition. Right, Ria?"

The woman in question went still, her gaze on Toren instead of her father. Fear radiated from her so strongly that Toren could feel it despite the grip he held on his power. What would she do? Belak gave her the slightest shake, and her eyes grew so wide and her breath heaved so harshly that he was certain she was about to give in.

Then abruptly, Ria jerked her arm free. "I have never been willing. He has threatened me with shame and ruin if I ever reveal the truth, but I no longer care. I was willing to feign death. At this point, I will accept actual death to escape him."

Satisfaction filled Toren at her courage, though he couldn't define why he cared that she'd stood up for herself. "And what is that truth?"

Her chin lifted, her expression going hard with pride. "My grandmother was part human, but my father didn't find out until my mother was pregnant with me. He married her instead of casting her out, but not out of generosity or love. She worked in his shop until her death, creating and augmenting his rudimentary designs until he was quite wealthy, and when I showed the same skill, he brought me into the shop, too."

"She was merely an assistant," Belak insisted. "As are you."

"You would have nothing but ill-conceived sketches without me," Ria said, though she kept her gaze directed at Toren's shoulder. "Your Majesties, please forgive the *elek terin*. I've had Enry searching for it for some time and gave no thought to the timing of his delivery. The authorities did not believe that my father had threatened me, but it is true. He swore that if I attempted to leave, he would hunt me down, and if I had children with the talent, he would take them, too. Pretending to be dead and then fleeing when I could was all I could think of."

Toren's magic trembled inside until he didn't dare to move, a clear reflection of the fury that also wanted to spill out. And it wasn't just the anger of a king who'd discovered that one of his subjects had essentially been held captive. This felt somehow personal. Ria had suffered this for years, and only a short walk away from the palace gates. It was unbearable.

"She is lying," Belak said, his voice going high with panic. "I have always treated her well."

Before Toren could form words, Ria fisted her skirts and tugged the fabric up. Mehl let out a choked sound as she extended her leg, but Toren wasn't sure if it was because of the motion itself or the mottled yellow-blue-black bruises marring her skin from the top of her knee to her hip. Then she held out her other leg, this one somehow worse.

"This is how my father has treated me," Ria said.

Toren's hands clenched from the force of the magic clamoring for freedom.

"Shield," he said, the command one only Mehl would fully understand.

But it had nothing to do with protection for himself.

No, this was to protect the others.

CHAPTER 3

THE TEST

Though High King Toren's expression had grown increasingly cold, Ria had forged ahead with her truth. But the look on his face when he snapped out a single word—shield—had her dropping her skirt in despair. He didn't believe her. No one ever did.

Any moment, the guards would—

Pain seared her skull as her father whipped her around by her hair. "I will not allow your wicked lies to ruin me."

For once, she didn't feel fear, not even from the relentless burn of her scalp. No, triumph rushed through her at the panic in his usually haughty blue eyes. His false lordly airs were gone now, weren't they? Despite his words, they both knew she'd already succeeded in destroying his carefully plotted world.

"Too late," she dared to say.

His other hand swung toward her face, and Ria braced for the impact. This time, it would be worth it. So worth it.

But another hand gripped her father's wrist, stopping the motion, and when she followed the arm to its owner, her heart slammed at the sight of King Mehl himself preventing the blow. Guards rushed up like useless ants to surround them, but the king didn't let go.

"Completing that action would be a deadly mistake," King Mehl said, so calmly he might have been discussing his preferred color for his new set of clothes.

Belak tugged against the king's hold.

It didn't work.

"If you do not release her hair, I will detach your hand from her at the wrist."

It took so long her father must have let go one finger at a time. But finally, the pain eased, and she let out a sigh of relief as the pressure on her scalp subsided. A relief that was short-lived. Something shoved hard against her shoulder, sending her hurtling forward until she slammed heavily against King Mehl.

Her breath left her in a rush with the impact, and fear clawed at her chest. She didn't have permission to touch the king. Had it looked like she'd attacked him? Ria stiffened, preparing for the cold bite of a sword through her body from one of the guards. *Any moment now.* Instead, King Mehl's arm curled around her, pulling her tightly to his side.

Ria dared a glance up in time to see the king release her father's arm, but it wasn't a victory for the wretched man. Two guards swarmed forward to detain Belak, and when he struggled, one of them cracked him over the head with the hilt of his blade. Before she'd processed what had happened, her father was bound at the king's feet.

"Take him to the dungeon," King Mehl commanded.

A few paces away, Feref's eyes narrowed on Ria. "And the woman, Your Majesty?"

"We will see to the woman," an imperious voice rang out behind her. "Leave us."

High King Toren. He'd been so still that she'd forgotten him for a moment, but she shouldn't have. Oh, she shouldn't have. He was renowned for his sometimes-harsh resolve.

And now it was settled on her.

MEHL HADN'T REACTED PHYSICALLY to anyone except his husband in so long that he was caught by surprise at the arousal surging through him. But he couldn't deny the effect of having the woman pressed up against his side. Though they were all in danger if Toren lost control, that didn't seem to matter to Mehl's semi-hard cock. Bad timing. He eased his arm from around her and made sure she was steady on her feet before stepping back.

As the door closed on the last guard, Ria sank to her knees, her head bowed. Mehl nearly groaned at the move. If she tipped her head back—

"Forgive me, Your Majesty," she said in a soft, fear-tinged voice. "I didn't intend to touch you without permission. My father shoved me."

"I know." Mehl swallowed, trying to ease the rough sound of his own voice. At least her fear cooled most of his ardor. "I am aware of that, Ria. I was not offended. I suggest, however, that you move to the other side of the room while I speak with High King Toren."

"Of course, Your Majesty."

Mehl had grown used to the honorific over the last century, but for some reason, he hated the sound of it from her lips. Not that he could tell her so without sounding like a fool. Instead, he reached out to grip her elbow, lending her support as she struggled to her feet. From her stifled wince, it was clear that the position had pained her injured legs, but the wide eyes she turned his way were more likely caused by his touch.

She stepped back and dipped her head. "Thank you, Your Majesty."

There was no telling what Toren intended to do about her, but Mehl had a sudden idea. Her father had claimed she had human blood, which would increase her fertility, and once her father had completed his punishment in the dungeon, she would need protection. Belak had even threatened to kidnap any children she produced. What child would be better guarded than the heir to the throne?

"Mehl," Toren whispered, startling Mehl guiltily from his thoughts.

At the sight of the stress on his husband's face, Mehl hurried over. "Can you contain it?" he asked quietly.

Toren slipped an arm around his waist and pulled him close. His voice was a bare whisper against Mehl's ear. "My body cries out to test her as I did you."

Mehl's eyes widened. "You want to marry her?"

"Not...I hadn't thought..." Toren's forehead rested against Mehl. "That doesn't have to be the end result. Something about her..."

"It made me hard to hold her against me," Mehl confessed. He never kept secrets from Toren, no matter how damning they were. "I was just thinking about her predicament. And ours. But a simple breeding alliance shouldn't require you to test her."

Toren's body trembled against his, and a tendril of power lashed at Mehl's shields. "If you disagree, send her away. Now."

Mehl glanced across the room at Ria, who did her best to avert her gaze. But she was watching them out of the corner of her eye. What must she think of them, ordering her to stay and then commanding her to the other side of the room? Few of the general populace knew of Toren's vast power. Would she accept it? Did he want her to?

"Decide. I can't…"

Abruptly, Ria looked up, and her eyes connected with his. The impact shocked him, and again, he went hard. Hell. Toren said she wouldn't be bound to marry him, though that had been a result of the testing Mehl had borne. But in that case, they'd already started their relationship after decades of Mehl acting as his bodyguard. They'd been close to discussing marriage already.

That needn't be so now. She wouldn't be chained to them, and the testing would reveal if she'd told the truth. Maybe—

"Mehl…"

"Fine," Mehl said. "But if she can't bear it, then what?"

"Then pull me away and call for the guards to carry her to safety," Toren rasped.

This might not be a good idea, but Mehl trusted Toren. There had to be a reason he was drawn to do this.

He would have to ensure she survived it.

RIA TRIED NOT to stare at the kings as they huddled against one another, but it was impossible. There was an intimacy between them that drew her, and her body burned at the sight of the High King nuzzling his face against King Mehl. She knew from experience how pleasant the latter's hold felt. Being tucked between both of them would be beyond compare.

Focus, she ordered herself. Her arousal didn't ease, but at least she was able to drag her gaze away from them. She should never have dared look in the first place. She was the part-human daughter of a tailor, not a fine lady or princess of a neighboring kingdom. They might need a breeding alliance, but she wouldn't even rank on an *If We're Desperate* list.

Movement caught her eye, but she tried not to glance at the kings again. Not that she had to. Energy surged toward her ahead of the advancing footsteps, a power so strong she caught her breath. It reminded her a little of the magic she used to create and add upon her father's designs, but the force of this was far different. Nearly crushing.

By the time his shadow surrounded her, her hair practically stood on end from the charge, but she didn't have to look to know that it was High King Toren. She'd noticed this very intensity growing around them since before the others had been dismissed. What was he going to do to her? Kill her where she stood? Cast her to some far-flung realm?

"Ria."

His raspy whisper had her lifting her head despite her best intentions, and her gaze collided with the pale blue-gray of his almost instantly. Oh, now she'd done it. She lowered her eyelids, but his hand darted up to grip her chin. Gently, he tipped her head back until their eyes met once more.

"I am not a god to require such subservience," High King Toren said softly. "You won't be stricken down for a mere glance."

Despite his reassurance, she wasn't so sure. Not with the mad power trembling in his hand. "Yes, Your Majesty."

His lips turned down in displeasure. "I must test you with my magic."

Ria had no clue if he was upset with her response or what he had to do, but she didn't feel confident enough to ask. There were more important things to discern. "Will it clear me of suspicion?"

"Yes. If you are innocent." His hand trembled harder

against her chin, and her skin tingled as his magic licked against her. He was losing control. "Can't... Must..."

King Mehl stepped to Toren's side. "I will see that you are safe, Lady Ria."

She opened her mouth to refute the title, but before she could utter a sound, the High King's power roared through her. Instantly, her vision went white as though she'd been sunblinded, and her muscles convulsed from the shock. Her legs went soft beneath her. She might have fallen if not for the strong arms that wrapped around her waist.

But there wasn't any pain. Gods, no. Anything but. Her body burned with pleasure, and hope, and life, and light. Her magic rose within her chest and poured into her hands until she was sure she could have created an entire wardrobe for the spoiled prince of Tenzick with little more than a wave.

Then the connection deepened—or perhaps became clearer. She brushed against something else, something beyond power. It was him. Them? A few thoughts flickered. A man's image, cruel and sneering. A hint of worry and fear. Protectiveness. She reached out without thought, her intent to soothe.

Then the power cut off, so abruptly she wanted to weep at the loss.

Her vision cleared, and her surroundings reformed around her. Ria stared at her hand against the High King's chest for a moment before she abruptly jerked away. But that only made her aware of the hard body at her back, the support that could only be King Mehl.

"I'm sorry," Ria gasped.

"She is innocent," High King Toren said through gritted teeth, his eyes on his husband rather than her. "There is much to talk about. Alone."

Ria straightened, and King Mehl let her go. "I didn't mean to touch you. My magic prompted me—"

"I am not angered by your actions." She wouldn't claim the High King relaxed, but some of his harshness smoothed. "And unlike your father, you are now free. You will be granted his business, properties, and other assets in return for the pain you have suffered."

"Toren..." King Mehl began, a strange note to his tone.

"I have decided. Unless you would like to argue now, husband dearest?"

"No," the king bit out. "But we will discuss this later."

High King Toren inclined his head. "As I have already suggested."

She should have been relieved that they were letting her go, but after the touch of his magic, a hard lump of sadness settled in her chest. Something had happened here that she couldn't explain. A connection in that soul-shaking moment. But they were the kings of Llyalia, and she was a tailor's daughter.

Although now Ria supposed *she* was the tailor.

Before she knew it, the High King summoned his servants, a couple of guards, and a scribe to record his decree. He even had the healer cure her injuries while he spoke to the scribe. Despite all he did, it felt like only moments before she was being ushered kindly but firmly from the palace and back to the home where she'd been raised. It was almost too much to process.

Ria dropped her newly returned basket beside the fireplace and sank down into a chair. She couldn't have said which one. Her mind was too busy racing through all that had happened that day.

Again and again.

CHAPTER 4

DESIRE AND INDECISION

The scribe rolled up the scroll and held it out. "Here you are, Your Majesty. The other copy will go to court for a formal announcement tomorrow."

After accepting the scroll, Toren gestured toward the door. "Thank you. That is all."

The man scampered toward the exit, but two guards and Feref remained at their places. Clearly, they had failed to read Toren's mood. Mehl hadn't—he'd already retreated to their bedroom. Toren barked out a terse order, and the others followed the scribe through the door.

Good. His control was near breaking.

Toren strode through the connecting door into their bedroom, only to find that perhaps Mehl hadn't read his mood after all. He wasn't reclining on the bed, ready to receive what Toren fought so hard not to have to give. Gods' blood. It would take hours—possibly days—to dispel this much energy without his husband's aid. Not even standard channeling would do in this case.

Mehl had to know the testing had ended too soon. Far too

soon to purge the energy scratching at his insides, searching for an intimate form of release. So why was his husband standing by the window, still in his dressing robe?

There could only be one reason.

"You're angry at me."

Mehl turned, his expression hard. "You should have listened to me instead of sending her home."

"I couldn't complete the testing without forcing far more than she would be willing to give," Toren snapped. "You want to be married to a stranger?"

Mehl marched over. "I didn't say you should have completed the testing. I said you shouldn't have sent her home. She belongs with us. I'd wondered before, but the way our magics blurred together..."

"I know. Gods, I know." Toren shoved his trembling fingers through his hair, and a shudder rippled through him as his energy surged to match his emotions. "I had to stop, or it might not have been undone. If any one of us had attempted to solidify the link, it would have been irrevocable."

"But to let her—"

"My control is thin." He grabbed Mehl's hand and pulled him close. "If you don't wish to help me temper it, leave now."

For a moment, he thought Mehl was going to do just that, but though his nostrils flared, he shook his head. "No argument would have me abandon you."

"I need rough."

"Then take it."

With a low growl, Toren walked Mehl back toward the bed. He didn't waste time on gentle caresses or heated kisses, but Mehl wouldn't expect him to. Instead, Toren ripped his husband's dressing robe off and tossed the shreds away. Then he gripped Mehl's cock and gave it one long stroke.

"Up on your knees."

Without a word of argument, Mehl climbed onto the bed, the lantern light gliding across the defined muscles of his shoulders and down to his perfect ass. There he waited, and that show of trust alone had Toren's desire rising almost painfully. Mehl was a powerful warrior, feared for centuries. He'd killed to protect Toren, yet he yielded that power now. But not out of subjugation. It was love.

Some of the tempest roaring through Toren eased, enough that he took extra time preparing his husband with the oil on their bedside table. Teasingly, he inserted one oiled finger. Then two. Mehl's back bowed, and he bit out a curse.

Toren smacked Mehl's ass with his free hand, just enough to redden the skin and startle another curse out of his love. "Watch your mouth in front of your king."

"I could...do other...things...with it," Mehl panted.

"Later."

After rubbing his cock with oil, Toren positioned himself behind Mehl and slid home. They both groaned at the pleasure, but Toren could only savor their connection for a heartbeat before his control finally snapped. With one hand, he gripped Mehl's hip, and the other tangled in Mehl's long, dark hair.

Then he began to move.

His hold on his magic disappeared, a fallen wall allowing everything through. Toren pumped almost mindlessly against Mehl as their energy merged, but it wasn't enough. They could never get close enough in body to match power and soul, though he tried.

Mehl's desperate cries intensified with each thrust, but he didn't try to take control. Perfect. Toren tugged at his hair until their eyes met over Mehl's shoulder. "You are mine."

"Forever." Mehl huffed. "No one...changes that."

"Good."

Power built with desire in Toren's head until he knew he would spend himself at any moment. He released his husband's hair, but only so he could reach around for Mehl's cock. As Toren's balls drew up, he gave several firm strokes, and with twin shouts, they both came.

And for the first time in days, his energy was calm.

MEHL SHIFTED himself deeper into the curve of Toren's arm and settled his hand against his husband's side. After the amount of power Toren had released through him, there was no way Mehl could sleep. But as his heartbeat slowed, he found his thoughts circling around to Toren's reaction. His husband was rarely so fierce without strong emotion behind it, and he'd developed enough control over his magic over the last century that he had to channel it through Mehl less and less often. Most times, it didn't actually require sex.

But Toren's tension had been increasing since they'd received that missive from Toren's brother. Ria's presence had clearly ignited it beyond all containing. Why did Toren seem reluctant to admit it? They'd shared women in the past without harm to their relationship, and he already knew he'd have to bed someone for an heir. Why was he so bothered by her?

"You're afraid," he concluded aloud.

Toren's muscles twitched beneath Mehl's cheek. "I have always been afraid. You know that."

"I'm not talking about the magic you must hold," Mehl argued. "Ria. You're afraid of what she could mean."

Toren surprised him by agreeing easily. "That is true. My goal in testing her was to determine whether she spoke the truth and to try to identify why she fascinated me. The answer to the first, I expected. But the second…"

"She wouldn't crumple beneath your power if you lost control with her." Mehl considered his next words carefully, but there was no good way to say it. Though if he found himself under Toren's mercy again, he *supposed* he could manage. "I know that's what's keeping you from selecting potential candidates. Ria would suit. Considering her father's threat, she might agree. He wouldn't dare try to kidnap a prince or princess."

Toren's breath ruffled his hair, but it seemed more exasperation than anger. "Have you forgotten I placed her father in the dungeon?"

"His crime is grave, but he can't be held there forever. And although your punishment was just, I worry that he will seek revenge," Mehl said.

"He will die for it," Toren replied coldly, and Mehl knew it was no idle threat. "See her guarded."

Mehl nodded against Toren's chest. "You know I will regardless. But you avoided the heart of what I said. Don't you think she would suit?"

The only sound that met his words was Toren's sharp huff of air.

"Tor." Mehl pushed himself upright until he could stare down into his husband's eyes. "It's rare for you to be evasive with me of all people. What is it?"

Toren's jaw clenched, and several tense moments passed before he would answer. "You are taken with her, and I will not lose you on top of this entire, miserable situation. I can fight my brother if need be. Without you, I would be nothing."

"I will be yours until my dying breath. That you know." Mehl brushed a lock of pale hair from Toren's cheek and bent to give him a soft kiss. Then he pinched him. "You are 'taken with her,' too, and that scares you. Admit it."

This time, Toren followed expectations and refused to concede. "A breeding contract must be a neutral agreement."

Mehl wanted to shake him. "A foolish idea if you hope for me to fuck the woman, and no child can be 'ours' otherwise. Think on that."

Toren fell silent, but Mehl didn't push the topic. He knew Toren too well for that. Instead, Mehl settled back down against his husband and closed his eyes with the possibly vain hope of getting sleep. He'd done what he could, and only leaving Toren to his thoughts would take the matter further.

It would be no good if Toren didn't agree, either.

RIA COULDN'T SLEEP. No matter how many times she reminded herself that her father was in the dungeon, far from able to do her harm, her body refused to acknowledge its safety. She'd lain in her bed for hours, startling with each creak and moan of the house. Each settling floorboard had been a footstep, each shake of the shutters a rap against the door.

Finally, she'd given up and started packing. The kings might have given her all of her father's property, but once he was free from his punishment, he would seek to reclaim it, decree or no. She would be better served to salvage at least part of her initial plan—starting a new life elsewhere.

Tomorrow, Ria would go before the kings to request an audience, hopefully a private one. She needed to know how long her father's punishment would be. Days, months, years? The longer he was in the dungeon, the longer she would have to sell off her newly acquired property before disappearing. If she was really lucky, the kings might offer to buy the lot from her and help her escape for good.

She had her most prized possessions in crates by dawn. Truth be told, there weren't many, and most of those were the few things she'd managed to save of her mother's. An antique dress, nearly a century out of fashion. A hand mirror and comb. A couple of journals.

Ria had only read one of the latter, the journal her mother had kept after Ria's birth. The other, her mother had warned, was best saved for a time when she was free of her father. Only once had curiosity tempted her to open that journal, and the harrowing account of an argument between her parents early in their marriage had convinced Ria that some things were better left unknown.

But she would keep it with her always.

Early morning light gilded the streets when Ria began the walk to the palace again. Many of the food shops were already busy, but the full crowds wouldn't be out for another hour or two when the rest of the stores opened. It was a relief in more ways than one, for there were fewer people who might offer a greeting. Like Enry. Thankfully, the dye merchant's shop was closed up tight.

Ria hurried her steps anyway lest Enry spot her through the window. He would want to know what had happened with the poison. Had she found it? When was she going to use it? But no matter how much she appreciated his help, she didn't want to talk about what had happened at the palace. Even she didn't know how to explain everything.

She walked between the open gates and did her best to blend with the nobles walking in small clusters along the path to the main entrance. Today, she'd donned a dress abandoned by a lady who'd decided she disliked the color, and she'd braided and pinned her hair up with a string of gemstones pilfered from their stock of dress trimmings.

No, Ria reminded herself. *My stock.*

It wasn't theft if it was hers, and she wouldn't claim to be a noble if the guards stopped her. But she hoped they wouldn't. The kings would hear court petitions this morning, so with any luck, she would blend in easily with the increased numbers entering the gates. It would be harder to notice differences amidst so many.

As Ria passed through the gardens and neared the inner gate, she increased her speed until she was behind a group of four ladies. They chattered on, not seeming to notice her presence, and Ria tipped her chin up proudly as they neared the guards. Though one of the two guards frowned at her, his concerns must not have been enough to stop her. In moments, she was through.

Ria followed her unwilling hosts all the way through the courtyard and into the palace receiving room, but she didn't dare stick too close here. They would notice her lingering for sure. In any case, the guards in this room appeared more bored than anything. Vigilant, of course, but not with the same intensity as those outside.

Now, she just had to see if she could make it into the throne room.

CHAPTER 5

INTO THE FIRE

Toren could barely focus on the inane stream of requests brought in endless procession. There was less than another hour of this, and then they would deliver any official pronouncements. Today, the decree concerning Belak would be read again for the court and a date set for the official hearing and final punishment. Mehl had suggested they summon Ria for the decree, but Toren had refused.

Both of them knew why.

He half-listened to a lordling's petty complaint about his neighbor's choice of garden flowers while his mind replayed Mehl's words from the night before. *She wouldn't crumple beneath your power if you lost control. You're taken with her, too, and that scares you. Admit it.* And it was true—all of it.

"If it pleases your majesties, I would like to request another color flower be planted to better harmonize with—"

"No," Toren interrupted, no longer able to listen to the foolish man. "Your neighbor is not obligated to match his garden to your preferred paint color, and you waste our time by coming to demand it."

The man's skin reddened all the way to the tip of his pointed ears. "I did not intend to do so, my king. I merely thought you might like our streets to be well-regarded in light of any alliance you might form."

Toren had to fight off the insane urge to toss his crown across the room and walk out, never to be seen again. He took a deep breath and reminded himself that he loved his people. Most of the time. Unfortunately, many of the courtiers who'd appeared this week had brought forth superficial problems, a poorly disguised attempt to bring noble ladies to his attention —or, like the current nobleman, to use Toren's need for a breeding alliance to further their own goals.

As usual, Mehl saved him. "No alliances can be formed with anyone who disapproves of our kingdom in all its variety."

"Yes, of course, Your Majesty," the lord mumbled, his disappointment palpable.

Not just because of the flowers, if Toren had to guess. The court had grown increasingly impatient for an announcement about a possible breeding alliance, either a contract signed or a search begun. He would have to find someone soon or suffer more coy flirtations and faux problems. There would no doubt be more of each, considering the line of supplicants lined up all the way to the door. With less than an hour left, getting through them all was beginning to seem impossible.

He listened to two more forgettable, pointless problems— missing hair ribbons and lost pets, truly?—before his thoughts began to drift again. Perhaps he and Mehl should consider a formal, public search for a woman willing to carry an heir, one that gave all citizens a chance. He stifled a snort. *Chance.* King or no, Toren would hardly be a blessing to be around, especially if he lost control.

Of course, he now had to find another tailor to create new ceremonial robes, one more bother he could have done without.

When the next courtier stepped away from the dais, Mehl leaned close. "What's wrong, love?"

"I can't..."

A commotion began at the throne room door as a woman's startled yelp sounded. Nobles shifted to see the cause, giving Toren a clear view. Beside the herald, a guard gripped a lady's arm—harshly, if he wasn't mistaken. Toren's brows lowered. He'd signaled a halt to new petitioners, not commanded harm to any who requested an audience.

Mehl's hand closed around Toren's. "Is that Ria?"

Toren found himself standing, and at the motion, the entire court lowered in a wave to their knees. It was the best thing they'd done all morning, for it provided no distractions for his regard. And he saw at once that Mehl was correct. The lady was dressed more elaborately than she had been the night before, almost like a courtier, but it was undeniably Ria.

"What is the meaning of this disturbance?" Toren snapped, his voice carrying like a whip across the crowd.

For the first time, the guard seemed to notice that Toren—and Mehl, apparently—had stood. He knelt at once, forcing Ria down with him until her knees cracked against the stone floor. At her whimper of pain, Toren's hands balled into fists. The guard would pay for that.

"She impersonates a lady, Your Majesty," the herald answered. "I ordered her removed."

"Does she, now?" Toren asked. Gods, this woman had poor luck. "Bring her forward. The rest of you may stand."

His temper slipped the slightest notch at the sight of the

guard jerking Ria to her feet and nudging her forward, but the brush of Mehl's hand brought Toren some measure of calm. Fortunately, Ria walked easily in front of the guard, earning no more harsh treatment. The strange protectiveness he felt for her wouldn't have withstood that.

When she reached the dais, Ria curtsied. Toren gestured for her to rise before pinning her with an impatient look. "Explain yourself."

Her cheeks went pink, but she didn't cower. "Pardon me, Your Majesties. I did not intend to cause a disturbance. I made no claim to nobility, but your herald thought I did with my clothing."

Toren could see the mistake. Her rich brown hair was braided and twined with expensive blue jewels, and her soft yellow gown fit in easily with the court style. "Is that so?"

"Yes." A hint of fear widened her eyes. "I give my word. These clothes are mine, granted with the rest of my father's assets. I only wished to dress well when I came to request a private audience."

Whispers and giggles echoed through the crowd, earning a frown from Toren that returned the room to silence. They thought her nothing but a foolish commoner, but the nobles gathered here knew nothing about what had happened the night before. None of those allowed in their private chambers would dare breathe a word.

"Is there some request that could not be made here?" Toren asked, unable to resist teasing her instead of granting her request for privacy. Not that anyone but Mehl would recognize it as teasing.

"I wanted..." Ria's shoulders slumped, and Toren regretted the impulse at once. "I wanted to know the length of my father's punishment. I need to make arrangements."

For some reason, that soft statement had dread pooling in Toren's gut. "For what?"

"To leave," Ria whispered. "Before…"

The memory of her bruises flickered through his mind, and her full meaning became clear. She wanted to run away before her father was released, and he'd forced her to confess it in front of the court. Gods' mingled blood. Why had he baited her instead of granting a private audience?

It was this blasted attraction, of course. Toren couldn't remove his gaze from her beautiful face, appealing despite the fear he abhorred. And not only because he'd amplified it. The thought of her in danger, afraid, calling for help—it scraped at his insides, threatening to shred his control. He already knew he would kill for Mehl. Now it seemed he might kill for her, too, and he didn't even know why.

He couldn't let her flee into the unknown, waiting for the day her father would hunt her.

"*Mehl,*" he whispered into his husband's mind.

"*Do it,*" Mehl answered, understanding at once.

"Curious," Toren said aloud. He stepped to the edge of the dais, and the crowd lowered to their knees once more. Thankfully, the guard had more sense than to drag Ria down again. "I thought perhaps you were here to discuss another arrangement. The breeding alliance."

RIA'S BREATH puffed out in surprise, the soft sound like thunder in the sudden quiet. Surely, she had misunderstood. Surely. But High King Toren stared down at her with a heated, almost possessive look in his eyes that suggested otherwise. King Mehl smiled slightly at her when she looked his way, a secret smile full of happiness. And maybe relief.

No. Absolutely impossible. She was the tailor's daughter.

That had to be it. Her father was no longer here to create the formal robes worn to celebrate a new breeding alliance, and the kings needed her help. These two perfect, powerful men didn't want anything else from her.

Just look at them.

The high king's pale hair fell, unbound, around a heavily embroidered, royal green robe that outlined his broad shoulders as lovingly as his dressing robe had the night before. His golden crown arrowed down across his brow like a circlet before rising to twine around his head in thousands of tiny, jeweled vines and flowers.

Beside him, King Mehl stood in equally gorgeous contrast, his robe a pale green and his silver crown designed to mimic the constellations. Each star a diamond. Part of his dark hair had been braided around the base of the crown, but it only served to highlight his sharp cheekbones and chiseled jaw.

They could have any woman—or man—in this room. Yes, she must have misunderstood.

"I see you are speechless," High King Toren drawled. "A rare event in this room today."

Ria gathered her resolve. She had no clue why he wanted to taunt her, but the sooner she escaped, the better. "I am uncertain I have properly interpreted your meaning."

Brows drawing down, High King Toren stepped from the dais until he was close enough to touch, and behind her, the gasps were practically forceful enough to blow her away. Unfortunately, she wasn't lucky enough to escape the king's regard that easily. He brushed his finger along her jaw to her chin and tilted her head up, holding her gaze to his.

At the contact, his voice rang in her mind. *"You understood well enough. Join with us and carry our heir."*

He couldn't be serious. *"I am a commoner with human blood.*

Last night, you thought I'd planned to kill you. If this is your revenge, it is a harsh one."

"No revenge." His lips thinned. *"Last night, you withstood my power. That is enough to prove your worth. As for your human blood, I find that is a boon. It will increase your fertility, and if I do not produce an heir within the next year or two, my brother will challenge me."*

Ria shuddered at that. His brother's ruthless cruelty was a barely concealed secret. *"But I am no one."*

Toren eased even closer. *"Yet you argue with me, your king."*

The growl in his mental voice should have alarmed her, but there was a sensual edge to it that had her heart pounding with something other than fear. He liked her defiance, though he must not realize it was more fear than bravado. Insecurity rather than confidence.

"I will not exist to serve your every desire," Ria found herself saying. *"Nor would I consider leaving my child to another to raise."*

Victory lit the harsh, cold lines of his beautiful face, and she knew at once she'd made a misstep. *"In such cases, the heir's mother is granted her own apartments in the palace, complete with a personal guard. You never need fear your father again."*

"You didn't address my first point."

"Neither I nor Mehl would touch an unwilling partner, but the purpose of this alliance is quite clear. We will spend much time abed." The finger beneath her chin shifted in a slight but somehow wicked caress. *"Afraid?"*

Ria jerked her chin upward, away from his touch. Now that they'd made mental contact, he didn't need physical. *"I am no virgin. Sex itself doesn't scare me."*

A slow smile crossed the high king's face, and she thought she might combust from the heat that speared through her. *"Then perhaps you will give us one night to convince you."*

CHAPTER 6
TWO KISSES

Mehl couldn't see Toren's face, but the expressions tracing across Ria's told a story all its own. Fear and desire were obvious—less so her curiosity. Yet even when she pulled her chin away, her body leaned toward Toren's. It was her insecurity that would cause the most trouble with convincing her to accept, but there was a spark in her eyes that promised great reward if they managed it.

Not by trickery or force, however. What she needed was truth.

"It seems the lady Ria has agreed to consider the arrangement," Toren announced aloud. "King Mehl, would you escort Lady Ria to the receiving room to begin discussions while I finish with court business?"

Mehl inclined his head, almost smiling at the quick, worried glance Toren cast his way before offering a shocked Ria his arm. It was a delicious scene, the way the nobles gaped at their High King leading a tailor's daughter onto the dais after naming her lady. There had been some dissatisfaction when Toren had married him, a bodyguard from a low-ranking noble house some hadn't even heard of. A mating alliance with a commoner? The whispers would go on for decades.

Well, it was time something shook up the complacent fae court. Better this than the vicious rule of Toren's brother.

Toren shifted Ria's hand to Mehl's arm in a smooth, practiced motion. *"Do not go too far in your convincing, not without me. No more than a kiss or a caress."*

Mehl's body stirred at the imperious command and the mental image it prompted, but he kept himself under control. *"I would not."*

"Good." Toren grimaced. *"Be gone before I regret this."*

Mehl took his husband at his word and swept Ria out the door behind their thrones as quickly as he could without causing a stir. Her fingers trembled against his arm, but she allowed him to lead her down a long corridor to the formal receiving room used for more confidential consultations. It was a neutral, rather impersonal spot, but private. Aside from the guard who stood outside the door in case of just such a meeting, there was no one to see them enter.

As soon as the door clicked closed behind them, Ria retrieved her hand and strode to the center of the room. "This is madness."

He smiled at the stiff line of her back and the lost wonder of her whispered comment. "Is it, my lady?"

Ria spun to face him. "I am not a lady. Not a titled one, at any rate."

"You are now," Mehl countered, his smile unwavering.

"That makes no sense." Her lips pinched together, and she lowered her gaze. "Your Majesty."

Mehl moved closer—but only a little. Too much haste would only scare her more. "Toren named you lady in front of the court, so you are. You'll have to ask him about the specifics of your new title, however. We haven't had a chance to discuss it."

"Did you discuss…" Her throat worked. "His offer? He didn't say much aloud. I can't imagine that Your Majesty would be pleased if you knew the full extent of it."

"Please drop the formality," Mehl said. The last thing he wanted to hear from her lips was another cold Your Majesty. "I was not born to the title and do not prefer it. Mehl alone will suffice."

Ria's brow creased. "That is your sole concern from my words?"

He risked another couple of steps closer until he could almost reach out and touch her. But unlike Toren, he wouldn't dare to do so. Mehl was well aware that he lacked his husband's mesmerizing pull. He was far more prepared to wait with endless patience like the bodyguard he'd once been—and always would be.

"Who do you think gave Toren the idea, Lady Ria?"

"I thought we were dropping titles," she retorted, her nostrils flaring.

His fingers itched to brush across her cheek. "I was the only one who gave leave to do so."

Ria huffed. "You have my leave, though it hardly matters. I'm still not sure you are correct about the title."

Silence rang through the large, nearly empty room as Mehl studied her. She stood as stiffly as the uncomfortable chairs lined up against the wall, her bearing as regal as the pair of thrones at the far end. But the way her fingers twisted in front of her waist revealed the nervous fear she was trying to contain.

"It is not my intention to scare you, nor is it Toren's."

"I know," Ria answered softly. "But all of this… It makes no sense. Everyone knows that High King Toren is seeking a breeding alliance, of course, but that is for the throne, not pleasure. I bring no prestige. No noble or royal bloodline. No riches, at least not compared to yours. The only benefit is to me in escaping my father for good."

His chest tightened at the true confusion filling her face. "Do you truly not realize we desire you?"

Her eyes went wide. "I... You've both implied such, but I don't understand. By all accounts, you've been committed to each other for a century. Not only is your preference for men, but any heir would have to be of the high king's bloodline. So—"

"You should know that since I am wed to Toren, your child together would also be mine." Mehl took another step forward. "And our preferences are not set the way you seem to believe. Toren and I have shared women before, though it was before we married. Rest assured that I'm more than capable of pleasuring you without getting you pregnant. You are correct that that would be Toren's job. Only afterward would we join."

She gasped, and with satisfaction, he noticed that her breathing went shallow. "Shared..."

"I've been given leave to test our compatibility," Mehl murmured.

"Here?" she asked, her voice going high as her worried gaze took in the room. "Now? You actually think I will—"

"Relax, Ria," Mehl interrupted with a chuckle. "Toren said I could have a single kiss and caress without him here, nothing more. With your permission, of course. Every alliance requires cooperation, and this one more than most."

Her shoulders went back. "Toren seems more inclined to take."

Mehl shrugged. "Only to a point. The mother of our child will be a rather permanent person in our lives even if there is no sexual relationship beyond conception. Neither of us is foolish enough to begin this with resentment."

"Then again that begs the question... Why me?" she asked.

What could he say to convince her? Because the truth was, he didn't have a clear reason. On the surface, everything she said was true. It wasn't unheard of for a king or queen to marry or produce an heir with a commoner, but it wasn't typical, either. She didn't bring connections, not even within the merchant community considering the way her father had treated her. They hadn't fallen into some great love like a tale out of legend.

And yet.

Something in Mehl was drawn to her in a way that defied logic. He didn't have Toren's gift, which required a mate who could withstand his magic, but it didn't seem to matter. Every time Mehl was near Ria, his body and soul called to hers in a way he hadn't experienced with anyone but Toren. If she accepted the breeding alliance, he would no doubt spend the next year convincing her to stay with them beyond the contract—and he couldn't even define why.

"I don't know," Mehl finally said. "Some things simply are."

She canted her head. "What is that supposed to mean?"

"Grant me a kiss, and I will see if I can show you."

Mehl braced himself for her rejection, so it took him a moment to process her nod of acceptance. But it wasn't victory that filled him. For the first time in decades, he had to fight against a moment of nerves. He hadn't kissed anyone but Toren in over a century, after all, and he rarely acted the assertive one anymore.

Then she licked her lips, her eyes filled with curious heat, and his uncertainty fled.

～

THE LAST THING Ria had expected when she'd decided to visit the palace this morning was to be tugged into King Mehl's arms in the center of a private receiving room. But even if she had considered the possibility, she never could have imagined the impact of his mouth on hers. Never. The desire she'd felt when he'd caught her against him the night before was nothing to this conflagration.

As his mouth toyed with hers, Ria ran her hands up his chest and around his neck, the long strands of his hair tangling in her fingers. Without prompting, she opened her mouth to his, and their tongues met in an endless duel. He'd said one kiss, and it was clear he planned to make the most of it.

He trailed his hand down her back and cupped her bottom, drawing her more firmly against his hard body. Even through their clothes, the heat of his cock seared her stomach, and she shivered at the force of the desire burning through her very blood. She hadn't lied about not being a virgin, but this went beyond anything she'd experienced before.

Some things simply are.

Ria moaned, and if not for the braids holding his crown in place, she would have threaded her fingers through to pull him closer. Or push him away. She honestly wasn't sure which. Did it matter?

"I do hope you haven't ignored my command," a smooth, cool voice drawled.

Almost leisurely, Mehl pulled his lips from hers, and Ria couldn't hold back a shiver at the loss. Her head spun and her body burned like fire. Then she glanced over to see the imperious heat in High King Toren's regard. And not just passion. There was a possessiveness in his eyes that set her heart pounding.

It's for Mehl, she told herself.

"You granted me one kiss," Mehl said. "But you didn't stipulate the length of time."

The high king's brow lifted. "And your single caress?"

Gods. Mehl's hand was still firmly cupping her behind. Flushing, Ria slipped from the king's arms. "That was the only one, Your Majesty."

"Did Mehl convince you of the merits of accepting our contract?"

The heat in her cheeks increased. "I'm afraid not, High King Toren. I didn't hear enough of the contract to decide one way or another."

"Just Toren," he snapped, closing the gap between them in a few sharp strides. "You needn't call me anything you wouldn't scream out in my bed."

Her breasts went heavy, and her sex clenched almost painfully. "There are many things I might call a person in bed, but I'm not certain they would be acceptable in general company. Or do you mean this moment only?"

"Much depends on your decision."

Her body seemed to have its own ideas, but she wasn't certain she could trust it. Could she truly desire two men at the same time? It appeared that way, but what if she was wrong? Beyond all else, she would have to deal with both of their touches for this to work. A massive risk.

"I'm not sure if I'm capable of wanting you both," Ria whispered. "And I can't imagine why you would both desire me if I could."

If Toren asked for Mehl's permission, it was telepathically. Ria heard nothing but the pounding of her heart as Toren pulled her tight against him, his lips slamming down on hers with none of his husband's gentleness. She gasped, and his tongue swept into her mouth. Claiming. Conquering. She gripped his shoulders as he took her lips without hesitation.

Before she realized his intent, Toren wrapped his hand around her thigh and lifted her leg around his hip, bringing them into sudden, intimate contact. Despite the layers of fabric between them, the feel of his hard cock at the juncture of her thighs had a moan slipping free. There was no doubt in him, and her body responded to his confidence with shocking clarity.

She did want them both. Urgently. Now.

Toren's lips trailed down her throat, and her head tipped back in a minor surrender. Then another pair of hands closed around her waist, and Mehl bent down to claim her lips again just as Toren's mouth reached the neckline of her gown. A strangled whimper vibrated in her throat. If this was a mere sample, would she survive months in their bed?

Her body unashamedly urged her to find out.

CHAPTER 7

NEGOTIATIONS

"Enough," Toren said, and Mehl pulled away at once. This time, the sound Ria made was pure frustration. "What—"

"Perhaps a night together would be unwise," Toren said as he released her leg and stepped back. His cool confidence slipped into place like a mask, so quickly she had the sudden urge to tear his restraint away. "I would want to take you completely, and no matter how I need an heir, I'll not risk fathering a child unless you've agreed to the breeding contract."

"Such a cold phrase, breeding contract," Ria murmured. "And I still don't know the terms."

Toren smiled tightly. "Then how about I enlighten you?"

To listen to his offer took her one step closer to actually considering it. Did she want to consider it? Her body still burned from both kings' touch, and her heart tugged her toward them. But that was dangerous. They might share women, but they were already committed to one another. To get attached would be to risk pain.

Then again, when hadn't her life been filled with pain in one form or another?

"I will listen," Ria said softly.

Mehl circled her until he stood at Toren's side. "It is a simple enough contract."

"Which you could have explained already," Toren said with an annoyed glance at his husband. "A breeding contract is just as it sounds. You agree to carry our heir, and we provide you with anything you might need during that time. As our child's mother, you may choose to live in your own suite of rooms until our child reaches adulthood, or you may go your own way with our full support. Monetary support, specifically."

She frowned. "That feels like…selling my body, I suppose. Or my child."

Mehl shook his head, and Toren cursed. "It is not," Toren said. "You may accept or reject anything you wish, including compensation. But it is no small inconvenience to carry a child to term, and that level of sacrifice deserves something in exchange. In the past, most mothers have stayed to help raise their child. It would be a grave insult not to offer them shelter and status for those twenty years. A couple of decades might not be a lot considering the centuries of our lives, but it isn't nothing, either."

His words made sense, but Ria wasn't certain she could accept anything in return. A place to live, sure. Compensation beyond that would be too much. "There is always the risk that my father will try to get to the child."

Mehl's expression went as hard as Toren's. "I will ensure he fails."

"But I still don't understand why you would ask me," Ria said, this time focusing on Toren. Mehl hadn't given a clear answer, but perhaps the other king would.

"Don't you?"

Toren lifted his hand, cupping her cheek in his palm. As it had the night before, his power rushed through her, and she shivered as flickers of memories flitted through her head, too ephemeral to process. Her body tingled and throbbed until a moan slipped free. The feel of it was beyond description.

Divine.

Ria bit back a whimper when the magic cut off, the loss strangely acute for such a short connection. After a few heart-beats, her eyes focused on Toren's once more, and the wealth of sadness within nearly crushed her. Then he blinked, and the emotion was gone.

"That is why," he murmured. "My power has grown greatly over the last century or two. Very few can withstand it if I lose my grip on it, and if I am overcome with passion... I fear what could happen. Then you appeared. Mehl and I both want you, and you can tolerate my power. You need protection, and I can provide it. No other obstacle is significant enough to matter."

What a terrible and lonely dilemma for him, to need an heir while fearing he would cause harm. But... "This seems too easy."

Toren let out a harsh laugh. "No one, including my beloved husband, would ever claim that living with me is easy. I am a difficult and demanding man at the best of times."

"Yet you are beloved throughout the kingdom for your fairness. Many have grown prosperous beneath your hand."

His fingers trailed down to brush against her collar bone. "As could you."

Ria flushed. "That isn't what I meant."

"See?" Toren smirked. "Difficult."

"But not unjust."

"One can be both fair and a pain in the ass."

Mehl's soft groan broke through their debate, and Ria glanced at him in concern. "What's wrong?"

"Would you please accept the breeding contract if you're willing?" Mehl let out a shaky breath. "This joust would be far better in the bedroom."

Ria winced at the assessment, but she couldn't say it was inaccurate. She did want this. But could she risk everything for that want? "I'll take some time to think through—"

"No," Toren said. "I must produce an heir in a little over a year, two at most. If you are unwilling, I must search in earnest."

She frowned. "How long have you known about this?"

"Only a few weeks. I've tried to search quietly since but have had no luck." Toren's expression turned fierce, and in that moment, she had no trouble seeing how difficult he could be. "Though it is tradition for a new king or queen to provide an heir within their first century of marriage, that has typically been waived for same sex pairings. I never imagined my brother would threaten this challenge, or I would have searched for a contract much sooner. I cannot delay much longer."

Speaking of unjust. Why would Toren's brother do this? But she supposed it was clear enough: power. He'd waited until time was almost up, giving Toren just the barest chance to successfully counter. A "mercy" he could tell the people he'd offered. Her father had shown such false kindness to her when others were around, but it was always a trap.

But she could help. This wasn't just a matter of desire, and it could be far more than escaping her father. She could literally save the throne and gain something for herself in the process—a child safe from her father's threats. And if it ended up being a mistake, at least her sacrifice would mean something.

"I'll do it," Ria said. "I'll enter into a breeding contract with you."

Mehl sagged in relief, but Toren's lips twisted up in a wicked smile. "Truly? I hope you're willing to prove it."

~

Toren's smile widened at Ria's confounded expression. In spite of her life experiences, there was a sweet innocence to her. Perhaps it was her relative youth, for although she was an adult by their standards, she was a young one. She hadn't spent centuries dodging the innuendo and intrigue of court like he had.

"I assume I can prove my intent clearly enough by signing a contract," Ria said.

"That you will," Toren agreed. "But that isn't what I had in mind at the moment."

Her breathing hitched. "Indeed?"

"Hmm." In a quick motion, Toren grabbed Mehl's hand and tugged him close. Toren kissed his husband long and deep, and his body went impossibly hard at the thought of Ria watching them. When he pulled back to look at her, his breath came in sharp pants. "First I should know... Does that bother you?"

Her eyes were wide, but the pulse at her neck throbbed a frantic beat. "Ah. No. Feel free to continue."

Beside him, Mehl chuckled, and Toren found his own lips curling up in another smile despite being almost painfully aroused. He released Mehl and spanned the short distance between him and Ria. She twitched at the rapid movement, and he froze, remembering suddenly the abuse she had suffered.

"I'm afraid I might be too forceful for you, Ria," Toren said softly.

"My father never did anything like *that*," she replied, her face going red. "I think I could tolerate some level of assertive-ness, so long as there's no...no hitting."

He curled his fingers over her shoulder, his thumb caressing the delicate skin at the base of her neck. "You will tell me at once if I go too far. Never hesitate to tell me to stop. If I should be too lost in my power to hear, Mehl will ensure I comply."

His heart pounded as she stared at him, and for the life of him, he couldn't define why her answer mattered so much. This was temporary. As soon as she was pregnant, she would no doubt flee to her own suite of rooms and see them as rarely as possible. He was happily married—what need had he of more than momentary acceptance?

When she nodded, he told himself the relief he felt was born of convenience. They wouldn't have to search for another woman to bear their child. That was all. But he couldn't resist drawing her against him and stooping down to capture her mouth with his. Her sweet, honeyed taste hit his tongue, and he devoured. Mehl's lips brushed against the back of his neck at the same time, drawing out a moan, as he pressed his hard body against Toren's back. Mehl curled his arm around Toren to caress Ria's waist, and Toren's own skin burned.

Didn't know it was possible to want to be inside two people at the same time.

Ria pressed closer, her breasts rubbing against his chest, and she wrapped her arms around his waist, right over Mehl's. Already, the control Toren held over his magic thinned, and they hadn't even shed their clothes. But they wouldn't have to for him to take her, and both of his mates could withstand his power.

With a low growl, Toren gripped Ria's thighs and lifted her against him, her heated core landing directly over his cock. Mehl eased back, and Toren started across the room, heading for the pair of plain wooden thrones on the far end. They sat high enough off the ground that he could take her there. Mehl would probably only be able to reach her breasts, but he was a creative lover. He would figure out a way to participate.

Toren sat her down on the cool wood and shoved her skirts up to her waist. She gasped in surprise, but she widened her legs, sending another wave of heat directly to his cock. Still, he paused to meet her eyes. "The contract will be a mere formality after this. Allow me to take you now, and you're mine."

Her eyebrows rose. "For how long?"

The word "forever" almost slipped from his lips, but that was foolishness. "The duration of our contract, of course."

She took a long, shaky breath—and nodded.

His husband came into view as he stopped beside the throne, exchanging a heated glance with Toren before trailing his fingers down Ria's arm. She shivered, and Toren smiled. This would be perfect. The only possible problem was the angle.

"Mehl," Toren commanded. "Sit and hold her on your lap. That should give us enough height."

Before Ria could stand, Mehl scooped her up and sat. She froze for a second, a flush rising up her neck, and then parted her legs once more. The blood pounded in Toren's ears as he stopped to stare at the sight of the two of them splayed on his throne.

Private court meetings would never be the same.

With an impatient tug, Toren loosened the bindings on his court robe and let it drop, leaving him in only a thin tunic and loose pants. He stepped over the puddle of fabric, only to pause again at Ria's wince. But she wasn't looking at him. Her frown was focused on the robe he'd left on the floor.

"That fabric could buy a small kingdom," she muttered. "You can't just..."

Mehl's laugh rang out. "Better pick up after yourself, beloved."

The mood might have been ruined by having to arrange his robe carefully across Mehl's throne—except Mehl rewarded them all by tucking Ria's skirts up around her waist and slipping his finger into the slit in her underclothes. She twitched and let out a startled cry, her head falling back against Mehl's chest as Toren returned to stand in front of them.

That delicious image had Toren's plan changing. Instead of preparing her himself, he let Mehl's talented fingers do the trick. Her soft moans began to echo around them, and Toren slid down her bodice, freeing her breasts. Usually, they weren't his favorite feature, but he found himself leaning down to tug one nipple into his mouth.

The guard outside the door surely heard *that* cry.

Mehl's other hand wrapped around Toren's cock over the fabric, but Toren batted his husband away. "Need to spill inside her. My control..." he whispered, his breath brushing across Ria's nipple, making her shiver.

"Soon?" she asked, panting. Mehl ran his lips down the side of her neck, and she whimpered. "Please?"

Toren freed himself from his pants and caught Mehl's gaze. "Brace her."

More than physically, but he didn't have to say those words aloud. He could see the comprehension in Mehl's eyes as he gripped her thighs and adjusted her for Toren's invasion. He would never be able to hold onto his magic during this. Never.

Toren positioned the head of his cock at her entrance and paused to ensure her consent. There would be no future question of her current willingness. "With this, our contract begins. I give my oath as High King that you and any children we create will be in my care."

"I give my oath as King that you and any children we create will be in my care," Mehl murmured against Ria's neck.

An impossibility unless they remained together after the first birth, but Toren refused to think about that.

Ria nodded.

"Say it," Toren said, his hands framing her face. "Swear it."

"I..." She swallowed. "With this, our contract begins. I give my oath that you and any children we create will be in my care."

The heat of her words slammed through him, the final part of her whispered promise one she wasn't obligated to give. One that brought more complications than he could contemplate. So he didn't. He let his willpower and his magic free.

Only then did he enter her.

CHAPTER 8
COMPLICATIONS

Ria thought she was prepared for his invasion, but she was wrong.

His thrust was unyielding, his expression harsh and almost pained. A wave of his magic swelled around them. Through them. But he didn't hurt her. Gods, no. Mehl's fingers still worked at her bud, and when he nibbled lightly on the side of her neck she screamed from the combined sensations. Satisfaction lit Toren's eyes at the sight, and he withdrew, only to thrust again.

And again.

She curled her arm around Mehl's neck and held on, grateful for his grip on her thighs. Another wave of Toren's magic crashed through her, but it didn't recede. It filled and filled until she feared she could take no more. Then Mehl turned her enough to kiss her, and some of the power bridged over to him, linking them in body and mind and power.

Thoughts and emotions crashed around her. Real or imagined? She could barely process them as Toren took her, his thrusts almost frenzied. Ria tilted her hips up for more. He had to fill her. The only thing better would be having them both.

"She'll sign the contract with my seed staining her thighs."

"If only she bore something of me."

Toren. Then Mehl. Were they speaking to each other mentally? Had she caught the edge of their thoughts? Ria didn't care. She cried out against Mehl's mouth, her body tightening around Toren with her release.

But it wasn't enough.

Ria pushed away from Mehl. "Wait," she gasped.

Though he groaned, Toren stopped at once. "You gave your oath that—"

"No, no," she said, panting. "Together. Mehl must find release, too. With us."

She didn't know why, but it was vitally important.

Mehl nipped at her earlobe. "I can't. The child must be Toren's. Only after you've conceived can I take you."

A heated look entered Toren's eyes, and his magic surged until she gasped. But he pulled from her body, drawing an involuntary groan from them both, and tugged her to her feet. Her legs trembled beneath her until he lifted her against him and kissed her, so thoroughly she barely noticed the sound of cloth rustling behind her.

He eased back, giving her bottom lip one last suck before turning her to face Mehl. The other king had removed his formal robe and freed his cock, and she couldn't draw her gaze away from the broad head. Her core clenched hard, sending a blast of heat through her body.

"If you want to do this together, you'll have to use your mouth," Toren muttered at her ear. "Are you willing to do that?"

Ria shivered. From the dark heat of his words and the hard press of his length against her bottom. From the sight of Mehl waiting for her decision, an almost vulnerable gleam in his eyes. As if she could refuse them. For some reason, she couldn't deny these men anything.

"More than willing."

Toren pushed gently between her shoulder blades, and she bent over, resting her forearms across Mehl's thighs. His hand cupped her cheek, his fingers tangling in her hair as she took him slowly into her mouth. A finger stroked across her entrance, and she hummed in pleasure. Mehl's startled twitch had his cock sliding deeper until she had to curl her fingers around the base to steady them both.

Then Toren slammed home, and all three of them cried out at the surge of power and pleasure. Magic moved between them in a constant ebb and flow, so strong and constant that Ria didn't try to grasp it. For the first time in years, she simply let herself feel. The salty taste of Mehl on her tongue and his soft, stifled moans. The slide of Toren inside her, hitting a spot that made her dig the fingers of her free hand into Mehl's thigh.

But most of all the nameless emotion she couldn't bear to fathom.

Someone's memories flitted through her mind, but she ignored them. She reached for something else, some eternal force she couldn't control or define. Her pleasure rose to meet it, and something sparked within her, like the magic she used to create clothes. But so much greater, especially when Toren's and Mehl's magics blended with it. Unconsciously, she smoothed the rough edges.

Ria couldn't pause to question. Her orgasm ripped through her with such force that light flashed behind her eyes. Then Mehl's cock pulsed in her mouth, and she swallowed his essence as Toren stiffened behind her with a cry, filling her with his seed. She shuddered from the perfection of the moment, an unbroken link connecting them.

They stayed that way for a moment, though Ria surely would have fallen if not for Toren's support. She let herself drift on a haze of pleasure before awareness slipped in with a slight movement from Mehl. Quickly, she drew back, releasing him from her mouth. A pinch against her scalp reminded her that his fingers were still tangled in her hair, something that only became clearer when he tipped her face up.

"Thank you for including me," Mehl murmured, his voice husky.

Her face went hot, and he chuckled as he drew his hand back. She understood why when Toren tugged her upright, turning her to face him. But she couldn't make out the expression on his face. Angry? Frustrated? Intense, most certainly, and not what she would have expected considering the situation.

"You shouldn't have done that," he said darkly.

"What?" Ria blinked, searching for understanding. "Include Mehl?"

Toren's jaw clenched as he shook his head. "No. Join our magics."

MEHL COULDN'T PREVENT the wave of hurt, so strong he almost didn't catch Toren's explanation. The thought of his husband wanting him left out of this... But, no. He'd mentioned joining magic. What did he mean by that?

"I don't understand," Ria said, obviously no clearer about the claim.

Toren scowled. "Couldn't you tell how our magics blended? You were the one who performed the task."

Quickly, Mehl searched inside himself, anxious to verify the claim, but the well of power that was uniquely his showed no sign of connection. Whatever Toren meant, it was not something ongoing. Mehl thought back to the flow of power between them while they'd been having sex. The blast of Toren's magic hadn't been unusual, but the thread that had come along with it...

Mehl's spine stiffened, and he leaned forward. "You were attempting to join our power together?"

Couples sometimes did that, either temporarily or permanently as desired, but it wasn't something undertaken without permission. Had they been mistaken about Ria after all? If she managed the trick, it would give her hold over them. Especially Toren, who was powerful but also vulnerable with it.

Ria's eyebrows drew together. "No."

"Then I hope you have a better explanation," Toren drawled. "We have given our oath to care for you in exchange for bearing our child. I hope we haven't bound ourselves in such a way to a traitor."

Mehl winced, though his husband's words echoed his own worries. He tucked himself back into his pants and stood, hoping to calm Toren enough to find the truth. But he should have worried about Ria, instead. Her skin flushed red, and before either of them could react, her hand cracked across Toren's face.

Before she could lower her arm, Mehl had her wrist in his grip. "You do realize you could be executed for striking the High King?"

The color that had risen in her face drained away, and her arm went limp in his hold. But a moment later, her chin tipped up. "I didn't consider that, but I don't care. He deserved it. Both of you do. To take my body like that and then call me a traitor... Go ahead and plan my execution, because just thinking about it makes me want to hit him again."

Although Toren's expression didn't soften, Mehl felt his own concern begin to fade. "Forgive us if we are mistaken. However, creating a link like that without permission would be obscene. If you did not attempt that, then what happened?"

Her expression twisted with dread. "When Toren's power rushed through me and into you, there was something unusual about it. Rough, like a snarled thread or fabric unevenly matched. I smoothed it so it wouldn't do harm."

"Interesting. Wouldn't you say, Toren?" Now, Mehl caught a hint of easing in his husband's demeanor. He slowly released Ria's arm and sighed. "How does your magic work?"

"I create," Ria answered at once. "My father shows me a design and provides a rough framework. Then I form it into what it's supposed to be. If I can get a hint of what the customer wants from their mind, I can do a more accurate job. His clothes would be average otherwise."

Mehl couldn't keep himself from chuckling as the problem became clear. "It was an accident."

The horror that spread across Toren's face erased the hint of humor Mehl had felt. He didn't need to link minds to understand what was bothering Toren. Twin problems, really. He'd made a serious accusation against the future mother of their child almost immediately after spilling himself inside her. But more—if she couldn't control the impulse, what would happen the next time they made love?

Not that the second was guaranteed after the first.

"I am sorry, Ria," Toren said, his expression turning grave. "You are correct. I deserved your blow."

Mehl rocked back on his heels at the confession. Did she know how rare that was coming from Toren? Would it matter? They'd made an oath to begin the contract, but the contract could be broken. With Toren's concession, she could sever the agreement and leave at once, child or no. Unfortunately, he didn't know her well enough to guess what she would do.

Though at the moment she appeared more confused than anything.

"What does it signify if our magics streamed together temporarily?" she asked. "It wasn't overly different from the testing you performed on me except that King Mehl was also involved. We didn't join, so there was no harm."

Mehl startled at the brief but shattered glance Toren gave him. Was Toren still upset that he'd called her a traitor, or was it something more?

"We could have," Toren whispered. "It was a near thing. And to link like that with me would no doubt destroy you both. You might be able to bear the testing, but..."

Ria took a step back. "I didn't realize I'd almost done that. I swear. But I don't think your magic would have hurt me."

"Because I didn't give it free rein." With a few sharp motions, Toren straightened his clothes and marched over to grab his formal robe. "We play a dangerous game."

Mehl's muscles clenched at the cold reserve that entered Toren's tone. Surely, he wouldn't send Ria away. There was no logic to it, but Mehl had been drawn to her from the moment she stepped into their dressing room the night before. He was certainly no less so after being inside her body, if only her mouth.

Toren held his heart and his loyalty, and Mehl would abide by his husband's decree if he truly believed the risk was too great. But that didn't mean Mehl would be happy about it.

CHAPTER 9

SEALING THE DEAL

Vibrating with power he could barely contain, Toren donned his formal robe as he fought to regain full control. He should summon one of his servants to guide Ria to a guest room, where she could stay in safety until they determined whether she'd conceived from their recklessness. He could have Mehl tie him to the bed if need be—one of the rare times Toren would ever allow that—while they waited. Anything to prevent himself from being tempted.

But he wouldn't.

Toren cursed beneath his breath at his own possessive nature. Ria was theirs now, and he could no more bear to release her than he could Mehl. Which was a problem in more ways than one. She wanted freedom from her father, not one more chain binding her where she didn't wish to be. And that potential link... Gods. He could never release the bulk of his power upon them like that. Neither Mehl nor Ria were likely to survive.

Still, he wouldn't let her go.

"Get yourself presentable, Mehl," Toren grumbled, his

tightening throat making the words nearly impossible to say. "We have a contract to sign."

Mehl's brows lifted in shock. "I thought…"

"We'll have to find a way to mitigate the danger."

Toren glanced at Ria, and a hint of softness curled through him at the way she stood, her arms crossed uncertainly. A rush of pride joined the tenderness at the memory of her striking him. Despite all she'd been through, she would not back down to injustice. Her beauty hid a will he couldn't wait to see turned on him in more…pleasurable ways.

"I know not to do that again," Ria said softly. "But you needn't be polite about the contract if you have changed your mind. I'm sure I can travel far before my father is released."

A bark of laughter slipped through Toren's lips. "I am hardly known for my immense politeness. Unless you have new objections, I'll hold you to your earlier vow. You are ours."

Her mouth slipped open on a soft "Oh," reminding him of how she'd looked with her mouth around Mehl's cock. Instantly, he went hard. If not for the multitude of formalities awaiting them, Toren would drag them both to his bedchamber at once. But he would leave nothing else to chance. They'd made their oaths, but they hadn't sealed them. He would not let her slip away if he could help it.

"Well?" Toren demanded, lifting a brow.

Ria's arms dropped to her sides. "Very well. Let's complete the contract, then."

It was madness, but Ria couldn't stop herself from following the kings from the room. Aside from the guard—his expression blessedly blank despite what he must have heard—outside the door, the hall was empty. Only when they reached another, larger corridor did they encounter any courtiers. Ria fought the urge to smooth her hair and dress, though she'd already done so before they'd left the audience chamber.

Stares followed them until they turned down another private hallway kept empty by a warrior who stepped aside as the kings approached. Neither Toren nor Mehl appeared to notice the arch glances and smirking lips, but Ria felt her cheeks warm. The heat didn't fade from her skin even after they were out of sight, the way behind them blocked by the warrior once more. Could the courtiers tell what had happened between them?

She'll sign the contract with my seed staining her thighs.

That errant thought from Toren haunted her with each step, and not, unfortunately, in the unpleasant way she might have expected. Normally, she would hate not being able to clean off immediately, but now, she could only remember the harsh possessiveness of Toren's mental voice. It built within her until her own desire blazed with it.

What was wrong with her? She'd enjoyed sex ever since she'd been old enough to take a lover—it was the one freedom her father had allowed her, so long as she didn't dare to form an emotional attachment. Any hint of that was harshly punished, but he'd openly hoped she would produce a child with the same talent. He didn't know about the enchantment she'd sought from a midwife that prevented conception, one she'd only had removed in preparation for her escape since she hadn't known if there would be anyone capable of doing so wherever she ended up.

But although she'd missed the freedom of taking a lover the last couple of months since the enchantment's removal, she hadn't craved another the way she did now. Her breathing hadn't hitched at the thought of a man's seed inside her. And two men? That she never would have imagined. Yet here she was, her heart pounding eagerly as she followed the kings into a large, airy office with a massive desk in the center.

Ah, the potential uses of that desk.

Her cheeks heated at the thought, especially when King Mehl cast her a knowing look. Unfortunately, a scribe sat to one side of the desk, papers spread out in front of him. That cooled a bit of her ardor. When High King Toren sat and gestured toward the chair across from him, she was able to settle herself into the seat with a reasonable amount of grace.

Then the true negotiations began.

Mehl leaned casually against the wall, his gaze trained on Ria as she listened to the terms of the contract. Toren must have given the scribe the details before meeting them in the receiving room earlier, for it was mostly complete. The provisions were fair, the expectations clear. None of them had reason to complain so far.

It didn't feel right.

They shouldn't be offering her a mere breeding contract— that was what his instinct screamed. Something deep inside urged him to demand more. To ask her to be their queen. Yet such a thing made no sense. Mehl knew what the hum of her pleased cries around his cock felt like, but he didn't know *her*. What did she enjoy in life? Hate? Fear? Did she have a favorite food? A preferred season? It was madness to marry someone you'd barely conversed with.

"Now," the scribe said. "Did you mean for the contract to have an unlimited amount of time for her to conceive, Your Majesty? I see that it is also exclusive. Considering your brother's threat, it might be wiser to consider more than one—"

"No."

Toren's hard voice cut off the man's words, but it made Ria frown. "Wait," she said. "What if something is wrong with me? Not that I want to share you with anyone, except for King Mehl, of course, but you don't have much time."

At her inclusion of him, Mehl's heart warmed. He'd wondered if it would be awkward to share a woman again after so long, but it had felt quite the opposite. Natural. But he couldn't deny his conflicted feelings about being unable to fully take her himself. The first child had to be Toren's, and Mehl wasn't exactly needed for that.

Yet neither had forgotten him.

Toren's expression softened. "I doubt there is anything wrong with you, Ria, but you are welcome to ask the palace healer to examine you at any time."

"Did he...?" Ria's voice trailed off, and she licked nervously at her lips. "Did he note anything when he healed me last night?"

Mehl straightened from his place against the wall, but he didn't rush forward to comfort her as he wanted. There was a brittleness to her demeanor any time her father or his actions were alluded to. Even now, her breathing was shallow, her body as motionless as prey caught out in the open. He couldn't help but fear that the slightest movement might make her bolt.

"I did not order him to examine you in such a way," Toren said softly. "Nor did I ask him what he might have found when he healed your bruises. Did you expect bad news?"

Ria relaxed against her seat, but her worried frown remained. "No. I confirmed with a midwife only a month ago that I could bear children once I escaped. But hearing it put so bluntly how much rests on me... I will check with the healer to be certain."

"Your Majesty," the scribe interjected, "If you might

consider contracting with others in the meantime, I do believe—"

"If you think I want to gather multiple women for this endeavor, you are mistaken," Toren said, his eyes narrowing on the scribe. "And you will not add such to the contract. If Ria has not conceived within the year, I'll reconsider then. Since any of us can end the contract at any time so long as Ria isn't pregnant, I see no need to specify otherwise."

Ria's frown hadn't entirely eased, but she nodded.

The scribe scanned the paper before turning the page. His throat working, he glanced up again. "The only other unusual clause, Your Majesty..."

"Yes?" Toren demanded in the imperious tone that never failed to make Mehl semi-hard.

Even now.

"Ah. Well." The scribe's throat bobbed again. "It is unusual to require King Mehl to bed the woman once the healer has confirmed her pregnancy. Normally, such contracts are only between the High King and—"

"I do not care what has been done in the past," Toren interrupted again. "This child will be *our* child, even if that is technically impossible. I can do nothing about the requirements of biology, but magic, ceremony, legal contract...those things I can control, at least in this. If Ria is not amenable, she should say so now."

Although Ria's skin reddened, the considering glance she turned Mehl's way was not scornful. Far from it. Her eyes heated, much as they had when she'd taken him in her mouth. He nearly groaned at the reminder. As it was, control over his body was hard won.

"I am amenable," she said.

The scribe's eyes widened. "You're, ah. You're willing to put that in the contract?"

A hint of Toren's magic brushed against Mehl's shields, prompting Mehl to stride to his husband's side. But before Toren snapped out an angry reply, Ria glared at the hapless scribe. "I just said so," she insisted.

Gods above. With time and confidence, she truly would make an excellent queen.

"Of course, Your—I mean, my lady," the scribe replied.

Mehl smiled at the slip. The man had almost called her Your Majesty. At least *one* other person sensed her ideal role.

"If that is all," Toren said, his expression indecipherable, "Then it is time for us to sign."

CHAPTER 10

THE DUCHESS OF NEVIAL

The scratch of pen nib against paper echoed through the room as Toren signed his name on the final page of the contract. As the ink dried, the scribe, Iyeth, tipped the melting spoon, allowing a precise amount of wax to pool beside the signature. It had to be habit that led to such neatness—the spoon bobbled in the man's hand as he pulled it out of the way. Toren nearly smiled. Out of all of them, the poor scribe appeared the most nervous about the contract.

Holding his palm just above the cooling wax, Toren triggered the spell that formed and hardened his seal. The force of his power trembled against his control, but he'd done this magic too many times for it to break free. Out of all the spells he'd struggled to learn without loosing his power, this was the most vital. Physical seals could be forged, but never this.

Mehl eased closer and settled his hand on Toren's shoulder. To an outside observer, it might have appeared casual, but Toren was well aware that it wasn't. His husband had already sensed his earlier flare of energy and stood ready to absorb any overflow. Warmth filled him, pure and light. Mehl always knew.

Perhaps he wasn't the only one. Across the desk, Ria studied him with a worried frown. "Does this distress you?"

"I am bothered only by my scribe's impertinence," Toren replied, though there was little heat to his words.

Iyeth had worked with him long enough to recognize that lack. "I merely worried for you, Your Majesty. With the threat of your brother and such unusual terms—"

"I am aware, Iyeth." Toren handed the pen to Mehl, who dipped the nib into the ink and signed his own name. "But in truth, this is mere formality. Our contract has already been sealed with more than mere words."

Any fool could surely tell what the three of them had been up to. Strands of Mehl's hair had come loose from his crown, and his clothes were clearly rumpled. And Ria. Her lips were red and swollen, and the bodice of her dress was slightly askew —not enough to reveal her breasts but more than hinting at the cause of the disorder. Toren had no clue what he himself looked like, but it couldn't be much better.

Iyeth must have been absorbed in his work, for as his glance shifted between the three of them, his eyes widened and his skin flushed. The scribe gathered the final page of the contract, the pen, and the inkwell without a word and carried it around the large desk for Ria to sign. Toren found himself leaning forward as she accepted the pen. This might be mere formality, but it was a formality he would see done.

She slid the paper closer and paused. Toren sucked in a breath as she rolled the pen between her fingers and stared at the blank area she was supposed to sign. Mehl's fingers tightened on his shoulder in an echo of his own tension. What was she waiting for?

"Ria?" Melh asked, his voice rough.

"I'm not certain what to do."

A surge of anger stiffened Toren's spine. "Did your father neglect your education, as well? Every citizen must be taught to read and write. Another law broken only adds to his crimes."

"What?" Her cheeks pinkened. "Of course I know how to write!"

This time, a hint of desperation curled around his anger like a vine. "You have already given your oath. Do you think I will easily release you from it?"

Iyeth sucked in a scandalized breath. "Your Majesty, you said the contract could be broken at any time unless there is a pregnancy."

"Which there could already be." Toren pinned Ria with his gaze. "Yes, the contract may be broken, but I never said I would make it an easy choice. Nor would Mehl, I imagine."

"Indeed not," Mehl said.

The flush on Ria's face darkened, but her eyes sparked with a hint of desire. "You misunderstand. I can sign, but I want it to be accurate. According to Mehl, I became a lady when you named me such at court. Do I need to add a title here the way you two have done? That would certainly require knowing what I am lady *of*."

Gods, he'd forgotten about that. Had it only been a couple of hours since the morning court session? He'd recalled the issue of her rank before joining Mehl and Ria in the private receiving room, but it had fled his mind entirely after burying himself in Ria's sweet body as she claimed Mehl with her mouth. The memory of that moment was all-consuming. He'd barely been able to focus on the contract when they'd first begun the meeting.

"I named you Duchess of Nevial," Toren said. "I suppose there's a contract to sign and seal around here somewhere."

Iyeth nodded. "Of course, Your Majesty."

With a wave of his hand, Toren gestured for the scribe to retrieve it. Ria didn't notice the man leave—she was too busy gaping at him. "You did what?"

Apparently, she wasn't pleased.

RIA MUST HAVE HEARD WRONG. She *must* have. High King Toren would not have named a tailor's daughter a duchess, especially not so casually. She knew little about the nobility beyond their names, their current fashions, and the few snippets of gossip she had overheard during fittings. They certainly hadn't acknowledged her as she'd worked. Though she'd outfitted quite a few nobles over the years, none of them had recognized her in court finery this morning, or if they had, they'd pretended ignorance.

They might have barely tolerated her if she'd been given some minor title, but they would never accept her as a duchess.. What was Toren thinking? Was he that blind to the biases of the upper class? He couldn't possibly be, or he wouldn't be such an effective king. Of course, he was at the top. He never had to worry about social rejection.

King Mehl frowned down at his husband. "Why that title, love?"

Naturally, Mehl understood. He'd been High King Toren's bodyguard before they'd fallen in love. Although that had been before Ria was born, she could imagine the furor that had caused. Few commented on his origins now, but Mehl had had nearly a century to win over the people. Not to mention the fact that he was *married* to the *High King*.

Toren lifted a shoulder. "Why not? It has been unclaimed since the previous duchess died without an heir. The title comes with an estate an hour beyond the city, and I thought

Ria might enjoy that as a periodic retreat from palace life. It will be hers even when our child is grown."

An estate to deal with, too? With a gasp, Ria jerked to her feet. "I don't know a thing about managing a household of that size. I've barely adjusted to the idea of bearing the next king or queen, and now you want me to oversee an estate?"

Mehl's lips twisted, but Toren chuckled without seeming to notice his husband's annoyed regard. "Absolutely not. It is one of many unoccupied holdings I have a steward administer. Believe me, I am far more concerned with our current, more pressing task."

As Toren's meaning became clear, her body flushed with heat. Even so... "I will be mocked by the entire court."

"Do you think so?" Any hint of amusement fled his face, replaced by cold resolve. "Anyone foolish enough to make that mistake will answer to me."

Ria shivered at the deadly certainty in his voice. High King Toren was renowned for his fairness, but it didn't always take the form a person expected. That was particularly true when King Mehl was involved in the decision—and if Mehl's sudden, fierce scowl was anything to go by, he would be. Life would become more than unpleasant for the first courtier or two who openly snubbed her.

And they would.

The door opened, and the scribe returned with another stack of papers in his hands. His worried frown was back, too. Though the man seemed the nervous sort, it was obvious that he held Toren in high regard. He wouldn't have fretted so much about this decision otherwise.

"Your Majesties," the scribe said. "Your advisers have arrived early for your afternoon meeting. I believe they hoped to share luncheon with you."

"Then they should have sent a formal request," Toren replied.

A hint of his energy pulsed in the air, and Mehl rubbed Toren's back in soothing circles. Ria couldn't take her eyes off the tender motion, done so absently it was obviously a habitual gesture. What would it be like to receive such casual, everyday love? Something sharp pinched in her chest. She wouldn't know.

"We may need their aid if your brother does return," Mehl said softly.

Toren's sigh ruffled the papers on his desk. "We need to finish the contracts. More, we must decide when to present the announcement. I would prefer to do so before Ria's father is brought before us for punishment in three days. The initial charge was read with the other decrees after the two of you left the room."

"I imagine we'll still need to eat." Mehl smiled. "Once the contracts are signed, we can delay the rest of the discussion until evening. Feref can show Ria to her new rooms while we attend to the advisers."

Ria didn't pay attention to Toren's answer—she was stuck on Mehl's comment about her rooms. A title, an estate, and a suite in the royal palace, where she would presumably sleep with the kings until she was pregnant. Was this even real? Her vision took on a hazy cast, like the time she'd drank too much of her father's wine. She blinked, but although her focus returned, she still couldn't quite believe she stood across the desk from High King Toren and King Mehl, her life changed by a stack of papers.

She straightened her spine and gripped her hands together in front of her stomach. Anything to regain her composure. Although Mehl studied her worriedly, Toren accepted another paper from the scribe without glancing up. He signed the bottom with a bold, confident flourish. No hint of her own doubt.

Is that for my new title? Ria wondered as he sealed the wax with his power.

In an odd sort of way, the title was more frightening than the breeding contract. The latter could be broken, or if she had a child, she could raise them here and then be able to do as she wished. But this title, signed by the High King's hand, would remain.

She couldn't begin to process the tangle of her emotions about that.

Once Toren was finished, the scribe returned to her side where the final page of the breeding contract still lay. This was the pivotal moment—an official binding. It was a formality after her sworn word, but one that couldn't be denied. With numb fingers, Ria took the pen from the scribe and dipped the nib into the ink. Then she took a deep breath and signed her name.

Ria Orindl, Duchess of Nevial.

She dropped into her seat, her eyes fixed on the ink as it dried.

Life was about to be anything but boring.

CHAPTER 11

NOT QUITE FAMILY

Satisfaction burned in Mehl's blood despite the niggling voice that called for a deeper, more lasting connection with Ria. However briefly, she was theirs. Too bad they couldn't take her to their room right now and claim her again. Toren might have hinted that he would ignore their advisors, but Mehl knew his husband would never neglect his duty. They might not have an official council like some countries, but their advisors performed essential tasks for the kingdom.

"Shall we leave for luncheon?" Mehl asked.

Ria stood uncertainly beside the desk, her gaze slipping back and forth between them, but Toren chuckled as he rose from his chair. "It might be wise to change out of our court clothes first, love. For more reasons than one."

Mehl glanced down out of reflex, only to grimace at the wrinkled state of his formal robe. "I confess I entirely forgot what I was wearing. I was too pleased after the creation of these wrinkles."

The papers bobbled in the poor scribe's hands, almost causing him to drop the entire pile. Ria reached out to steady them, and the red-faced man gave her a grateful smile. "Thank you, Your Grace."

Ever so slightly, she flinched, though Mehl didn't think the other two noticed. Toren's attention was on the scribe, who was too busy trying to hide his embarrassment to heed Ria. But Mehl understood that quiet little twitch very well, indeed, and not only because he'd learned to read others when he'd been a bodyguard.

He'd stifled his fair share of those reactions to his new title himself.

"Iyeth," Toren began, catching the scribe's attention. "Perhaps you should return to your office to copy and catalog the contracts. And if you could draft a formal announcement about the breeding contract for me to peruse later, I would be most grateful."

Ah, yes. Iyeth. Mehl rarely worked with the scribes, but his husband knew them all by name. Not for the first time, he was grateful to be merely king and consort. He oversaw the household and the palace guard, but he didn't have to tend to the minutiae of running the kingdom, not at the level Toren did.

"Of course, Your Majesty." Iyeth bowed toward Toren and then Mehl before inclining his head respectfully at Ria. "If you will excuse me."

Toren flicked his hand, and the scribe fled without waiting for a verbal acknowledgement from Mehl or Ria. She didn't notice, and Mehl didn't care. The constant obeisance was a willing price he paid to have Toren. He wasn't going to complain over the occasional lack.

"Come," Toren said. "We should go straighten up before I change my mind about eating luncheon with the advisors."

Ria stepped around her chair but halted before reaching Mehl's side. "What about me?"

A good question. Even had her new status been

announced at court, her presence would not be expected during a meal where important information might be discussed. He or Toren might choose to break that unspoken rule by inviting her, but it would be an unkindness. A tailor's daughter—now the tailor herself, he supposed—would hardly be trained in such formal etiquette. Mehl had only known the rules because of the long hours spent guarding Toren.

Would she be relieved or offended to be excluded?

"If you'll walk with us, I can show you to the suite I had Feref prepare," Mehl said. "I assume you will wish to become acquainted with your new rooms?"

Her shoulders lowered, and she smiled. "Yes. Very much so, thank you."

"We should hurry before Iyeth returns to blush at us again," Toren quipped, and Mehl's heart lightened at the teasing lilt to his husband's voice. It had been too long since Toren's guard had dropped enough to jest.

As they traversed the private hallways leading to the family wing, a sense of contentment hit him. The three of them together was simply...right. He suspected they agreed. A companionable silence had settled between them, and when Mehl looked at Toren to his left or Ria to his right, both wore easy, satisfied expressions. Only when they neared their rooms did he notice Ria tensing. Her steps slowed, and she cast him an uncertain look.

"Did you forget to stop at my room?" Ria asked. "We're almost to yours, if I'm remembering well enough from last night."

"You'll be beside Toren." Mehl halted at her door and tapped his finger against the wood. "This suite is for you. I'm technically in the consort's chambers on his other side, but I rarely use them for anything but storage."

Ria took a step back. "A breeding contract doesn't make me family. This seems…"

A scandalized Feref had given the same protest, but as then, Mehl cared nothing for useless traditions. "Convenient? I'm certain neither I nor Toren wish to go searching for your room, and I doubt you'll want to risk stumbling into some courtier in the middle of the night returning to yours."

"I don't." She nibbled on her lower lip. "Still…"

"Your rooms will be here," Toren said. "You will notify Feref if you need anything."

After a brief hesitation, Ria strode through the door, Mehl and Toren following. They were barely inside before she spun around to face them. "I need to retrieve my belongings."

"I will send someone to do so," Mehl replied.

She shook her head. "I want to go myself. I have to sort through not only my own things but also the shop's goods. We have a few outstanding orders that need attending, and there's a fortune in fabric and trimmings that need to be packed with care."

"With the threat of my brother hanging over us?" Toren frowned. "I do not like it."

Neither did Mehl. However, they couldn't keep Ria to themselves. She had the right to handle the disposition of her own belongings, and thanks to Toren's decree, the tailor's shop was now her responsibility entirely. She wouldn't let that go easily—nor should she.

"It is her business now, Tor," Mehl pointed out. "And there should be little danger so close to the palace. But I'll send several guards along with the servants just in case."

Although Toren's jaw clenched, his energy didn't surge. A good sign. Then Toren marched over to Ria and placed his hand over her stomach. "Take care to remember that you may even now be carrying our child. My heir. But more than that, *you* are ours. You will ensure your own well-being accordingly."

Her lips parted, and her eyes widened. If she'd formulated a response, Toren didn't allow her time to give it. He spun on his heel and strode from the room, a fierce expression on his face. Mehl sighed. Ever since his parents' death, Toren had struggled, both with attachment and fear of loss. It was a double-edged sword, one that could only be blunted but never dispersed.

"He worries," Mehl simply said.

Ria gave a shaky nod. "So I see."

He needed to change clothes and provide Feref instructions for Ria's trip into the city, but as Mehl bid her farewell and headed toward his and Toren's room, he hesitated. His husband's magic had appeared to be under control, but his temper wouldn't be. If that hadn't cooled... Well. There was a fair chance they would be late for their own luncheon, after all.

RIA'S EXIT from the castle was far less subtle than her entrance had been this morning. How could it not be? In the time she'd taken to freshen up in the bathing room, Feref had gathered at least fifteen servants, and they'd barely reached the end of the royal wing before four guards, fully armed, had flanked her. If she'd thought people stared before, that was nothing compared to walking through the palace with such a large entourage. The only thing that might have garnered more attention was the kings' presence.

At least her dress and hair were in order again. There were still whispers and sly looks from the courtiers lingering in the halls, but she received far fewer knowing smirks. Not that she could blame them for those after she'd seen herself in the mirror. She'd never looked so thoroughly tumbled—but she'd never been with more than one partner, either.

As soon as she stepped foot out of the palace gates, another guard melted from the shadows and strode forward, taking position in front of her. Ria's eyebrows knitted. Was there some imminent, direct threat that she knew nothing about? There'd been no announcement about the breeding contract, so there was no reason for anyone to target her.

Not that they would *need* an announcement after this. First, Toren had mentioned in front of the entire court that she was considering a breeding alliance, and then she'd been seen looking decidedly disheveled on the way to the kings' office. And now...now she had an honor guard and team of servants just for a trip to her own home.

The reason had to be obvious.

As they advanced into the trade area where many of the nobles shopped and almost everyone Ria knew lived, she had to contend with more than courtiers. Business stopped as she neared, and now noble and commoner alike gaped at her. Although her skin heated with a blush, Ria held her head high and continued her unreasonably slow progress toward the shop. Had it been anyone else causing everyone to freeze like statues, Ria might have laughed at the scene.

Only Enry shook off his surprise quickly enough to hurry toward her, though he halted a couple of paces away when the nearest guard drew his sword partly from its sheath in warning. "Ria!" Enry called.

"He's a friend," Ria said, her words nearly tangling in their haste.

The lead guard's expression hardened. "The High King ordered us to see you safe at all costs."

"I'm certain he didn't mean I couldn't speak to anyone," Ria argued. "Toren is hardly so thoughtless as that."

An indrawn breath sounded behind her, and the guard's eyes widened. It took her a moment to realize why—her casual use of the High King's name. Gods above. Less than a day had passed since she'd met the kings, but in a strange way, they felt more familiar to her than the shopkeepers currently gawking at her, though she'd known the latter all her life. At some point this day, she'd started to see the kings as men first and royalty second.

Ria scoffed at herself. *Maybe when you had them inside your body?*

"Speak to her quickly," the guard said, catching her attention again.

Fear and worry filled Enry's eyes. "Are you well, Ria? Is this...? Did I cause you trouble?"

Oh, no. Poor Enry must think the herbs he'd given her had brought her grief. Truthfully, they almost had, but it wouldn't have been his fault. "I'm fine. My father's perfidy was discovered, and I'm safe."

"But you're being escorted through the streets by..." Enry's voice trailed off as he took in the line of servants behind her. "I'm not sure what to make of this. Do you need aid?"

Ria smiled. "No. They are helping me sort through the shop. That's all."

Enry opened his mouth, probably to ask another question, but the guard interrupted. "We should go before His Majesty grows worried, Lady Ria."

A few murmurs went through the small but ever-growing crowd, and Enry paled so abruptly that she had a moment's fear he might faint. Thankfully, he steadied himself, because she wasn't sure she could have risked stopping to help. Not with the avidly curious group pressing closer. If they didn't get out of here soon, it might take Toren and Mehl themselves to disperse the crowd.

"I'll speak to you later," she assured him.

The guard wasted no time moving them forward after that. A few scowls and harsh words—and one sword being loosened in its scabbard—had them reaching the shop sooner than she could have managed on her own. But once they made it to the front door, Ria allowed herself a few moments to study the building's façade, from the stone tiles on the roof to the freshly painted sign swinging beside the door.

So many memories, and few of them good.

Swallowing against the lump in her throat, Ria led the others inside. Then she had little time for reflection as she directed the servants in their work. There were completed orders to send to the appropriate customers—she assigned two people to box up the clothes and another two to deliver them—and countless bolts of fabric to properly store.

As that work began, Ria showed several more servants to the crates she'd packed the night before. "These will go directly to my rooms," she said before glancing around at the remaining furniture. "The rest can stay for now."

What should she do with it all? She'd planned to sell it before she left, and selling still seemed to be the best solution even though she was staying closer than she'd expected. But what about the shop itself? Did she want to close it entirely? Give up her talent for making designs come to life? Without her father to command her, they would be *her* creations for the first time in her life.

But selling clothes wouldn't help her fit in with the nobility, and Toren might find it unseemly for the mother of his heir. Did she want to create clothing badly enough to deal with snide remarks and blatant disapproval? It was a question she couldn't answer, at least not for the long term. For now, she needed to catalog all incomplete orders and have the necessary supplies sent to the palace.

Perhaps fulfilling that duty would reveal the truth of her feelings about her gift.

Ria had just given the final directions to the servants when the shrill sound of a horn cut through the walls and vibrated the windows. She rushed over to peer outside, just in time to see several warriors ride by with banners held high. A richly dressed man rode in the center, and the woman at his side lifted her bugle to her mouth to sound another call.

The group slowed, and Ria peered at one of the banners dancing gently around its pole. Purple and silver, with a stylized mountain in the center. Her blood chilled. That was the flag of Centoi—the kingdom that had given refuge to Toren's brother.

Not good.

CHAPTER 12

THE CHAMBERMAID

Toren tapped his fingers against the table, startling the scribe beside him. But Caidis was a steadier sort than Iyeth. She barely paused her writing as the advisors shared their observations in a more formal location than the lunch table. Not that they'd had much time at the latter. He would never force his servants to work harder because of his ill manners, so by the time Toren and Mehl had arrived, they'd all had to choke down cold food.

And now the endless deluge of problems.

"Accordingly," Lord Aievo said, "we will need to replace both ships sooner rather than later. Lady Meble intends to order the required timber from the western forest."

Toren leaned forward. "The Howling Woods? No."

Lord Aievo was an excellent advisor when it came to trade, but other segments of the kingdom often went unconsidered. "Your Majesty?" he sputtered. "The Howling Woods possess fine, straight trees that make excellent lumber. Several ships have been created from their wood."

Things like diplomatic relations. "That is precisely the

problem. We are granted a certain number of unclaimed trees by the dryads, and we're nearing that quota already. Two ships worth? No. Coordinate with Lady Iryne to have timber teleported from Honor's Forest to the south and The Merry Woods to the east."

Aievo sucked in a breath. "Ah, the costs..."

"I will bear them myself if need be." Toren's nostrils flared, his patience slipping. "We will not break our word to the dryads."

Perhaps sensing his anger, Lady Iryne was quick to turn an admonishing glance Aievo's way. "I am certain the mages guild will be willing to assist for a reasonable price, particularly if the alternative risks a conflict with dryads. Earth and nature mages would suffer greatly were that to occur. I will speak to them."

"You will carry my recommendation with you." Toren nodded toward the scribe. "If you would pen such, Caidis? A copy each for Lord Aievo and Lady Iryne."

Caidis pulled a few pieces of clean paper from the stack. "Of course, Your Majesty."

Beneath the table, Mehl's hand squeezed his leg in a show of support, but only when Lord Aievo gave his consent did Toren fully relax. His brother's threats had him too on edge if a minor challenge like this had his temper so close to slipping. His trade advisor always grumbled about costs. Nothing new about that.

As soon as Caidis finished, Toren read over her words, nodded his approval, and then waited for her to write out the second copy. But he'd barely managed to sign his name and harden the seal on both when the door opened to admit Feref. Toren's blood chilled at the tense worry on the man's face. Had something happened to Ria?

"Forgive me, Your Majesties. Ladies and lords." Feref

bowed. "I regret the interruption, but I've just received word that a contingent from Centoi just reached the palace gates. I have no doubt they will seek an audience momentarily."

Mehl's fingers spasmed around Toren's leg. "Centoi?" Mehl demanded.

Toren wanted to ask much the same, but shock left him grateful that his husband had beat him to it. Could Ber have come already? His missive had said he would arrive within the year, not a handful of weeks. Of course, it could be a coincidence. Ber had fostered in Centoi in his youth, and the king had taken a liking to him. That was true. However, there were plenty of reasons for King Ryenil to send an envoy beyond the fact that Ber was currently staying at his palace.

"The banners they carry proclaim such, Your Majesty," Feref said to Mehl.

Toren pushed his chair back, forcing Mehl to remove his hand quickly. While Toren normally would have apologized, he couldn't bring forth the words. "Who?" he asked instead. "Who is part of this contingent?"

Understanding filled Feref's gaze. "No one the guards recognized, Sire."

It wasn't Ber, then. Toren's tension eased a notch. "Have formal court gear brought to the antechamber, please."

"Already done," Feref replied.

Whether a messenger or more official envoy had arrived, Toren would be prepared to greet them properly. The less weakness he showed, the better. There was only one possible problem—Ria. It would be best to prevent word getting back to his brother that Toren had formed a breeding alliance. If she returned to the castle with a trail of servants carrying her belongings to the family wing, there would be no hiding it.

Mehl caught his eye. "What about...?"

Toren nodded, then stood. "Forgive me, honored guests,

but as you can see, we have pressing business. We will continue this discussion later. If you will accompany us to the antechamber, Feref?"

Neither Toren nor Mehl waited to see if their advisors would complain. He and his husband had already reached Feref before their murmured words of acceptance reached his ears. In truth, the advisors were probably relieved to be left to gossip about this newest arrival and what it might mean. They had to have similar fears about the contingent from Centoi.

Once they were well away from others, Toren slowed, catching Feref's attention. "See that Ria's return goes unnoticed, and place her in a less conspicuous room until our visitors are gone."

At his side, Mehl let out a relieved sigh. "That was my thought, as well."

"Once I have assisted you, I will ensure it is done, Your Majesties," Feref said.

"No," Toren insisted. "Mehl and I can don our own robes. Assist Ria."

Feref's brows twitched, a sure sign he was repressing a frown, but he'd been with Toren too long to argue. "I will do so at once."

As their chamberlain bowed once and then hurried away, Toren picked up his pace. Free of distraction, his thoughts turned back to the group from Centoi. His energy surged with his anger and worry, but Mehl slipped his fingers through Toren's, a silent symbol of comfort and support. Toren squeezed his husband's hand and offered him a smile, if a tense one.

Together, they would never let his brother prevail.

〜

RIA LINGERED beside the window after the group passed, uncertain what to do next. Part of her wanted to hide, and another part urged her to rush back to the palace to offer her support. But to what purpose? She might be the Duchess of Nevial in title, but she had no place in court. No right to stand beside Toren and Mehl. It wasn't as though she had knowledge that would be of benefit.

One of the guards stepped to her side. "The packing down here might take some time to complete, my lady. If you prefer, we can accompany the servants carrying your personal belongings from upstairs to the palace."

It seemed a reasonable suggestion, so she nodded. "I've already given directions to those working down here, so I suppose there is no reason for me to linger."

A handful of servants carried crates down the stairs, setting the boxes beside the front door before returning upstairs for more. By the time they were finished, there was a greater stack than Ria had anticipated. Had she packed so much in the dark hours before dawn? Perhaps they had added a few more things at their own discretion.

The door opened, and a servant wearing the fanciest of palace livery entered. He bowed to Ria. "Feref sent me, my lady. I am to ensure you return as subtly as possible. He has been directed by the High King to keep you from the envoy's notice."

She drew back in surprise. "How?"

"You're to arrive without escort, though a guard or two should trail you for safety's sake. Your belongings will be brought slowly and without fanfare." The servant skimmed her body with a critical eye. "If you might have plainer clothing...?"

There was logic to request, however unusual. Toren wanted her to return largely alone after assigning her so many guards on the way out? He had to be concerned about the

Centoi learning of their contract for him to change his directions so abruptly. Well, if he wanted subtle, she was well-prepared for that.

"My simple day dress should still be in the dressing room, if it hasn't been packed."

Ria hurried across the workroom to the door closest to the storage area. Just that morning, she'd changed into the court garb she now wore, and she hadn't thought to direct anyone into the usually empty room. Thankfully, she found her dress still there. It seemed none of the servants down here had taken the liberty to work outside the areas they'd been assigned.

She slipped out of her court gown and hung it carefully on its hanger. Her fingers sank into the soft, worn fabric of the blue day dress she'd left folded on a bench. So familiar and yet so strange after a day spent wearing the finest silk. Her old dress, though...it was a different kind of soft, one born of years of use. The familiarity eased some of Ria's tension as she donned the gown.

Quickly, she unwound the jeweled strands from her hair and took out the pins holding the mass up. Then she braided her hair into a simple plait before studying her reflection in the mirror. Good enough. If she grabbed her basket—minus any hint of the *elek terin* or the royal green dye it had been packed with—she would look like any commoner moving around the outer edges of the palace on her business.

The disguise was a mixed blessing. As she entered the main gates to the palace, Ria hesitated before heading toward the main doors where she'd exited. No matter her clothing, she was a duchess now, and the nobility rarely if ever used the other entrances. But the guard at those doors directed her firmly to the servants' entrance in the very back, not even the middle gates where she'd entered with her father the night before. Was it because of her clothing?

Unease began to tremble through her as she followed the long path around. It wasn't a status thing. Even if she hadn't been named a lady, it wouldn't be a slight to be considered a royal servant. The highest placed of those held more prestige than a mere tailor's daughter. No, it was the abrupt shift. She *had* completed the breeding contract, hadn't she?

It felt like a different lifetime at this point.

After a seeming eternity of being shuffled from servant to servant, Ria finally ended up in front of Feref. He entered the small sitting room where she'd been sent to wait, a neutral expression hiding his feelings on the matter. But even so, there was a stiffness to his demeanor that hinted at unhappiness or disapproval.

"Ah, Ria." He gestured toward the door behind him. "I've had a place prepared for you amongst the higher-ranked chambermaids. If you'll follow me?"

She froze. "The chambermaids?"

A hint of a sneer appeared, then was gone. "You should go unnoticed there."

Ria had the uneasy feeling that it wasn't just the Centoi whom Feref hoped would forget her, but she had no cause to argue. For all she knew, Toren or Mehl had ordered this very location. So she swallowed the sick feeling rising up her throat, nodded, and followed the kings' servant toward yet another room.

An abrupt change of circumstances—that appeared to be her new norm.

CHAPTER 13

INVITATIONS

By the time they resumed their places at their thrones, Mehl's tension had grown to nearly unbearable levels, a contrast to Toren's apparent calm. An illusion, of course, one that Mehl's husband had long perfected. But here, Toren was the High King in his element, even his immense well of power attuned to his role.

Not so for Mehl. He held his hands in loose fists in his lap, but he kept scraping the fingers of his right hand against the base of his palm out of the instinctive urge to grasp his sword. The one propped on the weapons' rack in his room, more decoration than anything else these days. He'd been king for a century, but not protecting Toren was simply unnatural.

Two guards opened the doors to the otherwise empty throne room, allowing the Centoi entry. A handful of warriors, unarmed, entered first and quickly spread to the side to admit a woman in purple livery with a richly dressed man following close behind. The pair halted, and the woman trilled out a few notes on her horn. Mehl struggled not to wince at the ridiculously loud display.

She bowed low until the jaunty feather on her cap brushed the floor. "Greetings, Your Majesties. If I may beg your indulgence, please allow me to announce my king's own messenger?"

Good gods, had King Ryenil sent an actual bard to introduce an envoy? She had the drama for it. But if Toren found the pretentious formality odd, there was no sign of it on his face as he gave his assent. Mehl only nodded, lest his voice give away his amusement.

"Thank you, Your Majesties," the herald answered, though she hadn't yet straightened from her bow. She had the muscle control of a warrior. "Then I present to you His Grace Lord Ormero Abret Naiess Hayl, Duke of Aony and Earl of Woifen, who is here under the auspices of King Ryenil Breren the Mighty, Sovereign of the Kingdom of Centoi."

For the first time since they'd sat down, Mehl sensed the rise of Toren's magic, but it wasn't out of control—yet. Nor did Toren appear disturbed as he regarded the herald. "We receive Lord Aony in peace. Stand and give him passage forward."

At Toren's command, the woman straightened with impressive ease. Mehl eyed the corded muscles of her calves beneath her tights as she stepped aside. There was something to her grace that reminded him of more than a simple herald, a careful fluidity reminiscent of the spies he'd trained beside in his youth. Assassin or added bodyguard?

Hopefully, they would have no cause to know.

"Thank you for the welcome, Your Majesties," Lord Aony proclaimed, the booming cheer in his voice setting Mehl even more on edge.

"Of course," Toren replied. To most, he likely sounded bored, but Mehl caught a hint of the strain beneath the calm. "We are pleased to greet an envoy of King Ryenil. Do you bring a message from your sovereign this day?"

Lord Aony gave a quick bow. "An invitation, Your Majesty. An honor that could only be delivered by one of my high status."

"Is that so?" Toren flicked his fingers. "Do tell."

Mehl never would have dared such a casual response, but although Lord Aony flushed slightly, he made no complaint. "King Ryenil Breren the Mighty, Sovereign of the Kingdom of Centoi requests the presence of High King Toren Eyamiri and King Mehl Eyamiri, Sovereigns of the Kingdom of Llyalia, at the marriage of his daughter Princess Lora in three months' time."

Mehl's fingers ceased their glide against his palm. A wedding invitation? That was all?

"I had not heard that Princess Lora was affianced," Toren said politely.

A hint of smugness flickered on Lord Aony's face. "Had you not? I thought this a mere formality since Her Highness is to wed your brother. Perhaps his message was delayed."

Everyone in that room, down to the scribe tucked into the corner taking notes, knew exactly why Toren hadn't heard that Prince Ber was wedding Princess Lora, but not even Lord Aony dared say it. A good thing, too. Toren's expression hadn't changed, but his energy had. Mehl formed a mental connection at once, and the rush of power was strong enough that he had to hold back a wince.

"I am certain you are correct," Toren replied, his words chillingly precise. "If you would leave the formal invitation with my chamberlain, we will give it due consideration. A guard will escort you to Feref now, and he will see that you have lodging for the night if you so require it."

"That is very kind of you, Your Majesty." Lord Aony's gaze darted briefly to the sunlit window. "Especially since it is not yet dark."

"We'll be well into afternoon once you've delivered your

invitation to Feref and traversed both palace and city," Mehl interjected. The man startled slightly, probably forgetting Mehl's existence—or maybe relevance. "And it's a fair journey to the next large city. Though our roads are generally secure, I'm sure my husband thinks only of your safety and comfort."

More likely, Toren thought to observe Lord Aony and the others from Centoi, but that hardly needed to be said.

"I will consider your kind invitation, High King," the lord replied.

Only time would tell if the man refused.

TOREN MAINTAINED his composure all the way to the family wing, but as soon as he and Mehl were alone, Toren released a harsh curse. "I cannot believe that King Ryenil would marry his only daughter to Ber. He has to know of Ber's threat to me. *Everyone* knows. Despite that, our long-standing alliance is intact. Could there be more enmity between us than I realized?"

His husband squeezed his shoulder. "Considering your brother's skill with lies, the king might not be aware of the full, true story."

"Possibly."

Even so, something about the situation was...off. Royal weddings tended to be as much alliance as affection—Toren's excluded. For King Ryenil to affiance his only child to Ber and then send a formal invitation to Toren? There was a statement behind that. A potentially dangerous one. What could Ryenil be plotting?

"This invitation bears the stench of trickery," he muttered.

His magic hammered against his mental shields until he ached with it, and his vision flashed. Toren halted, bracing himself against the wall as he struggled with the surge. Vaguely, he felt the brush of Mehl's arm around his waist, but it was a pale sensation against the burn of magic repressed.

"Toren?"

"It's as though my magic senses the threat," Toren gritted out, "When I know it's my own upset to blame."

Mehl's hold tightened. "Channel through me."

"I have done that too many times this day."

His husband *could* bear his magic, but the process wasn't without risk. In the throne room, Toren had sensed Mehl's pain when channeling his latest overflow. He shouldn't have risked it then, not after doing so before the luncheon, but showing such a severe weakness in front of Lord Aony had been a greater threat.

"It will take much agony for this to dispel on its own," Mehl insisted. "I'll be fine."

Toren shook his head. "No. I hurt you earlier."

Mehl's huff brushed his cheek. "Then find Ria."

Before he could answer, his husband nudged him forward, half-supporting and half-guiding him with the arm around his waist. Ria wasn't experienced in channeling, but just a small release of energy would help. He'd meant to check on her anyway.

Toren took deep breaths and fought the power back with each step. Fortunately, his vision cleared by the time they reached her door. Mehl turned the knob and shoved the panel forward, then helped Toren through. But the only person they found inside was a maid, who let out a yelp and dropped her cleaning cloth at the sight of them.

When she lowered into a deep bow, she snatched the fabric up. Toren pretended not to see. "Your Majesties! May I help you?"

"Where is Lady Ria?" Mehl demanded.

"Lady?" The maid's brow wrinkled. "Do you mean the woman that Feref moved to the servant's quarters? We thought she was a guest here until that happened. Now I have to clean the whole room again before we close it up."

If anything was capable of distracting Toren from his unwelcome invitation, it was this affront. Feref had sent Ria to the servant's quarters? Toren had ordered nothing of the sort, and Feref would have known that. It was a betrayal of the highest order. Pure, cold rage filled him until not even the discomfort of his magic could compete.

Toren spun from Mehl's hold and strode back to the door without a word. Once in the corridor, Mehl hurried up beside him with an expression furious enough to match Toren's own mood. They strode together toward the door at the far end that led to the servant's stairs. Ria would be returned to her rightful place.

And Feref would be searching for a new appointment.

At least the room had a proper window.

Ria had heard of nobles who kept their servants in bare, windowless quarters in the less favorable parts of their homes, but that wasn't the case at the royal palace. Really, it was a fine room. The bed was the same size as the one at her father's house, and if the linens were less luxurious than those in her initial guest room, a brush of her fingers revealed the fabric to be soft and sturdy. The solid wardrobe would hold all of her clothes. Even the tub she found behind a privacy screen in the corner had magically heated running water.

Regardless, it stung. She tried not to think of the abrupt change in her circumstances as she sat beside the window and watched the rush of people below. This room was situated above and to the side of the back entrance, so her observations were confined mostly to deliveries and dinner preparation—not exactly the best distraction.

Based on the baskets just carried in, freshly roasted vegetables were on someone's menu tonight. Too bad she had no idea if it was hers.

Would she dine with the servants? The kings? Alone in her room? Perhaps she would be forgotten entirely, as Feref clearly hoped. The man had given her no instructions on what to do. She had no clue if it was safe to leave her chamber or if she was *supposed* to leave when she needed something. A chambermaid wouldn't wait to be served, after all.

It wasn't that she minded attending to herself. She was accustomed to that. But—

The door swung open, and just like that, the kings stormed through. Ria leapt to her feet out of instinct, but the raw fury on Toren's face locked her body with fear. Even Mehl's jaw was set with anger, his eyes flashing with it. Had *she* done something wrong? She'd only followed Feref's directions, but she might have misunderstood. She was the stranger here, not him.

Abruptly, Mehl halted, and his hand darted out to grip the High King's arm. "Toren, stop."

Toren glared at his husband. "What?"

"Look at her," Mehl said, then leaned close to whisper in Toren's ear.

Either his voice was too low, or her heartbeat drummed too loudly in her ears, but Ria couldn't hear what was said. Whatever it was, Toren's expression blanked for a moment before dismay crossed his face. He went still, even his posture relaxing.

"Forgive me for scaring you, Ria," Toren said softly. "My anger was not for you."

She pressed her palm against her breastbone and inhaled through her nose. Once her frenzied heartbeat slowed to normal, she nodded. "I didn't know what I was supposed to do, so I've just been...here. Waiting. I thought I'd chosen wrongly."

Toren's jaw clenched. "You should be in your room upstairs."

"Oh." Her palm dug into her chest until it stung. "I only did what—"

"Feref is to blame," Mehl interrupted with a quick, frustrated glance at his husband. "Toren didn't mean to imply it was you. We came to bring you back upstairs. Please?"

The tension unwound from her muscles until she nearly slumped. Whatever had led to her move here, they hadn't forgotten her. Ria didn't know what shape her life would take in the coming days, but with the kings, she could truly find out. How could she refuse Mehl's quiet request?

But then, she was coming to fear she'd accept any invitation from these two.

"First to our room," Toren said tightly.

Heat replaced the chill of fear.

Especially an invitation like that.

CHAPTER 14

COAXING

Under any other circumstances, Ria would have laughed at the spectacle their passage through the servants' quarters caused. Even in the middle of the afternoon when most were working, the hallways were fairly busy with people passing through as they changed tasks. Or in this case, freezing like statues at the sight of the kings before dropping hastily to their knees. Toren's expression twisted with frustration each time he had to gesture for them to rise.

Eventually, he halted beside one of the women, her lined face revealing her great age. Even fae with human blood lived unchanging for millennia. "Margil, please stand. You would not do this in the palace proper, or no work would get done. None of you would. Why now?"

The woman wobbled on her feet as she rose, and Ria's eyes widened when Toren held out a hand for her to grip. Surprisingly, Margil did so. With a grateful smile, the woman regained her balance and patted the High King's arm lightly. Then she took a small step back.

"Thank you, Your Majesty," Margil said. "As for the other?

It is unprecedented for you and your husband to walk these halls. That's why."

A hint of softness lightened Toren's eyes. "Is that so? I seem to recall racing down this very corridor more than once in my youth. Someone who looked much like you kept chasing me away from the kitchens."

"Curious, that." Margil smiled slyly. "I'll have to seek my face sister, Your Majesty. I was unaware another resembled me so closely."

Ria couldn't help but stare at the High King as he asked after the woman's family. Did Toren know the names of everyone who worked in the castle? Surely not. Considered to be fair but firm, he was a powerful king whose rule was obeyed without question. Even so, she'd never heard rumors suggesting this level of kindness.

"Would you please ensure that word of this doesn't travel to the outsiders from Centoi?" At her nod, Toren smiled. "Also, I would greatly appreciate it if you would precede us and ask the other servants to cease these displays. I wish to return Lady Ria to her proper room without delay, but I did not intend to cause such a disruption in the process."

Margil bowed. "Of course, High King Toren. I would be pleased to give aid."

After the woman rushed ahead to spread the word, their way was much easier, though the curious stares didn't exactly cease. Regardless, Ria found tension drawing her muscles ever-tighter with each step. What would happen when they reached the kings' room? Her skin heated. Aside from the obvious, of course, although the obvious was perhaps the problem.

Even as she grew wet at the memory of being taken by Toren in the throne room, uncertainty heightened her nerves. That had been...fire. A spontaneous moment born of sudden passion. This time was more deliberate. She was giving herself to the kings with purpose.

And few things were scarier than that.

SOMEWHERE BETWEEN THE family wing and the servant's quarters, Toren seemed to have lost a bit of the hard edge that had threatened his control. Mehl had shifted in the other direction. Now his husband walked calmly up the stairs while Mehl fought not to stomp his temper into the stone. The threat of Toren's brother picked at him, but it wasn't really that.

It was Ria's frozen expression when they'd first rushed into her room.

He'd seen that look before on his sister's face when her new husband had grown angry during a family gathering. There was a haunting stillness to it, but not quite that of a predator in front of prey. For alongside the fear, there was that little hint of frantic hope. That idea that if one reacted *just so*, all would turn out well.

Mehl had watched Klerah carefully after he'd first seen her worrisome reaction, but it had taken a couple of months to prove the abuse. When he'd come upon his sister being punched in the stomach, he'd beaten her husband severely before binding the man up for the authorities. Mehl had received a mild rebuke from his superior for that, but it was a formality at best—and entirely worth it.

Even though several centuries had passed, that hell spawn still bore the scars as he limped through the recesses of the dungeon near Mehl's hometown. And Mehl knew because he made it a point to check yearly. Fortunately, Klerah had remarried a couple of decades after Mehl had wed Toren, and she and her current husband now lived half a day from the palace.

To see another woman he cared about—

Mehl stiffened. Another bit of craziness, that. He surely didn't have the same level of feeling for Ria—not even close. She wasn't family, and he didn't think of her like a sister. He wrinkled his nose. Definitely not like a sister. Yet somehow, he *had* come to care for Ria with a fierce, protective urgency. Like most things involving this situation, it defied logic.

Her father had much to answer for. If Mehl were once again a simple guard-in-training and not king, he would have slipped into the dungeon to mete out his own justice, but even kings had limits. He rather suspected their subjects would protest if either of their monarchs began beating prisoners before any kind of trial.

As soon as they reached the family wing, Toren slowed until he walked at Mehl's side. "Thank you for the warning."

Mehl nodded. "We must take care."

He might have said more, but Ria stepped up to his right. "Take care? Do you think there might be spies even here?" she asked.

His answer wasn't a lie, though it skirted the truth behind the words she'd overheard. She didn't need to know they'd been talking about startling her. "I doubt it, but it would serve us well to be cautious while the Centoi are here."

Toren opened the door to the High King's suite, and Mehl followed him through. Had Toren shivered when passing through the protective shield on the door? Mehl frowned at his husband's tense shoulders and the tight expression he wore when he turned. That calm he'd shown as they'd retrieved Ria was at least partly feigned, Mehl would wager.

The room grew quiet as he and Ria joined Toren in the center of the sitting room. Had it only been a day since she'd entered this room with her father and set off the wards? It felt like much longer. In that time, she'd agreed to have Toren's heir. She'd taken Mehl into her mouth as Toren had claimed her.

Yet her very demeanor shouted her uncertainty. Her eyes were averted like they'd been the day before, almost as though she was afraid they would chide her for glancing their way. Her fingers were twisted together so tightly that her knuckles had gone white. It was as though they'd never been intimate at all.

"Ria," Mehl said softly, but her gaze darted to his as though he'd yelled. "Are you afraid of us now?"

Her teeth sank into her lower lip. "Not exactly."

Toren eased closer until they formed their own little triangle. "I am sorry if my anger caused you distress. It was not because of you. My control was thin after our visit from the Centoi, and finding you gone did nothing to help."

"Was Feref not supposed to send me downstairs?" Ria asked. "He sounded confident that it had been on your orders."

Toren's jaw clenched hard enough that Mehl reached over to rub his arm soothingly. "I told him to make sure your return went unnoticed," Toren said. "And to place you temporarily in a less conspicuous room. As a duchess of the realm, you should have been given a place among the other noble guests."

Ria's brow furrowed. "They would definitely notice that."

"Not necessarily." Mehl smiled at her. "There are many rooms here. Whole corridors that are only opened for special occasions."

He could see that she didn't quite understand the scope of Toren's anger. Like him, she hadn't been born to the nobility. Royal servants were well-regarded, but it was a terrible insult to house a noble amongst them. To people like himself and Ria, it was simply a less fancy room. To the highborn, it was a shift in their entire world.

Mehl lifted his hand slowly, ready to stop at the slightest indication that Ria was uncomfortable. She tracked the motion, but instead of flinching, she relaxed as he brushed his fingers gently along her cheek. Somehow, his anger had shifted almost entirely to tenderness.

"What is wrong?" Mehl asked.

Her sigh warmed his wrist. "It's silly, but...I don't know what to do now that we're here. Deliberate action is so much tougher than sudden passion."

Beside him, Toren tensed, a sudden fire lighting his eyes. But he stared at Mehl instead of Ria. *"If she seeks passion... I cannot touch her first, Mehl. Not when I am so volatile. Can you ease her uncertainty?"*

Toren's mental voice held the burn of his power, the magic barely restrained. Ria had so much spirit, but that kind of intensity after they'd scared her once already? It wouldn't go well. Mehl gave Toren the slightest nod.

"Contract or no, we would never force you," Mehl said. "In fact, I believe the contract forbids such a thing."

Ria's hands lowered to her sides, and she straightened. "I know. It's just strange to be so deliberate about it all. So matter of fact. I'm unaccustomed to bedding someone for any reason save pleasure."

Even as Mehl's heart softened, his body heated. This time, he eased closer and cupped her cheek in his palm. Ria stared up at him in surprise, her lips parting on a gasp. Slowly, he slid his fingers through her hair until he could tip her head back for his kiss.

"Then perhaps we should begin with pleasure?" Mehl murmured.

Ria licked her bottom lip. "Yes."

Still, Mehl hesitated. "Toren?"

"Yes," his husband growled.

Permission granted, Mehl swooped to claim. Her mouth was heaven, and his cock went painfully hard at the memory of how she'd felt sucking him to completion in the receiving room. But this time, *he* would take care of *her*. He would stretch her atop their bed, spread her legs wide, and pleasure her until she begged. Then Toren could fuck her if she wished.

Mehl pulled his lips from hers, but he tucked her body against his. Her eyes widened as his cock pressed into her stomach. Someday, Toren's child would rest within her there, and Mehl would finally be able to claim her fully. It was all he could do not to lower her to the floor now and damn the consequences.

The rumble of Toren's low groan helped Mehl gather his control.

But he couldn't reign in his frustration when a knock sounded on the outer door.

CHAPTER 15

THE JUDGMENT

Toren was so focused on the delectable sight before him that he nearly missed the knock at the door. But then Ria jerked out of Mehl's arms, a furious blush lighting her face, and Mehl groaned and glared at the door. As his energy surged, Toren turned his own scowl in the same direction.

Unfortunately, he recognized the knock's cadence—Feref. For multiple reasons, Toren wouldn't ignore *his* presence. "Enter."

His chamberlain no doubt heard the bite to his tone, for he entered more slowly than usual, his eyes downcast. Only when Feref had closed the door soundly behind himself did he skim his gaze over the room. He froze at the sight of Ria, and his skin went as pale and blotched as a cloud at sunset.

"I see you are aware of your transgression against me," Toren said coldly.

Feref dropped to his knees. "High King, I swear I did not intend to act against you."

Out of the corner of his eye, Toren saw his husband take

Ria's hand and draw her closer to Toren. A show of solidarity, but safety, too—for Feref. Toren's magic was far too uncertain for this, but it had to be handled.

His expression hardened. "Because of your years of service, I will give you a chance to explain."

Feref nodded, but he didn't look up. "I want no harm to come to the woman, but I could not bear to place her closer with yet more danger in the palace. She arrived here with poison, Your Majesties. I have served you proudly since you were a prince, High King Toren, and it goes against my heart to see you in danger. I had...hoped you might forget. Or simply reconsider."

Forget? Was he daft?

Mehl let out a snort-chuckle. "We have a binding contract, Feref. You might not have been in the room when it was sealed or signed, but I know you are aware."

The chamberlain's skin mottled to a sunset red. He understood exactly what Mehl meant by "sealed," and it wasn't the wax affixed to the contract. The guard outside the receiving room would have heard their sounds of pleasure as they'd claimed Ria, and what one servant or warrior in the palace knew, Feref soon learned.

"It will be a shame to lose you as my chamberlain," Toren mused. "I count on you immensely."

Feref nearly choked on a gasp. "Your Majesty? You cannot be... I thought only of your well-being. It is my paramount concern."

"You shared that concern with me earlier, and I appreciated it. However." Toren stiffened his spine. It truly was a shame, but he had little choice. "I cannot allow you to countermand me in such a way. After so many centuries of service, you cannot convince me you weren't aware of what I wanted. You are also aware that Ria is now the Duchess of Nevial, and yet you didn't even grant her a noble's rooms."

The chamberlain flicked a quick, angry glance Ria's way. "I thought it safest, since she was returning from the *merchant's* area."

"You were to do as I asked, nothing more," Toren snapped. "You will tell me what happened with the Centoi, send your apprentice to me, and then pack your belongings."

"But Your Majesty," Feref began before his voice choked off.

Suddenly, Ria darted around Mehl, shifting until she was half in front of the chamberlain. "No, Toren. This is unnecessary."

"I told you anyone foolish enough to mock you would answer to me." He allowed the barest hint of temper to enter his eyes. "Feref's actions were an insult that cannot be tolerated, especially considering his insubordination."

Ria placed a shaking hand against his chest. "He's right to be concerned. Please."

Feref was *right?* Toren's magic shoved hard against his shields.

What did she mean by that?

RIA KNEW one thing for certain: she couldn't let Toren dismiss his chamberlain over her. It didn't matter whether he had a point about the man's disobedience—nearly every servant in this castle would hate her over it. Besides, Feref had acted out of loyalty, not malice. There had to be a better way.

"What do you mean by that?" Toren asked, and she hated the sudden gleam of suspicion in his eyes.

Perhaps she could have phrased her last comment better.

"If he cares for you, it is normal and right for him to see to your health," Ria said. "What if you believed I'd threatened Mehl? Wouldn't you be angry at my continued presence?"

His eyes narrowed. "Of course. But I told Feref there was no need for concern."

Ria tapped her forefinger against Toren's chest. "I suspect your explanation was...sparse. You tested me yourself, so you know. No one else has reason for the same certainty."

Feref gasped behind her. "Tested? I did not know you'd..."

"It was not a full test," Toren said, his voice rumbling beneath her hand. "But it was enough."

"Forgive me, Your Majesty."

Toren's expression didn't yield, but the tension leached from his muscles. He appeared to be considering his chamberlain's plea. What might sway him? It was understandable that he would be concerned about such a highly placed servant disobeying his command. What sort of punishment would be fitting?

Mehl stepped forward, catching her gaze in the process. The slightest hint of a smile appeared and then was gone. "Toren. Might we consider a sort of probation for Feref? Have him seek approval for decisions before they are made? He might also serve Lady Ria as he does us, at least for a time."

Though she didn't consider herself particularly troublesome, Ria refused to turn around to see what Feref thought of that extra duty. She almost hoped Toren didn't agree to that part. The chamberlain clearly disliked her, so interacting with him even more wasn't precisely appealing. But if it would save them all future grief, she would do it.

"Perhaps," Toren said. "Ria, go with Mehl into our bedroom and await me there. I would like to speak to Feref alone. Continue as you were before his interruption."

Her heartbeat slammed and skittered, and her entire body went hot. Had she misunderstood? Was Toren actually ordering them to resume their heated embrace even when he wasn't there? That couldn't be right. But the flicker of fire in his gaze when their eyes met suggested otherwise.

Mehl's arm circled her waist. "Come. Toren will judge Feref fairly."

She didn't glance at the chamberlain as Mehl guided her toward another door, his warm hand lowering to rest just above the curve of her ass. His thumb caressed her lower back in a slow circle, and she shivered. There would be no doubt about what they were doing.

None at all.

As soon as the door clicked shut, Toren advanced on Feref, who still knelt. A host of emotions beat through Toren along with his magic, both threatening to break free. Something his chamberlain clearly knew, for he neither spoke nor looked up when Toren halted in front of him.

"You realize the source of my anger, don't you?" he asked softly.

Feref's gaze made it to his chest. "I do, High King. But I swear that I had no ill intent."

"Very few know how my mother's chamberlain betrayed her." Toren clenched his hands at the memory. "But you do. We've been together for a long time. You must have guessed I would not take disobedience lightly."

"May I speak plainly, as I would have when we were young?"

Toren inclined his head. "Yes."

Only then did Feref glance up. "I know you need an heir. That is vital with your brother's challenge hanging over us all.

I'm also aware that Ber worked with your mother's chamberlain to administer the poison that killed her. Your brother is beyond ruthless, and fighting him allows no distractions. Ria… Lady Ria has more of your attention than may be wise, and her arrival here under suspicious circumstances does her no credit."

There was truth to what Feref said, even if Toren didn't want to admit it. But at the same time, his instincts cried one thing: *she is the answer.* He just didn't know why.

"How am I to sire an heir without that attention?" Toren asked instead.

Feref's lips twisted wryly. "I have no doubt you have that part covered, Toren. But your eyes draw toward her for more than sex. Mehl's, too. I haven't noted the like since I watched you and Mehl pretend you weren't falling in love with each other. It concerns me, since she may not be what she seems. But if you tested her with your magic, then I will do my best to give her my trust regardless of my future place here."

Sighing, Toren pinched the bridge of his nose. What was the best course of action? Surely not dismissing the man who'd been more friend than servant before rank came between them. Feref hadn't called him by name alone for decades— maybe a couple of centuries. That was something that should perhaps change.

But not yet.

He dropped his hand back to his side. "Stand up, Feref. I believe Mehl's plan to be a sound one."

Feref rose to his feet, cautious relief crossing his face. "I'm appreciative. However, if you are uncertain of me, I understand—"

"You'll not talk your way out of the job just to save yourself the extra duties," Toren said with forced sternness. "For the foreseeable future, you will tell me how you intend to complete all orders I give, and you will attend to Lady Ria's requests whenever possible."

"Of course, Your Highness." Feref bowed. "I will do my utmost not to squander this chance."

Toren nodded. "Good. Now, tell me what happened with the Centoi contingent."

Whatever the news, it ultimately wasn't likely to be good.

RIA HAD BARELY MANAGED to get a look at the huge, sumptuous room before Mehl tugged her close, his mouth claiming hers so thoroughly she no longer cared where they were. Her world became the tangle of their tongues and the smooth slide of his hair between her fingers as she anchored herself to him.

Needy, she rubbed against him and groaned at the spear of pleasure. Mehl growled low, the hum rumbling between them as he grabbed her thighs and lifted her. Ria wrapped her legs around his waist, then nearly yelped when he started walking. Each stride rubbed his cock against her, only a few thin layers of clothing between them.

Ria expected him to toss her onto the bed, but he lowered her gently—almost reverently—to the coverlet. He crawled up beside her, bracing himself on one elbow and staring at her intently. Instead of kissing her again, he cupped the side of her face, then traced his hand gently along her throat and down to her breast.

His thumb toyed almost absently with her nipple. "Are you still eager for a bit of pleasure, Ria?"

"Yes," she breathed. "But last time, Toren granted you one kiss only."

Mehl bent his head and nipped gently at her lower lip. "He

fears taking you with his magic so heightened. He'll be less concerned if you're not nervous."

Ria chuckled. "And you aim to ease that?"

"One does what one must." Abruptly, he pinched her nipple, and her back bowed off the bed. "If you're amenable to distraction?"

"They'll hear if I—"

"No." Mehl's grin turned wicked. "There's a spell on the walls to muffle sound. Is that all?"

Ria threaded her fingers through his hair once more and gave a tug. "Yes."

But he resisted. Instead, Mehl straightened from the bed and gripped her legs, tugging until her bottom was at the very edge. He ran his hands up her calves, then thighs, and with the glide of his palms, he slid her skirt higher. A quick tug of her underclothes, and she was bare to him. Completely open.

Mehl's heated gaze met hers. "Ready to see a king on his knees?"

Then he dropped down beside the bed and showed her just how talented he was with lips and tongue.

CHAPTER 16

BLESSED DISTRACTION

Ria tasted divine.

Mehl flicked his tongue against her nub and smiled at her stifled squeal. Just the kind of tangy sweet he loved. He teased her for a moment longer, circling and nipping before he dove in deep. He could take her this way, at least.

Her knees drew up, and he rested his arms against her thighs, holding them wide. Ria moaned and undulated against him, but her hand darted into his hair to hold him close. He chuckled against the warmth of her cunt, sending a new quiver through her. This was the kind of torment he could deliver for hours.

By the time the door clicked shut across the room, Ria had already cried out in release twice, and his cock was so hard it hurt. The latter was in no way helped by the sound of Toren's ragged in-drawn breath. The kind that inevitably preceded a good fucking.

Mehl pulled back, grinning when Ria's hand tightened in his hair. But when Toren growled low, her head jerked up, and she scrambled back on her elbows before Mehl caught her thighs in a tighter grip. Her wide eyes stared up and to the side where his husband no doubt hovered over them.

Toren's hand dug into his shoulder, and Mehl tipped his head back to meet his eyes. Gods, yes. Desire blazed there. Toren leaned down and licked Ria's juices from Mehl's chin before devouring his mouth. His husband's tongue danced with his in much the way he'd tormented Ria.

Magic throbbed in the room, and Toren pulled back, panting. "Someday," he said, "I will taste your flavors more fully entwined."

Groaning, Mehl palmed his cock. The thought of spending in Ria, only to have Toren take him into his mouth… "Hopefully not long."

Toren tugged him to his feet and kissed him once more, their hands brushing as Toren gripped his cock through his clothes. His energy pulsed so strongly that Mehl vibrated with it even though it was still contained. A slight ache began to build in his head from all he'd had to channel of late, distracting him from pleasure. They had to do something about Toren's magic.

But could Ria help? Was she ready?

Gods, he hoped so.

Toren knew the moment Mehl's mood shifted, and after their decades together, he understood instantly what it meant—discomfort. When he'd entered the room to the sight of Mehl pleasuring Ria, Toren had wanted nothing more than to lift his husband from where he knelt and take him hard and fast. Then take Ria. His control was like the finest gossamer, easily torn, and Mehl would bear the brunt if they continued.

He would hurt his husband like this.

Reluctantly, Toren drew back. Heat filled Mehl's eyes, but there was a hint of a headache, too. Toren brushed his finger along his husband's lower lip. "I dare not…"

"I'm sorry," Mehl said.

"Do not," Toren snapped before forcing calm back to his voice. "The sight of you two nearly severed the remainder of my restraint. It is not your fault that I didn't stop to consider your comfort."

A rustle of cloth caught his attention as Ria sat up. Hastily, she tried to shove her rumpled skirt back down her legs. A pity, that. "I'm sorry," she said. "We did too much without you here. I worried, but—"

"No." Toren's voice stopped her hands mid-tug. "I wanted you to be ready for me. Usually, Mehl helps dispel this energy, but that type of sex is…intense. Now, I fear I've distracted away all his work."

Ria's throat worked. "Not entirely."

"Shall I attend to you again?" Mehl asked in a low voice.

Before Toren could urge them on, Ria shook her head. She averted her gaze for a moment, her teeth sinking into her lip. Then she met his eyes directly. "Maybe you should continue as you were. With…fewer clothes."

She wanted to watch them? Fire scorched his veins, nearly burning away that gossamer-thin control. Toren pinched his eyes closed and let out a curse. He would like nothing more than to grant her wish, but he would never make it through, not without hurting Mehl. Possibly even hurting all of them.

As always, Mehl knew. "Removing clothing is a simple thing, my duchess, but I have a better plan for the rest. One that will see us all well-served."

Toren couldn't help but stare as Mehl tugged his formal robe over his head and tossed it across a chair. Gods above, he was handsome. His muscles flexed and flowed in the light, and the vee of his hips arrowed down to the mouthwatering bulge tenting his pants. But that last bit of clothing remained, Mehl's fingers hooked in the waistband.

"I believe it is your turn, Ria," Mehl said.

Ungh. Toren led as often as not, but when Mehl got in a mood like this... Apparently, Ria agreed, for it only took her a moment to ease her dress back up her thighs and then higher. She wiggled her bottom back and forth to free the fabric, and Toren's mouth went dry. Whatever Mehl planned had better work quickly.

Before Ria's dress had even hit the floor, Mehl shucked his pants, giving Toren another delightful view, and then crawled up beside her on the bed. Mehl eased her up to the center of the mattress, and as he did, her legs fell open. Something equally delightful to see.

Toren's magic surged until it physically hurt to restrain it, but he only fisted his hands around the fabric of his robe as Mehl settled on his side and palmed Ria's breast. "The plan, Mehl?" he gritted out.

His husband gave him a wicked smirk. "Fewer clothes, my love. Then you can join us."

Was that so? Toren didn't have to be told twice.

HAD she really asked the kings to strip naked and kiss each other for her pleasure? It had been a moment of insanity, a dare she wouldn't normally make. But something in the way Toren had lapped her juices from Mehl's mouth had set her aflame. Too bad her wish hadn't been granted.

At least not completely.

She watched through heavy-lidded eyes as Toren finished

undressing. Every line of his body was perfect, from his leanly muscled frame to his proudly jutting cock. Between him and the more muscular Mehl, it was a miracle she hadn't already drooled onto their sumptuous bedding.

Ria sucked in a breath as Mehl's hand slid down her stomach, his fingers tracing her folds where his mouth had just been. At the end of the bed, Toren froze, his gaze trained on the dance of Mehl's fingers over her core. Her heart pounding, Ria widened her legs more.

That goaded Toren into action. Before she could blink, he knelt between her thighs and plunged two fingers deep at the same time that Mehl gently pinched her clit. Her release crashed over her so hard and fast that she screamed, and her vision went white around the edges. But as her muscles began to relax and her breathing to steady, Toren curled his arms beneath her knees, spread her wide, and entered her in one stroke.

All while Mehl's fingers continued to torment her.

Oh, gods, it was so much.

Whatever control Toren had held onto must have snapped, for he took her relentlessly. Almost ruthlessly. Mehl flattened his fingers, two on each side of her clit, so that each time Toren pounded against her, his fingers rubbed her *just so*. But the fire only grew, higher than before, the pleasure never breaking.

She couldn't take this much longer.

She needed—

Then Mehl took her nipple in his mouth and tweaked the tip with his teeth, and she exploded.

Ria barely noticed when Toren's magic rushed through her. She didn't even try to grasp it, for the force of his energy almost paled in comparison to her pleasure, a diamond pure and sharp and cutting. She could do nothing but ride the wave as Toren stiffened and cried out above her.

Finally, he collapsed against her, his panting breaths cooling the fine sheen of sweat between her breasts. Ria wrapped her free arm around his back and held on, stunned. Shaken. This time felt different, but she couldn't process how.

Mehl slid his hand from between them, his damp fingers making her shiver as they traced up her belly. But rather than seeming aroused, Toren levered himself up on his elbows to frown at his husband. Had Mehl done something wrong?

"No one saw to your pleasure," Toren growled.

With a half-pained grin, Mehl gripped his cock and slid his hand down its length. "True enough."

"Well." Toren brushed a kiss across Ria's lips before sliding free of her body and releasing her legs. Then he sat back on his heels and turned his attention more fully on Mehl. "That cannot stand. But perhaps I can grant Ria's wish after all."

She shivered with cold without the warmth of him upon her—within her—but the chill didn't last long. Toren shifted to kiss Mehl, first on the mouth and then in a line down his chest. By the time he reached his husband's cock, she was hot enough to heat the entire room. When Toren took Mehl in his mouth, Ria was certain of one thing.

If she were to die anywhere, it would surely be in this bed.

A ray of light from the window annoyed Mehl awake, and he turned his face into Toren's neck to block the piercing glow. Unfortunately, he couldn't go back to sleep. It had to be nearing sunset to hit his face at that angle, and that meant there was dinner to attend. He'd grown accustomed to being a king for the most part, but at times like this, he would far prefer to stay abed with his lovers and let the world take care of itself.

Being wrapped around Toren, his hand resting on the dip of Ria's waist while she slept against Toren's other side, brought Mehl more true peace than he'd felt in some time. At least since Prince Ber's threat. The only thing that marred it was being unable to fully participate in the lovemaking the way he wanted, but Toren and even Ria had made that up to him in the end.

It could have been an awkward thing, marred by jealousy or spite, but somehow, the three of them in bed just...worked.

Toren shifted and mumbled something, but Mehl couldn't make out the words. Regretfully, he lifted up to his elbow, squinting against the light as he glanced down at his husband. It only took a second for Toren's eyes to blink open.

"Nearing dinner?" Toren murmured.

"I would say so." An unpleasant one, if the Centoi had stayed. Mehl stifled a curse at that reminder. "I should have asked what happened with the envoy. Are we to dress for the highest formality and suffer hours of forced, awkward discourse?"

When Toren's brow lowered, Mehl assumed the answer would be yes. Until Toren said, "No. According to Feref, they left."

"They..." Mehl rubbed his palm against his ear. "They left the palace? That, I did not expect."

"Nor did I. It is suspicious."

Mehl thought back to the group who'd entered the throne room, especially the "herald," and nodded. "Did Feref have them trailed?"

"That he did," Toren replied.

With a huff, Ria rolled to her back, flinging her arm wide across the covers. But the move was more indolent than annoyed, and her expression was sated rather than angry. An "I don't want to be awake" sort of huff, then. She was surely tired. Their first round of lovemaking had been followed by a second, and it wasn't even evening yet.

"You didn't end up dismissing Feref because of me, did you?" she mumbled. "Please tell me you didn't."

Toren smiled. "I did not, but I fear he may bemoan that choice after all the extra work he'll be doing."

Ria relaxed against the bed. "Thank you."

Abruptly, Toren sat up, giving Mehl a view of his gods-wrought back as he leaned over Ria. Mehl had just started to contemplate which muscle he'd lick first when Toren spoke.

"You may regret the thanks, my lady." Toren twined a strand of her hair around his finger. "Feref's next job will be seeing you properly prepared for dinner with the court. I've decided to announce our contract there. Tonight."

Ria's eyes widened, and her mouth dropped open. Mehl had a feeling he looked much the same. Hadn't they decided to discuss this later? Where had this resolve come from? For resolve it was. Mehl had long learned it was a waste of time arguing when Toren took on that kingly tone. The amount of effort required to change his path then was rarely worth the effort.

The question was...would Ria agree?

CHAPTER 17

DINNER PLANS

Toren wanted to do *what?*

Had his expression looked less determined, Ria might have thought he was jesting. But although his tone had been light, there was no humor on his face. "Did I miss a vital conversation?" she demanded.

His lips thinned, but he stroked his thumb gently against the strand of her hair he still held. "I will not have today's mistake repeated. The Centoi refused our hospitality, so I see no reason to delay."

Of course he didn't. He'd spent centuries at the High Table. The rules and expectations were practically ingrained in his blood, and if he did stumble, none would dare to challenge him. Any mistake in etiquette would probably become a new trend. But as soon as the announcement of their contract was made, all focus would be on her.

Not in a nice way, either.

"It would be bad enough at court," Ria said softly, her hand going to his chest. "But that is short-lived. A formal dinner? That takes hours, and I would be trapped at the table for all of it. Would I even be seated beside you? Either of you? I'm not royalty. We aren't married or engaged."

He dropped her lock of hair and leaned his weight on both arms, caging her in more thoroughly. "You will be seated where I wish."

Her body went hot—he'd looked much like this when he'd claimed her earlier—but she had to ignore her desire. It was more important to discover the reason behind the intensity in his eyes. "I'm clueless about royal protocol. We all know it. So why are you so determined to do this tonight?"

The muscles in his cheeks flexed. "There should be no doubt, not by anyone, that you belong to me and Mehl. I will not return to the family wing to find that you have been shuffled elsewhere. Never again."

Ria held his gaze, though her heart thumped a heady beat. She didn't want to think about the thrill of his claim, one he couldn't fully mean. This arrangement was temporary. Wasn't it? She was too afraid to delve into the heart of that question. They'd given her rooms in the family wing, and Toren called her his. But once she'd borne his child, that would no doubt change.

Especially after she humiliated him with her lack of knowledge.

"Toren..." Mehl began. "Perhaps this is too much."

Ria grimaced. It was good that one of the kings understood her limitations, but the embarrassment still stung. "You can't want me to sit at the High Table while the nobles study my every move," she said. "As soon as you announce the breeding contract, I won't be able to hold a fork slightly off without it being the evening's gossip."

Toren's nostrils flared. "Would you prefer I hide you away?"

"Maybe," Ria answered at once. "At least when it comes to

formal events. I suspect I will not be popular amongst the nobility, so the less I am seen, the better."

Mehl sent her a sympathetic smile. "They do eventually grow accustomed to our ignoble intrusion."

"When they must." Why couldn't either king see how different things were for her? Even Mehl only partially understood. "I am temporary. A means to an end, which makes me open to contempt. If I'm not careful, the mockery might cause you trouble, too. Or our child. Do you want whispers about your heir's mother?"

"No one will dare." Despite his harsh words, Toren brushed a soft kiss across her lips. "Come. You must show them from the beginning that you will not cower. There will already be whispers after our foray into the servants' quarters, and hiding will only make things worse."

He did not, of course, refute that she was temporary, but she had no right to the pain that omission caused.

Mehl gripped Toren's forearm. "Her concerns are not without merit, Tor."

"I am aware." As soon as his husband released him, Toren pushed up to a sitting position by Ria's hip. "Thus my decision. The Centoi's departure is cause for concern, but it opened up a new opportunity. We appear together tonight and end the speculation about the woman we escorted from the servants' quarters before the rumors get out of control."

Part of her had hoped that his resolve was not as strong as it appeared, but those words quashed that dream. Even Mehl's worried expression had shifted to resignation. Should she fight it? These two men were the final law of their land, Toren most of all, and yet she didn't think they would force her.

Unfortunately, Toren's explanation made sense. Palace servants were renowned for their discretion, but even they had limits. Others outside the castle might not hear a whisper, but inside? Everyone from the top down would be watching each step she took for clues to her presence in the family wing instead of the rooms usually granted during a breeding alliance.

It was only a matter of time before one of the nobles heard. They would guess that she'd agreed to the contract after Toren's words to her during court that morning, but her placement beside the High King was unusual enough to cause greater speculation. Even though not all of that would be stopped by a show of unity at dinner, the announcement would provide her greater protection from the worst of it.

Nothing like a necessary disaster.

Fortunately, no one could enter the dining room before the High King, because once again, they were going to be late.

By whatever miracle, Feref opened the door to Ria's room just as Toren and Mehl neared, and Ria glided out to meet them. Toren halted, his breath catching at the sight of her. The pale gold dress hugged her body, a thin, turquoise over-dress flowing around her with each step. Her hair had been swept up into intricate braids, but she wore no crown or tiara.

All normal for a king's consort. In fact, Feref had seen her outfitted perfectly for the role. She wasn't royalty, but she would bear the heir to the kingdom. As such, she wore a color that hinted at royal green without appearing to mimic it. Turquoise was included in the portrait of nearly every past consort for a reason.

"Well?" Ria asked.

Mehl stepped forward to offer his arm. "Perfection."

Both looked to Toren, but it took him a moment to formulate words. The sight of them together squeezed his chest, but not in a bad way. There was something—there *could be* something between the three of them. He had the uncomfortable feeling that more of his heart stared at him than he wanted to consider.

He barely knew Ria, yet somehow, she was no stranger.

Mehl quirked a brow, so Toren forced a smile despite his discomfiture. "You look lovely, Ria." He caught his chamberlain's eye where he hovered in the doorway. "Feref is to be commended for guiding you properly."

Feref practically sagged against the doorframe in relief.

Toren pretended not to notice.

The three of them made their way out of the family wing in silence, Mehl and Ria no doubt as lost in thought as he. Or perhaps worried. Despite Ria's assumptions, Toren was well aware of her precarious place amongst the nobles. But they were as constricted by tradition and law as he was, and the primary law was obedience to the royal family. Their magics were bound into their oaths more thoroughly than Ria or even Mehl realized.

Toren had spent his life in service to his people, fighting for their health and safety before he understood what those words truly meant. Acceptance of Ria was not an unjust request, and he would not yield on the matter. They didn't have to like her, but she would not be disrespected.

After tonight, that would be perfectly clear.

As a bodyguard, Mehl had watched everyone without being noticed. As a king, it was nearly the opposite. The closer the three of them came to the dining room, the more eyes fastened on them like raptors sizing up mice. Hungry and wanting.

None of them saw Toren and Mehl, much less Ria. Only High King and King.

He no longer stiffened beneath their regard the way he'd once done, but the same couldn't be said for Ria. By the time they neared the doors to the dining room, her arm was a tight knot of muscles where it rested on his. And no wonder. The long hallway they traversed was lined with nobles awaiting entry. This would be no easy meal for her.

How well he knew.

Before they reached the doors, Mehl tipped his head toward hers. "You'll have to enter behind us," he murmured.

She gave a slight nod and loosened her hold. After a kiss to her hand to show he meant no slight, Mehl released her to join Toren. This time, it was Mehl who settled his arm on Toren's. As a servant intoned their names, the doors opened, and they strode in. Etiquette forbade them from looking anywhere but forward at the High Table on the far end of the room, but when Ria's new name and title rang out at his back, Mehl was tempted to turn.

Whispers echoed into the room along with Ria's footsteps, and Toren's breath hissed out beside him at the low, building murmurs. But neither of them faltered. Would Ria? Only when they rounded the table could Mehl see her out of the corner of his eye. She followed without hesitation, though her skin was a hint flushed.

The servants lined up along the back wall kept their expressions impassive, but Mehl didn't miss the quick glances at Ria, sometimes only the slightest movement of their eyes. Not even the cook at the head of the line managed to resist. Only one remained statue-still, a young man he'd never seen in this post before.

Hadn't he? There was something familiar about the lad. Mehl had spent most of his life amongst the soldiers, so he didn't know the palace servants as well as Toren did. Even so, having taken on a great deal of the palace management, Mehl could identify most regardless of whether he could name them. He should know the man's usual task.

Anything unusual bore watching.

Once they reached their seats, Ria faltered, but before Mehl could invite her to sit at his side, Toren gestured to his left. "You will be seated beside me, Lady Ria."

It was a pointed, powerful show of favor. No other noble had been invited to the High Table tonight, and by the strained glances many sent their way as they were announced into the room, it hadn't gone unnoticed. A few brave ladies even directed glares at Ria before schooling their features into something more pleasant. Without guests at the table, it might have been a boring dinner, but reading body language and facial expressions would likely be more interesting than any conversation.

For some reason, his gaze went to the young servant as they took their seats. Mehl didn't know why, but instinct screamed that interesting might come in other forms. A newcomer in such a tense situation? He would listen to instinct and watch that one closely.

Now, Mehl had two people to guard.

CHAPTER 18
A RAT IN THE LARDER

I'm such an imposter.

Ria kept her grip relaxed on her spoon, but she didn't dare scoop up more than the slightest bit of the rich stew. And not only because of nerves. Once again, she was in a borrowed dress, though at least the one she'd worn to court that morning had technically been hers, only designed for another. The gown she wore now was more elaborate than anything her father would have kept in stock, and she dared not spill a single drop of soup or scatter a crumb of bread on the rich fabric.

"Is something wrong with your food?" Toren asked in a low voice.

She sighed. "No. Just nerves."

There really wasn't any point in going into greater detail than that. He was so accustomed to such luxury that he might dismiss her concern over her gown, and the rest of her worries he surely knew, considering they sneered up at her from more than a few faces. Toren was a shrewd enough king to see the glances and stares, the intense scrutiny on her every action. Why draw attention to herself more by discussing it?

She had enough to focus on. Dress aside, a misstep as great as spilling food would be tittered about for days. Maybe weeks. For that matter, even a minor mistake would provide a barb for their arrows. So she did her best to mimic the ladies at the closest tables—small, measured bites. Delicate motions. Slight smiles.

Gods, this was awkward, and Toren had yet to make the announcement. Voices rose and fell in a murmuring wave from the tables in front of them, but neither Toren nor Mehl seemed inclined to speak beyond Toren's polite enquiry. Were they truly going to endure this entire dinner in silence while the court pretended not to stare incessantly?

She couldn't stand it.

"Toren," Ria said softly, surprising the serving maid into bobbling the bowl she was removing. Ria breathed an apology to the maid before focusing on the High King. "Tell me about yourself. You, too, Mehl. We should know each other better."

Both men smiled, but the differences made a fascinating study. There was no softening in Toren's formal demeanor, a sort of polite detachment that gave away nothing of his feelings. But Mehl's lips curved up with a hint of his usual humor, and his posture eased a fraction. One born to court life and one trained. How would they answer?

"It is kind of you to inquire, Lady Ria," Toren replied. Her cheeks warmed at the reminder of her title—and her lack of use of his. "What do you wish to know?"

So cool and reserved, as though he hadn't been buried to the hilt in her body only an hour before. Ria set her spoon down with a soft click and fixed a polite smile on her face. What could she ask him? Certainly not about family. Even had his demeanor been more open, she would not have ventured there.

"Perhaps I am too forward, Your Majesty." Ria paused as another servant placed a new plate in front of her. "But I find myself curious. What do kings do when they are not occupied with the kingdom's business?"

Mischief danced in Mehl's eyes. "Some might say we *do* a great deal, particularly of late."

The innuendo was so light that Ria almost missed it, but Toren's lips twitched. "Behave, husband."

"I was merely referring to our sword work." Mehl's brows rose. "You're a bit rusty, but I've enjoyed the indulgence. One never knows when one might need such skills."

A hint of Toren's reserve slipped, enough to reveal his exasperation for a moment. Hastily, Ria lifted her goblet to her mouth to hide her grin. Was Mehl doing this on purpose to put her at ease, or did he always enjoy needling his husband in such situations? It was a curious dynamic.

"I am certain you would be heartbroken if I did not indulge you," Toren said smoothly. "You've never been fond of taking your blade in hand without me to direct you. How *did* you make it through your early years?"

It was fortunate that Ria had tipped the glass to her lips in show, for she surely would have choked on her wine at that teasing barb. Toren's statement had been delivered with polite calm, but the implications beneath his words were more than clear. For his part, Mehl merely chuckled low and lifted one of the tiny pastries from his plate.

Setting down her glass, Ria studied the trio of matching pastries on her own dish. What course was this? The third? It seemed a waste of effort to present three such tiny foods as an entire dish, but she had no idea how many more rounds would be served. Probably more than she wanted to sit through, but at least the meal hadn't been too bad as yet.

She watched the way Toren ate his serving before copying the motion. A laugh tinkled up from the lower table, and Ria stiffened. But when she peered toward the source, the lady chuckling with her friend seemed to be paying no attention to Ria at all. Not a slight, then, only her imagination.

Perhaps she would make it through this after all.

Centuries of practice allowed Toren to maintain a calm, disinterested demeanor, but there was little he missed at the tables below. As he ate the last bite of pastry, he added yet another name to his list of people to watch—Lord Bielen. The man was too shrewd to reveal his feelings openly, but Toren was not fooled by the veil he attempted to throw over his contempt. Bielen had hoped one of his three daughters would be in Ria's place, and he might yet cause trouble in an attempt to make that so.

Mehl's mind brushed his. *"When are you going to make the announcement?"*

"After this course," Toren assured him. *"I wanted everyone well settled."*

And less guarded. Aside from Ria's presence, the only real difference in this meal from any others was that he hadn't invited a handful of courtiers to join him and Mehl. Those invitations generally rotated enough that the nobles were accustomed to their current seating arrangements, and easing into routine allowed the courtiers to relax into greater complacency. Their reactions to the announcement would thus be more genuine.

More servants approached to remove their plates again,

and Mehl went still beside him. Though his expression didn't shift in an obvious way, Toren knew that watchful pose well. But who had inspired it? Toren followed his husband's gaze to the young man who'd just reached for Ria's plate. A new servant? Could that be the cause?

Kerelin had warned Toren a week or so back that she might need to replace some of her staff. With Mehl in charge of many of the household details, he should have learned the same, but even after all this time, he wasn't as comfortable as Toren with the myriad servants. No doubt only love kept Mehl from fleeing to the training grounds instead of listening to menu ideas and cleaning schedules.

The servants stepped back, and Toren no longer had time to consider Mehl's caution. Lifting his hand, he caught Feref's eye and gave a slight nod to signal him. While the chamberlain ensured the next course was held back, Toren waited for the room to quiet. It didn't take long. Too many had been eyeing the High Table for the gesture to go unnoticed.

"Now that the edge of hunger is sated, I bid you direct your attention to my words," Toren said, projecting his voice. "It has surely not gone unnoticed that our table boasts only one guest, and a stranger to you, at that. As was announced upon her entry, a new Duchess of Nevial has been named. You will give Lady Ria Orindl all the respect due her station."

This time, there were no murmurs, simply an expectant hush. Only the foolish hadn't guessed what was coming.

"In addition," Toren began, placing his hand on Mehl's, "It is our honor to announce that Lady Ria has accepted the role of consort in order to carry our heir. She is therefore afforded the highest honors and will be treated accordingly. As all know the threat of my brother's challenge, I expect each noble in this court to place Lady Ria, royal consort and your future sovereign's mother, in your highest regard."

It wouldn't stop the worst of them from slighting Ria, regardless of Ber's threat—a simple glance around the room had Toren rearranging his mental list of potential troublemakers. But at least now, his intentions would be indisputably clear. They would mistreat Ria at great peril.

Message delivered, Toren gestured at Feref to resume the meal.

IF NOT FOR that blasted servant, Mehl would have trained his attention on the lower tables during his husband's announcement so he could make note of potential trouble. Instead, his every instinct screamed to keep an eye on the man waiting behind them. Not literally, unfortunately. Until he stepped forward to deliver the next course, the servant was out of sight. Even with his face turned toward Toren, Mehl couldn't see the other man out of the corner of his eye.

But he couldn't stop trying.

For the second time that day, his hand clenched reflexively around an invisible sword hilt. His mind couldn't pin down the source of the danger, but deep inside, he *knew*. And if Mehl had learned one thing during his decades of training and centuries of service, it was to heed that inner voice.

He barely registered when Toren stopped speaking and almost missed his husband's signal to Feref to continue the meal. With the announcement done, Mehl couldn't keep staring without raising questions, so he shifted his attention momentarily to Ria. He tipped his lips into a smile that was more show than substance.

Let the courtiers believe he was paying extra attention to their new consort—looking at her also allowed him to view the approaching servants.

He sensed Toren's gaze on him. *"What is it?"*

"I'm not..."

The mystery servant appeared at Ria's side, depositing her plate on the table with a flourish. A familiar one. But where—? Sudden memory cut through the disguise, superimposing the image of the jaunty bard on his mind's eye. The woman had donned a wig and applied cosmetics to add illusion to the lines of her face, but there was no mistaking the truth.

It was the Centoi's herald.

"You," Mehl said, and alarm flashed for a moment in the traitor's eyes before she covered it with feigned shock.

Before he could say more, Ria lifted her fork, and Mehl's attention was drawn to her plate. Were those the usual spices the cook sprinkled across the roast vegetables? The normal sauce drizzled over her cut of roast? He couldn't let her take a bite.

Formality be damned.

Mehl leaned over Toren to grip Ria's forearm in a strong hold. She gasped, but he ignored the hurt in her questioning eyes. "Drop the fork, Ria."

The clatter of metal on wood echoed through the tomb-quiet hall.

But it didn't quite cover the rustle of fabric as their spy turned and fled.

CHAPTER 19

OLD HABITS

Time slowed and surged in an uncanny dance. Mehl's hold on Ria's arm. Her startled, hurt expression. A scowling Toren muttering "What are you doing?" Every action compressed into a breath's time, and yet Mehl could have described every nuance.

In truth, only a few heartbeats passed before Mehl released Ria and shoved away from the table, but it was long enough for the spy to reach the back entrance to the dining room. When the cook and another servant attempted to block the exit, the spy slipped between them before darting into the hallway beyond.

Without thought, Mehl leaped to his feet and ducked between the pair of stunned servants who'd just delivered his and Toren's plates.

"Stay," he barked over his shoulder. Then he connected to his husband telepathically. *"It's a Centoi spy."*

Before their mental connection was even closed, Toren's voice rang out. "Stop him!"

The two nearest guards had already been moving, but at the High King's command, they picked up their pace. Mehl reached the doors first. Whispers and cries of alarm followed him as he dashed through, but he blocked them out. His focus was on scanning the servants in the corridor that stretched the length of the dining hall. This area was a wretched mess at the best of times with dishes being carried back and forth for so many guests.

Cutting left would go toward the kitchens, while right would lead to the service corridor between the dining hall and throne room. He paused to consider the correct path. If the spy had been clever enough to blend in, there was no way to know which direction she would have taken.

Glass clattered and crashed to his left, and a man cursed. Mehl's head whipped in that direction in time to spot the intruder darting away halfway down the corridor, a mess left in her wake. He rushed to follow, gaining his own share of attention. Between the crash and Mehl's sudden presence, most of the servants froze, though a few attempted to waylay the spy.

Once again, time seemed to rush and suspend as Mehl wove his way through the chaos. But by the time he reached the trio cleaning up the broken, overturned plates and scattered food in the center of the hallway, the intruder was nearly to the end of the hallway. Mehl cursed. He needed to move quickly, and this wouldn't help.

Fortunately, a couple of servants beside the wall slid out of the way so that he could skirt the mess. Alas, that was his only bit of fortune in the situation. Even that pause allowed the Centoi woman to slip into the small hallway leading to the kitchens and the scullery.

She would be out the back entrance well before he could catch up at this rate.

The soft clink of metal armor heralded the guards' arrival behind him. "Your Majesty, please wait," one of them called.

Mehl ignored the man and continued dodging his way through the servants, but as he reached the L-shaped corridor to the kitchens, the guard rushed ahead of him. When the man held up a hand, Mehl paused. Sir Macoe, one of Toren's most trusted knights and the head of the palace guard.

"She's escaping," Mehl snapped. "Move."

"I cannot let you proceed, Your Majesty," Macoe said, his chin set with resolve. "By the High King's command, I must protect you, and that includes preventing you from charging into danger."

Helpless fury sent a flood of fire through Mehl's blood. "The spy will be gone if we stop to argue this. Again, move. That is *my* command."

Sir Macoe flushed, but he didn't yield. "Which I would normally obey at once. However, we are all bound by the High King's orders. Even you." Macoe released a long sigh. "Let the guard handle this, King Mehl. I've ordered every exit blocked. Mages have been summoned to scan for spells, and the healers are checking the food. It is no longer your job to rush after danger."

The guard's words were logical and true, yet Mehl's anger didn't ease. He could have ended this if he'd managed to catch the spy, but instead, he was being forced to wait. Why? Toren knew Mehl would never give up on protecting him, even if tradition said he should. Why would his husband order this?

Mehl gritted his teeth and turned away. There was only one way to find out.

∾

THE DINING HALL was a teeming mass of barely contained fear, and Toren had to remain calm to reinforce control. So as a handful of healers and mages streamed into the dining hall, he relaxed in his chair and pretended he couldn't incinerate half the castle with his anger alone. This evening's mistakes could cost them dearly. What had he been thinking?

He never should have made his announcement so close to the Centoi's arrival.

"What's going on?" Ria whispered, the fear in her voice heightening his fury.

Toren could barely look at her without his magic surging frightfully. "Mehl had concerns about the new servant," he answered.

She snorted in disbelief, but the simple explanation would have to suffice. He was hardly going to announce that there was a spy on the loose, even if most of the nobles had surely guessed as much. Some rumors were best left unconfirmed, and this was one of them. He didn't even dare tell Ria telepathically since he couldn't be sure how she would react. The High Table didn't have the luxury of showing open emotions.

Fortunately, Ria kept her expression neutral in spite of her doubt.

"Shall we resume the meal, then?" she asked. "While we wait for his return?"

Toren clenched the hand in his lap until his nails bit into his palms, but he was careful to keep the tension out of view. "Not as yet. I believe there is also concern about the quality of the food."

Before she could ask another question, the lead healer reached the table and bowed low. Toren had already contacted Serae telepathically with his orders, so he only needed to nod before she moved forward to check their food. It was an obvious tell to anyone with sense—the head cook would have ensured that each dish was of the highest quality before sending it out. But Toren reclined almost indolently, all save the clenched fist that the rest of the room couldn't see.

Ria's gaze flicked to his lap and then back to her plate. She saw, of course.

His magic pounded against his shields, but he tamped it down ruthlessly.

He could not lose control. Not now. He hadn't established a strong enough relationship with Ria to have her dispel his extra magic in this sort of situation, and even if Mehl was in the room, he was still too mentally raw. Toren had to keep his grip.

Finally, the healer stepped back. "His Majesty King Mehl must have been mistaken, High King. There is no sign of spoilage or other problems."

Toren held back a frown. It was good news yet worrisome. He doubted his husband was wrong about the Centoi spy, but if she hadn't been there to tamper with their food, then why had she placed herself where she could serve Ria specifically? Had the woman hoped to infiltrate the staff for longer than a night?

He connected mentally with the healer. *"No poison? No herbs that would prevent or harm conception?"*

Serae gave the slightest shake of her head. *"Only the standard spices. The other healers have found nothing amiss in their scans of the lower tables."*

"Thank you, Serae," Toren said aloud. Most of the mages had already disappeared into the back hallway, but one who'd remained sent him a signal that there was no one cloaking themselves by magic. "It appears that all is well. Please forgive the inconvenience."

"It is our honor to serve, Your Majesty," Serae said before

bowing once more and then retreating toward the entrance to the dining hall. Silently, the other healers followed.

The nobles didn't appear particularly reassured. Not that he blamed them. Toren lifted his wine glass and took a slow, casual sip. "Please continue your meal," he said. "King Mehl will return momentarily. I am certain he will solve the problem causing him such discord with all haste."

A few of the bolder nobles cast doubtful glances his way, and there was a fair bit of mumbling. But as soon as Toren braved a bite of the now-cold roast, they began to eat once more, if somewhat tentatively. Except Ria. Her hand rested atop her fork, but she didn't pick it up. He could sense her distress like his own.

It tore through him like the phantom poison. Why had he decided to make the announcement tonight? He'd told himself it would be best to make her position clear sooner rather than later, but he should have considered deception on the part of the Centoi. It was his job to anticipate such things. He'd been too distracted to think properly, and that was a danger.

He could have lost Mehl tonight.

The savory roast turned bitter in his mouth. Toren had been so mesmerized by Ria that he'd dismissed Mehl's worried glances toward the servant. After a century together, it was easy to forget that his husband was trained as a bodyguard, and those instincts hadn't gone away with the king's crown. At the first sign of Mehl's unease, Toren should have made a discreet inquiry about the new servant. His husband could have been killed chasing after her.

He observed Ria out of the corner of his eye. She toyed with her food now, clearly unnerved by the evening's events. His distraction had put her in danger, too. Unforgivable. He needed to regain his focus. She was here to bear their child and nothing more. Certainly not to be all but claimed in the dining hall like a betrothed or wife.

It was best he remembered that.

WAS this what her life was to be, then?

Ria stared down at her plate, but she couldn't bring herself to take a bite. She still felt the tension of Mehl's fingers around her forearm, and his command echoed through her head. *Drop the fork, Ria.* There'd been a steely, frantic edge to his voice that had forced her compliance more surely than any spell.

It had been no idle threat that prompted that tone, no matter how Toren had tried to dismiss Mehl's actions. Not that she believed Toren's excuse about something being amiss with a servant. What king ran from the room for something like that? And of course, she could see and feel what others didn't —the tension the High King so carefully hid from the rest of the room. His palm probably had bruises from the tightness of his grip.

Then there was his magic. Having channeled his energy, she could not miss the building force of it at her side. Her own power vibrated from it, almost as though hers wanted to join with his. For what purpose, she couldn't divine. But she wasn't going to ask him. He clearly didn't want to confide in her concerning any of this.

The High King's fertile bed-warmer and subsequent target for his rival's ire—perhaps that was the life of a royal consort. No explanations. No sympathy. Merely food to be rushed away and—no doubt—knives to be dodged in the shadows, all beneath the weight of the noble court's scorn.

And she'd signed her name to this—or someone's name. If she waited, maybe the real Duchess of Nevial would appear from the aether to relieve her of this mad decision. *How* could she have lost herself so thoroughly in less than two days?

From the increasing glances directed at the door behind her, Ria anticipated Mehl's return before he slid into his seat. She dared only one look, but the thinly veiled anger in his demeanor had her averting her gaze at once. Had she misread things entirely? Maybe he hadn't been worried for her but upset at her. She could have done something wrong concerning the servant.

No. That doesn't make sense.

Unfortunately, logic made little impact on the increasing whispers of self-recrimination, especially not as the meal continued in cold silence. The tension between Mehl and Toren alone was as palpable as the airy confection served as dessert—but certainly wasn't as sweet. If she had to guess, she would say they would all be sleeping alone tonight.

CHAPTER 20

RIFTS

Mehl managed to hold his temper until they reached the family wing, but just barely. As soon as they made it well beyond the guards at the end of the corridor, he let the façade drop. He wouldn't hide his anger from Toren, not over this. The spy had surely gotten away because of his husband's overprotectiveness.

"You should not have ordered me stopped," Mehl snapped.

Toren halted in the middle of the hallway, so suddenly that Ria continued on a couple of steps before turning around to frown at them. "I disagree," Toren replied coolly.

"Do you know what this has likely cost us?" Mehl longed to throttle his husband or, barring that, at least pace the corridor. Something. As usual, he couldn't. "We haven't heard a word from Sir Macoe, which means the Centoi informant escaped. I could have caught her."

Abruptly, his husband's reserve evaporated. "I don't give a fuck about the spy. We'll capture her or we won't. It's you who concerns me. If I must protect you from your own impulses, I will do so."

Ria gasped, but Mehl couldn't focus on anything but Toren's words. Protect him from his own impulses? Protect. Him. Apparently, he had returned to his youth and now needed a minder.

Mehl scowled. "Has your regard slipped for me, then?"

"My regard?" Eyes narrowing, Toren stepped into his space. "What madness is this? I cannot believe you would ask me such."

"There was a time you trusted me and my *impulses* implicitly," Mehl said. "For decades, I stood guard over you against every danger, but now you treat me like a fool."

"I don't mean to. But you are now *king*, not a *bodyguard*," Toren gritted out.

And that was the problem, wasn't it? Mehl loved his husband and for the most part bore his current role well enough, but there was a core of discontent he'd refused to face until the current threat from Ber had forced it to the surface. For truly, what purpose did Mehl serve? He offered opinions on issues and helped manage the household, but Toren didn't need him for those things.

Toren could rule the whole blasted kingdom alone.

"I don't know what I am," Mehl said. "And neither do you."

He shoved past Toren and hurried around a shocked Ria, only to be pulled up short by his husband's grip on his arm.

Toren circled him, expression furious. "You are mine."

That wasn't in question—or perhaps it wasn't *the* question. "And what else?"

"You needn't do anything." Toren advanced, crowding him once more. "As my king—"

"I am useless." A wave of his husband's energy crashed against him, a sign that Toren was near his limit. But Mehl couldn't yield. "I am a warrior, but I have no battle or task. No purpose beyond your bed."

Toren stumbled back as though Mehl had shoved him. He might as well have. Gods, had he just said that? Horror washed over him, followed promptly by shame and regret. Toren was his heart, and he'd never doubted being loved in return. What had come over him? He knew very well that he wasn't a mere bedmate.

A small, distressed sound from Ria caught his attention, but he could barely take in the upset on her face. His gaze was for Toren and the stark pain in his eyes a few heartbeats before it was shuttered away. Mehl's stomach lurched. It was a rare hurt that his husband hid from him.

"I see," Toren said. "I will be in our room. If it is still ours."

Then Toren spun away and strode off, his footsteps sharp against the stone.

Mehl wanted to call him back, but his tongue felt awkward and frozen. A useless thing, much as he'd claimed to be. He closed his eyes, unwilling to look at his husband's retreating back. Or Ria. She was no doubt terrified by their argument.

What had he done?

For a moment, Ria couldn't move. She and Mehl could have both been statues, turned to stone in the center of the corridor and left for future generations to gawk at. But she doubted they were stunned for the same reason.

A Centoi informant? She'd been suspicious of the situation and had guessed there was danger. Of course she had. But she'd tried to ignore her disquiet, especially after Mehl returned and the meal continued. *It could have been anything,* she'd eventually told herself.

The fact that she'd been served dinner by an actual spy from the enemy kingdom and Toren hadn't breathed a word...

that was a blow to the gut. Toren could take her body. He could trust her to carry his heir. Yet he couldn't confide in her when her life was in actual danger? If not for Mehl's outburst, she wouldn't even know that the spy was still on the loose.

How could Toren do that?

Mehl's shoulders sagged, and harsh, naked pain twisted his face as he stared down the empty hallway. Just like that, the shock holding her in place cracked. As much as she was bothered by Toren's actions toward her, she couldn't deny the old pain behind his argument with Mehl. She'd never thought of the kings as anything but a unit, as solid and ever-present as the palace itself, but they were clearly more complicated than that.

It wasn't really her business, yet how could she ignore Mehl's obvious need? Before she could stop to think, Ria crossed the space between them and stopped in front of him. He seemed to peer through her for a second before he blinked and focused his gaze on hers.

"I'm sorry, Ria."

This time, she was the one who blinked. Had he somehow guessed her thoughts, or was it something else? "For what?"

"I should not have started this argument in front of you," Mehl answered softly. "I fear my anger has harmed both Toren and you. I hope you aren't too frightened."

A little frown of worry wrinkled his brow, and Ria melted inside a little at his concern, one that usually would have been accurate. She'd been too distracted about the newest revelation to heed their argument, though. Had Toren even told him that she didn't know about the spy? Mehl clearly wasn't oblivious in general to her feelings, but he hadn't mentioned it. Curious.

"Ria?" Mehl asked.

Now she was the one causing distress with her silence. She

forced her thoughts back to what he'd said. "I'm not scared, but I suppose I am upset. You're not the only one who needs to have words with Toren."

"Not words like mine, I hope," Mehl said, his voice rough with regret. "I need to go after him, but I don't know what to say."

Ria couldn't resist giving his upper arm a comforting rub, but his startled glance down at her hand had her jerking away. "Sorry. I shouldn't have…"

"No."

Her heart dropped at his pained response, but before she could back away farther, Mehl wrapped his arms around her waist and pulled her close. He buried his face against the side of her neck, his breath tickling and heating her skin. But there was no apparent desire behind the embrace, not that she could detect. This seemed more like comfort-seeking.

Ria softened against him, curling her arms gently around his head to hold him close.

When he finally eased back, his eyes held chagrin. "Forgive me. Again. I should not have grabbed you in such a way without permission."

In that moment, there was something…different about him. A vulnerability. Mehl had never seemed as imperious or commanding as Toren, but he possessed his own kind of strength, one as steady as bedrock. To see him so shaken made her long to hold him again.

To comfort.

"I wasn't offended," Ria said. "Only surprised. And you're right. You need to go after Toren."

Mehl started to shove his hand through his hair, only to be stopped by his crown. She nearly smiled at his frustrated curse, for it so echoed the sentiment behind the argument she'd witnessed. Unfortunately, he probably wouldn't appreciate the humor.

"I'm not sure I have ever said anything so cruel." Mehl averted his gaze. "I didn't mean it. But I don't know if he will listen."

Ria could have lied and told him it would be an easy apology—they clearly loved one another deeply. It would do him no favors, though. Even without knowing Toren nearly so well, she'd been able to see how deeply he'd been wounded. She had no clue what insecurity Mehl's comment had slashed open, but she thought she understood the effect. No one wanted to be dismissed as an interchangeable lover. No married pair, at least.

She wasn't exactly fond of the feeling herself. But that was her own burden, wasn't it?

"Go on," she said. "You'll not forgive yourself if you leave it to fester."

"You—"

"I'll sleep in my room tonight," she assured him. In a way, it would almost be a relief. She needed time to process her anger with Toren. "I could use the rest after the events of the last couple of days. It *is* safe to be alone, right? With a spy on the loose?"

"As safe as anyone can be. There are wards on the family wing, and mages scan frequently for danger."

Ria forced a smile. "Then go."

Mehl peered at her a moment as though he might argue, but he finally nodded. "I'll tell Toren. If he lets me."

"He will." Impulsively, she lifted on her tiptoes and kissed Mehl on the cheek. "Have some time without me. I'll get some sleep."

Gods, she hoped she'd be able to sleep.

TOREN PACED circles around the sitting room, but he couldn't escape Mehl's claim. *No purpose beyond your bed.* His stomach churned at the endless refrain of those words. They'd been married nearly a century and together for several years before that. Had his husband spent the entire time believing Toren had used him for sex?

So often, Mehl yielded to him. To his barely leashed magic. His temper and possessiveness. Toren had thought of it as a gift—a blessing. But maybe it had been a lie. Had he taken what he'd believed offered?

Gods of all, but it was repugnant.

He strode past the floor-length mirror situated beside the door, and the flash of gold caught his eye. He halted in front of the glass, his scowl directed at the crown fixed atop his head. So many saw it as a symbol of status and power—for him, it was more often a weight. One he currently couldn't bear.

In short order, he found himself in his dressing room, almost frantically removing the pins and braids that held it in place. Once freed, he dropped the gold-and-emerald piece atop his dressing table and tugged off the ceremonial robe he'd donned for dinner. Only the memory of Ria's frown had him placing it carefully on the hanger instead of flinging it to the ground and stomping on it like the memory of the argument he'd prefer to erase.

But even without the trappings of his rank, he couldn't face his reflection in the mirror again. Not with this shame burning through his blood. He couldn't have mistaken his relationship with Mehl so thoroughly, could he? For a few years, perhaps, but not an entire century. He wasn't such a tyrant to force that kind of subjugation.

Was he? Gods, what if Ber was right? His brother had always called him a danger.

His magic pulsed against his shields with each beat of his heart, a drumming reminder of Ber's claim. *You call me ruthless, but you could kill countless people if you lost control.* And it was true. Only Mehl knew how much stronger Toren's energy had grown, too. Had he taken advantage of Mehl's help?

Toren sank down onto the bench beside the dressing room door and dropped his head into his hands. Pain and self-loathing blurred into the ache of his building magic until he could barely stand it, but he couldn't bring himself to seek any kind of release. He couldn't ask for help. How could he approach Mehl or Ria right now? There was too much unresolved with Mehl, and he hadn't missed the anger in Ria's eyes as he'd walked away.

With his energy so heightened, he sensed Mehl's approach before the door opened, but he didn't lift his head. He didn't dare to. Just a hint of recrimination or rejection on his husband's face could shatter his control.

And then he would truly become what he feared.

CHAPTER 21

BRIDGES

The sight of Toren's slumped form nearly shattered Mehl's heart. What had he done? He'd anticipated anger and hurt, but nothing like this. Toren had his insecurities, but he rarely crumpled. Not this way.

Abruptly, his husband straightened. Toren's long hair tumbled around his shoulders, the strands still bent and crinkled from the braids he'd removed. Shadows beneath his eyes lent a dark aspect to his face, and the agony twisting his expression did nothing to help. And all it had taken was one foolish statement spoken in anger.

They'd argued before without...this. Why?

"Tell me I didn't force you," Toren whispered.

That was where he'd taken it? Bile burned a sick path up Mehl's throat. "You have never forced me," he said, his voice sounding rough to his own ears.

His husband slumped against the wall. "Thank the gods. If I had..."

Hesitantly, Mehl approached. "I'm sorry, Tor. My words were thoughtless and inaccurate."

"What if they *are* accurate?" Toren murmured, his distant gaze fixed on the ceiling. "Perhaps I am too blinded by my own needs, a servant to my power. First you. Now Ria. I take and take, but what do I give? Certainly not contentment."

"I am happy for the most part." Mehl sank to his knees in front of Toren and settled his hands on his husband's thighs. "You bring me great joy. It is simply... Something has been off, a discontent I couldn't name. I only realized what it was after your brother's threat. I do not mind being your king, but I need to fill my warrior's heart with something outside of royal duties. That's all."

Finally, Toren's pained gaze met his. "To say that your only use is in my bed is not quite that, Mehl. With sex our favorite way to dispel my power, there is no way to ignore the implications. Was it ever 'our' favorite?"

Mehl's fingers tightened involuntarily on his husband's thighs, and his head lowered until he was staring at Toren's chest. Gods, he'd messed up. He'd realized that the moment the ill-thought words had left his lips, and now the effects would take months to repair. Maybe years.

"Never think it wasn't," Mehl said. "It brings me nothing but pleasure each time I yield to you. It's always my choice. Every time."

Toren's hand cupped his face, and Mehl allowed his gentle hold to tip his head back until their gazes collided once more. "I don't know how to banish this new doubt," Toren said.

"It was merely anger speaking, my love," Mehl said. "A feeling that is not gone, I might add. I still don't think you should have stopped me from detaining the spy. I'm one of the few to have seen her up close in the throne room and again wearing her disguise in the dining hall, and I have the training to follow. To be stopped like a child... I felt disrespected."

Toren's sigh drifted between them. "I am sorry for that. But you were unarmed and acting in haste."

Mehl couldn't hold in the short chuckle-snort. "Beloved. There are at least ten things in this room I could kill a person with, probably more if I put some thought into it. I'm trained to protect under any circumstances. I can also assure you there was no haste involved. I had my eye on that new 'servant' from the moment we rounded the table."

A bit of the fire returned to Toren's eyes. "Oh, certainly. No haste at all. You surely planned to chase them in a mad dash through the back hallways. How could I think otherwise?"

Mehl grinned. "No doubt the court will *tsk* over it for months."

As expected, Toren stiffened, his eyes narrowing. "Not in my hearing."

"That I know." Mehl leaned closer and slid his hands further up his husband's thighs. Perhaps some things could only be shown. "Come on, Tor. Help me out of this blasted finery. Then you can yield to me for the night so you'll know we're forever even."

Toren's breath hissed out, and for a moment, Mehl thought he might refuse. There was no perfect way to restore his husband's shaken faith, but it seemed a good start. Had he interpreted the need wrongly? Toren was less inclined to yield at the best of times.

Worry settled in, and Mehl started to ease back. But Toren's hand slid from his cheek to his neck, preventing the motion. "Very well," Toren whispered. "Tell me what to do."

Desire and relief—an interesting combination.

Mehl's lips curved up. "Indeed I will."

∼

Toren's heart pounded a frantic beat as he waited for Mehl to make his move. Giving up control filled him with a heady fear, a daring sort of excitement. It was like racing his horse across the open fields at breakneck speed or leaning over the parapet atop the highest tower to better admire the view. As with those things, the pleasure would be worth the danger—and with his rogue magic, there was always danger.

"Will you unbraid my hair?" Mehl asked, his hands slipping a little closer to Toren's cock as he braced himself and stood.

At Toren's muttered curse, his husband grinned and turned away, presenting his back. For one mad moment, Toren savored the mental image of shoving everything off the nearby table and bending Mehl over it. But no. His husband wasn't the one who was supposed to be yielding this night.

He had to take quite a few calming breaths before he approached Mehl. His hands trembled as he lifted them, his fingers diving into the mass of dark, smooth hair twined around the crown in simple braids. Simple, because Toren had plaited them himself while Feref focused on Ria. It made untwining the strands a blessedly simple matter.

In short order, Mehl's crown rested beside his, their formal robes together on their hangers. Now what? They faced one another, and Mehl took his hands. But neither of them made a move. Toren couldn't have coaxed his body into motion if he'd wanted to, not with Mehl's tender gaze pinning him in place.

"I hope you don't expect me to be rough in my command," Mehl murmured. "My intent is to show you my love so thoroughly that you'll never doubt it again."

A weight settled on Toren's chest at the worried slant of his husband's brow. He felt in his soul that Mehl loved him, but recent events had him off kilter. Apprehension was a constant companion, ready to latch onto anything it could. It joined with fears that had lived in his heart for a lifetime. All it needed was for him to falter.

Mehl's earlier words had been bad. That was truth. But one misspoken phrase shouldn't destroy over a century of love. "You've already succeeded in that regard. You needn't—"

"Surely you aren't arguing." Mehl's lips curved into a wicked smile. "Since you are currently under my command."

Toren's cock went so hard he couldn't hold back a groan, eliciting a laugh from Mehl. When Mehl tugged him toward the door, Toren followed without complaint. Even as his magic surged, shallowing his breath with its force, he allowed his husband to strip him of tunic and pants. Slowly.

Far too slowly.

Mehl's hands glided gently over Toren's skin with each bit of clothing removed until he feared he would go mad from it. The delicious torment didn't cease when every stitch they'd worn was strewn across the floor, either. Mehl nipped and kissed and stroked his way down Toren's chest. Toren froze when his husband traced the line of his hip with his tongue. Straight toward—

He gasped, a ragged sound, when Mehl's mouth closed around his cock.

Gods of all.

Sadly, Mehl didn't linger, only bobbing his head a few times before drawing away. Toren's head fell back, and his long hair danced along his ass. He hissed out a breath, his skin so sensitive the teasing brush could have been fingers. Whatever Mehl planned, it had better not require endurance, because tonight, Toren feared he would have little.

Mehl kissed his way back up to claim Toren's mouth. No gentleness this time, only claiming. Toren burned hotter with each duel of their tongues until he nearly shoved his husband onto the bed behind him. Instead, it was Mehl who spun them. Mehl who eased Toren onto the mattress.

The muscles of Mehl's arms strained as he caged Toren in, but Toren didn't feel trapped—he felt cherished. And in that moment, he allowed himself to be free of all, save the grip he held on his magic. That had too much power to hurt Mehl, who was still raw from channeling so much energy the last couple of the days. But kingdom and rank and treacherous family?

They had no place here.

He watched through heavy eyelids as Mehl grabbed the jar of oil from the side table to prepare them both. Each touch fired his blood and muddled his senses until he squeezed his eyes closed, his back arching from the pleasure. His breath caught when his husband parted his legs wider and poised at his entrance.

But he didn't push forward. "Look at me," Mehl growled.

Toren couldn't resist the pull of his husband's harsh voice. His heart slammed and squeezed at the sight of Mehl above him, his expression twisted with love and passion and possession. The kind of fierce claiming he rarely displayed.

"Whatever you may fear, you are mine," Mehl said through clenched teeth. "My love. My life. Mine. Remember it always."

And then he took.

It was difficult to settle with one's potential assassin on the loose.

And so Ria paced.

There wasn't much else to do. She'd already changed from her fancy court dress into her own clothes. She'd riffled through the array of beautiful gowns hanging in the dressing room and admired their fine craftsmanship. She'd skimmed the titles of the books on the shelf in the sitting room, but none had caught her interest. Her thoughts were too chaotic to give proper attention to a story, anyway.

Finally, she settled onto the bench built beneath the broad window in her bedroom. Night had fallen, so the full glory of the view was hidden from her sight. But with the royal quarters situated so high, she could admire the soft glow of countless lights below her. Mage-lit lanterns created beautiful patterns in the gardens where they followed the lines of flowerbeds, hedges, and groves. Periodically, someone would walk within the circle of their glow, giving her a glimpse of the nobility at their games.

Were they undaunted by the drama of dinner? From here, it was impossible to tell if they moved with ease or trepidation, and there was no way to know what they said to one another. No doubt speculation ran freely, especially in the absence of the kings. How strange to think of the courtiers lingering like unwanted guests despite their hosts having left the party, though she supposed that was the norm with some of the nobles living here.

Ria hadn't heard a sound from the kings' bedroom. Due to some kind of muffling spell, no doubt. Were they arguing? She hoped not, but she wasn't about to knock and ask. She'd promised Mehl time without her, which they clearly needed. Her lingering annoyance with Toren wouldn't help, either. If he answered the door, she might end up assaulting the High King again.

Not a good habit for certain.

Really, she should have given greater consideration to the threat of physical danger. If Prince Ber sought the throne so ruthlessly, he wouldn't hesitate to have her murdered, would he? There might be countless dangers to her life, and now she couldn't trust that she'd be notified about any of them. How many spies could be on the loose without her knowledge? Could she even trust the servants?

Her gaze flicked to the huge bed. Ridiculously sumptuous and regretfully empty. Ria couldn't fathom sleeping alone in the intimidating space when she *wasn't* already scared. While wondering if every vibration of the window was a possible murderer or a simple breeze? Impossible. She had to find something to do. Somewhere else to be.

When Feref had helped her prepare for dinner, she'd asked him to have the shop goods delivered to a room close at hand. He'd told her he would have her fabric and sewing supplies placed in the unused sitting room at the end of the corridor, right beside the guard who kept intruders from the royal wing. That should be safe enough. It was still in the shielded area, and the guard would hear any trouble. She could at least check to see if her things were there.

Resolved, Ria headed toward the door. It wasn't as though Toren or Mehl would notice her absence. Not this night.

CHAPTER 22

IN THE FLOWERS

Mehl trailed his fingers through Toren's hair and lifted one of the strands to his nose, the spicy-sweet scent of his husband's shampoo a balm to his soul. Toren had tucked himself beneath the crook of Mehl's shoulder, his arm across Mehl's waist. For the first time in ages, his husband was completely relaxed—from his deep breathing, probably asleep.

But then Toren's finger began an absentminded swirl against his side. "Where's Ria?" Toren mumbled.

Mehl had forgotten to tell his husband Ria's words. Whoops. Not that it had been a priority, considering. "She decided to return to her room alone. She said she needed rest after the last few days, though I suspect it was as much for our benefit as hers."

"She was upset," Toren said flatly.

"Yes," Mehl confirmed, releasing Toren's hair. "I take it you didn't tell her about the spy?"

Toren squirmed against him. "We were at the High Table,

and I didn't know how she would react. Of course, I didn't tell her."

With his anger purged, Mehl felt amusement—and its mismatched sibling, sadness—at the admission. It was so typical of Toren, for good or ill. Protecting others and himself, yet mangling it badly when it was someone he cared about. His fear of loss overrode good sense in those situations.

"Don't you think she might have been bothered to learn that she'd been in danger?" Mehl asked, careful to keep his tone soft. The last thing he wanted was another argument. "She's trusting us to protect her as part of our contract. It might be difficult to maintain that trust if you hide pertinent details."

Toren's sigh warmed his skin. "I didn't consider it that way, but you're right. If she weren't asleep, I would apologize."

"I'm surprised you aren't doing so, anyway." Mehl chuckled, but he rubbed his husband's forearm soothingly. "How is it both normal and strange for her not to be here? It isn't exactly a lack, and yet…"

"I know," Toren whispered.

Neither of them moved, and Mehl refused to be the first to do so. After all that had happened with Toren's family, loss was Toren's greatest fear, and he'd already worried that he might lose Mehl to Ria. Mehl knew otherwise, but there was no logic in it. Toren would have to see for himself that not all change was destruction and that sometimes adding truly did create more instead of somehow turning out less.

If Ria was destined to be theirs, Toren would have to be the first in their marriage to embrace it. Mehl might be a warrior, but he couldn't conquer another person's doubts.

No matter how much he wanted to.

⁓

It wasn't necessarily a bad space to set up a little workshop, but it would definitely require some changes. Ria frowned down at one of the decorative tables situated between two chairs. Better work surfaces, for one. The large, airy room was full of both smaller seating areas like this and a couple of larger groupings, but none of them had a substantial table.

She could no doubt have Feref bring those in and arrange them near the back wall where the goods from her shop were currently stacked. But how would she manage fittings? This room could be divided for such a purpose, but this was the royal family's personal wing. No courtiers allowed, as far as she was aware.

Could there be another nearby room that would serve? Ria nibbled on her upper lip as she considered the possibilities. They'd passed quite a few doors before reaching the family area, but any of those rooms could be occupied. If it weren't so late, she might have summoned Feref to ask. Not tonight, though. The poor man had nearly lost his job over her already.

Ria could ask the guard at the end of the corridor. Surely, he would know whether there were people in the nearby rooms? But what would she do if they were empty? She couldn't forget that there was a spy out there. The guard had to stay at his current station or risk Toren and Mehl, and it seemed silly to have him call someone to escort her. It would be foolishness indeed for her to go by herself.

Sighing, she sank down onto one of the fancy, stiff chairs. If she wandered the palace alone under these circumstances, she would deserve whatever mockery the bards wrote after her demise. She'd had her fair share of beatings from her father— no reason to risk worse from the spy. She would have to find some other way to appease her restlessness until she could get a proper workroom arranged.

Maybe she could work on the fabric experiment? Ria

scanned the bolts stacked along the wall. She'd added subtle designs to plain cloth with success, but she had yet to try altering something more complicated. Which of these could use a change in pattern? There was the floral motif, with its too-large flowers, or the eye-watering geometric design that made her dizzy any time she stared at it too long.

Hmm. Probably the first one. Dizziness never worked out well while doing magic.

Ria's thighs twinged when she stood, and she flushed at the lingering reminder of her time with Toren and Mehl. She'd never had sex so often in a single day. How long would it take for her to get pregnant? She rested her palm on her belly as she strolled toward the bolts of fabric. The warmth of her hand felt comforting, but it didn't exactly answer the question. She was neither a healer nor a seer to divine that.

Of course, she would have to get over the urge to throttle Toren before she gave him her body again. The ache of her muscles as she hefted the fabric told her that might not be a bad thing. Yet it was terrible, too. As angry as she was, she found she missed both kings. Madness to do so on such short acquaintance, but she couldn't seem to resist.

Lost in thought, Ria nodded absently at the guard as she hauled the bolt of fabric out the door and headed toward her room. Would Toren and Mehl have settled their argument by now? Part of her wanted to knock on the door to check, but despite their physical relationship, it didn't seem appropriate.

They were royalty—she was merely a vessel.

Ria shifted her awkward bundle until she could nudge the door open to her suite. She was so focused on keeping hold of the fabric that she was halfway through the sitting area before she noticed the servant standing by the bedroom door at the other end. Yelping, Ria dropped the heavy bolt, barely jerking her foot out of the way before the cloth thudded against the floor.

"Oh, my lady!" the woman cried. "I was just fretting about where you'd gone."

Pressing her hand against her chest to soothe her racing heart, Ria frowned at the servant. "And you decided to linger in my bedroom?"

The woman went still, her eyes widening. "Isn't...isn't that customary for a lady's maid? I saw the light shining beneath the door and thought to offer you some tea. For calming?"

Of course. Ria wasn't accustomed to servants, but it made sense that the kings' consort would receive the best service possible. She should have thought to request tea herself. "Ah, yes. I would appreciate that, thank you."

As the woman bustled out the door, Ria glanced down at the fabric. Where should she attempt the experiment? She could always do it here instead of draping the cloth over the bed. Resolved, she gathered a cushion to kneel on before shoving the bolt until it rolled toward the wall, leaving a trail of flowered fabric in its wake.

Ria lowered herself to the cushion and held her hands over the cloth. This was much like forming a dress into its ideal shape, and yet it wasn't. For one thing, the designs were woven into this fabric, not painted, so it was more complicated to shift. To rearrange the pattern meant transmuting the composition of each strand to change its color. It took a fair bit of time and a lot of energy.

Perfect for when she couldn't sleep.

Her vision went hazy as she connected with her magic, but she didn't close her eyes. Not with this. There were too many tiny details in the pattern to trust her inner vision alone. Instead, she focused her gaze on a single flower. So many shades of pink. How could she best minimize the size without ruining the overall look?

Bit by bit, she altered, shifting some shades and erasing others. Compressing. Her energy drained into the cloth, and she let it pour freely. She had more than enough after channeling for Toren. Truly, if he were here to provide more, she could transmute the entire bolt. Maybe even an entire room of the stuff.

High King Toren, the tailor's secret power source—an amusing thought.

She barely processed the sound of the door opening, but the rattle of porcelain caught her attention. The tea. Time to stop, then. Ria shifted one last color and prepared to release her hold on the spell. Ah, but one more nudge on the pink there, and—

Pain exploded in her head, and pink blurred into black.

DESPITE MEHL'S comforting warmth at his back, Toren couldn't settle into sleep. It was too impossible to shake his husband's words. *She's trusting us to protect her. It might be difficult to maintain that trust if you hide pertinent details.* Nothing but the truth, and yet here he was, resting while Ria fretted over a possible spy all alone.

Had Mehl told her about the wards on the family wing? Only the guards and servants entrusted with special amulets could make their way through unless directly guided in, as Ria and her father had been, or officially attuned to the magic, like Toren and Mehl. Even the amulets were bound to their user so that they couldn't be stolen. It had been so for millennia, the spells renewed for each new monarch.

When the spell had shifted to him... Toren shuddered. *That* had been an agonizing day of uncertain magic. A task done blessedly infrequently, but it was vital, nonetheless. At least attuning Ria wouldn't be as taxing. That would need to be completed sooner rather than later, no matter the state of his control. She wouldn't relish being kept from her own room.

Gods, she was no doubt cursing his name. Or was she too terrified for that? Ria was braver than he'd expected, considering her history, but the threat of physical harm couldn't be easy on her. How could he contemplate sleeping without ensuring she was well?

Mehl's annoyed huff tickled his neck. "Tor—"

"I know. I'm sorry." Toren tugged free of his husband's arms and sat up. "But if I don't speak to Ria, I won't rest. She's surely upset."

"More angry, I think, which is why she chose to be alone." Mehl crossed his hands behind his head, leaving the fine expanse of his chest on display. And the way the sheet draped —No. Toren yanked his gaze back to Mehl's face in time to catch the flash of his wicked grin. "Go on. I'll wait right here."

A cock-stiffening thought, one made no easier to disregard when he considered the possibility of bringing Ria back with him. But first, he had to bear the brunt of her anger. He slid from the bed and donned his discarded tunic and pants. A little wrinkled, but they would do.

Fortunately, her room was next to his, so it only took a matter of moments to reach her door. But when he knocked, the wood shifted beneath his hand, and fear chilled his heart as the door swung open. She wouldn't have left it unlatched, would she?

Toren sent a mental call for Mehl as he peered into the room beyond. There was nothing apparent amiss, except...was that fabric unrolled across the floor? Perhaps she'd decided to work on her designs and had left her door ajar while going for more supplies. Aside from the cloth, he spotted only a tea tray on a side table.

When Mehl hurried over, it was with knife in hand and sword belt strapped over equally wrinkled clothes. "Did you call the guard?" he murmured.

"Not yet." Toren pointed at the fabric. "She could be working."

The hard lump of fear in his stomach said otherwise, but he tried to ignore it. There had to be a simple explanation.

Had to be.

"I'll go in first," Mehl said.

Unlike earlier, Toren made no effort to stop Mehl, though he burned with the urge to do so. Nothing about this situation felt right. But Mehl had made his point, however much Toren hated it. His husband was a trained warrior, skilled enough to have guarded royalty. It was an insult to suggest otherwise.

Toren followed Mehl as he crept beyond the sitting area and through the open bedroom door, but it didn't take a body-guard to see that both rooms were empty. Nor did a search of her new workroom provide any hints. According to the guard, he'd last seen Ria carrying a bolt of fabric to her bedroom.

Her now empty bedroom.

Please let there be a simple explanation.

"Where could she have gone?" Toren scanned her sitting area once more for clues, but there was no sign of a struggle. "The wards have not been activated. Unless the guard is remiss..."

Mehl stopped beside the tea service. "If she were quiet enough, she could have slipped into one of the empty chambers. I ordered them checked."

Something Toren should have thought of, but the sick twist of his stomach and the pounding of his magic clouded his mind. In so many ways, this was his fault. But had she fled or somehow been abducted? He walked over to the fabric and frowned down at the cushion some distance away from the cloth.

Had she been sitting there? Why? He knelt down to take a closer look, and the sudden taste of magic had his vision going white before he controlled it. This was Ria's energy. Had she done a spell on the fabric? One of the flowers seemed smaller, but...

Smeared. That edge of color looked smeared, though this design didn't seem to be painted. And there, nearly blending into the pattern, were several red drops.

"This tea set," Mehl said, his tone cold and hard, "Is remarkably absent of tea."

Awareness coalesced into one sickening lump of fear and rage.

Ria had been taken.

CHAPTER 23

SECRETS AND DELUSIONS

T raining smothered all but a single, tightly held core of fury, chilling and deadly. Mehl nourished it as much as stifled it, but balance between the two took care. And as he watched Toren's face go white, Mehl had a moment's fear that his well-honed balance might fail. But he couldn't allow it. He had to keep his mind clear and focused.

A wave of Toren's magic washed over him, stealing his breath. This could topple everything, beginning with his husband's control. As Mehl sent a quick, mental summons to Feref, he rushed across the room to Toren, who still knelt beside the fabric. Carefully, Mehl gripped his husband's shoulders and tugged him to his feet.

"Tor," he said sharply. "Look at me."

Energy streamed through his body from the physical connection, and despite the twinge of pain in his head, Mehl channeled and grounded the power as usual. He had no choice. Though the family wing had few residents, Toren was like contained lightning—if he lost his grip, there was no telling who or what he might destroy.

Mehl tightened his hold. "Toren Eyamiri. Look. At. Me."

After the longest heartbeat of Mehl's life, his husband blinked a few times before his unfocused gaze sharpened on Mehl. "Ria…"

"Needs you to not level the castle before we find her," Mehl said, keeping his voice matter-of-fact. "Send me what you have to, but get control."

Toren shuddered in his hold, but after another endless moment, energy slammed into Mehl like a blow. Though gasping from the force, he again channeled the power into the ground and did his best to ignore the increasing pain in his head. Only when the energy cut off did he truly recognize the extent of the hurt—the agony pounded in his very blood.

"Fuck," Toren cursed, his voice ringing in Mehl's ears. Mehl swayed, and his husband grabbed his waist to steady him. "I'm sorry."

"Don't." Mehl took a deep breath through his nose. "Just summon the healer. And think of how Ria disappeared."

The command felt as muddled as his thoughts, but Toren nodded. Then his husband helped him over to the nearby sofa.

The healer better hurry.

A TINNY, musty scent slid through the darkness, bringing a touch of awareness in its wake. Long-formed instinct had Ria springing fully awake at that hint, and she braced for another blow. Pain was her inevitable reward. It bounced and skittered through her skull like a bobbin of thread clattering its way down a shelf. What…?

She sucked in a breath, and dust tickled her nose until she couldn't hold back a sneeze. The bobbin tumbling in her head turned into a pin cushion, poking and stabbing. She couldn't help but moan, though she did her best to hold it in. More noise only meant more pain. If the neighbors heard...

"Don't move," a kind, soft voice said from somewhere beside her.

Wait. That wasn't her father. "Who?"

"Call me Tes," the person said.

How had she ended up with someone named Tes? That name didn't sound—

Memory hit, and she gasped. She'd been in her room, working on altering the pattern on that fabric. Then something had struck her. Quickly, she took stock of her body. The back of her head felt sticky with wetness. Blood? And she was stretched out on her side with her hands bound behind her back.

Someone had captured her and taken her...somewhere. Not a well-frequented place if the dust and the musty smell were things to go by. Finally, she cracked her eyes open the barest amount, but the light was so dim she could barely make out the shape of a person beside her. Small and slim, but she couldn't discern more than that.

"You're the spy," Ria said before she could think better of it.

A soft chuckle met her ears. "I am not, but I imagine that's what your kings have told you."

The words made no sense. "You're hardly a friend."

"I can see why you think that, too," the person said. "For what it's worth, I hit you harder than I intended. Ber will be furious if I've caused you harm."

Ria attempted to process that statement, but it didn't provide greater clarity. Prince Ber was known to be cruel, harsh to his servants and reckless with the soldiers he'd once had under his command. There were even whispers that he might have murdered his mother, the previous queen. No official word had ever been passed down about that, but Ber had been banished just after her death.

Yet Ria's captor sounded rather fond of the man—and quite familiar, too. What was going on? "I don't understand," she whispered.

The person lifted their hand, and a pale light sparked above their palm, giving Ria her first clear view of her captor. Thin, delicate face, pinned up hair, serviceable dress—it was the maid. The woman who'd been standing in her bedroom door when she'd returned with the fabric. Too bad Ria had been foolish enough to believe the woman's lies.

"So much for the comforting tea," Ria muttered.

Surprisingly, the woman winced. "I've never actually been a lady's maid, but my own used to offer such a thing. It seemed like a good cover while I reevaluated my plan."

Was the ache in her head causing delusions, or had she heard her captor correctly? Because a spy with her own lady's maid didn't exactly make sense. And what had been the previous plan if the alternative was clocking her over the head?

Ria wrinkled her nose. "I don't think I want to know your first idea."

"Oh, it was much nicer," Tes said in a rush. "Had you been abed, I could have used magic to send you into a deeper sleep."

But she couldn't have done that while Ria was awake? Something was off about this, and she didn't think it was her own muddled brain. A spy skilled enough to blend in with the servants, evade Mehl and the guards, and blend in again as a maid didn't exactly match Tes, a cheerful woman who didn't seem particularly adept at using magic. Or altering plans.

"Why are you doing this?" Ria asked.

Tes shrugged. "To save you, of course. Ber told me that if his brother had found a woman to force into carrying his heir, I was to bring her to safety. Whatever Toren has over you, we'll get around it. But I'll need to get you home first."

Ria tried to roll onto her back, but the bite of rope around her wrists reminded her of her current position. Not to mention the woman's hypocrisy. "You're the only one using force," Ria grumbled.

"Well, I didn't want you to flail around and make noise." Tes leaned over Ria and studied the rope before shrugging again. "Doesn't look too tight. Once we're out of here, I'll unbind you, though, I promise. I just don't want anything to go wrong."

Whoever this woman was, she was surely mad. "I don't want to leave. I'm with Toren and Mehl willingly."

"Only because you don't know the truth." Her captor frowned. "Toren is dangerous, and he sent his brother away to hide that fact. Ber is only trying to keep the kingdom safe."

The woman delivered those words with the force of conviction, but Ria couldn't grasp what reasoning might lie behind it. Why would the Centoi invite Toren to his brother's wedding and then abduct the royal consort in such a blatant way? It would have been more shrewd to simply slip in unannounced. Was there even a marriage taking place? Perhaps the entire thing was a ploy from start to finish.

"He wants to keep the kingdom safe by kidnapping the person who could be carrying the heir to the throne?" Ria asked slowly, her head pounding with increasing force. "Did he make up the wedding, too? That invitation made a good excuse to get you here so you could ruin Toren's breeding alliance."

Tes's skin flushed dark in the dim light. "The invitation wasn't entirely false. It's only that the wedding already took place. In secret."

There was something very personal in that blush—both shyness and passion, almost like...a bride. But no. It had to be the headache prompting that odd thought. This could not possibly be the princess of the Centoi. What princess would act as herald for her own wedding announcement, much less a spy?

Maybe this woman was Ber's mistress. She could be trying to prove her loyalty with this unusual stunt. Then again, for all Ria knew, the three of them might have an arrangement much like she had with Toren and Mehl. She certainly wasn't going to ask.

Either way, it wasn't good news for Ria. Tes appeared nothing but earnest, but it was impossible to discern whether it was an act. Even if the woman wholeheartedly believed that Prince Ber was nothing but goodness and light, that didn't make it true. The last thing Ria wanted was to end up in his clutches.

To escape, she would have to learn more about Tes's plans so she could counter them. At least she had a lifetime of practice with pretending cooperation. "If what you say about Prince Ber is true," Ria began, "Then he'll want me taken from here safely, I presume?"

"Of course," Tes agreed.

"Well, how do you think to accomplish that? You don't look strong enough to carry me far, and as soon as the kings realize I'm gone, the palace will be swarming with even more guards than the ones already looking for you." Ria's stomach took the opportunity to growl. "And I'm hungry. I was too nervous to eat much at dinner, and I doubt he'd want me starved."

For the first time, true annoyance pinched the woman's face. "I am not so foolish that you'll trick me into running down to the kitchen for you. As soon as you're capable, we'll walk. Ber told me how to get out of the tunnels."

Tunnels? Ria's gaze darted around the dim room, but Tes's

mage light revealed boxes and old furniture, not narrow passageways. "This isn't—"

"I took you up to the storage area," her captor said. "But the sooner we head down, the better. I don't know how long it will be before you're discovered missing."

Unfortunately, Ria wasn't sure, either. She'd told Mehl she wanted a night alone, and the kings were busy arguing—or making up. They might not look for her until morning. But was there a true lady's maid who might check on her? She hadn't thought to ask whether the servants would appear on a schedule or would need to be summoned.

Ria couldn't rely on anyone but herself for this escape.

Ah, well. It wouldn't be the first time she'd been on her own.

THINK OF HOW SHE DISAPPEARED—A command easier said than done. Toren could barely drag his mind free of the morass of fear and worry long enough to contemplate it. Not only was Ria gone, but he'd hurt his husband. He struggled to get beyond anything but the mental image of a pale, swaying Mehl.

Only when the healer rushed in a blessedly few minutes later could Toren manage to comply. As he stepped back so the healer could work, Toren forced his mind to consider the problem. How could someone abduct Ria from the family wing without being noticed?

It would have been difficult but not impossible for an intruder to pull Ria into a nearby room, but by now, those had been searched. The servants' stairs were at the far end of the corridor, so it was unlikely that the guard would have missed someone being carried that far. In fact, the guard hadn't seen anyone else except Ria and a maid.

A maid who brought an empty tea service. Could she have been the spy? But if so, how could she have entered the family wing without having one of the amulets attuned—

Oh, gods.

Ber could have adjusted that spell if he'd gained one of those amulets. Ber could have adjusted that spell if he'd gained one of those amulets. The two of them were so similar, by blood and magic, that his brother could do so. But if Ber hoped to be king someday, it would do him no good to give such an important talisman to just anyone, which meant the spy was someone he trusted. Someone close.

Someone he might also entrust with the knowledge of the secret passages.

Those didn't lead throughout the entire palace. Some went up to the floor above, which held the nursery as well as rooms for older children and visiting family. A mostly unused section, considering how the royal family had shrunk over the years. Aside from that, a few passages snaked down to the throne room, study, and other vital locations. But all of the tunnels eventually led to a single branching point that then split into three escape paths—and each emptied out beyond the city walls.

The Centoi's refusal to stay made a sudden, sick sense.

He had to go after Ria. Now.

CHAPTER 24

ALTERATIONS

Ria had to come up with a plan, and fast. Her captor kept eyeing a spot on the wall, probably where the tunnel emerged, and then frowning down at her. It was only a matter of time before Tes decided to make Ria try to walk. So what would be her best option?

When the other woman glanced away again, Ria tested the bonds around her wrists. The rough bite of rope scratched at her skin, but there wasn't much give. There didn't have to be. With a little magic, she could alter the threads, either stretching or fraying them. The trick was getting Tes away so she didn't pick up on it.

"Can you at least bandage my head?" Ria asked. "I can't tell if it's still bleeding, but it feels uncomfortable, regardless."

A lie—Ria was reasonably certain from past experience that the wound had clotted. Fortunately, her captor appeared less knowledgeable about the aftermath of violence, considering the worried frown crossing her brow.

Tes leaned down, holding her tiny spark of light lower. "It doesn't look like there's more blood."

"Maybe clean it off?" Ria sighed at her captor's blank look. "You could tear a strip of fabric from the petticoat of your dr—"

"I'll not ruin this poor servant's dress!" Tes exclaimed in horror. "As I am not a thief, I have every intention of seeing it returned in one piece. That is not an acceptable solution."

Ria stared at the daft woman. Tes had no trouble stealing *her* from the castle, but a pilfered dress was too much? "You're not a thief, huh?"

"You know nothing about me," Tes said, flushing once more.

"I don't think I care to," Ria snapped, and her captor flinched. Why did the hurt on the woman's face make her feel a little guilty? It was probably all feigned, anyway. "Look, maybe search the room for some kind of cloth? It's a storage area, so it shouldn't be too hard."

Lips thinning, Tes spun away and stomped toward the nearest pile, taking her light with her. Ria smiled into the sudden darkness, but her satisfaction didn't last long. Her head pounded and spun as she reached for her magic. Had she thought doing a spell when dizzy was bad? Adding pain to the mix wasn't precisely a help.

Desperation, though...that worked. Although her stomach heaved and rolled, Ria managed to weaken the rope by the time Tes returned with a dusty scrap of fabric. But she didn't free herself yet. It really would be a good idea to ensure that her head had stopped bleeding before she attempted to make a run for it.

"That's covered in dirt," Ria couldn't help but point out as her captor leaned close with the cloth.

"By all the gods," Tes muttered between clenched teeth. "If I'd had any inkling this rescue would be such a pain in the—"

"Rescue?" Ria laughed. "I could be in bed with two

gorgeous kings right now having my every need met. Instead, I'm tied up in a storage room that probably hasn't been visited since Toren was a baby, and I have a raging headache. I'm not sure why you expect friendly cooperation."

Tes's nose wrinkled. "You could meet your death in that bed. King Toren is dangerous."

She could meet her death, all right, but not in the way her captor seemed to believe. "So is grinding dirt into a wound."

Tes let out a low growl and held the bit of fabric in front of her face. A hint of magic shimmered on the air before the cloth went pale in the thin light. Then the scowling woman bent over Ria and began to poke at the back of her head. Ria had to admit her captor used a lighter touch than her expression had suggested she would, but pain still spiked through her skull with each dab.

After straightening, Tes squinted down at the scrap. "A little red from your hair. But it didn't look like there was fresh bleeding when I examined your scalp."

That prognosis was probably as good as it was going to get. At this point, it would be better to risk fainting than to trust her inept "rescuer" with more wound care. As far as she was concerned, whatever cleverness had seen Tes through to finding Ria was gone now.

"Fine," Ria said. "Then let's get on with it."

Getting to her feet was easier said than done, though, especially without breaking the frayed rope before she was ready. But with help from Tes, no small amount of cursing, and a great deal of awkward shifting, Ria finally managed it. Sort of. She couldn't help but sway on her feet a little.

Getting away might prove…difficult. She would do it, though. She'd worked entire days in the shop after beatings, hadn't she? A head injury might be a bit trickier than the hidden wounds her father had inflicted, but disconnecting from the pain was much the same.

Tes's arm wrapped around her waist for extra balance, but no matter how much she wanted to, Ria didn't shrug her off. Not yet. It kept them side-by-side, and that might make it easier to slip away than if her captor was behind her. Besides, it took her several steps for the dizziness to ease.

After setting the tiny sphere of mage light on a dusty side table, her captor pressed a series of spots on the wall, and a small door opened. Instinctively, Ria dug in her heels, forcing Tes to a halt. There was nothing but darkness beyond that door. If she stepped through, what would happen? Her captor tugged, but Ria couldn't move.

"Dizzy," Ria whispered, though it wasn't the reason for her hesitation.

How could she stay out of that darkness?

The door had opened toward them, and the thick stone was almost within touching distance—provided Ria's hands were free. If she could get Tes to go first, maybe she could finish breaking the rope, close the woman in the tunnel, and run for it? Tes obviously knew how to open the secret entrance, so it wouldn't be much of a head start.

Unless...Ria lowered her head as though trying to ease her dizziness, but she used the opportunity to study Tes's skirts. Ria could spell-alter dresses in her sleep. Why not make this one unexpectedly small? Her captor would have to fight her way free of shrunken fabric before attempting a pursuit.

"You're just going to have to manage," Tes said. "We can't stand here all night."

A tinge of fear coated Ria's tongue, but she ignored it. She would not be abused again. "Could you light the tunnel a little? I think the difference in light is bothering my head."

Frowning, Tes peered at her for a moment before reluctantly releasing her waist. "Fine. But don't you dare move."

As her captor stepped reluctantly into the doorway, Ria broke the few remaining strands of the frayed rope with as little movement as she could manage. Then she waited. A moment later, Tes glanced toward Ria, nodded as though satisfied, and turned back toward the tunnel to begin her magic.

The world tilted and swirled slightly as Ria rushed into action, but desperation steadied her enough that she managed not to fall when she shoved against Tes. Caught off-guard, the other woman flew into the tunnel with enough force to smack against the opposite wall before tumbling to the ground. It was difficult to tell in the thin light if she'd caught herself with her hands or landed more roughly, but Ria wasn't going to check.

Instead, she used her magic to grab the fabric and twist. It required little thought to narrow and snarl the skirts until walking would be nearly impossible. Although she had to grip the edge of the door to keep herself from toppling next to Tes on the floor, Ria managed the job before her captor did more than let out a moan.

Ria's body trembled, and she had to fight back a surge of sickness. But within moments, she'd managed to close the narrow door with a decisive thud. Slowly, she turned to face the room. In the dimming glow of Tes's mage light, Ria could make out a door on the far end of the cluttered room.

Now she just had to reach it.

The healer had barely completed his work before Mehl was on his feet. "Well?" he asked Toren.

Fear and fury tightened his husband's expression, but Toren said nothing, merely gesturing for the healer to leave without a word. Only when the door closed did he hurry toward Mehl. "The secret tunnels. That has to be where they've gone."

Mehl's blood chilled at the thought. If that were the case, Ria's abductor would have a significant head start, possibly enough to be out of the city. He exchanged one worried glance with Toren before they strode as one toward the fireplace.

With shaking hands, his husband pressed the correct pattern into the stone wall beside the mantel, but he didn't rush through after the panel swung open. A change, that. Mehl gave him a grateful smile as he moved around his husband to take the lead. Toren followed, closing the door behind him. Complete darkness enclosed them, but a hint of Toren's magic sparked a thin line of light above, so pale it barely shifted the tunnel to gray.

Mehl drew his sword, but he didn't move forward. Which direction should they go?

"I ordered Macoe to begin in the throne room and head toward the branching point," Toren sent. *"Let's go up before we descend to meet him."*

Mehl started walking at once. *"Besides Sir Macoe, who else knows of the secret passages?"*

"No one outside of the royal family," Toren replied grimly.

Truth be told, Mehl hadn't even been aware that the head of the guard knew. With each person entrusted with the secret, the risk increased. *"You're certain he hasn't betrayed us?"*

"If you'd been king when Sir Macoe undertook the oathing cere-mony, you would have no doubt of his loyalty." Toren went silent as they climbed a narrow staircase. *"More than words are bound in that vow. Despite the increased security the ceremony provides, it is not something I would have required myself."*

It must have involved either Sir Macoe's inherent magic or his very soul. Possibly both. The ancient founders of this land had been harsher than most realized—than *he* had realized before becoming king. What appeared to be tradition or changeable law was sometimes an immutable rule, made so by the magic underpinning the kingdom.

Such as the heir-challenge that Prince Ber planned to exploit.

And no one was more bound to obey than the high king. It was a sad reality, being chained into such power while unable to change it. Toren's strength was such that he could barely contain the force of his own energy, and yet he'd never been capable of shifting any of the Iron Laws, so-called by the royals for their poisonous immobility.

They were as endless as these blasted tunnels.

Surely, they were near the end of the upper passages, which only stretched to the end of this floor. Mehl's grip tightened on his sword. This was taking too long, and it might be fruitless, besides. If the spy had detailed knowledge of the escape tunnels, she could have taken Ria through one of the connected rooms. Otherwise, she probably would have fled below, not lingered up here.

Mehl was about to suggest that they turn back early when a pale lump huddled ahead caught his eye. Was it a person? He dropped into a crouch and eased forward, ready to confront any kind of trap. But the closer he got, the less the sight made sense. The tangled fabric made such an odd shape that any person inside would have to be mangled.

"Ria's magic is strong in the air," Toren sent.

Shutting out the surge of emotion those words brought, Mehl edged closer to the unusual lump. *"Can you increase the light? Slowly? Or will that risk your control?"*

Toren didn't answer, but the glow intensified—as did the force of his husband's magic. But Mehl couldn't worry about the latter. His focus was for the mass of cloth taking on ever-greater detail. It didn't take long to discern that it was just cloth, either.

The discarded fabric might have once been a servant's dress. The color was right. But it was twisted together until he couldn't imagine how anyone had ever worn it. A dark splotch marred one maybe-sleeve. Blood or mud? Either way, the person inside was gone. He looked up, searching the tunnel for the wearer.

But the passage was empty all the way to the dead end.

CHAPTER 25

UNBALANCED

Ria had been too nervous to grab the tiny mage light left by her captor. Its magic was failing, and there was a chance it could be tracked. But as she stumbled her way down the darkened corridor, she almost wished she'd risked it. This was clearly some kind of neglected side hallway, for the only glow to be found was at the far end where it met the main corridor. Did the kings truly have so little family that they could forget part of an entire floor?

She stepped as carefully as she could, her hand on the wall for balance. Why was it so dark? Maybe more time had passed than she'd thought. It would make sense to dim the lights to save magic if most were sleeping, and that was doubly true if the area wasn't being used. It was rather inconvenient for her, though. Her vision was already blurry, and—

Pain seared through her left toes as they connected with something hard. Hissing out a curse, Ria squinted down into the darkness and managed to make out a small table. She ran her hand carefully across the top, hoping for a discarded mage globe, but nothing was there. Drat. It would have been nice to get something out of the mistake besides an aching foot and an increased risk of being recaptured.

Gods help her if Tes had heard the slight commotion.

Ria braved a quick but unenlightening look over her shoulder—it was far too dark to discern detail. But it was best not to tarry, regardless. She eased around the small table and kept going. Each step sent more pain and dizziness through her poor head, and her limbs were growing heavy with exhaustion. She needed a healer—sooner rather than later.

By the time she neared the end of the hallway, the floor had a slight tilt she felt confident didn't exist outside of her own spinning head. Even the faint glow filling the main corridor speared into her eyes and through her pained skull until she had to lean against the corner with her eyes closed for a moment. Her skin crawled as though anticipating phantom hands taking hold at any moment, and her heartbeat pounded in her ears, the only sound in the eerie place.

Then a slight clink and the *shoosh* of fabric echoed from somewhere around her. But which direction? Ria pressed her fist against her breastbone and lifted her eyelids a fraction. A mistake, for the light sent another dart of pain through her. Why did it keep getting worse? She couldn't account for it, because she *had to* see if someone was there.

Swallowing against the lump in her throat, Ria turned her head slowly and squinted into the darkness behind her. No difference that she could tell, though that didn't mean much in her current condition. She tried to peer left, then right down the main corridor, but between her blurred vision and the poorly spaced and barely lit mage lights, she couldn't make out a great deal more detail.

She spotted another of those little tables to her left. Directly across from her, Ria saw a massive vase with a decorative plant spearing from the top, and the pattern of table-vase-table seemed to repeat down that side. She leaned farther around the corner to see better and nearly groaned. Vases on this side, too. Since she needed the wall to maintain her balance, she would just have to do her best not to knock one of the things over.

Ria took a chance on turning left, where the light glowed slightly brighter and the corridor looked like it stretched for longer. If she could reach a more populated area of the palace, there would surely be guards around. For that matter, if this was still the family wing, shouldn't there be someone preventing entry as there was on the kings' level? She tried to peer into the shadows at the far end but didn't have much luck. For all she knew, the guard had hidden himself behind a plant for a quick nap.

Of course, details like that might have been more evident if the world wasn't growing hazier and more tilted with each moment. The dull glow here bothered her worse than the deep shadows of the previous hallway. With her hand against the wall for balance, the sconces were directly in front of her face. Each time she neared one that held a mage globe, blurry light clouded her vision in shimmering rings, and those rings eventually refused to fade.

Ria lifted her free hand to shade her eyes, but she still couldn't bear to do more than squint through the hazy kaleidoscope. A dark, distorted something loomed along her path. Was that another vase? Perhaps a different table was...no. Tables didn't move. And the blob was too tall. *Why* couldn't she get her vision to cooperate? Her world was nothing but dull shadows and badly refracted light.

She longed to let out a curse in frustration.

"Stop right there!" a deep, stern voice commanded, and she froze out of instinct.

Should she run? It clearly wasn't Tes, but that didn't mean

Tes was working alone. Did it even matter? At this point, Ria had little hope of escape. Her head was one giant mass of pain, and the figure emerging from the deeper shadows curved and bowed like fabric twisting in the breeze. The more she tried to focus on it, the more it spun—along with her stomach. What she needed was to sit and close her eyes until the world went steady.

Abruptly, her mind and body agreed, and everything spun and lurched as her legs lost their strength. With her hand on the wall, she was barely able to manage a controlled slide. Or something resembling. Pain radiated through her backside from her abrupt landing on the hard floor.

If someone else intended to capture her, they could have at it.

So long as they let her rest.

TOREN HAD SENT out an immediate command to have this floor searched, but it didn't seem like enough. For the first time in ages, he wanted to throw caution aside and leap into danger as surely as Mehl would. But what good would it do to rush through every room connecting to this section of the passages in hopes of being the one to find the spy?

Thinking logically was paramount.

It was impossible to know for certain when or why the spy had abandoned the dress. Ria's magic indicated her involvement, and the mangled state of it implied why it had been left behind. But where could they have gone afterward? He hated the thought of Ria waiting for rescue in one of the nearby rooms while he and Mehl simply left, but if there was a chance that her captor had hauled her through the tunnels, Toren and Mehl were among the few who could pursue.

"Back down?" Mehl sent, a frown creasing his brow.

"Unfortunately, yes."

Too bad he didn't dare connect fully with the shielding. Had his hold on his power not been so shaky, he could have altered the key attached to the pendants, making everyone in the family wing immediately evident, but that was a major working. Far too risky. Toren cursed his own weakness as he and Mehl hurried back the way they'd come.

Mehl touched his shoulder. *"I know that look on your face. This isn't your fault."*

"Oh, but it is," Toren argued. *"I decided to make that announcement tonight without watching the Centoi more closely. I prevented you from following the spy, causing the argument that saw Ria left alone. Now, I can't even use my magic to find her."*

His husband's frustrated sigh echoed down the staircase as Toren stepped back to follow Mehl down. *"You aren't a god, Tor. Self-recrimination is useless."*

So it was, but he seemed unable to stop.

They'd just cleared their own floor and started down into the lower passages when he sensed Sir Macoe's presence at the edge of his mind. *"Yes?"*

"One of the guards found a woman, Your Majesty," the captain of the guard sent. *"But her identity is unclear. She fainted and has not awakened. He carried her to the Bronze Room."*

Toren's heart leaped with nervous excitement, but he kept his emotions to himself. *"Continue searching the passages. I'll go."*

Grabbing Mehl's arm, Toren drew them both to a halt. But for a moment, he couldn't answer the questions gathering in his husband's eyes. Too much feeling swelled within him. Earlier, he'd prevented Mehl from going into danger, but it had been the wrong choice. No matter how much he feared for his husband's life, he had to make the logical decision.

"Toren?"

"Sir Macoe sent word that an injured woman was found," he replied. *"I need to go see if it's Ria."*

Mehl nodded. *"We can exit just ahead, then."*

"No." Toren squeezed Mehl's arm. *"You continue searching for the spy. Or Ria, for that matter. We don't know for sure that it's her."*

"You want…" Surprise resounded in Mehl's mental voice, and his brows rose. *"You're actually telling me to go alone this time?"*

Toren's nostrils flared. *"I don't like it, but it's the best option. Be certain you return to me safely."*

After a quick grin, Mehl gave him a hard but brief kiss. *"So I will. You'll surely remember to have a bodyguard accompany you in my absence for the same reason?"*

"Of course." Toren released his arm as he calculated where they were and the best place to exit. *"We'll part after the next turn."*

He had to hope it wasn't a mistake.

WHEN RIA SURFACED THIS TIME, it was with no greater clarity. Her head pounded, and the tang of sickness filled her mouth. Her arms ached. She attempted to lift them, only to feel the bite of rope around her wrists. Again? Fear burned a path up her throat, though she didn't think she was in the same place. Her arms were in front of her this time, light glowed behind her eyelids, and the surface beneath her had more cushion.

Nevertheless, she was captured.

Ria didn't want to look. She didn't want to open her eyes to find Tes and her accomplice staring down at her. She might have idly thought she'd welcome this for a chance at rest, but she hadn't meant it. No matter what the woman claimed, there was no reason to believe she had good intent. The blinding headache and sticky, matted hair at the back of her head were counter enough to Tes's assertion.

Should she pretend to be unconscious? Last time, waking up had prompted her captor into leaving the castle. The longer she feigned sleep, the more time she had to be found. Hours had to have passed at this rate. Surely someone had checked on her by now. If nothing else, Toren was eager to produce a child, so he might have been less inclined to leave her alone than Mehl.

The click of a door caught her ear, and she couldn't help but tense. *Blast it*, she cursed to herself. She was supposed to be unaware. Even so, it took all her self-control not to open her eyes to see who had entered.

"Where—" The low voice cut off abruptly, but not before she recognized the rough timbre of it.

Toren.

Her eyelids shot open in time to see Toren glare at a guard standing beside the door. "Were you not given a description of Lady Ria by Sir Macoe?"

The soldier paled. "This is Lady Ria? Forgive me, Your Majesty. With her plain clothes and dirtiness, I would not have thought it so."

Without another word, Toren strode toward her, leaving the guard fretting in his wake. The High King's expression was so cold and blank, his posture so rigid, that she suspected he held onto his rage—and his magic—by the thinnest thread. That wasn't good. Thinking to reassure him, Ria shifted, only to groan as her vision blurred and her head throbbed.

Stark fear filled his eyes as he dropped to his knees beside her. "Where are you injured?"

"My head," she whispered, then snapped her mouth closed against a wave of nausea.

Toren glanced over his shoulder at the guard. "You didn't think to summon the healer?"

"If she were the criminal—"

"Then you would summon the healer," Toren snapped. "Go. Do so now."

No matter how right he was, the volume of his words pounded directly into her skull. Too much. She tried to reach for his arm to get his attention, only to remember rather painfully that her wrists were bound. As the guard hurried toward the door, Ria swallowed down bile and prayed she could speak without being sick.

"Toren," she said. His head whipped back around. "Quieter. Please."

Even as his eyes continued to burn, his expression softened. "I'm sorry," he murmured.

Ria licked her dry lips. "Wrists."

Frowning, his gaze trailed downward, and his lips whitened when he saw her wrists. "Who bound you?" he snarled.

"Guard? Maybe," Ria answered. "This time."

Toren froze, the fight for control obvious to her even in her muddled state. When he reached for the rope, his fingers trembled against her skin whenever they brushed. Unfortunately, a hint of his power leaked through, too, and she whimpered against the increased pressure in her head.

He drew back. "Ria?"

"Your magic," she whispered.

She hated the pain that brought to his eyes and the way he stiffened against it. But what could she do? He wouldn't want her to suffer in silence, nor would she do so. Not again.

Never again.

Carefully, Toren reached out once more, but all she felt this time was the tug of rope as he picked at the knot. It seemed to take forever. But once the rope fell away, she let her arms settle at her sides. So much better. Ria sighed in relief and gave Toren a grateful smile. Unfortunately, he'd averted his gaze.

"Not your fault," she said.

His eyes burned into hers once more. "Mehl said much the same, but you're wrong."

"Where?"

"Mehl?" he asked. "He's searching for the spy."

Ria let her eyes drift closed. "Secret tunnel."

"All we found was an abandoned dress," Toren said, his tone going tight.

Well, that was unfortunate news. Ria's handiwork might have slowed Tes down, but the woman was still out there somewhere.

And now Mehl was in danger.

CHAPTER 26

SHADOWS AND LIGHT

Without Toren there, Mehl could move faster and with more stealth. His husband was far from helpless, but he was no trained warrior, either. That always had to be taken into account. Working alone also meant there was no risk of triggering Toren's magic if Mehl used his own. So he allowed his senses to open and expand until he could scan ahead and around for signs of life.

In the distant past, it hadn't caused trouble for Mehl to sweep their surroundings with magic, but the closer he and Toren had grown, the riskier it had become. The worst of it started the last decade or so when Mehl had needed to channel more of his husband's magic. That energetic link was no doubt to blame.

One of many reasons Toren had other bodyguards when outside the family wing.

The tunnel descended ever lower, passing from floors filled with guest rooms to those of the servants. At that point, not even Mehl's magic helped a great deal, for there were many servants asleep in their rooms at this hour. He slowed, searching for anything out of place. Every person he scanned appeared to be sleeping—or otherwise occupied—in their beds, no hint of unusual magic or unexpected tension.

Unless he wanted to question every single servant, he would have to rely on that as truth. But how far could the spy have gotten? If she left the secret passages, she would be noticed quickly, especially if she was in her underclothes as he suspected. Neither the uniform she'd worn at dinner nor the clothes she had on as an envoy would fit under a servant's dress without being noticeable. The gowns weren't particularly low cut, but the high-necked line of the former two outfits would be quite obvious.

Perhaps it would be more productive to consider where the spy might have acquired her stolen dress. The amulet providing passage through the family wing had likely come from Prince Ber, since he was the only one with the potential to modify it, but the current fashion in maids' gowns was less likely to have made its way to the Centoi. If she hadn't stolen that dress from an individual, she would have purloined it from either the laundry or the servants' storage closet and might have stashed her other clothes there in the process.

Both rooms would have been easy to access after she escaped the dining hall through the servants' areas, but only the storage closet had an entrance to the secret tunnels. Not that the servants were aware of that fact—it was nestled at the edge of a shelf and was a narrow squeeze to reach. According to Toren, that section had been planned as the royal seamstress's suite when the castle was built millennia ago, so the access point had been added.

Funny how things shifted even amongst the seemingly timeless.

Mehl slowed as he neared the entrance to the storage room. A sweep of his senses had a smile curving his lips. There were fewer people around at this time of night, yet he detected a presence in the very room he sought. Coincidence? It was certainly possible that some industrious soul was working in the room holding excess clothes and accessories for the servants, but it hardly seemed to be the most likely explanation.

As he reached the entrance, he sensed Toren at the edge of his mind and had to drop his magic in order to communicate. He leaned his back against the opposite wall and tightened his grip on his sword. Fortunately, he'd grown accustomed to using all his senses. He kept watch on the entrance and surrounding tunnel as he opened his thoughts.

"Is all well?" he sent Toren.

"They found Ria," his husband answered. *"I'm with her now."*

Mehl sagged against the wall. *"How is she?"*

Anger slipped across their link. *"A bit dazed and ill from being hit on the head, but the healer should be here soon."*

Hit on the head? The hilt of Mehl's sword dug into his palm from the strength of his grip. *"I may be nearing the spy. I'll let you know."*

"Take care."

Though he sent a wave of love, Mehl ended their link before his husband could linger on his worry about the coming confrontation. Mehl needed to move. So he let his magic sweep out once more, and almost at once, he noted that the person in the storage room had shifted position. They'd moved much nearer to the entrance he sought.

Better, then, to lie in wait.

Mehl shifted around until he could press his back to the opposite wall, just beside the secret doorway. Sure enough, the other person grew ever closer until they were unmistakably beside the entrance to the tunnels. There was no reason to be squeezed into that spot unless planning an escape.

But then the stranger began to move away, and Mehl recited a litany of curses to himself. Was he mistaken, or had they detected his magic? If the spy was a mage, it was possible, especially with closer proximity. She might choose to risk leaving through the main rooms to avoid him, and then he'd never find her.

As the person eased farther from him, Mehl pulled his magic back into himself and swung around to open the door. He would have to go in blind, but the other person would no longer be able to detect him, either, not without him sensing the scan. But the entrance...that would be the tricky part. It was a tight squeeze, and that meant vulnerability. He would lose most of the range of movement with his sword, but since he had neither a shield nor a knife, it would have to do.

He would rather risk injury than allow her to escape again.

The door slid open with a soft whoosh of air, and Mehl turned sideways, sword arm first, to sidle through the gap. Unexpectedly, pitch black darkness greeted him, all the more stark for the slight glow he'd become accustomed to in the tunnels. Had the spy been working without lights, or had she extinguished the mage globes when she'd sensed him? Too bad Toren controlled the light in the secret passage. It put Mehl at a disadvantage since it framed him clearly in the doorway.

As he waited for his eyes to adjust, he attuned his ears to the slightest sound. The irregular hiss of ragged breathing. The slight scuff of shoe against stone. Both expected. Then the swish of a blade cut through the air, and he turned his sword to counter a blow even as he stepped back.

Sharp pain exploded across his forearm. He sucked in a

breath from the bite, but he couldn't let himself be distracted. He could make out the other person's form now as they danced back farther into the room. The barest light glinted off the knife they held, one no doubt dripping with his blood. Well, no reason now to withhold his magic.

Unlike in the secret passages, Mehl could connect with the spells lighting this room. He let his senses rush out once more as he slowly increased the light to highlight the spy. Once again, she wore her Centoi clothes, and she held her knife with skill. Yet her eyes...there was an increasing fear as he approached—an uncertainty not typical of an assassin.

"King Mehl?" she whispered.

He watched, physically and magically, for her to attack once more, but now that they were at equal advantage, she didn't seem inclined to proceed. She was too busy staring at his face in horror. More the pity for her.

"And you are?" Mehl asked, though he didn't care.

As her eyes fastened on his mouth, he sprang forward, cracking the end of his sword against her hand so hard he heard the crunch of bone an instant before her scream. The knife slipped from her hold, and she reached instinctively toward the injury with her other hand, only to cry out again at her own grip. With his own arm burning with pain, he couldn't summon sympathy.

Mehl grabbed her uninjured arm at the elbow and spun her around, shoving her against a shelf full of folded clothes. As she sputtered into the fabric, he dropped his sword to grip her other arm and twist it behind her. Her sharp, panting gasps turned into a low moan as he gripped her wrists in his uninjured hand and leaned his weight against her.

"Please," she gasped. "The shelf is digging...can't..."

He eased up the slightest fraction, but he didn't let her go.

Instead, he glanced around the room until he spotted a shelf full of accessories, including a bit of silken ribbon used for belts and hair ties. Good. He could bind the spy with that, then find something for his arm. The bleeding had slowed, but a trickle still trailed down until it dampened his palm.

Even if the woman made it to the dungeon with no further injury, there was no guarantee Toren wouldn't kill her for that.

Mehl shoved the woman over to the other shelf, and using a combination of his teeth and his free hand, he managed to tie a loose binding around her wrists. She squirmed in his hold and tugged at her arms, but he leaned his weight against her once more until he could get her better secured with a second ribbon and his own free hands.

Only when he had her securely bound—at wrists and ankles—on the stone floor did he tend to his own wound.

Gods, Ria loved healers.

Sweet relief chased away pain and dizziness, leaving her with a light and slightly giddy feeling. In that moment, it was probably best that she didn't remember the healer's name, for she surely would have insisted they name their first child after him. Possibly even their second. That wouldn't be too confusing, would it?

But as the healer shifted his magic away from her head to heal her chafed wrists, Ria's mind began to clear. Her cheeks warmed. What had she been thinking? She was contracted for one child. Once Toren and Mehl had their heir, she would be relegated to some suite close to the nursery. Probably near the place she'd been held captive.

In any case, she wasn't likely to have a say in the child's

name—a depressing thought that wiped away the pleasant feeling she'd gained from the healing. Not even the easing of the other aches and pains in her body helped after that. How could it when her heart burned in her chest from the sad, undeniable reality of it all? She was never chosen for anything other than what she could give.

Never for herself.

Unbidden, her gaze slid to Toren where he paced on the other side of the room. With his green tunic against the overriding brown of the walls and decorations, he was a bright spot of life against the dull. So vital—and growing alarmingly dear to her heart in such a short time.

He drew her, though he was taken. She couldn't help but long for him, though she was a means to an end to him. It was a dangerous place to be. Perhaps her father had been right to call her foolish all these years.

The healer's magic cut off, but the comforting smile he wore faded after he studied her face. "Do you still feel unwell? I thought I found everything, but with the possibility that you might be—"

A guard rushed through the door, and the healer glanced over his shoulder, his words forgotten. Ria wanted to shake the rest of the sentence out of him. The possibility that she might be *what*? Seriously ill? Needing more intensive healing? Pregnant?

It couldn't be the latter. Could it? Not enough time had passed for that—nowhere near. Gods above, she needed to know what the man had been about to say. Ria glared over at the guard speaking to Toren, but her annoyance faded a little at the concern on Toren's face.

"And he's bleeding?" Toren asked.

A chill passed through Ria. Mehl. How could she have forgotten the danger he was in?

"There is blood on him, but it's unclear whether it's his, Your Majesty," the guard said. "Sir Macoe is assisting him with the prisoner now, so King Mehl sent me ahead to warn you. He said he's too tired to connect telepathically."

Toren let out a vicious curse that had the guard's throat bobbing convulsively, but Ria was fairly confident it was directed toward Mehl, not the hapless warrior. Because the reality was likely somewhat different from the message given —if Mehl was in pain from being injured, he would never risk a mental link with Toren for fear of overloading him. Exhaustion was quite possibly a coded excuse.

The healer seemed to come to the same conclusion. "I suppose I should stick around."

Ria eyed Toren. He was scowling at the door, his attention eons away from her. She grabbed the healer's wrist and tugged softly until he leaned close. "What were you going to say earlier? The possibility of what?" she whispered.

"Ah, that." His soft smile returned. "You aren't pregnant yet, but you could be soon. It'll be at least a couple of weeks before we know if it takes. Until then, it is a mere possibility, and many things can go wrong."

She blinked. "What?"

The healer shrugged. "Even if the seed does fertilize the egg, it doesn't always work out properly. And when *that* works correctly, implantation may fail. Really, it is a complicated process that—"

This time when the door opened, Ria was grateful for the interruption. Anything to save herself from this awkwardness. Then Mehl stumbled through, one arm slung around a wriggling Tes and the other hanging at his side, blood-soaked fabric wrapped tight around the bottom. With a gasp, Ria sat up just as another warrior entered. The second man took hold of Tes, only to force her to her knees in front of Toren.

Tears tracked down the woman's face, and dirt and blood coated her clothes. But Ria couldn't find any sympathy in her heart.

All she could see was the blood that trickled down Mehl's finger to land on the floor with a wet plop.

CHAPTER 27

DISCERNMENT

At the sight of blood on Mehl's arm, Toren almost lost every shred of his control. He pinched his eyes closed as his magic slammed painfully against his mental shields like a sudden flood in the rainy season. Then he held on tight, bolstering that shield piece by piece until he was certain nothing would seep free. Only then did he meet Mehl's gaze—but no lower.

"How bad?" he asked, his voice rough.

"Nothing dire," Mehl answered, though Toren could see the pain pinching the corners of his eyes. "A mere gash I reopened hauling our little spy into the room."

After bracing against another surge, Toren finally allowed himself to study her. She'd donned the clothes she'd worn as herald to the Centoi, but now the fine fabric was coated in patches of dirt and blood—some of it dark enough that it might not be fresh. Ria's? His vision flashed white, and the floor trembled slightly beneath his feet.

"I didn't realize it was King Mehl," the woman whispered. "I thought only of protecting myself. Please don't kill me."

There was real fear in those teary eyes—as well there should be. She'd drawn the blood of one of the kings after abducting the royal consort. He could kill her where she knelt, and none would question it. Yet the way her breath heaved and her body trembled gave him pause. More often than not, the worst among the guilty displayed anger with their fear, a hint of the defiance that had carried them through their poor decisions in the first place.

Not so for their spy.

Although she was clearly terrified, she didn't bow or even lower her head. There had been no fawning with her whispered plea, and she hadn't used an honorific beyond Mehl's title. Who was this strange woman who had introduced the Centoi envoy like a carefree bard and attacked Mehl like a warrior, only to quiver at his feet? Something was off about her presence here.

"What is your name?" he snapped.

Her eyes widened. "Tes."

"You would do well to consider the full truth." Toren turned his attention to Mehl for a moment. "See the healer, love. He should be done helping Ria."

Mehl frowned. "But if you need—"

"Please, Mehl," he interrupted in a tight voice before his husband could mention Toren's weak control of his energy. The less revealed about that to the spy, the better. "I am capable of interrogating this criminal."

Out of the corner of his eye, he caught her wince.

Though Mehl didn't look pleased, he complied. Toren watched his husband until he settled onto the now-empty side of the sofa where Ria had lain. Ria, who studied Tes with equal parts anger and curiosity—but no real fear. Why? If it wouldn't threaten his control, he would have asked her telepathically.

Instead, he glared down at his captive once more. "Well?

I'll have your full name, including any titles. I will not ask again."

She licked her lips. Gods, was even her tongue trembling? What had she heard of him? He could be stern, but he was hardly known for killing those who displeased him. Murder might earn the culprit an official death sentence, but this?

That sort of cruelty was more Ber's style.

"I am Princess Lora Etessa Breren, the Jewel of Centoi and Heir to King Ryenil of Centoi," she said, her chin tilting up in sharp contrast with her thin, shaky tone.

Shock tempered his anger into a cold ball in the center of his chest—an unexpected boon for his control. But surely, she was lying. King Ryenil would not have sent his only child here as a spy, not under any circumstances. What game was she playing?

Toren lifted his brows. "That is a bold claim, one that is difficult to countenance."

"It is nothing but the truth."

Her shoulders drew back at her words, and he could discern nothing but earnest resolve in her expression. But that brought its own complications. "Am I to understand that the Kingdom of Centoi wishes to court war by attacking one of our sovereign kings?"

"No." Princess Lora flushed a bright red. "My father isn't aware that I'm here. As soon as I saw King Mehl's face, I knew you would claim such, but I give my word it is not so. The king believes I'm on my wedding trip."

His stomach twisted as all too many things became clear. The invitation to Ber's wedding, the unusual spy who could enter the family wing, Ria's abduction—his brother had planned every bit of it, and he'd used this woman in the process. His wife, if she were to be believed. Wasn't it enough to issue his challenge for the throne without involving Princess Lora?

Without causing injury to Mehl and Ria?

The chill of shock morphed into frigid rage.

"Where is he?" Toren snarled.

She swallowed. "Waiting for me somewhere safe."

His surging magic practically begged to be freed, but Toren kept a ruthless hold on it as he bent down, lowering his face close to the princess's. "If you value your life at all, you will tell me what you know. Where is he waiting? What was your mission here?"

Princess Lora tried to ease back, but with her hands bound, she nearly toppled over. Toren gripped her shoulder, his thumb digging into the soft spot above her collarbone just shy of causing pain. So badly, he wanted to tighten his grip until she cried out, but he would not allow himself to be that kind of person.

Not like Ber.

"Last chance," Toren said, the words sharp and precise.

Although her nostrils flared with anger, she averted her gaze. "I was only to observe. That...and to help any unfortunate consorts escape death."

Escape death?

Releasing the woman's shoulder, Toren straightened. What had Ber told the princess? Yes, Toren's magic was unpredictable, but he'd never harmed anyone he'd bedded. In fact, he *wouldn't* sleep with someone who couldn't tolerate his power, especially since it had grown more...erratic over the last decade or so. His brother was well aware of Toren's restraint, if not his strengthening magic.

It did make for a convenient excuse, though. Convince the princess she was saving some poor, doomed woman, and if she succeeded, Toren would be without his chance at an heir. The first part had clearly worked. Lora's expression was filled with such disgust that an outside observer might think she'd caught him in the middle of some debauched murder.

"My brother has misled you greatly," Toren said. "I have never in my long life harmed a bed partner. And unlike Ber, I've never killed anyone. Not by my own hand, though I've sentenced my share of criminals."

Princess Lora gasped, her lips a perfect O of shock. Then her mouth pinched tight, and she twisted her body, sliding one knee forward as though attempting to stand. Mehl surged to his feet despite the healer's protest, but before Toren could tell him to stay back, Sir Macoe had his knife at the woman's throat.

Instantly, she stilled. "You lie."

That slur was one more offense to add to her tally, but Toren turned away from her without comment. His frown was for Mehl. "Is your healing complete?"

"Nearly." His husband strode over. "I'm no longer bleeding, and the scab is almost gone."

"Mehl—"

"I shouldn't have unbound her legs," his husband mused as he scowled down at Lora. "Sir Macoe, see her fully tied once more. She can be carried to the dungeon once we're through."

With a nod, the captain knelt behind the princess and tugged a length of rope from a pouch at his waist. She didn't bother to struggle this time, though her fear seemed to have shifted mostly to anger. Had she the power, she surely would have glared a hole in the floor.

Until Macoe gripped her hand to connect the rope to her other bindings.

Then she screamed.

∼

Gods, her injury. Shame burned through Mehl to settle in his gut.

He'd forgotten entirely.

"Stop," he commanded as he grabbed the woman's shoulders to keep her steady.

The captain lifted his hands away. "I did nothing untoward."

"She was injured in the capture." Mehl peered at Tes and winced at how her face scrunched with agony and tears poured from her eyes. It was one thing to hurt a foe in battle but another act entirely to do so to a captive. "In the chaos, I forgot."

"Vesset," Toren said, gesturing for the healer. "Help her."

As Vesset hurried forward, even Ria took a few steps their way, her brow creased with worry. A surprise, that. Why wasn't Ria afraid? She'd been hurt by Tes. Held against her will. Yet if she felt anger or fear, he saw no sign of it.

Curious.

Tes shuddered in Mehl's hold, reclaiming his attention. Sweat slicked the woman's forehead, and her gaze had gone distant and unfocused. Whatever strength had seen her through to this point had apparently been wiped away by Sir Macoe's unfortunate tug on her hand. She might hyperventilate before the healer could repair the wound.

Surprisingly, Toren knelt at Tes's side as the healer sat behind her. "Should we unbind her? Where is the injury?" Toren asked.

"I believe I broke her hand when I knocked the knife free," Mehl admitted.

An unfortunate action, but one he didn't regret. Becoming too distracted by his own healing and her interrogation to ensure she received help sooner? That was definitely a point of shame.

Toren's chiding glance only added to the emotion, though his words were directed at the healer when he spoke. "What course of action do you suggest?"

The healer caught Mehl's gaze. "Hold her."

Mehl barely had time to tighten his grip on her shoulders before a surge of power from the healer made her eyes roll back and her body go limp. Vesset must have rendered her unconscious. Likely a good thing, since his next action was to work at the bindings on her wrists.

Mehl peered over her shoulder and grimaced at the swollen, blue-and-purple mess of her hand. How had she blocked the pain enough to argue with Toren at all? It must have been agony *before* Sir Macoe had touched her.

"She's bleeding," Vesset murmured.

As the bindings slipped away and the healer gently separated her wrists, Mehl caught sight of the thin, red trail along her unbroken hand, the source hidden by her sleeve. He frowned. That injury he knew he hadn't done. Not directly, in any case. Had she been hurt before? A memory flashed into his mind of the abandoned dress in the tunnels.

One sleeve reddened.

Toren frowned at him, but Mehl shook his head. "I didn't do it."

"I think..." Ria's soft voice drifted around them. "I think it was me."

RIA BIT HER LIP, her gaze focused on Tes's blood-stained hands. She'd meant to stay out of the way, but she just couldn't. There was too much wrong here. Not with the kings or the healer, exactly. But as she'd listened to Toren interrogate Tes, her own thoughts during her captivity had crystallized into a more solid form.

Tes was no villain—she was merely the hero of the wrong story.

"How could this be your fault, Ria?" Toren asked.

She winced. "I shoved her rather hard when I escaped, and I wasn't sure how well she caught herself against the tunnel wall."

The healer shifted Tes's sleeve upward, and Ria winced again at the gash on the woman's wrist. Tes *had* hurt herself, then. Ria's own skin ached as she watched the healer pull a tiny bit of stone from the wound before settling his palm just above the gash. As his magic trembled through the air, she cast a worried look at Toren, but for once, he seemed unbothered by the increased energy.

Without a word, Toren stood, and as he trudged the short distance to Ria's side, his demeanor had her studying him more closely. Before, he'd paced with sharp, almost frantic steps as they'd waited for Mehl, and he'd questioned Tes with all the regalness of the High King on his throne. But now, exhaustion lined his face and haunted his eyes. Only the magic that hummed around him stood in contrast.

"How do you feel?" Toren asked.

"Perfectly fine." Should she tell him what the healer had said about a possible pregnancy? Perhaps not. There'd been more doubt than anything in the man's words, and Toren had enough trouble after Tes's revelations. "The healer did an excellent job."

Though the guards and healer were present, the last bit of the cold reserve he always wore in public melted from his expression. He tugged her against him, so abruptly she couldn't hold back a soft *oomph*. But she didn't complain. Instead, Ria wrapped her arms around his waist and sank into his embrace. Her heart thrummed a frantic beat even as wild, reckless joy filled her soul.

She couldn't keep him, but Gods, how she wanted to.

After a moment, he released her, his hands trailing down her arms as he stepped back. But instead of letting go entirely, he twined his fingers with hers. "I am sorry you suffered because of me."

"You didn't—"

"I might not have hurt you, but you were injured on my behalf." His hold tightened slightly. "I underestimated Ber's boldness. That he would send his own wife...it is difficult to fathom."

That was true enough. Ria had dismissed that possibility herself. "What are you going to do with her?"

Toren sighed. "Once she has been healed, I'll send her to the dungeon."

"The dungeon?" Ria's brows lifted. "If she's married to your brother, she's technically family."

"If she's married to my brother, she's my enemy," he retorted.

Ria opened her mouth to argue, then pressed her lips together just as quickly. Toren wasn't wrong, but he wasn't entirely right, either. There was more to the woman who called herself Tes, an inherent kindness at odds with her actions. When Ria had awakened in that dusty storage room, she hadn't been mistreated.

She'd been cared for—in a fashion.

Tes had seemed earnest in her claims of rescue, but she hadn't been the most adept at handling the situation. Now Ria understood why. The princess had obviously received some training in combat and subterfuge, but not much else. She'd probably never been in a situation like that in her life.

If they could figure out the full truth of why, it might give them an advantage against Prince Ber. That meant befriending the woman, but Ria doubted that Toren would entertain that suggestion right now. Possibly not even a week from now.

But there were secrets to be gleaned, and Ria had the sudden urge to discern them.

CHAPTER 28

BEFORE THE DAWN

Toren felt every hour of the endless night in the tension of his muscles and the ache in his heart. More, there was a heaviness that weighed down his shoulders. Maybe his very soul. How did he process all that had happened in such a short time? How could he separate lies from truth?

In Ria's eyes, he could see a spark of curiosity. Deliberation. Part of him felt the same. Princess Lora held fascinating contradictions, and he could understand the desire to explore them. But with his brother involved, there was too much risk. Anything Ber touched suffered from it. Toren didn't have the time to determine if Lora could be saved.

"Shall I awaken her, Your Majesty?" Vesset asked.

Toren gave Ria's hands a quick squeeze before he released her to return to the healer. The man had shifted Princess Lora around until she leaned against him instead of Mehl, her hands in front of her now. While so deeply asleep, her face was the picture of youth and innocence, though she was only a handful of years younger than he and Ber were.

He'd seen little of her over the centuries. On his very rare visits to the Kingdom of Centoi, she'd emerged only for the occasional court dinner. King Ryenil had claimed she was timid and needed protecting, the delicate "jewel" of Centoi. But perhaps it had been her penchant for trouble that had been the root cause of her absence.

And here he was, wondering like Ria.

"Awaken her once Sir Macoe has secured her in the dungeon," Toren decided. "I need rest before morning court, and there can't be more than two or three hours left before that. Perhaps some discomfort will prompt her to speak of my brother's plans."

Macoe stepped forward. "I will carry her myself, Sire."

"Very well." Toren nodded, then glanced down at the frowning healer. "I do not mean to imply that her health should be put at risk by this discomfort. Accompany Sir Macoe and ensure that it is so. I'll summon another healer to finish repairing Mehl's injury."

Mehl touched his arm. "It is merely a scab now."

"Nevertheless," Toren insisted, already sending out the mental command. He couldn't bear for his husband to have a moment's lingering discomfort because of his poor judgment. "They will meet us in our suite."

Mehl merely sighed.

After all the chaos, it took only a few quick moments for Macoe to carry the princess from the room, Vesset trailing behind. Toren returned to Ria's side, linking arms with her as Mehl joined them. She would not be left in danger this time. She didn't know it yet, but she would be sleeping with them.

Tonight and every night.

"What were you doing to that fabric?" Toren asked as they walked toward the family wing again. "In your room, that is. Your magic was all around it, and the pattern was skewed."

"Skewed?" Ria's nose wrinkled. "I suppose it shouldn't surprise me that Tes made me mess it up."

Toren nestled her arm closer to his side. "It was a good thing. If I hadn't noticed the disturbance in the pattern, we wouldn't have realized you'd been taken. Not that we truly provided rescue."

"You must have been near to it since Mehl found Tes," Ria said. "As to the fabric...I've been working on expanding my skills. I can alter fabric to match my designs. What else can I alter? Perhaps I will have more time to explore my magic now."

"You're more than welcome to use the royal library," Toren offered before he could think better of it. But a moment's consideration did nothing to change his mind. "I'll notify the head librarian that you're to be given access. The rooms already open to everyone might have some books about your type of magic, but the royal collection likely has more detailed texts."

Ria gaped at him, but over her shoulder, Toren caught Mehl's smug smile. She might not fully realize what an offer like this indicated, but it clearly hadn't slipped his husband's notice. Yes, Toren's feelings had shifted toward Ria—or rather, clarified. He'd been denying the unusual link between them and the protective urges that goaded him. No longer.

He was beginning to believe what Mehl had said from the start—Ria belonged with them.

"You truly don't mind?" Ria asked. "I could always petition for entry to the mage's library if you decide otherwise."

"It is fine, Ria. You're the—" By the gods, he'd almost called her queen. He resolutely avoided looking at Mehl this time. "You're the royal consort and hopefully the mother to our next monarch. You have every right to use the royal library."

A fine flush pinkened her skin, and she nodded. Then they passed the guard to enter the family wing, and her arm tensed against his. Was she nervous about being here now? He supposed he couldn't blame her. But neither he nor Mehl would be so careless with her again.

As though summoned, Mehl's mind brushed his. *"Please tell me she's coming with us."*

Toren gave him a quick, amused glance. *"You seem to agree with my own thoughts. Ria sleeps with us."*

"Until Ber is no longer a threat?" Mehl asked.

"Of course." Toren hesitated, though he was fairly certain of his husband's feelings on the matter. *"Possibly longer if we're all in accord. You above all."*

Mehl's lips curved upward. *"I've believed she is ours since the beginning. Difficult to fathom, yet undeniably true."*

"Perhaps," Toren allowed.

It would take time before he could claim certainty.

But he was close.

WITH EACH STEP nearer to her room, Ria found herself growing increasingly tense. But why? All had turned out well. She was safe, and the healer had done an excellent job fixing her every pain. Even so, the thought of walking back into the sitting room where she'd been attacked caused her muscles to tighten as though preparing to flee. How would she be able to sleep?

But although her steps slowed automatically as they approached, Toren didn't so much as glance at her door. Instead, he led her straight into his and Mehl's suite without a moment's hesitation. She was so stunned by the shift that it took her a moment to notice Mehl hurrying ahead to speak to the healer waiting on the other side of the room.

"You are staying with us," Toren said in a low voice as he drew her to a halt.

Ria's heart pounded harder in her chest, but she wasn't certain if it was in anger or anticipation. "During Mehl's healing? Or for longer?"

"All night, or what's left of it." Somehow, Toren managed to appear both exhausted and imperious. "And each night after. We will see you safe."

Oh gods, but the fierceness in his tone made her chest squeeze with ill-advised hope. "I suppose I am not safe alone?"

Toren inclined his head. "No room is entirely secure, it seems, while my brother stands against us. He would do anything to prevent me from producing an heir."

His heir. Of course.

"It seems so," Ria said softly, her shoulders sagging like a wet bolt of fabric.

Suddenly, she wanted nothing more than to crawl into bed —any bed—and sleep for a solid year. Maybe then she could untangle it all. Her abduction, her tumultuous feelings, her new place in life—so many things weighed heavy on her heart. Both body and spirit needed rest.

"I told you I was nearly healed."

At the sound of Mehl's voice, Ria blinked, her attention slow to shift his way. When had he reached them? Yet there he stood, close enough that he could have taken her hand and Toren's to form their own little semicircle. Already, the healer crossed behind him, stifling a yawn as she ducked out the door.

Then once again, they were alone.

"Let me see," Toren demanded.

With an indulgent smile, Mehl extended his arm, and even Ria felt a spark of amusement at the way Toren studied his husband's skin for signs of lingering injury. Only when he was satisfied did true relief cross his face. Some of the tension eased from his demeanor as he released Mehl.

Surreptitiously, Ria eyed Mehl's arm, but she also found no hint of injury. The torn and bloody state of his sleeve, though—that struck her. He'd truly been hurt trying to capture the woman who'd abducted her.

"There." Mehl's smile shifted from Toren to warm her, too. "Let's go to bed. We've merely an hour until the dawn."

The simple walk to the bedroom door felt like a slow, awkward trudge, and she couldn't prevent her skin from heating in a fierce blush at the sight of her nightgown on the foot of the bed. A servant must have brought it here. They'd known before she had that she'd be sleeping with the kings.

Mehl rubbed her shoulder soothingly before heading for a door over to the side, but Toren circled the bed, tugging his tunic over his head as he walked. His gaze flicked her way before he draped the tunic over a chair, and that small gesture had amusement taking the place of awkwardness. It was certainly something to have the ruler of the kingdom picking up after himself to avoid displeasing her.

Carefully, Ria took off her own bedraggled gown, but this time, she was the one who had to drop her clothing to the floor. At Toren's lifted brow, she grimaced. "It would dirty the furniture. I hesitate to consider the state of the sofa I rested on, but at least it was brown."

"Perhaps that's why the guard took you to the Bronze Room," Toren said, his voice light but his brows drawing down. "I should have thought to show you the bathing room. Your hair..."

Her hand darted to the dried, matted mass at the back of her head, and her grimace deepened. "Yes, please."

"Come with me, then."

Ria followed him to the door where Mehl had disappeared, and her gaze caught and held on the lean, well-formed muscles of Toren's naked back. Her fingertips tingled with the remembered feel of those shoulders beneath her grip. And the flex of his arse with each step... Swallowing hard, Ria jerked her attention away and commanded herself to behave. They all needed sleep.

A resolution that was sorely challenged by the sight of Mehl, completely nude beside a dressing table.

"The gods are testing me," she muttered beneath her breath.

Toren's back muscles went taut a moment before his head whipped around. "What?"

Mehl laughed. "Perhaps we should all bathe together."

Her mouth watered—actually watered. Had she thought she needed sleep? As heat flared in both kings' eyes, rest was suddenly the last thing on her mind.

Mehl took a moment to savor how the surprised consideration on Toren's and Ria's faces shifted to desire. Unlike the two of them, Mehl wasn't particularly tired. It would be hours before the adrenaline from Ria's abduction and Tes's capture wore off, and healing sessions always left him full of energy—a useful side effect unless it was bedtime. That meant he'd have to find a way to use the excess if he hoped to sleep.

The sight of a naked Ria trailing his shirtless husband certainly provided plenty of ideas.

"Really, Mehl? We have, what...three hours until court?" Toren asked, though there was no conviction in his voice.

Mehl shrugged. "That little bit of sleep will hardly make a difference."

Toren let out a low groan, and Ria shivered, making her breasts jiggle delightfully. But then Mehl's gaze narrowed in on something else—the line of dried blood along her collarbone.

Oh yes, he would bathe her. He would ensure that all memory of her ordeal was erased.

"Let's go," Mehl prompted.

Silently, they trailed into the large bathing chamber. Two large, raised pools consumed the bulk of the space, the water filled and removed by pipes and magic, and a narrow alcove in the corner allowed water to drip from the ceiling for quick cleaning. Mehl grabbed several bottles containing soaps and oils from a shelf while Toren led Ria to the alcove.

As usual, he and his husband needed no words to be in accord.

Together, they cleansed the blood from Ria's hair and body. Carefully. Reverently. Only when she was clean did Toren gather her against him so that Mehl could wash his own body. As he scrubbed dried blood from his stomach where it had seeped through his clothes, he trembled from the heat in Toren's eyes as he watched each movement. With Ria nestled softly against his husband's chest...

Already hard, his cock twitched. "The soaking pool?" he gasped.

Toren's smile grew wicked. "A pleasant idea, indeed."

CHAPTER 29

GRATITUDE

Toren couldn't bear to release Ria for even a moment. She was warm and safe against him, and that was where he preferred she stay. So he bent slightly until he could boost her up higher in his arms. Although she let out a soft *eep* of surprise, she wrapped her arms around his neck and her legs around his waist.

Over her shoulder, he met Mehl's eyes, and they exchanged understanding smiles. Perhaps they all needed this more than sleep. Not sex, exactly, but the connection of being together. Alive and well. Toren needed to feel them both—with him, around him, inside him. That would give more contentment than a couple hours of sleep.

Carrying Ria, he followed Mehl up the short flight of stairs to the narrow platform backing the raised soaking pools. The smooth stone had been shaped by mages some generations past, and Toren sent them a fleeting thought of gratitude as he entered the water after Mehl by another set of steps built into the pool. No need to release Ria. One hand gripped her thigh and the other curled around her waist to steady her as he descended.

On the far side of the pool, Mehl settled onto one of the shaped benches, and his heated gaze only made Toren harder. Water lapped up his thighs like tiny fingers, and Ria yelped when it finally brushed her skin. But it only took a second for her to relax against him once more.

"It's warm," she said against his chest.

He smiled at the surprise in her tone. "This one, yes."

The heat wrapped around them with each step until the water sloshed around their chests by the time they reached the center. This lowest dip in the pool allowed the most immersion, but Toren was more interested in the shallower edge where Mehl waited. The angle there would be best for the three of them together.

And that was what he wanted most.

Mehl held out his arms, and Toren lowered Ria to his husband's lap. Although she settled easily enough, her fingers tangled in his hair, and she tugged him down for a kiss. Without hesitation, he let himself devour. And as their tongues met and dueled, he felt the slow glide of Mehl's hand down his side, enflaming him further.

Toren pulled back. "Touch her, too," he whispered against Ria's lips.

Her gasp slid into his soul, and in that moment, he was lost.

ONCE AGAIN, Ria perched on Mehl's lap, her thighs spread wide and his fingers playing skillfully at her core. Just like the throne room—but different. Now, he trailed tender kisses down the side of her neck while Toren cupped her breasts in a gentle, reverent hold. It was that softness that was different, she decided.

So sweet, but she burned all the same.

Then greed darkened Toren's eyes a heartbeat before he bent to suck her nipple into his mouth.

The first wave crashed through her with sudden force, sweeping away thought, and her cries echoed from the stone walls. Gods, she was so ready for Toren to take her. But this time, he showed no signs of the dark intensity that had driven his frenzied claiming during their first time together. Instead, his hands trailed her body in slow, patient sweeps that had her every nerve singing and the wave building again.

Ria wiggled against Mehl, and he groaned against her skin as she rubbed against him. A wicked smile crossed her face as she shifted to the side enough to wrap her fingers around his cock. This time, both men moaned, and through slitted eyes, she watched Toren's rapt gaze as he peered through the water at her hand on Mehl.

"I dare not—" Mehl sucked in a sharp breath. "If I release in the water..."

Ria couldn't hold back a frustrated *mmph* as she pulled her hand away. Forget heirs—in that moment, she wanted to be pregnant already so they didn't have to worry over such things. So they could be together fully. Unfortunately, the healer had given her only possibilities, not certainties.

"Sorry," she said.

Mehl's lips curved against her shoulder, and his finger flicked against her nub until she gasped. "One of you will see to me soon enough," he murmured against her skin.

From Mehl's clever fingers and the mental images his words evoked, Ria's body trembled with the fire that rushed through her. Moaning low, she caught Toren's gaze. "Please."

Some of that dark intensity returned as Toren gripped her

thighs in a gentle but firm hold, lifting her lower body until she half-floated. Wordlessly, Mehl anchored her upper body against his chest, and the vulnerable position sent a bolt of nervous excitement through her. But she wouldn't be hurt—both men would see her safe.

In one thrust, Toren entered her, just as Mehl tweaked her nipple between his fingers. She screamed from the strength of the combined sensations, but the force of her release didn't relent as Toren took her body without hesitation, Mehl steady behind her. Like she was—had always been—theirs.

Then Toren's magic crashed through her, and her world went blissfully white.

MEHL HAD no clue if he would be able to hold on. Not to Ria—she was secure in his arms. But his control was another matter entirely. His balls were drawn up so tight they ached, but releasing in the water might bring disaster. Ria had a ridiculously small risk of getting pregnant that way, but they couldn't afford even a slight chance.

Suddenly, Toren's magic bolted through Ria and into him, and Mehl let out a strangled cry. "Lift her from the water," he gasped out.

Toren's jaw clenched. "No time. I..."

This was it—Mehl was going to die right here. He wrapped his hand around the end of his cock in an almost-painful grip. He needed to look away. Think unpleasant thoughts. Anything. But he couldn't take his eyes off Toren's face as his husband came. Gods, what a perfect sight.

Even as Toren shuddered from the aftershocks, he gathered Ria from Mehl's hold and stepped back. Shivering, Mehl watched Toren rub gentle circles on Ria's back as she trembled against him. Then his husband walked over to the platform and settled her gently on the edge. Mehl's heart squeezed as he watched Toren wrap a drying cloth gently around her shoulders.

"Stay here, love," Toren said. "And I'll see to Mehl."

This time, it was Mehl's moan that filled the room.

DAZED, Ria gathered the drying cloth close to stave off the chill air and stared at Toren's back once more as he returned to the other side of the pool. Tremors still shook her body from the force of their passion, but she couldn't be annoyed at Toren for leaving her here. Of all of them, poor Mehl had it the worst. He deserved release.

Part of her wondered if she should avert her gaze to give the kings privacy, but as Toren swept Mehl into his arms for a long kiss, she couldn't force herself to do so. Surely, they would have commanded her to leave if they wanted privacy? Gods, she hoped that was the case. As Mehl boosted himself onto the narrow rim of the pool near his earlier seat, Ria couldn't hold back a little whimper. The way the water rolled down his body to caress every line...

Toren glanced at her. "Ria?"

He must have heard her whimper. Blast it. She couldn't pretend ignorance now. "Should I look away?" she asked. "Or leave?"

His slight smile took on a wicked slant. "That depends on your own comfort. I'd rather expected you to watch."

"Yes," Mehl bit out, his head thrown back. "Stay."

Toren hadn't been joking about leaving the decision to her, for he turned back to Mehl without another word. Well, with their permission granted, she certainly wasn't going anywhere.

As Toren kissed his way down Mehl's chest and along the line of his hip, her own skin flushed with heat. She didn't know why, but the sight of them together flamed her desire nearly as much as physical touch.

Ria's moan was lost beneath Mehl's as Toren took his husband's cock in his mouth. She squeezed her thighs together, and the drying cloth slipped from her loosened grip as she stared, transfixed, at the sight. Mehl's muscles stood out in sharp relief as he clung to the edge of the pool, and Toren's pale hair tangled around his thighs, the tendrils connecting them in an unbearably intimate way.

Gods. Tes had claimed that Ria would die in the High King's bed, but Ria was fairly confident that if she were to die anywhere, it would be here. Watching Mehl grip Toren's hair to guide him to a more frenzied pace. Feeling the burn in her own body. She could bear almost any torture after this.

Then Mehl cried out as he came, and she found new depths to the blessed agony.

By the time Toren returned to the bedroom with the others, he felt as though he'd purged some kind of darkness in himself. Fear, perhaps, of losing Mehl and Ria. Possibly even of his brother's theat. Whatever it truly was, his steps were lighter, and the harsh press of magic that constantly plagued him had lessened to dull annoyance.

Mehl carried Ria now, and she drowsed adorably against his chest. Toren hadn't been able to resist taking her again after her reaction to watching him with Mehl. Truth be told, he felt as blissfully replete as she looked, but he wouldn't be able to appease the pleasant exhaustion that filled him.

Gods help anyone who brought foolishness to morning

court. His mood might be light now, but he was far too tired to have patience for the silliest requests, not when he could be here in a sated pile with Mehl and Ria. He would have to ask Feref to carefully screen for the worst of those. With luck, Toren's reaction to any that slipped through would dissuade the rest.

When they reached the bed, Toren pulled back the covers, and Mehl settled Ria between the sheets. She frowned up at them. "Aren't you joining me? It can't be time for court yet."

Toren eyed the pale glow of dawn outside the window and sighed. "No, but it takes time to don court finery and prepare. You should sleep."

"Alone?" Abruptly, Ria sat up, her gaze darting around the room. "Will it be safe?"

"I…" He stopped himself before the reassurance could slip free. After Princess Lora's incursion, he could give no guarantees. "Mehl should stay. I can deal with the court."

Mehl's lips thinned. "I haven't had cause to miss in years. Decades. After last night, the rumors—"

"No, please." Ria swung her legs over the edge of the bed and stood. "I'll come with you. There must be somewhere out of the way for me to stand."

She wobbled a little on her feet, and more heat than regret flashed through him when he considered why. He would not have her standing for hours, not when her muscles were shaky from his repeated taking. Yet only those on the dais sat, unless they were aged or physically unable. There were traditions connected to court, and she was not their queen.

They were joined only through the breeding contract. She hadn't even reached out to link their energies when he'd been unable to hold onto his magic earlier—an odd regret he tried not to examine too closely. After all, he'd been the one to adamantly command her not to connect them in such a way.

"Sir Macoe could wait with her," Mehl said.

For some reason, the thought of her relying on the captain turned Toren's stomach. "No. She will sit with us."

The court's traditions weren't magically bound laws, after all, and he was High King. If he wished for the royal consort to have a seat on the dais, then she would. Every tradition had to start somewhere.

But Ria paled. "I'm grateful for the consideration. Truly. It's only...the dais? I received enough rancorous looks as a guest at the dining table."

"They will obey, or they will lose their invitations to court," Toren insisted.

"Then rescind mine." Ria's shoulders jerked back, and her nostrils flared. "Because *I* am not going to obey."

CHAPTER 30

PROCLAMATIONS

Time slowed as Ria watched Toren's expression morph from resolved to shocked to angry. Coldly, deeply angry. Her heart leaped and pounded in her chest until she found herself pressing her palm between her breasts. Gods, his lips were practically white, he'd pinched them together so tightly. But she couldn't back down. She just couldn't.

If she had to sit in front of a crowd of nobles while they speculated on her position there, she would vomit. The thought alone made her stomach turn. No matter what title she now carried, everyone knew she was the kings' consort. A mere vessel, really. She had no place on the dais. And after all she'd been through in the last day... No. It was too much.

Toren's hands clenched, and he took a step forward. Ria froze, her gaze locking on his fist and her body going tense in anticipation of the blow. He could punish her however he liked for defying his order. She'd taken beatings for less. It would be a familiar pain, more so than the agony of being gawked at and whispered about for hours.

"Ria," Toren said, and the raw, broken sound of his voice startled her enough that she dared meet his eyes. "I would never strike you. Never."

Cold sweat broke across her brow at his words, and her hand trembled against her chest. There was a horrified pain in his gaze as it held hers. He meant it. She knew he meant it. But her body couldn't seem to catch up. She sucked in a ragged breath and gave a jerky nod.

"Even if you change your mind about that," she whispered, "I won't do it. You can't ask me to after all I've been through."

Toren's skin paled, much the shade it had been when he'd hurried into that brown sitting room after she'd escaped Tes. Slowly, he eased back until there was more distance between them, and she couldn't help but note that he'd relaxed his hands at his sides. Still, her tension remained.

Beside her, Mehl shifted, drawing her gaze. "Toren wasn't thinking, I'm sure. You needn't sit on the dais, especially after last night. Forget the rumors. I'll stay."

The chiding look he shot his husband was far from subtle, but it was lost on Toren. His eyes hadn't left her face even when her attention had shifted to Mehl for a moment. She'd felt the burn of that regard down to her soul. But when she turned to Toren again, she found his expression closed. Unreadable.

"Forgive me, Ria," he said, each word carefully measured.

Was he angry? Worried? Upset? It was impossible to tell, and that was almost as terrible as his unthinking advance had been. A lot could hide behind a shuttered wall—including the worst violence. Some of her father's most terrible rages had come from nowhere. Instinctively, she shivered.

Toren's face fell. "Perhaps you cannot," he murmured.

Relief rushed through her at that sign of emotion, but it was a bittersweet giddiness. She hadn't meant to hurt him.

"It's not that," she said. "I thought you were still angry. You closed yourself off, and I…"

"Didn't know what to do," Toren said, running his hand through his hair in a frustrated sweep. "I thought my lack of emotion might help, but I see now that I was wrong."

Mehl reached out a hand toward her, a question in his eyes. At her nod of consent, he rubbed gentle circles between her shoulder blades, and some of that final bit of tension began to leech from her muscles. She was fine. She'd known in the pool earlier that they would keep her safe, and they would do so now. It was simply going to take time for her instincts to catch up.

"I would much prefer to know what you're feeling," Ria replied. "Even the potential fear of that is better than the mystery. Always."

Toren nodded. "I will endeavor to remember, though I may be unable to oblige in formal settings."

Without conscious direction, her nose wrinkled. "Which brings us back to the problem at hand, I suppose. Toren…I want a quiet day. More than one quiet day, if possible. Standing around at court isn't precisely that, but it's better than being a spectacle."

"There's no need to worry, Ria." Mehl's hand slowed in its soothing sweep. "I'll stay with you, rumors or no."

Though his lips twisted with displeasure, Toren inclined his head. "Very well. Mehl will keep you safe here."

Curling up in bed with Mehl was an incredibly tempting thought, even if they only caught up on sleep. The soft comfort of their mattress tugged at her until she almost sat back down, but the hint of exhaustion on Toren's face held her back. He'd had as little sleep as any of them and nearly as much trouble. It would hardly be fair to leave him alone to handle the entirety of the aftermath.

"That wouldn't be right," Ria said with a decisive shake of her head. "The rumors must already be brutal after last night's unusual dinner. Between the abrupt announcement of our contract, the potential poison, and Mehl running after Tes... Well, none of that will be improved by our absence."

Toren sighed. "No. And since even guards gossip, there might be whispers about your abduction. I'll no doubt have to make a proclamation about the matter whether you're there or not. Otherwise, there's no telling what kinds of rumors will spread."

"They'd be whispering about our deaths in the village taverns by noon," Mehl said, his tone wry. But his touch was gentle as he ran his hand down her arm to link their fingers. "More so if Ria and I are absent, it is true."

Her body swayed toward the bed in one last rebellion before she stiffened her spine. "I'll stand near the wall close to where one of the guards is stationed. It won't be as quiet as I'd prefer, but it will ease things in the long run. But you'll have to think of a way to ensure my safety afterward, because I'm returning to my room to sleep whether you have business or not."

A hint of her earlier tension returned at that bold claim. What had her time with the kings done to her? It was the second time in a matter of minutes that she'd been so assertive in the face of power, and the first had been open defiance. Had the slight tremor she felt on the inside echoed in her voice? If so, neither king made note of it.

"We'll consider this issue while we prepare," Toren said, and this time, she was surprised to see a hint of admiration in his eyes. "I sent out a call to Feref to assist you again, and once he's seen you properly dressed, he'll find you a secure spot in the throne room."

She'd won. The glory of that brought a smile to her face

and lightness to her heart. Her father might have called her a coward more than once, but she'd stood against the High King and won. Few joys in life could compare with the rush of *that*.

Bathing rooms notwithstanding.

MORNING COURT WAS NEVER ENJOYABLE, but Mehl was more than ready for escape as the tedious couple of hours drew close to an end. The number of veiled complaints, innuendos, and offers they'd rebuffed appalled him. Toren, though—his building anger was like a pending storm, a strike waiting to happen. At least by this point, only the foolish failed to notice the signs, and Feref could easily keep them at bay.

Mehl's gaze was drawn toward Ria, but he kept his face resolutely forward. He couldn't gawk at the royal consort, especially not with their current petitioner. Lord Vayan bristled at the slightest hint of insult, and as he was the nephew of one of their closest advisors, offending the man would do them no good.

But blast it all, Ria looked tired. And lonely. She hadn't been actively snubbed, but no one had bothered to speak to her, either. Mehl was more than familiar with that treatment, in fact. No doubt as soon as he and Toren left, the subtle slights would begin. He'd put up with the same for several decades himself, but few people had been bold enough to take it very far. There would be less hesitation with Ria.

"Do you agree with my decision, King Mehl?" Toren asked.

Feck. His mind had wandered even if his eyes hadn't. "As you decree, my king," he replied.

Only Mehl was close enough to hear Toren's slight huff, a blend of amusement and annoyance. "Then let it be so. Thank you for bringing the problem to my attention, Lord Vayan."

The young lord bowed low before resuming his place in the crowd. Mehl still had no clue what the man had wanted—which Toren knew full well after his answer. But it didn't matter. The only thing left was for Toren to make his proclamations, then Feref would conclude court by reading the day's official announcements.

If Mehl could stay awake during the listing of new alliances, weddings, and births, he'd be able to go curl up with Ria in bed for an hour.

Detecting the slight shift of Toren's body, Mehl stood at the same time as his husband. But as the courtiers sank to their knees, he kept his face pointed ahead and his expression impassive. Sometimes, being a king bore a great resemblance to being a guard. Showing no reaction during boring functions was perhaps the most shared skill.

The room went entirely silent.

"I have no doubt there are rumors concerning our dinner last night," Toren said, his voice ringing through the quiet. "And for more than one reason. First, allow me to reiterate that I will tolerate no disrespect toward our new royal consort, Lady Ria Orindl, Duchess of Nevial. A formal presentation will occur in two weeks' time, as is proper, but considering my brother's threat, I believed an informal announcement was prudent. That should imply no lessening of her status."

His husband paused for the crowd to process those words, but Mehl had to stifle a wince. When had Toren decided on a formal presentation? Ria would be upset by the display, and they were hardly prepared, besides. They'd never even managed to commission the formal clothes, something that generally took weeks. Not to mention all the other countless formalities.

"However," Toren continued, "There is a more pressing problem. One of the Centoi contingent attempted to infiltrate our staff at dinner and later tried to bring harm to the royal family. While no visiting citizen of Centoi should be accosted in any way, since most, if not all, are innocent of wrongdoing, I do advise you to remain vigilant in the castle while I handle this matter with their king. Any future envoys from that kingdom are to be considered a possible threat and watched accordingly."

Even prior knowledge of Toren's announcement didn't quite dull the shock of hearing it said aloud. Their kingdoms had been allied for at least two millennia, which was why Ber had been fostered there in his youth. A potential conflict between them was nearly unthinkable. And the further implications of possible war? There hadn't been so much as a hint of such a thing during Toren's reign.

Uneasy glances passed around the room like fire over dry brush, a hint of fear left in their wake. Mehl was no empath, but the silent worry building in the room made the spot between his shoulder blades itch. Especially when a few of those looks were cast toward Ria. He would like to believe the courtiers were too rational to blame Ria, but he was all too aware of what fear did to logic.

"*Toren,*" he sent to his husband.

"*I see it,*" Toren answered at once. "*Make note of any whose suspicion lingers.*"

His husband continued his proclamation in a hard-edged tone. "I have reason to believe my brother is ultimately responsible. He would do anything to establish his dark rule here, including deceive the royal family of Centoi. He will most certainly attempt to interfere with my breeding contract. As such, I will expect each of you to guard Lady Ria as you would me or King Mehl. My brother must be stopped at all costs."

Mehl scanned the crowd, noting the bows of acknowledgement but also the tight, false smiles. As at dinner last night, he could see that some would obey more readily than others. Fortunately, they were to receive more exacting instructions to counter any loose interpretations of Toren's orders.

After the courtiers' movements had ceased once more, Mehl finally spoke. "Further directives will be sent to the head of each noble family by the end of the day, but it is expected that all nobles will encourage calm amongst the citizens. Any caught spreading false rumors will be dealt with harshly."

Their proclamations delivered, Toren and Mehl resumed their seats. Usually, the courtiers stood rather quickly, but today, it was an uneven and hesitant rise. Mehl's hand settled on the dagger he'd hidden beneath his formal robe as he studied each face again, looking for signs of potential conflict. Most still appeared concerned or afraid, but a few had a hint of calculation in their eyes.

The power hungry always bore watching.

Feref stepped forward from his place beside the dais and unwound the long, traditional scroll used for formal announcements. But as the man began to read, Mehl found he couldn't sink into his normal half-listening state. Something was building. The source of his uneasiness wasn't likely to appear so soon, but he couldn't cease searching.

Had he missed something? That itchy feeling between his shoulder blades increased until it crept up the back of his neck, and his hand twitched against his hidden dagger. Why? None of the courtiers appeared threatening.

But when the door opened and a messenger in Centoi livery stumbled through, he understood.

CHAPTER 31

MIXED MESSAGES

As the newcomer staggered into the room, his appearance sent a chill down Toren's spine. The messenger's livery was rumpled and dirty, and sweat trickled down his face in dusty lines. His stiff, awkward walk spoke of a hard ride—a sleepless one, if the dark circles beneath his eyes were any indication. It was highly unlikely that he'd been with the envoys who'd left the day before, for they were still too close for him to have ridden this hard.

Two guards stepped forward to block the messenger's advance, but the nobles lining the carpet leading up to the throne shifted farther back. They'd apparently taken his words seriously. Perhaps too much so. Toren knew from long experience that the threat the messenger posed was far from physical.

His *message* held the real danger.

Toren beat back his own exhaustion, lest it ring in his voice. "Allow him forward."

The guards parted, and the messenger shuffled his way up the carpet in what felt like an eternal march. Beside Toren,

Mehl leaned forward ever so slightly, and if Toren wasn't mistaken, his husband's hand rested on the knife he'd strapped to his thigh before donning his robe. Though against tradition, Toren hadn't said a word. Not after yesterday. With this new potential threat, he was doubly grateful.

When the messenger drew near enough, he lowered into a deep bow. His body swayed like a tree branch in the wind—but an insecure one. The slightest motion might send him toppling to the ground.

"Rise," Toren said quickly.

The messenger straightened in ridiculously slow degrees, but Toren made no comment. Gratitude crossed the man's face. "Forgive my intrusion, Your Majesties. I come bearing an urgent message."

Toren tensed. "Then deliver it."

Inclining his head, the messenger spoke. "King Ryenil Breren the Mighty, Sovereign of the Kingdom of Centoi requests the aid of all allies in this most difficult time, the abduction of his daughter, Princess Lora Etessa Breren, the Jewel of Centoi and Heir to King Ryenil of Centoi."

"Her abduction?" The earlier chill settled into Toren's bones. One way or another, Ber was almost certainly involved. "When and how was she taken?"

"Some three weeks prior, she disappeared from her chambers. The king ordered the entire kingdom searched, and when that yielded nothing, we messengers were sent forth. Both the king and her betrothed, Prince Ber, are distraught as they await her return." The man paused, a flush returning color to his cheeks. "Announcements about that happy event had not yet been sent out, Your Majesty. Forgive me for the clumsily delivered news of your brother's betrothal."

He thought the betrothal hadn't been announced? Something was very, very wrong. Toren exchanged a frowning glance with Mehl before focusing his gaze on the messenger.

"That is curious," Toren drawled. "Just yesterday, a formal envoy from Centoi arrived, and word of Princess Lora's and Prince Ber's betrothal was delivered by Lord Aony. The group departed from here in the evening, but one of their contingent remained behind to attempt harm on the royal family. Yet you claim that no announcements have even been made? Someone is clearly lying."

Fear etched lines on the messenger's face, and he frantically shook his head. "It could not have been Lord Aony, Your Majesty. He's in the north, preparing his estate for the impending winter. He sent an official missive in response to the king's demand that his lands be searched. The magic of such a document could not be feigned."

It was true that if the duke used a magical seal similar to Toren's that the message was unlikely to have been forged— but did it have to be? If Ber and Princess Lora had drawn Lord Aony into some plot, he could have penned the note in advance of meeting with the "missing" princess. But why?

One possibility came immediately to mind—Ber wanted to frame Toren for the supposed abduction. It wouldn't be difficult if the princess was discovered in his dungeon. Fortunately, no one else in the palace knew her identity. If that was discovered before they figured out what was going on, though...

They needed more time.

Suddenly, Mehl spoke up. "If someone is impersonating Lord Aony, he most certainly will want to know. We will have our soldiers apprehend the so-called envoys who claimed to come from your land. In the meantime, our chamberlain will ensure you have a place to rest."

It wasn't an offer, but a command. Recognizing it as such, the messenger bowed his head. "Thank you, Your Majesties."

Toren lifted a finger, and from his place beside the door, Macoe nodded and slipped silently out the room to see Mehl's first order done. One of the higher-level servants approached Feref, who bent to give his own commands. In a matter of moments, the servant was escorting the messenger from the throne room, leaving an expectant hush behind.

Once again, Toren stood, his husband only a breath behind. "There is much to consider, but I urge you to remain on your guard," he said, even before the courtiers had finished sinking to their knees. "Feref will complete the announcements while we withdraw to handle this matter. If anyone has additional information, I expect it to be brought to us immediately."

He glanced toward Ria's position as he turned to leave, but he didn't have time to find her in the crowd. He connected with Mehl. *"Did you see Ria?"*

"As she slipped out of the room a moment ago," Mehl replied. *"I've sent a guard to tell her to meet us in the study."*

Ria had slipped out? Why? Toren had no suspicions about her, not anymore, but dread filled him all the same. Perhaps she'd merely grown tired and had chosen to leave while the courtiers were distracted. Surely, she wouldn't do anything foolish after last night.

But his fear wouldn't abate.

RIA WONDERED FLEETINGLY if she'd lost her mind as she hurried down the corridor after Sir Macoe, but instinct told her she couldn't delay. Toren and Mehl would deliberate for hours on this latest development—for good reason, since they had the entire kingdom to consider. If she were brave enough, she could help them.

Who could have expected that the entire delegation had

been false? It had seemed bad enough that Prince Ber and Tes were working together to infiltrate the palace, but the princess hadn't appeared to be malicious. If the messenger's story were true, it implied that something more sinister was going on, something at odds with Tes's earnest "rescue" attempt. They wouldn't go to the effort of recruiting a high-ranking lord to deliver a pretend message just so they could save a random woman from a breeding contract.

Besides, Tes had claimed she'd already married Prince Ber and that they'd pretended to leave on a wedding trip. He'd been waiting for her somewhere safe, the princess had said. Yet the messenger claimed her "betrothed" Prince Ber was with the king. Which was the truth?

If only Ria had pressed Toren harder about questioning Tes before sending her to the dungeon! The woman surely held the key to much of this. But would the princess confide in Toren? Considering their interaction after Mehl had caught her, no.

Ria had to hope Tes would be more open with her.

Sir Macoe paused to speak to a guard, giving Ria time to catch up. Though her legs began to tremble with each step closer, she didn't slow. No matter how much she wanted to. *I can do this*, she thought. She'd stood up to Toren earlier, hadn't she? The captain of the guard would be nothing compared to that.

When he pinned her beneath his sharp gaze, she reminded herself of that again. "Lady Ria," Sir Macoe said.

She barely noticed when the guard left—she was too busy commanding her knees not to buckle. "Sir Macoe. Please forgive my disruption, but I need your aid."

"I have a great deal to do for the kings, my lady," he replied.

"I am aware." Ria gathered her resolve. "However, I require you to see me safely to the dungeon."

His brows rose. "Pardon? Did you say the dungeon?"

"I did."

"Forgive me, my lady, but that seems unwise," Sir Macoe said, his regard even more piercing. "And I have no orders to do such."

Ria shoved her shoulders back and channeled every noble client she'd ever had. "You do now. I am the Duchess of Nevial and the Royal Consort. As I outrank you, I suggest you obey my command. I doubt the kings would be pleased if you left me to find the dungeon on my own."

Sir Macoe's eyes narrowed on her face, and at first, she thought he would refuse—and probably laugh for good measure. But whether it was her words or something he saw in her expression, he finally nodded. He gestured toward the hall with a flourishing bow.

"I will escort you part of the way myself, my lady." He started down the corridor, and she wasted no time following. "But only until I reach my own destination. After that, you'll have to rely on a pair of my most trusted guards. Is that sufficient?"

"As long as the kings would consider them such," Ria replied.

She had a feeling Toren and Mehl wouldn't consider an entire army sufficient so soon after her abduction, but they couldn't accuse her of being reckless. She was no fool. There could be a new threat at any time, and she wasn't going to rush out to find it. Perhaps even trusting Sir Macoe was a mistake, though if that were the case, the kings had far more to worry about than her.

But speaking to Tes was worth the risk.

~

BY THE TIME they reached Toren's study, Mehl was ready to turn back the way they'd come and chase Ria down himself. He couldn't, of course. This situation with the Centoi had too much potential for disaster, and he and Toren would have to decide what to do fast. If word got back to King Ryenil that his daughter was in their dungeon, he'd have his army at their border in a matter of weeks.

Frowning, Toren leaned his hip against the edge of his desk. "We have to figure out what my brother is planning."

"Yes." Mehl dropped into a nearby chair, heedless of his formal robes. "Although it might not be your brother alone. The princess claimed her father believed them to be on their wedding trip, but no one else in the kingdom knows of the marriage? This is either one elaborate ploy or two confounded ones."

"King Ryenil might be keeping the wedding a secret in hopes of Ber winning his challenge against me," Toren mused. "It would be a fine thing for him if he could claim to join the two kingdoms through marriage, and that's doubly guaranteed if they are already wed. But to then send her here? That makes no sense."

In truth, it went against everything Mehl had ever observed of the other king. The man was beyond protective of his only daughter, so much so that Mehl had barely caught a glimpse of her even during their state visits. He couldn't fathom any plan that would prompt the king to send his princess to infiltrate a foreign household. But Ber's involvement brought other possibilities.

"It's more likely that your brother intended her capture," Mehl said.

Toren nodded. "My thought, too. It certainly creates complications. Even with witnesses, Ryenil might refuse to believe her crimes, so any action we take might still end in ruin."

Their army was mighty enough to defeat the Centoi, but the loss of life would be horrendous. It would be a terrible price to pay, especially for a misunderstanding. But how could they avert it? A great deal depended on how they dealt with Ber and Princess Lora. They might have to release her, and that rankled after her treatment of Ria.

Speaking of.

Mehl glanced at the door, but of course, the guard he'd sent after her didn't appear on cue. What was taking so long? She couldn't have gone far before the man caught up with her, but she still wasn't here.

He made mental contact with the guard. *"Where is she?"*

"I'm consulting with Sir Macoe. I..." A pause. *"It seems Lady Ria requested an escort to the dungeon."*

Mehl leapt to his feet as he cut off the mental link. "Feck."

Toren straightened. "What is it?"

"Ria." Mehl tugged his formal robe over his head and tossed it over the chair, leaving him in his tunic and pants. He would not be left fumbling for his knife beneath the layers of cloth. "She's going to find the princess."

His husband's low oath matched his own mood perfectly.

CHAPTER 32

EVASIONS

Ria tried not to look too hard at the doors they passed as she followed one of the guards down the surprisingly well-lit corridor. She'd expected a dim, dirty place with open cells full of wicked-eyed people, but that was far from the case. The entire hallway was plain, smooth stone, nothing like even the servants' area, yet there was no more sign of dirt here than anywhere else. Even the doors were solid, no barred windows in sight.

Her father was behind one of them.

A muscle in her neck twitched, but the shudder in her soul never made it down her body. He was locked up here, unable to hurt her. Unable to claim her future children no matter what talent they had. Soon, he would be tried by the kings, and she couldn't imagine Toren and Mehl would go easy on him.

Her eyes wanted to drift toward the closest door, but she kept her gaze resolutely forward. There was every possibility he was along another corridor or on another level. How large was the dungeon, anyway? Perhaps this section was relatively nice because nobles were housed here. It would explain why it wasn't as large as she'd expected.

Finally, the guard halted at the last door on the left and slipped a chain from beneath his shirt. A large key dangled from the end, and he slipped it into one of two keyholes below the doorknob. The second guard stepped around her with a second key and placed it in the other spot. Together, they turned the keys, and a loud *clack* split the air.

Unsure what she would find, Ria braced herself as the door swung open. Devices of torture? A sumptuous room little worse than a guest chamber? Neither matched what she would expect of either king, but they hadn't exactly been the ones to establish the dungeon. Although if they had, it might reveal more than she wanted to know about them.

The lead guard stepped aside, allowing her entry, and Ria took a hesitant peek inside before entering. Sparse—that was her first thought. An average-sized bed was situated against the far wall, and there was a small table and a single chair to the right. In the far corner, she spotted a retiring area. Otherwise, the room was more plain stone.

Tes was stretched out on the bed with her eyes closed. Just as Ria wondered if she'd have to wake the woman, Tes's eyes popped open, and she shoved herself into a sitting position. Metal clanked together, and Ria's gaze landed on the chain attached to the princess's ankle. Only then did she notice the thick metal circle embedded in the wall near the foot of the bed where the other end of the chain was connected.

So Tes wasn't allowed free movement even in the locked room.

One guard snapped to attention against the wall while the other moved to close the door. They were obviously intending to stay, but that would never do. "You may leave us," Ria said.

"Alone?" the second guard asked, halting with the door

half-closed. "Sir Macoe said that you were not to be left unattended."

Though she felt more than a little foolish, Ria prepared once again to channel one of her haughtiest clients. "I outrank Sir Macoe. Shall I tell Toren that you have disrespected the royal consort and disobeyed the command of a duchess?"

The man's face went as red as an *apelli* fruit. "I am merely concerned for your safety, my lady."

Ria eyed Tes, who glared at them with a tired, resigned kind of anger. "How far does the chain stretch?" Ria asked.

"No farther than the table," the other guard said.

"Then I will remain here where she cannot reach," Ria said. "The questions I wish to ask are of a private, feminine nature. Leave me with a knife if you need, but *leave*."

Neither seemed inclined to ask what private questions she could possibly have for the captive; instead, they both made hasty exits, the final guard handing her a small dagger as he passed. Tes didn't bother to hide her confusion, though. Frowning, the princess stood, a symphony of clinking metal accompanying the movement.

"Feminine questions?" Tes asked wryly.

Ria shrugged. "A fairly certain way to gain privacy. Fortunately, we didn't have a female guard."

The glare crept back over Tes's face. "What do you want?"

"For you to tell me who you really are," Ria answered at once. "And the truth about what's happening."

Tes plopped back down on the side of the bed. "I tried to help you, and this is what I got. I have no reason to tell you anything."

Ria skimmed her gaze down the princess, taking note of the wrinkled, blood-stained clothes she still wore. In fact, smudges of dirt covered her face, and her hair was a tangled mess. A quick look at the retiring area revealed a distinct lack of water in the washstand. Hadn't Toren ordered the captain to see to her health? Lying around in blood and filth wouldn't exactly help that goal.

"I'll make sure you are brought clean clothes and water," Ria offered. That put a considering light in the princess's eyes, but she remained silent. "You know, I might be the current royal consort, but I was a mere tailor's daughter a few days ago. I know little about the Centoi royal family. No court loyalties or hidden schemes."

"Everyone wants something," Tes muttered.

"Oh, I do. I want to help Toren and Mehl. They *did* save me from my abusive father," Ria said. She held Tes's gaze. "And for some reason, I don't want to see you hurt, either. Maybe it's my ignorance of politics, but I would swear you were telling the truth about wanting to rescue me. Do you think Toren will really believe the same?"

Tes's shoulders slumped. "I know he will not. He'll no doubt have me executed soon, if quietly."

Executed? What had Prince Ber told this woman? "I can't imagine why. I've only heard of one such sentence in his entire reign, and that was for a murderer who slaughtered two families before he was caught. Why do you believe the worst of Toren?"

"Ber said his brother is cruel and volatile, his magic a risk to all." Tes lifted her chin. "I felt the terrible force of that magic myself."

"Yet here you are, unharmed by it," Ria pointed out. She thought back to their last encounter and smiled. "He even tried to help you when you were in such pain earlier. Don't you remember him kneeling at your side? Your claim makes no sense."

"A ploy, surely," Tes said.

But she averted her gaze.

"Look, Tes. Or is it Princess Lora?" Ria shook her head. "Either way, I hope you'll listen. Because if you don't confess to what's going on, there's certain to be a war."

"You're exaggerating." The princess glared at the floor. "And do not call me Lora. I despise that name. When possible, I do go by Tes. I didn't lie when I told you to call me that."

Well, then. There was surely a story behind those bitter words, but Ria wasn't going to try to learn it. "Fine. But I wasn't exaggerating. If you don't cooperate—"

"Ber will save me," Tes said firmly.

Gods, the princess was serious. She really thought the man was nearby, ready to charge in to rescue her. It was painted into every resolved line on the woman's face. But unless he had the rare ability to teleport, that was impossible—so long as this latest news was true.

"According to the messenger who just interrupted morning court, Prince Ber is at the Centoi palace with your father. It seems he is very upset by your abduction."

Tes's entire body jerked as though Ria had stabbed her with the dagger. Then the princess leapt to her feet. "That is a cruel lie. He trailed us at a safe distance."

So safe that the princess hadn't seen him, Ria would wager. How many times had her father promised great things—kind things—only to go back on them without a qualm?

"What if you're wrong?" Ria asked. "Because the messenger claimed that your father had been searching for you for three weeks. He sent missives around the kingdom and requests for aid to all his allies. Isn't that an odd thing to do if he believed you were on your wedding trip? Think, Tes. What if no one is waiting to help you?"

Ria expected more anger. Instead, Tes crumpled into tears.

～

Toren marched down the corridor at a rapid pace with Mehl at his side. A few times, they had to pass through public areas, and the courtiers who'd made their way out of the throne room gawked and whispered at their passage. With Mehl wearing his court crown but no overrobe and Toren still in full, formal regalia, it was an odd sight even without their haste. Gods knew the rumors it would cause.

Normally, he might have worried more about the impression they were giving, but at the moment, Toren was too tired and upset to truly care. What would be the point? It wasn't as though the rumors weren't already raging, and he didn't need to hear them to guess their substance. Fear-fueled speculation was its own beast.

"I can't believe we're chasing Ria once again," Mehl muttered into his mind.

Toren sighed. *"According to Sir Macoe, we needn't. He saw her properly escorted."*

Mehl cast an annoyed look his way. *"Yet you're walking as quickly as I am."*

It was true, of course. Toren had learned from the captain that Ria wasn't in trouble, but he was charging after her just as readily. But blast it all, the princess had held Ria captive only hours ago. The woman had a talent for subterfuge and an unreasonable bitterness toward Toren after Gods knew what stories she'd heard from Ber. Fear burned a path up Toren's throat at the thought of Ria alone with her.

By the time they reached the upper dungeon, his hands shook with it. But seeing two guards standing *outside* the door? That made him shake with a different emotion entirely. According to Macoe, those two should have been with Ria.

"Did you leave Lady Ria alone with the captive?" Toren snapped as soon as he was close enough.

Both guards winced a moment before sketching quick

bows. "She ordered us to do so, Your Majesty," the nearest guard said. "It seemed unwise to ignore a duchess of the realm without your direct command."

Unfortunately, there was truth in that. Beside him, Mehl cursed beneath his breath.

"Open the door," Toren commanded.

If only the guards did so at the same pace as Toren's racing heartbeat! Instead, it felt like forever before they pushed the door open. Mehl stepped neatly in front of Toren as they entered, but Toren didn't say a word about the protective habit. He was beginning to understand the depths of fear that prompted the action.

He searched instantly for Ria, who frowned at them from beside the nearby wall. As he and Mehl stopped at her side, Toren skimmed her with his gaze. No sign of injury. In fact, she held a dagger in one hand and appeared ready to defend herself. Or to stab one of them with it for interfering.

Finally, he glanced at their captive. The princess shuddered on the bed, and the face she'd turned up at their arrival was wet with tears. Why was she sobbing? Ria wouldn't have hurt her, surely. There hadn't been blood on the dagger. But the stains on the princess's clothes... Toren frowned as he studied the rest of the room and its distinct lack of basic necessities.

He spun back to glare at the guard standing uncertainly at the door. "I cannot believe you left her in this state. Retrieve fresh clothing, water, and food at once."

The guard's throat worked, but he bowed without a word and hurried away.

Then the other warrior took uncertain hold of the door as though unsure if he should close it. "Sir Macoe spoke with the healer, but he gave us no orders, Your Majesty. We did not want to act against your wishes."

"You may consider it a given that any prisoner of any rank

should receive those three things as a matter of course," Toren said. Predictably, his magic began to pulse against his shields like a headache at his increased annoyance, but he did his best to shove it down. "Please close the door behind you, but bring in the supplies as soon as they are gathered."

Only after the guard complied did Toren turn his attention back to the woman on the bed. "Forgive the ill treatment. You'll remain here until you reveal the truth of your plot with my brother, but I'll not see you so neglected, Princess Lora."

Anger flashed across her face like lightning. "Princess Etessa or Tes. Never Lora. *Lora* was my father's favored mistress."

Good Gods, had King Ryenil truly insisted on naming his daughter after his mistress? Toren had never heard of discord between the other king and his wife before her death, but the woman couldn't have been happy about such a thing. The princess never showed this type of distaste when her father called her the name at court, so Toren never would have guessed. What else lurked beneath the surface in the Centoi palace?

"Princess Tes, then," Toren said. "Perhaps Ria came to offer kindness, but I cannot. If your father learns that you're in this dungeon, he'll send his armies at once. I suppose that was your plan?"

Tes's tear-drenched eyes widened. "No! I was not to get caught."

"Convenient." Toren took a step forward, and Mehl shifted nervously at his side. "But we had the rest of your contingent followed. Even now, they are being brought back to the palace. Will they tell us the same?"

"I don't care," Tes snarled. "Ber swore to save me if I failed. The secret passages—"

"Do not extend anywhere near the dungeon." Toren's

energy flared, and once again, he had to beat it back. "Ber lies. Trust me, princess. Ber *always* lies."

He regretted the words as soon as he said them, but not for their truth. What he hated most was the shattered, betrayed look in Tes's eyes, a pain he knew too well—along with the hope that still lingered. It had taken several centuries for that hope to be demolished in him, but it seemed the princess might learn the quick and hard way.

"Then prove it," Tes whispered. "Prove that he deceived me, and I'll tell you everything."

CHAPTER 33

INTERFERENCE

Mehl sucked in a breath at the princess's bold words. Even bound to the wall by a chain and huddled in a disheveled mess on the bed, Tes maintained her defiance. How would Toren react to her demand? Mehl cast an uneasy glance his husband's way, but aside from the energy thrumming through the room, Toren showed no reaction.

"Very well," Toren finally said, his expression closed. "Give your bound oath to it, and I'll find your proof."

Tes's brows rose, and her lips parted as though his response had caught her by surprise. "I...I cannot. The chains suppress my magic too much for a formal binding."

The muscle in Toren's cheek twitched, and Mehl didn't have to ask why—his husband dared not use his magic for the task, either. Without hesitation, Mehl stepped forward, catching Tes's immediate attention, and pulled a simple binding spell into his palm. Hopefully, his well-known protectiveness would be a boon, for the princess was more likely to assume that was the reason for his interference rather than Toren's troublesome magic.

"Princess Etessa," Mehl said as he approached. "Do you bind soul and word into this oath, that you will reveal all you know about Ber's plans and your presence here once provided proof of Ber's betrayal?"

The hand she lifted trembled, but her eyes were steady on his. "I do so bind my soul and word," she replied.

She touched a single finger to the swirling energy above his palm, and light flared around them. Power surged through them both, for a moment stealing his breath. His own magic thrummed in time with the binding, though the force of it was on her. Even so, Mehl knew his husband never could have borne it without losing control.

Once the light faded and the spell was complete, he stared down at the princess, and what he saw had him more than a little concerned. She was gasping for breath, her skin was practically gray, and her body shook and shuddered. Had she been in worse condition than he'd thought? Even with her magic suppressed, she should have withstood the spell with ease.

Mehl knelt before her. "Princess Tes?"

Ria rushed over and sat on the bed beside the princess. Quickly, Ria tucked the dagger in her belt and grabbed the other woman's hand. "I knew I should have been the one to talk to you," she muttered. "Mehl, what did you do?"

"No." Tes freed her hand from Ria's grip. "Not his fault. I haven't eaten or slept in a day or two. I'll be fine with rest."

Behind him, Toren snapped a command out the door, and footsteps rushed over stone. Mehl focused on the princess. She kept her eyes averted, and her body swayed where she sat. Had she always been so thin? Her muscles were too well-formed to suggest her health had been neglected long—one of his first observations of her had been the visible signs of her training. Even so, something was off.

But he had the unfortunate feeling that they wouldn't learn what until she told them the rest of it.

Things were obviously not what they seemed in Centoi, though Mehl had to admit that he'd always been uneasy in that land. Without fail, King Ryenil hosted perfectly pleasant state visits, but there was a slight edge to everything there that was difficult to quantify. Like his overly protected, mild-mannered daughter. Had the man done something to keep her that way? The defiance they'd seen here hadn't been in evidence in Centoi.

Several servants bustled in, bringing pitchers of water, food, and a stack of plain-but-clean robes. Mehl stood and moved out of the way, tugging Ria up with him, so that a small table could be situated in front of the princess. One servant placed a plate of simple bread and cheese on the surface, and another set down a mug of water.

"You," Toren said, pointing to one of the guards. "Stay in here until the servants have finished tending to her. The healer is on his way to examine her again, and you will guard him, as well. I will send a summons for Princess Tes later today. See that she is in good health."

Toren spun on his heel and strode from the room, clearly expecting Mehl and Ria to follow. "Come on," Mehl said softly.

"I wanted..." Ria began, but her voice trailed off as she watched Tes nibble weakly on a piece of bread. "Blast it."

Silently, they left, but Mehl could guess some of what Ria wanted to say. She'd come here with intention, and it seemed they'd interfered with her goal. With luck, it wouldn't be to their detriment.

～

RIA SPENT the entirety of the walk to Toren's study attempting to restrain her temper. Why had they marched in and so confidently messed up everything? She'd been so close to coaxing the truth out of Tes, and without a difficult binding spell, too. But as soon as the kings had walked in, the princess had turned guarded.

Had it been only worry for her that had brought the kings to the dungeon? Ria had known they would be upset by her actions, but she hadn't expected them to charge in while she was there. Toren, especially. What did it look like to the courtiers to see their kings rushing to and from the dungeon right after the messenger's news? Just the night before, Toren had chided Mehl for such a hasty action at dinner.

Ria thought back to the moment they'd entered Tes's cell. Both men had looked for her immediately, and Toren's face had been pinched with fear. Worry was most likely, then. And if she were honest with herself...Toren's initial interference had been to see to the princess's health. After that, though, one of them could have at least asked Ria about her plan. Something. Instead, they'd treated her like an annoying afterthought.

When they finally entered Toren's office, Ria halted near the door, crossing her arms hard over her chest while the kings continued toward the desk. She could see why they might have been concerned about her, but she still had to fight the urge to flee before she lost her temper entirely. Only hurt ever came of that.

"The two of you should go rest," Toren said as he turned, only to frown when he noticed her distance. "Ria?"

Ria's fingers dug into her upper arms. "I hope you don't think a nap is going to distract me from being annoyed at you. I think I could have gotten the full truth from Tes if you hadn't interfered."

Toren's frown deepened, but unlike during their disagreement in the bedroom, he remained perfectly still. "You were the one interfering without permission."

"Do I need permission for everything?" Ria demanded.

The High King froze, and his eyes grew shuttered. Had she challenged him too often? She glanced at Mehl to see his reaction. He'd stopped halfway between them, but he was looking back at her with a grimace. Whether in sympathy or annoyance, she couldn't quite tell.

"You do not," Toren said tightly, "But interrogating a prisoner is no simple, everyday matter."

Ria shrugged. "I'm the one she abducted. Who else has more right?"

Toren's mouth pinched closed at that.

"She has a point," Mehl finally said.

"Indeed?" Toren's eyes narrowed. "And who was it who threw off their overrobe and charged out of here like a madman?"

The question was delivered like it was supposed to be a revelation, but Ria wasn't at all surprised. It was exactly the kind of thing Mehl would do.

"I didn't know if she was properly guarded," Mehl said, defensiveness creeping into his tone.

Silence fell around them, only her sigh disturbing it. Did she really have the right to be upset? Discovering Tes's secrets was important, but it wasn't Ria's job. Perhaps her annoyance was born of her desire to prove useful. To do something besides wait to produce an heir. She hardly minded the latter, but the former might grant her more...permanence?

A foolish hope.

With a shake of her head, Ria turned back to Toren. She was merely exhausted, and that turned every annoyance into a life-changing problem. As the rest of her anger drained away, she lowered her arms to her sides. Maybe she simply needed time to herself—if she could manage it. The kings hadn't wanted to let her out of their sight earlier.

"We need to figure out some solution to this." Ria gestured between them with the words. "I can't stay with you every moment of every day, and neither of you need to be charging after me constantly. Surely, you don't have to chase me down each time I leave your presence."

Toren cleared his throat. "As Mehl said, we didn't know you were properly guarded at first. And after last night... Even after I'd checked with Macoe, I needed to see for myself that you were safe."

Tenderness squeezed her heart, but Ria couldn't bear for him to consider her so imprudent. "I'm not a fool. My entire life has been one of caution, and I have no plans to forget that now. In fact, I'll probably keep my new toy with me," she said, tapping her hand on the hilt of the dagger she'd stuck in her belt.

Eyes flashing, Toren strode toward her, only stopping when he was in arm's reach. "I do not consider you foolish."

"Then assign me bodyguards, but grant me enough respect to choose where I go." Her hand itched to rest against his chest, but his visible anger kept her from moving closer. "After Tes's little trick, I'll be cautious around nearly everyone."

Toren eased closer until she could feel the warmth radiating from his skin, and when he bent down, his breath caressed her lips. "I vow to see you so safe here that you never need think about knives or bodyguards. It is galling that I have failed to do so already."

She gave into temptation and lifted her hand to his chest. "Is there true safety anywhere?"

"Maybe not." Toren's nostrils flared. "But Mehl and I will do our best to provide it to you and our children."

Our children.

He had to mean his and Mehl's with whatever consorts they might choose to take over the coming centuries. She didn't dare to hope otherwise. Ria was hardly special—not to anyone.

Mehl approached, stopping beside her and Toren. "That is so. You know I would see the both of you safe above all, and I will do no less for any children."

Why was her mouth so dry? Her tongue felt too thick to function, and her mind scrambled to find words. Her fingers flexed helplessly against Toren's chest. Why couldn't she think of something to say?

"We are too intense," Mehl said softly.

"No," Ria managed. They were perfect—so why would they have such tender protectiveness toward *her?* "I..."

Toren's eyes went unfocused for a moment. Then his muscles went rigid beneath her hand a moment before he cursed. Ria's heart skipped a beat.

"What is it?" Mehl asked.

"I just heard from Macoe." The barest shiver vibrated from him into her palm. "Lord Aony was already on his way back to the palace before our orders reached the soldiers trailing his group. They have a body tied to one of the horses, and one of our warriors heard them mentioning the princess. Unfortunately, he couldn't make out enough to say why without breaking his cover."

Ria gasped. "Could they have encountered another messenger? Oh, but a body..."

Pulling away from her and Mehl, Toren began to pace. Ria stood frozen, uncertain whether she should try to soothe him or leave altogether. Neither king would blame her for returning to her room to sleep while they dealt with the crisis. She was consort, not queen. But her feet wouldn't budge.

As she straightened her spine, Ria caught Mehl's gaze on her. "What can I do?" she asked.

His smile held kindness, not mockery. "I believe I have an idea."

CHAPTER 34

SUSPICIONS

Toren circled his office three times before he could clear his mind enough for rational thought. A body. Could his warrior have been mistaken? It was remotely possible, since the man had been forced to keep his distance to avoid detection, but Toren had the sinking feeling the information was absolutely correct.

He connected with Macoe again. *"How long until they arrive?"*

"A couple of hours, Your Majesty."

The group must not have traveled much if at all after breaking camp this morning. Well, at least he wouldn't have to wait too long. *"Have them escorted immediately into the throne room. Consult with Mehl about which courtiers are to be allowed in, and ensure that there is at least one healer present."*

"As you will it, High King," Macoe answered before disconnecting.

Mehl's talent for observation would no doubt prove beneficial here. To confront Lord Aony without any nobles present would fuel the rumors to ridiculous heights, but if they were careful, they could fill the throne room with the most useful courtiers. They could also hide Princess Tes in the crowd. A risk, but it was their best chance to find evidence for her quickly.

Toren returned to Mehl and Ria beside the door. "Mehl," he said. "Macoe will consult with you on the courtiers we'll let in, but I have another idea to speak to you about."

Mehl nodded. "It may align with mine."

"I want the princess to see this," Toren said, "If we can find a way to have her in the throne room without garnering attention."

A smile crossed his husband's face. "Somewhat aligned, then. Since Tes already knows about the secret tunnels, I thought to have her stand in the hidden observation point off the escape tunnel. Sir Macoe and Ria can accompany her."

"Ria?" Uneasiness filled Toren at the thought. "Why?"

"We'll want more than one witness in case the woman says something, and it prevents her from claiming mistreatment," Mehl replied. "Ria is one of the very few here who know Tes's true identity. Sending her with them makes the most sense."

The sick feeling in Toren's stomach didn't abate. "Macoe is one of my most skilled warriors, but if something were to go wrong, it would leave Ria vulnerable to the princess. In the tunnels, no less."

"I won't be caught unprepared again," Ria said, her hand settling over the hilt of her new dagger. "Mehl and I were just speaking of the plan, and I think it's excellent."

Toren couldn't resist tracing his finger along her cheek. "You aren't afraid?"

Although Ria shivered at his touch, she answered levelly enough. "Only a little. Last time, she hit me over the head when I wasn't looking. I'll be ready this time. And if she's still bound in the magic-dampening chains, I won't have to worry about spells, either."

Hmm. A large part of Toren hated the idea. Abhorred it. But he couldn't deny the logic of it. Princess Tes had spoken more to Ria than anyone, so if she were to let anything slip, it would be to her. And with the royal consort accompanying her, King Ryenil couldn't claim that they'd left their precious "jewel" to the mercy of a soldier who might take liberties with the princess's person. Macoe wouldn't, but it would be his word against hers without a witness.

Toren pursed his lips. "We could watch her ourselves in the throne room without the risk to Ria, but your idea does have merit."

"Won't the courtiers notice Tes's reaction if we're standing in the throne room?" Ria asked. "She isn't likely to remain silent for unexpected news."

"And she might call out to her people." Mehl pointed out. "We could have a mage cast a muting spell, but that would almost certainly draw attention. It is too rare to have mages lingering in the throne room unless there's a major threat."

Mehl's hand settled on Ria's lower back, forming them into an earnestly united front. Their arguments were well-made, but he almost hated to admit it lest he ruin their camaraderie. If there were more time, he might not have. But at his hesitation, Mehl's forehead furrowed, and Toren could practically see the next line of reasoning forming in his husband's head.

Quickly, Toren lifted his hands in defeat. "Very well. If a former bodyguard believes it safe enough, I'll not argue. Provided the healer will be able to help the princess regain her strength before Lord Aony arrives."

That was the primary risk to the success of their plan. Whatever news the Centoi duke delivered, Toren had no doubt the princess would need to hear it. Her strange weakness, though... He hadn't thought her so drained of energy that she wouldn't be able to tolerate the binding spell. It was a sadly amusing contrast—he'd had too much magic building inside himself to safely *do* the spell, and she too little.

Although, he had to admit that at the moment he was strangely calm. Worry beat in his blood alongside excitement, but for some reason, the intense weight of his energy remained tolerable. And more importantly, controlled. Had he grown accustomed to the current level after so much stress these last few days? An intriguing thought, but one he didn't want to test further.

"I don't suppose you've arranged those bodyguards for me?" Ria's brow wrinkled. "Now that I've stopped moving, I find that I'm rather hungry."

Gods. None of them had managed breakfast, had they? Suddenly, Toren felt the full force of everything that pressed upon him, from his crown and court robes to the nagging hunger and exhaustion he'd been trying to ignore. Ah, how easy it would be to slump beneath the weight, but he couldn't.

For himself, he might have—for his people, he never would.

So he stiffened his spine and led the way to the dining room. Too bad the rest of his problems weren't as easy to solve as simple hunger.

AT BREAKFAST, they'd discussed every possible scenario they could think of, but Ria still felt jittery with nerves when they re-entered Toren's office to retrieve Mehl's formal overrobe. It couldn't be long before they needed to take their places in the throne room—or in her case, the secret tunnel. According to the latest report, Lord Aony would be here within the hour.

But would Tes be ready?

The healer had sent word that he would escort the princess to the office himself, but the two of them still hadn't arrived. How long had it been? As Toren helped Mehl straighten the wrinkles from his robe and smooth his hair, Ria eyed the door. She didn't recall it being such a long walk. It wasn't a good sign of the princess's recovery.

Why do I even care? Ria found herself wondering. An excellent question that she didn't have the answer to. By all logic, she should have been happy that the woman who'd abducted her was too weak to hurt her again, but instead, a ball of worry lodged in Ria's gut. It made no sense.

Maybe it was that hint of hope and optimism that surrounded the woman? Ria might have dismissed the blend as naiveté, but there was too much bitter darkness in the princess's voice when she spoke of her father for that. Besides, Tes's talent for blending in suggested she was far more familiar with hiding than a princess should need to be.

Or so Ria assumed, never having been one.

The door opened, and Sir Macoe entered. The healer followed, Tes leaning heavily against his arm. Four guards slipped in after to surround the group, but Ria suspected it was unnecessary. Although Tes's skin had some color to it now, there was still a fragility to her demeanor that suggested she wouldn't be fighting anyone.

"I have brought her as promised, Your Majesty," the healer said. "However, I must recommend that I remain. I don't know what you have planned, but the lady is in too delicate a condition to withstand much."

Toren's brows shot up. "I'm hardly intending to torture her. In fact, unless she attempts to hurt another, no one will touch her at all except to offer physical support. She should face nothing more strenuous than listening."

Tes herself stared at the floor, but the healer's expression was upset enough for the both of them. "Considering current events, that alone could cause harm. These chains barely allow enough energy for a woman in her condition."

As Toren spoke to the healer, a sudden suspicion had Ria peering closely at the princess. Was it annoyance or embarrassment prompting the flush spreading over Tes's face? Her shoulders were curled in a little, her head slightly bowed. With her left hand, she gripped the healer's arm so tightly her fingers were pale, but her right hand was curled over her stomach.

Tes was with child.

No. No, Ria had to be wrong. It would make even less sense for her to be here in that case. Why would she have taken such a risk? Why would Prince Ber have encouraged it? The pregnant princess of Centoi, the king's own heir, would not have put herself in this much danger, especially not for the sake of a royal consort.

"I will not allow your interference," Toren said, the hum of his energy increasing as he stared coldly at the healer. "You may remain outside the door, however. Macoe will support her while the rest of you leave."

"As you command, Your Majesty."

The healer's tone could have cut a piece of Ria's thickest fabric, but the man bowed smoothly enough before allowing Sir Macoe to take Tes's arm. As he stepped back, Ria caught Mehl's eye, and the others' movements faded from her attention at the pain she saw there. He'd gone so pale that for a moment, she feared that he'd been injured, but a quick scan of his body revealed no sign of that. What was it, then?

The door clicked shut, and Ria blinked. It was only the five of them now. Even the extra guards had gone. For a heartbeat, they stared at one another—all but Tes, whose gaze remained locked on the floor. Then Toren took a step forward.

Mehl grabbed Toren's arm. "Wait, Tor."

"What is it?" Toren demanded, his brows pinching together.

A question Ria wanted to ask herself.

Mehl slipped in front of Toren, half blocking him, but his gaze was on Tes. "How far along are you?"

The princess's head jerked up, and her mouth dropped open. Just as quickly, she pinched her lips closed, a hard look entering her eyes. Would she refuse to answer? It hardly mattered—her reaction was telling enough. But why was Mehl so upset?

Toren pushed past his husband, and his expression was just as hard as Tes's eyes. "You believe she is with child?"

"What other delicate condition would have the healer this concerned?" Mehl's expression turned grim. "And I fought with her. Broke her hand. Had I known..."

"You would have let her go," Toren finished.

So that was it. Ria's heart melted a little at Mehl's distress. But Tes still hadn't confirmed their suspicions, and from her expression, the princess might never do so. What was she hiding? There was so much buried beneath her unyielding façade, and for once, Ria saw no hint of the kindness that had led her to attempt her "rescue."

Ria eased closer to Sir Macoe and the princess, and Tes's wary look saddened Ria in a way she couldn't explain. "Why won't you admit it? Toren need only ask the healer for confirmation."

The princess shook her head. "I bound my secrets safe until you've given me proof. Until then, I have no reason to trust you."

To Ria's mind, it sounded fair, but if the surge in Toren's

magic was anything to go by, the High King disagreed. Fortunately for Tes, he had no time to argue. Sir Macoe stiffened a moment before he raised his hand for the kings' attention.

"Forgive me, Your Majesties." Sir Macoe cleared his throat. "According to my sentries, Lord Aony is entering the outer gates."

It seemed it was time to get into position.

CHAPTER 35

ILLUMINATION

As soon as the door to the secret passage closed behind Ria, the princess, and Sir Macoe, Mehl spun to face Toren. Exhaustion and worry lined his husband's face, but only for a moment. Already, Toren was slipping into his role as High King, and by the time Mehl formulated what he wanted to say, all hint of emotion had disappeared from his husband's regard.

"This could turn bad," Mehl said. "We both know it's not a coincidence that Lord Aony was on his way here with a body not long after we caught the princess. Even if he's unaware of her capture, he has a plan."

Toren nodded. "I would wager Ber is involved, whatever it is. Princess Tes appears to be truly convinced that my brother was nearby and would come for her. I'll be curious to learn whether Lord Aony has the same belief."

Mehl didn't want to say what Toren was no doubt beginning to suspect—Ber had used Tes and would be happy to dispose of her, even pregnant. For if they had married, then Tes was all that stood between Ber and the throne of Centoi. King

Ryenil would have no other heir but his daughter's husband if said daughter died.

No matter what Toren claimed, he still held a sliver of hope that he was wrong about his brother. It would be difficult indeed to believe Ber capable of such a foul plot. And if Ber actually attempted to murder Tes? The thought of the grief that would cause Toren filled Mehl with dread, and he couldn't stop himself from giving his husband a quick kiss before turning toward the door.

"What was that for?" Toren asked at his side.

Mehl didn't dare glance over, lest his husband see the worry reflected in his eyes. "Merely a moment's joy before yet another unpleasant meeting."

They exited into the hallway before Toren could question him further, and then they were no longer alone. Directly across from the door, the healer waited, and at the sight of them, a frown creased the man's brow. It seemed he'd taken them seriously about waiting outside for the princess.

"Pardon me, Your Majesties, but if you have finished speaking to my patient—"

"She remains here until our return, Vesset," Toren said, his tone implacable.

Toren continued toward the throne room, but Mehl halted in front of the healer. "Do not enter without our express permission or unless requested by Sir Macoe," Mehl said. The healer flushed, but he nodded. "And Vesset? I would like to know how you missed the lady's pregnancy during her first examination."

"It was shielded from my sight," the healer replied. "The energy required for the oath-binding must have dissipated the shield. I suspect she'd been using most of her personal magic to maintain it."

"An interesting possibility." Mehl smiled, an acknowledgement rather than a sign of pleasure. "Thank you."

As Mehl hurried after Toren, his uneasy suspicion began to congeal into certainty. The pregnancy had been intended to remain a secret, but Tes herself had clearly known. With her unswerving faith in Ber, she'd likely told him, too. And still, he'd left her here. Whatever Ber was up to, it was very, very wrong.

If she'd been abandoned, of course. Lord Aony could be intending some type of rescue. There was even a chance that the messenger had been wrong about Ber's whereabouts. With that unpleasant possibility in mind, Mehl sent a few additional orders to Sir Macoe.

It was paramount that Ria and even Tes were protected from the wayward prince.

~

Toren resisted the urge to rub his fingers against the worn armrest of his throne as a handful of courtiers trickled into the room. Unfortunately, the smooth stone was the only thing potentially soothing at the moment. He and Mehl hadn't been here long enough for the stone to warm, and for a fleeting moment, Toren wished for the simpler wooden thrones in the secondary receiving chamber where they'd first taken Ria.

Of course, he would have been forced to hide an altogether different discomfort with those memories running through his head. Toren directed his thoughts away from that at once. He could not afford distractions. Lord Aony was not arriving with the intention of being questioned. The man had to know that Tes was missing from his group, and his planned return suggested a duplicity that bore watching.

Would the Duke of Aony accuse Toren of abducting the Centoi princess? Pretend the woman had never existed? What? At this point, Toren had to brace himself for anything. And from the stiff stance and uneasy glances of the Centoi messenger where he waited to the right of the dais, there was likely good reason.

If Toren had time, he would endeavor to discover what the messenger was expecting.

Mehl gave him a mental nudge. *"Send me some of your energy, beloved. I can handle it."*

Toren tensed at the comment. Gods, his power had heightened, hadn't it? Rather than a surge, the energy had built slowly until he'd barely noticed how it pounded against his shields. It was under control despite the increase, but the level was dangerous with Lord Aony still to confront.

"I didn't notice," Toren replied. *"Thank you."*

Gently, he channeled the excess through the link to his husband. As the pressure waned, relief deflated the strain he hadn't been aware of. Not for the first time, he wondered why. Why did he hold such a well of power so intense he couldn't even use it? Was it a curse—or a misunderstood blessing? The head of the mages hadn't been able to explain the phenomenon.

His brother had always hated him for it. Ber was his twin, born second by nearly an hour, but unlike Toren, he possessed little natural magic. As a child, he'd called Toren a thief, and sometimes Toren couldn't help but wonder if he was right. Their mother had sent Ber to foster with the Centoi years too early just to stop the constant bickering.

Ber had never forgiven any of them for that.

Mehl's mental voice broke through his thoughts. *"The others are in position. I had Sir Macoe place Ria and Tes in the corner of the alcove so he can watch the tunnels, too. Just in case."*

In case Ber was there after all? An unfortunate possibility. *"Good."*

When the Centoi contingent stepped through the doors this time, there was no jaunty herald trilling on her horn—said herald was currently hidden in the wall near Mehl's throne. But the entrance was no less spectacular for the lack. Instead of a bard, four soldiers marched through, each holding the corner of a funeral bier.

An honest-to-gods funeral bier with a woman who greatly resembled Tes stretched out atop. Not Tes in her herald's garb, either. This woman wore an elaborate gown, white with autumn leaves embroidered at the hems, and a jeweled tiara atop her head. This was what one expected of a princess. Except she was clearly dead, and he knew very well that Tes had no sister.

His skin prickled, and he gave thanks to Mehl for his foresight as his diminished magic started to hum in tune with his worry. This wasn't right. Initial reports had indicated a body tied to a horse, not a funeral procession. Even Lord Aony played the part, his clothing a deep black and his eyes redrimmed and swollen from apparent tears.

Only habit kept Toren impassive.

Unlike the messenger, who released a strangled gasp-cry before stumbling forward to drop to his knees beside the long runner leading to the dais. "How?" the man gasped.

Very much what Toren would like to know.

The procession halted near the base of the dais, and Lord Aony sketched a bow. But Toren wasted no time on preamble. "You have much to explain to us, Lord Aony."

This time, the duke was too smooth to let any emotion slip. "Of course, Your Majesty. I must confess that our earlier message was a ruse designed by Princess Lora herself. She wished to see in person how you would react to the news of her marriage to your brother in light of the challenge he has recently issued."

"We were not greeted by the lady lying in state before us," Toren said coldly.

"She acted as our herald." Lord Aony's voice began to crack with each word. "But brigands set upon us in the night. They killed a sentry, Princess Lora, and her bodyguard before the rest of the camp roused."

Based on his soldiers' own reports, Toren knew the statement for a lie, but something told him not to fully challenge it despite the shocked murmurs sweeping through the courtiers. "Is that so? Intriguing that your group should encounter violence on the same night one of your warriors tried to hurt a member of the royal family, and more so after the arrival of a messenger from Centoi claiming the Duke of Aony is currently on his lands to the far north."

The man inclined his head. "The princess gave great thought to this subterfuge, Your Majesty, including my supposed retreat to the north before the winter. As for my warrior, she claimed to be visiting family in the city. I have no idea why she might have accosted you."

Both of them were aware it wasn't true. But how far would Lord Aony carry the deception? "Attacking a member of the royal family typically warrants a death sentence."

"Naturally." Not a hint of concern flickered across the duke's face. "It is the same in Centoi. Please, execute her. It will save us the trouble of doing so ourselves."

There it was, then. Lord Aony knew exactly who Toren had captured, and he had no qualms about seeing her killed. Whatever plot Tes thought she'd concocted with Ber had been a ruse —against her.

Ber wanted his pregnant wife dead.

BESIDE HER, Tes swayed, and Ria wrapped her arm around the princess out of instinct. Only the barest light illuminated the tiny alcove through the magically cloaked observation hole, but it glowed like the moon against Tes's pallor. The woman's ragged breaths sounded loud in the small space, enough so that Ria cast a worried look out of the hole to see if noise was cloaked, too.

Probably. None of the courtiers had glanced their way, even after Tes's initial gasp.

"That ill-born piece of slag," Tes muttered beneath her breath.

Ria's nose wrinkled as she stared out at Lord Aony. "Which one?"

"Ber," the princess snapped. "Though Aony can join him in the dross heap. They planned this, complete with the body-guard who looks like me. Just in case there's suspicion, Ber said. Someone who could pretend to be me if there was danger. Hah. She's wearing my wedding dress and tiara. The ones I left at home."

Gods above. Ria tightened her hold on Tes, but it was as much a hug as it was physical support. The poor woman. At this point, Ria couldn't be mad at her for the attempted abduction. That was nothing next to hearing one's former ally order one's execution, likely at the behest of one's own husband.

Toren's voice reached them. "Shall we do so today so that you might carry her body back, too?"

Tes went rigid against her.

"Release her body to her family here," Lord Aony said. "It will be grievous enough to present this bier before King Ryenil, not to mention the princess's grieving husband."

"Husband?" This time it was Mehl. "Didn't she present her wedding invitation to this court yesterday?"

Lord Aony gave a semblance of a sad smile. "A ruse, as I said. Princess Lora was too afraid to invite you to her actual wedding. Under the circumstances."

"One of the few truths he's uttered this day," Tes whispered.

As the discussion in the throne room shifted to a proper escort for the duke and the funeral bier, Ria peered at the group, searching for any details they'd missed. Everything appeared normal, on the surface. Even the poor, murdered woman dressed like the princess atop the bier would pass for her to any who didn't know Tes particularly well. Surely, this wouldn't fool King Ryenil?

She didn't want to know what Ber planned to do about that.

Too bad Ria couldn't see Toren's and Mehl's faces during this. For whatever reason, Toren wasn't challenging Lord Aony's lies. He'd even offered to execute Tes, though Ria couldn't imagine that he'd been serious. Could it have been a test? She hoped so, because like it or not, the princess was his family now through marriage.

A surprising surge of protectiveness rushed through Ria. Lord Aony's request to turn Tes over "to her family here" might not have been made in kindness, but it was the truth of the matter. Unless there was some other revelation to require otherwise, the princess was staying here.

This would have to be her home now—if they could keep her alive.

CHAPTER 36

FAMILY CONNECTIONS

No one else in the room could measure Toren's anger, but Mehl knew. He felt it in the pulse of his husband's energy along their link and in the absolute, cool reserve in his demeanor. Each word his husband spoke was a chilling blow, delivered with such precision that the recipient couldn't be certain they'd been struck. Only the most experienced courtiers had started casting uneasy glances between the High King and Lord Aony.

The duke appeared largely oblivious—Mehl didn't trust that it was so. Lord Aony skated smoothly across the crackling ice of royal displeasure, a skill no doubt honed while living in the court of the prickly King Ryenil. He'd appeared less adept when delivering yesterday's message, and that had Mehl studying him closely.

"It will take a great deal of time to reach Centoi, especially with a large entourage," Lord Aony said.

"Aren't you concerned about further brigands?" Toren asked, a hint of mockery in his lilting voice. "I would not wish to send you with insufficient protection."

The duke didn't so much as blink. "Once they'd finally roused, my soldiers dispatched all of the criminals who attacked. However, it is not the size of the escort that bothers me. We must move slowly with Princess Lora's precious remains, and I would like to see her home quickly."

"If you are suggesting I go to the expense of creating a magic portal for you after your deception, I'm afraid you will be disappointed." Toren's frosty tone nearly made Mehl wince, but Lord Aony showed no reaction. "However, I will grant you permission to request such from the Mages' Guild in the city and encourage them to accept. The cost will be theirs to determine and yours to bear."

It was a noticeable slight—but reasonable enough to avoid offense. That type of spell took several mages and a massive amount of energy, and that much effort deserved ample compensation. Even those among the nobility rarely went to such expense, especially since the mages didn't always grant such requests. Only the High King's order could guarantee it.

But a gate being opened directly between their palace and Ber's new home? Toren would never allow the court mages to take such a risk. Access through the portal outside the city wasn't entirely safe, either, but it was more easily mitigated. Mehl made note of who he would need to contact amongst the mages to ensure the access point was well-monitored. At least additional soldiers in their "honor guard" wouldn't draw attention.

"I see," Lord Aony said, a hint of his unhappiness slipping through. Perhaps intentionally. "I suppose I understand your reticence under the circumstances."

Toren inclined his head. "Do pass along my condolences to my brother. Despite our current discord, I would not wish him to experience the loss of a wife."

After all his smoothness, that simple statement appeared

to take Lord Aony aback. "Ah, yes. Of course. I will tell him so. That is...kind."

"I do not forget family, Lord Aony. You may be assured of that." Toren waved a hand toward the door. "I will not keep you. Outside, Feref will direct you to your escort to the Mages' Guild. Oh, and as one last assurance... We will be happy to take care of the problem soldier who dared to sneak into our palace. King Ryenil and Prince Ber will have no need to worry over her dispensation after her incursion here."

Mehl caught a hint of relief on the duke's face before he bowed, but the man surely hadn't understood the undertones of Toren's statement. Even if no one else in the room had enough information to recognize the promise, Toren was taking formal responsibility for Tes. He would leave Ber to assume what form "dispensation" would take, and the prince would no doubt assume the darkest outcome had occurred.

Killing the princess was clearly what Ber would do, after all.

Of course, the *how* of sheltering Tes held its own complications. Toren would insist she be placed in the family wing now that he'd tacitly accepted her, but her true identity would need to be hidden since Ber and Lord Aony wanted her dead. There had to be a way to reconcile the two. Some excuse for her presence.

While Toren oversaw Lord Aony's departure, Mehl considered his husband's sad family tree. He did have some cousins, but they weren't close enough—in age, interest, or proximity —to visit often. The guest rooms of the family wing remained empty more decades than they were used. Could Toren pretend that Tes was one such distant relation?

A question that would need answering sooner rather than later.

"Let's go back to Toren's office," Ria said gently as Lord Aony exited the throne room.

Tes cast her a bewildered glance. "Why are you being so nice to me?"

"Your initial actions weren't good, but your heart seems kind." Ria tightened her arm around the princess's waist in another awkward hug. "And you've obviously been through a lot."

"More than you know," Tes said with a sigh.

Ria nudged the princess in the direction of the tunnels. "Come on. You need to rest."

"Only because I wasted my energy on that useless oath-binding," Tes grumbled, though she finally began to move. "Apparently, I should have saved myself the trouble and told the kings everything. Gods above. Ber said I needed to experience the kind of man his brother was for myself, but Ber was the one I should have been watching. Unless High King Toren does have me executed, of course."

"I don't think he will," Ria said. Sir Macoe slipped his arm around Tes as they moved into a wider portion of the tunnel, and Ria let him take over support. "It might be a law that he *could* do so because you attacked Mehl, but he seems allowing of unusual circumstances. Toren didn't punish me for slapping him."

Sir Macoe let out a choked sound, and Tes snorted. "You struck the high king?" she asked.

Ria shrugged self-consciously. "I assure you he deserved it."

"If only I could do the same to Ber," Tes said. "That and far worse."

After that, they fell into silence as they made their slow

way through the tunnels, and Ria found herself trailing the other two. Her hand went to the hilt of her new dagger. With nearly every step, she darted glances around the dimly lit passage. The slight glow hadn't extended into the alcove, but she was grateful for it here. It felt like danger could come from anywhere.

Especially since the person who most wanted Tes dead also knew about the tunnels.

Though Ria had to admit that Ber had already chosen a strange method of murdering his wife. Sending Tes here under the pretense of learning about his brother, enlisting Lord Aony, having the kingdom searched...so much effort. Couldn't he have arranged one of a million possible accidents in the Centoi palace? A trip down the stairs, a fall from the parapets, an assassin...even Ria could think of more options than this. There had to be more to the plan.

Maybe Tes would be able to tell them.

Ria half-expected the prince himself to spring out of one of the side tunnels, so when they emerged into the office, she practically sagged in relief. The princess's tension didn't appear to ease, though. Not at first. When Sir Macoe led the woman to one of the more comfortable-looking chairs in the corner, she sat stiffly on the very edge, her fearful gaze sweeping the empty room.

The captain frowned down at her a moment before striding toward the entrance. But he didn't leave. Instead, he took position next to the door like any of the other guards. If his protection brought Tes less fear, she didn't show it. Despite her rigid posture, her hands trembled in her lap, and her lips quivered.

Then abruptly, the princess dropped back against the soft cushions with a huff. Was Tes unwell? Worry carried Ria forward, but no sign of illness showed on the princess's face. Tes merely tipped her head back against the headrest and closed her eyes. Had the walk worn the woman out enough to require a sudden nap?

Tes's whisper broke the silence. "I don't know what I'm going to do."

Not napping, then. Fretting.

As she considered the problem, Ria sidled closer to the chair. "You'll stay here," she determined. "That seems like the best choice."

Tes opened one eye. "Even if the kings actually agree to that, I still have to worry that Ber will find out. I might risk it if it were only me, but…"

The princess's hand drifted to her stomach, and suddenly, Ria understood. In other circumstances, Tes might have chosen to step forward and reveal Ber's lie, but she had a child to protect. Ber might ultimately be foiled, but he would no doubt lash out in the process. She would forever have to fear assassins if he knew she was alive.

"You could pose as a companion for me," Ria offered. "Maybe even a relative? My father was a tailor. No one knows a thing about me."

With a jerk, Tes sat up straight. "You would do that?"

It probably did seem strange after everything, but it felt just as right as accepting the breeding contract. Why not continue to follow instinct where it led? "Sure, so long as the kings agree to it."

Suddenly, Toren's voice rang out behind her. "Agree to what?"

ALTHOUGH MACOE LOOKED relaxed for a guard and there was no sign of strife in either woman's demeanor, Toren couldn't help the sharp slamming of his heart at the sight of Ria standing so close to the princess. To hear that they'd been forming some plan before he'd entered? That had energy pounding through him so abruptly that Mehl placed a hand on his shoulder and Ria took a quick step back.

Cursing at himself, Toren sucked in a deep breath and channeled a little of the power through his husband to calm himself down.

"Nothing kingdom-shattering, I should hope." A line formed between Ria's brows as she looked at him. "I had just recommended to Princess Tes that she act as my companion. Maybe even a relative since no one knows about my extended family."

Toren blinked. "You want her to be your companion? After..."

"After she hit me?" Ria tilted her head in thought, then nodded. "Yes. Really, you could say we're even after I shoved her into the tunnel too hard and she gashed her hand open on the wall."

How could Ria be so matter of fact? Toren glanced between the women, only to find Tes studying Ria with equal surprise. Clearly no one, including the princess, had expected Ria to become the woman's champion. Then again, Ria *had* been caught carrying poison into Toren's and Mehl's private rooms on their first meeting. Perhaps it inclined her to examine the undercurrents of any supposed wrongdoing with more care.

"Your plan has potential," Toren allowed. "But I'll hear the full tale from the princess before I decide."

Her teeth tugging at her lower lip, Tes squirmed in her chair. "So you'll not be executing me and then delivering my body to some mysterious 'family' before the day is out? You did make the offer to Lord Aony."

He lifted his brows. "I did not. I asked if that was what he preferred I do, but I never said I would follow through with his demand. In truth, your 'body' has already been delivered to family. *Us*. Even if you prove treacherous after all, I will not have you executed."

A squeeze on his shoulder heralded Mehl's movement a heartbeat before his husband slipped around him to claim a seat near Tes. Toren longed to ease his own tired body in much the same way, but family or not, he couldn't bring himself to relax in front of the princess. Not until he knew the truth of her plan.

"Will you reveal the whole story now?" Mehl asked Tes. "Or should I activate the terms of the oathbinding?"

Tes flinched. "Please don't. I'll tell you everything. Upon my word."

Dread filled Toren at the quiet but insistent statement. He already knew he wasn't going to like what she revealed.

CHAPTER 37

STORYTIME

"It isn't as sordid a tale as you might expect," Tes said softly, the heavy sadness in her voice pinching Ria's heart. "Not considering the way it has turned out."

But it was likely to be a long one, Ria suspected. She moved back a little and sat on the arm of Mehl's chair. Thankfully, this seat was as comfortable as Tes's, so it was no inconvenience—and when Mehl's hand circled her waist to keep her balanced, it became a pleasure. Only Toren remained standing, his posture as stiff as his expression.

Toren's lips pinched together. "That is difficult to believe."

"I understand, but I give my word that I'm telling the truth," Tes replied. "And the truth is, this began centuries ago when Ber first came to Centoi. We were both quite young, and I saw...or thought I saw...a kindness in him that everyone else overlooked. He was the first person to view me as something beyond a remote, precious 'jewel' of the kingdom. Because of him, I learned ways to cloak myself from others well enough to explore the palace more freely. Without expectations. And he taught me to defend myself."

Mehl's fingers tensed against Ria's waist. "He trained you in combat?"

The princess nodded. "As best he could. We were friends. I was devastated when he returned here after his fostering. Then he came back to Centoi a couple of centuries ago when he was banished from here. He said little publicly, but he told my father and I that High King Toren was at risk of going mad from too much power. My father offered him quarter while he determined what to do."

Ria could see the scene clearly enough to anticipate where her story was going. The prince had used Tes's loneliness to gain sympathy, and then he'd drawn her into his plans. She suspected poor Toren had guessed the same, for he had such an air of lonely, painful anticipation around him. If he hadn't been likely to rebuff comfort in front of Tes, Ria would have gone to him.

"I do not believe he was in Centoi the entire time," Toren said tightly.

"That's true." The princess's fingers picked at the thin, plain fabric of her borrowed gown. "He did travel around, but for the most part, he's remained in our palace for the last decade or so. Our friendship grew. And deepened. We fell in love. I...I thought."

Ria's heart twisted. "I'm sorry," she couldn't stop herself from saying.

Tes gave a quick, sad smile. "Thank you. As am I. It brings me deep grief to see the depths of the deception. He told me so many things about High King Toren, but mostly that his magic was a danger to anyone who came in close contact with him. Ber claimed to worry for King Mehl, and he was certain that Toren would kill any woman he ordered to bear his child. That's why Ber waited until it was nearly too late to issue his challenge for the throne. He hoped you either wouldn't bother or would be unable to find someone suitable in time."

"And in the event he was wrong, he sent you as some kind of savior for any woman I might have trapped?" Toren demanded.

The low hum of Toren's magic thrummed against Ria's shields in increasing waves, and Tes squirmed uncomfortably in her seat. "Could you...could you sit? Your magic alone is making me nervous, but to have you hovering..."

Ever so subtly, Toren flinched, but then his face went so cold and remote that Ria expected him to refuse. But to her surprise, the High King eyed the closest chair, a less comfortable looking but lighter seat, before sliding it nearer. He sat stiffly, almost as though passing judgment from his throne, but at least the waves of his magic receded.

"I'm not sure I really knew the plan," Tes finally continued. "Only what was disclosed. You see, when I told Ber that I was pregnant, he was adamant that we should wed in secret, and because of the baby, my father agreed. Ber claimed that you would interfere in our wedding, possibly even by harming me, but despite the stories, I thought that sounded rather extreme. I wanted to issue the invitation in person. Maybe even see if the two of you could make amends. But Ber said you would have him executed if he accompanied me. Then *he* suggested I disguise myself as a herald for Lord Aony while the invitation was delivered so that I could judge you for myself."

A small V appeared between Toren's eyebrows. "I can't imagine that my response to the invitation confirmed such terrible rumors about me."

Ria felt a pinch of regret that she'd been packing up her former home when Tes's group had arrived. "What happened?"

"Nothing," Toren bit out. "I accepted the invitation and offered lodging."

"But your magic..." Mehl began.

Tes nodded sharply. "Yes, that. Your voice turned frigid, and your energy pulsed through the room like the side of a blade slapped against a palm. Ready to cut at any moment. It was exactly what Ber described happening before one of your rages."

"I do not have rages," Toren argued.

As if in mockery, the hum of his magic increased, and Mehl shifted restlessly behind Ria, his fingers flexing against her side. *He's worried about Toren*, Ria realized. Considering Tes's sudden pallor, the princess was worried as well—though for different reasons.

Someone needed to help him settle before he scared the woman back into silence. Ria twisted from Mehl's hold and rose. Then she marched across the space between them almost defiantly and slipped behind his chair to place her hands on his shoulders.

As soon as she touched him, his energy swelled through her, and her breath hissed out in a surprised rush. She forced herself to relax and let it channel through. Although Toren's muscles hardened like rock beneath her fingers, he didn't rebuff her comfort as she'd earlier feared he would. Ria began to rub soothing circles over his tense shoulders, but they barely yielded beneath her touch.

"I don't understand this," Tes said, her soft voice tinged with confusion. "That type of power is exactly what Ber warned me about, and my own instincts tell me it is dangerous. Yet you have shown me more kindness than my own father."

Ria winced in sympathy. How well she understood *that*.

"Holding power does not always equate to abusing it," Mehl replied when Toren remained silent.

"Perhaps," Tes said. "I wouldn't know."

The matter-of-fact statement bothered Ria nearly as much as the full story, but the princess didn't linger on the trouble it implied.

"In any case, Ber told me that if his brother had formed a breeding alliance, I should try to help the woman escape if at all possible." Tes sighed. "I'd expected Lord Aony to accept the invitation to remain overnight, which would have given me a valid reason to be here. When he didn't, I remained behind in the city and slipped into your household. I'd thought my disguise was strong enough to observe you at dinner, but it seems King Mehl is better able to identify me than my own father is."

Did the princess mean that she'd once spied on her own father in such a way? Ria's brows rose at the daring feat. "If you were just observing, I guess that explains the lack of poison."

"Indeed." The princess's low chuckle held little humor. "Gods, I thought I was so clever. Ber was supposedly following me, and he'd claimed he would wait near the far exit of the escape tunnels in case I found some poor woman to lead to freedom. Lord Aony didn't know about that exit, but he'd been directed to camp in a nearby clearing if we became separated."

Mehl's lips straightened into a sympathetic wince. "According to reports, their camp was nowhere near that location, princess. I'm sorry."

"I guessed as much."

Toren remained silent, and from the tight line of his shoulders, Ria suspected he was holding back a great deal. Not just words, either. Emotions, energy, recriminations—she couldn't imagine how he bore it all.

Near the door, Sir Macoe shifted on his feet. "Please forgive the interruption, Your Majesties. Your Highness. But as the one who checked the tunnels, I would like to add that I searched the area surrounding the exit point myself. No one was there."

For a handful of moments, Tes's pain lay bare in her crumpled expression, but she rebuilt her composure quickly. Her sadness echoed only in her voice. "I see. Thank you."

It was the final confirmation—Ber had abandoned her.

No matter how much Toren had braced himself for it, the princess's story still ricocheted painfully through his heart. She'd trusted his brother, much as Toren once had, and for what? It was plain that she'd been used. Yet another victim of his twin's dark nature.

"What did he hope to accomplish by risking you?" Toren asked.

Tes startled at the unexpected question. "We were preventing harm. To whomever you'd chosen to carry a child and to the kingdom as a whole. He said you would be bound by the magic of the challenge. He could have you imprisoned once he was king. And once my father died, we could consider uniting the two kingdoms to the benefit of all."

As if it would be so easy to unite anything.

"But Ber was aware of your pregnancy," Toren countered instead. "If he believed me so dangerous, why would he have sent *you*? The beloved wife who carried his child?"

"I don't know." Tes's eyes pinched closed in pain. "I should have thought of those contradictions, shouldn't I? I suppose I'd been hiding in plain sight so long that I never expected to get caught."

Toren always felt uncomfortable in the Centoi palace, but he'd never imagined the shadowy thread her confessions now revealed. Why should the heir to the throne have needed to cloak herself to leave her rooms? How could her father not have recognized her? Tes's every word hinted at the king's neglect, and Ber had obviously taken advantage of that rift.

What else was wrong in Centoi? Their status as ally needed...examination.

"And you have no inkling of why Ber might have planned this?"

Abruptly, the princess fastened her gaze directly on his. "We can both guess why. He knew you would catch me, and he hoped I'd die in the process. Since he and my father are close, he was counting on being named heir at my death, and as my husband, there would have been little argument. If I *had* managed to successfully interfere with your breeding alliance, all the better, but no matter what, he would still have Centoi. Too bad I let love cast my good sense into the shadows."

After decades of avoidance and denial, Toren couldn't fault her for it. "Is that all you know about the plan?"

She nodded. "For what it's worth, I truly thought I was helping."

He believed her. Even so, he glanced toward Mehl. "The oathbinding?"

"There is no strain on the spell," Mehl replied. "She told the truth."

It should have been a relief, but like Ria's touch on his shoulders, it did nothing to ease the ragged stone lodged in his gut. Would the painful weight ever be lifted? He didn't dare hope for it.

"I suppose we need only settle on a way to interject you into the household, at the very least until your child is safely born," Toren said.

"Yes," Tes agreed. The hard gleam in her eyes suggested that her revenge would follow that blessed event with remarkable swiftness.

Toren would be more than willing to help her.

CHAPTER 38

CLARIFICATION

The walk back to their bedroom seemed to drag on forever—or perhaps it was Mehl's mood. He'd expected some sense of closure after learning Tes's story, but in a way, it was almost the opposite. Rather than settled, matters felt incomplete, and overriding it all was a looming sense of foreboding. Ber wasn't through with them, challenge or no.

Of that Mehl had no doubt.

The princess needed to be secured quickly—but carefully. As such, Toren had ordered the healer to escort Tes back to her cell in the dungeon. It hadn't felt right to Mehl to house the princess there, but if Tes disappeared from their prison right before Ria gained a companion, the truth would be obvious to anyone with sense—and no few without it.

Once Toren had made an afternoon appointment with the head of the palace mages and Mehl had given Feref several orders to carry out, they'd decided to get some rest. Gods knew they deserved an hour or two of sleep after such an intense morning. Ria shuffled along on Toren's other side, her steps dragging, and for once, Toren's energy was merely annoying rather than borderline dangerous despite so much turmoil.

Even a couple of the courtiers they passed showed a glimmer of worry at the sad sight they made.

At least Feref would see some of their plans put into action while they rested. Once Tes—in the guise of Ria's kinswoman—penned a letter to Ria, Feref would ensure it was anonymously delivered to the tailor's shop. The guards stationed there to protect Ria's store would forward it to the castle without knowing the origin, lending authenticity. Within hours of their rest, she should be able to read and respond.

Tomorrow would bring the feigned execution that would allow them to smuggle Tes from the castle to a safe location. Sir Macoe and two trusted bodyguards would see to the task with the aid of an illusion spell. Then after a week or two, she could reappear as Ria's relative, a genteel merchant's widow seeking companionship during her confinement. It wasn't a perfect plan, but with luck, there wouldn't be any problems.

Maybe that was the source of his uneasiness—the need for luck.

"Mehl?"

At the sound of Toren's voice, Mehl pushed his musings aside. "Yes?"

"You seem...distracted." Toren's brows lowered. "It isn't like you, at least not when we're outside the safety of our rooms."

Ria glanced at Toren. "We're all tired. A little distraction sounds normal."

Mehl smiled at her automatic defense, unnecessary though it was. "I was deep in thought, but I was still aware of our surroundings. We're one turn from the family wing. Our bodyguard is trailing at a respectable distance, and approximately fifteen courtiers have gawked at us since we've left your office."

Ria's eyes widened, but Toren chuckled softly. "I see I was mistaken, love."

"Not entirely," Mehl countered. "I didn't get an exact count of the courtiers."

As they turned down their private corridor, his husband's chuckle deepened into a laugh loud enough to startle the guard stationed beside the wall. Mehl's heart melted at the sound, as welcome as rain falling on water-starved ground. Truly, there hadn't been enough cause for humor of late.

When they reached Ria's door, she halted, her hand settling gently against the wood. Her solemn expression suggested that their moment of happiness was about to come to an abrupt end. At Mehl's side, Toren fell quiet.

"I'm sorry to ask, but now that our intruder has been soundly caught and the mystery of her solved..." Ria's words trailed off. Then she licked her lips nervously before squaring her shoulders. "Would you prefer I sleep in my own room now? I will understand if that is the case."

Mehl caught a low, quickly stifled growl from Toren, but his husband didn't speak. He appeared to be too busy grinding his teeth together. "Is that *your* preference?" Mehl asked for them both.

Ria's gaze shifted to the floor, and this time, it was her teeth that worried her lip. "You are the kings here, and married at that. I'm mostly a temporary necessity for you, easily forgotten. Maybe it isn't wise for me to consider my own desires."

Mehl's chest squeezed. To think that she believed them so cold toward her....

"You paint us as heartless," Toren practically snarled, and Mehl's own emotions caught with a similar fierceness. "And at the same time, you undervalue yourself."

Her head whipped up. "I didn't mean to do either. You've

both been very kind. I only...I don't want to impose myself upon you if you wish for time alone."

So it wasn't them, precisely. It was her fear of not belonging *with* them.

"Why shouldn't you consider your own desires?" Mehl asked. "You have every right to express them."

She froze, and for a moment, he thought she wouldn't answer. Then her soft voice filled the space between them. "I dare not become attached, lest my own heart be broken. Once I give Toren an heir, my purpose here is done. But I won't be gone. I would never abandon my child, so in the years to come, I'll see you both constantly."

Mehl longed to pull her into his arms, and from the way Toren vibrated with tension beside him, his husband likely fought back the same urge. "We would not intentionally hurt you."

"Of course not." Her lips trembled, giving Mehl another hint of the insecurity that goaded her. "But love doesn't require multiple participants to cause pain. One's own heart can do its worst damage alone. I learned that as a child longing fruitlessly for my father's love, an emotion he could never give."

Toren's breath hissed out. "I am not like him. Neither of us are."

Her free hand gripped the fabric of her skirt until her knuckles whitened. "Of course you aren't. That's not what I meant. It's only...I wasted years trying to earn my father's love. If I let myself turn into a lovesick fool, forever longing for you both against all odds, then I'll become an annoyance and will cheat myself, too. I might miss a chance at happiness in the centuries ahead. Perhaps someday, I'll find a merchant or a soldier to love. Even a minor noble, since I'm now a duchess."

Mehl could have told her that those were...not the right words. Not with Toren's mood. But before Mehl could intercede, Toren snapped, and between one breath and the next, he tugged Ria hard against him. "You'll use the title *I* gave you to find another man to fuck?"

She gasped. "I was speaking of love. Far in the future, if at all."

"Didn't I tell you earlier that you're ours?" Toren demanded.

Mehl gripped his husband's shoulder. Hard. "She didn't understand the scope, Tor."

Indeed, there was no reason that she would. Hadn't Toren accused her of trying to trap them in a permanent bond the very first time they'd slept together? Even Mehl could see that their messages had been mixed amidst the chaos of it all. Her caution made sense.

Toren turned his head, and his heated gaze burned Mehl to the core. "Then it is time we show her."

IT WAS CERTAIN MADNESS, but Toren could not allow Ria to contemplate some nebulous future mate. Not for a moment. She belonged with him and Mehl, and the length of their acquaintance truly meant nothing. Didn't she feel the link between the three of them? Or was the problem that she felt too much?

Mehl's hand fell away, and Toren shifted forward until Ria was trapped between his body and the door. "Tell me now if you wish to sleep alone. And I want to hear *your* wish, not mine."

Ria licked her lips again, and it took all of Toren's control not to kiss her. "I...don't," she said. "I like sleeping with you two. But—"

"You don't wish to become accustomed to it?" he interrupted.

Another slow lick over soft pink flesh. She sought to torment him.

"Exactly," Ria whispered. "Once you're done with me, I want some pride left."

Toren gave in and nipped her lower lip with his teeth. At her gasp, he caught her gaze. Held it. "Dearest Ria. We'll never be done with you."

She let out a choked sound. "That's quite a claim."

Over Toren's shoulder, Mehl spoke. "And a claim it is. If you'll accept it."

"I..." Her wide eyes shifted to Mehl, then back to Toren. "You can't mean that the way it sounds. Unless you want more than one child? Surely not me as a woman."

"If you'd like proof of how much I want you as a woman, I would be happy to take you now against this door," Toren said, one hand slipping down to cup her ass. "So hard they'd hear your screams in the public corridors and none could deny your claiming. And I wouldn't care if there was a child from it."

Her breath hitched, and Toren's heart stuttered and then raced at the truth that rang clearly beneath his desire. Down to his soul, he'd meant those words. His brother's threat remained, but he couldn't bring himself to care. He, Mehl, and Ria were meant to be joined. Children or no children. He couldn't let her go.

"You can brace her against me instead of the wall," Mehl murmured by his ear. "I'm forever willing to keep our lady from feeling discomfort."

Panting softly, Ria squirmed against him, and the mental image of slamming into her here while Mehl held her steady nearly made Toren come where he stood. But she cast a frantic glance back down the hallway where the guard protected the entrance to the family wing and then shook her head hard.

"I do *not* want to be an exhibition," Ria insisted.

Mehl's huff ruffled Toren's hair. "He's not facing our direction."

"Oh, sure," she said. "There's no chance he would look despite his orders. Anyway, with my luck, it would be time for a shift change the moment you lift my skirts."

A streak of jealousy, hot and unreasonably strong, rushed through Toren at the thought of either Ria or Mehl being seen by others in such a way. In one swift motion, Toren knelt enough to boost Ria into his arms. She wrapped her arms and legs around him with a surprised *oof*, and Mehl chuckled from somewhere behind him. But Mehl was no stranger to his possessiveness.

How would Ria deal with it?

He could only hope it wasn't the one thing that pushed her away.

RIA'S entire body burned and ached, and for the life of her, she couldn't remember how they'd gotten to this point. To think that she almost hadn't admitted to the depth of her worries over the future! For somehow in the revealing, she'd unlocked a fierceness in Toren that she hadn't expected.

He'd shown signs of possessiveness before, but there was a different tenor to it this time. More strength to his hold. More emotion in his eyes. Even now, he grumbled beneath his breath with every step—unless he was turning his hot gaze on Mehl to ensure that his husband didn't fall behind. Toren was like a wolf trying to carry two treats back to his den at the same time.

Gods, she hoped he devoured her.

As he hurried through the sitting room straight into the bedroom, Ria couldn't resist kissing the side of his neck. She grinned at the telling surge of his magic, but when she looked up, her eyes collided with Mehl's. Like Toren's, there was enough heat there for a solid devouring.

Toren dropped her on the bed a moment before his lips claimed hers. No gentle taking, either. Their tongues were dueling almost before she'd realized the battle had begun. Ah, she loved it. Ria slid her hands up his sides and around until she gripped his shoulders. The rich embroidered fabric of his formal robe dug into her fingertips, but this time, she relished the thought of wrinkling the expensive cloth.

Finally, he dragged his mouth from hers. Their gazes met and clashed over their panting breaths. "I thought I might die if I didn't kiss you like that."

"Glad to have saved you," she managed to get out.

The slightest hint of a chuckle slipped out before he pulled against her hold. "I'll not neglect Mehl, though."

At that, Ria released him. Toren straightened, and only then could she see Mehl, his robe and tunic already gone. With annoyed tugs, he was attempting to remove the pins holding the elaborate twist of gold and silver vines atop his hair. And though Toren was clearly aroused—a glance down his robe allowed no doubt of that—he leaned over to help with patient, gentle pulls.

Why did that only make her body flush hotter?

Though her limbs felt heavy, Ria sat up to provide the same help for Toren. She could have left the silver-and-diamond circlet. But no. She wanted to dig her fingers in the fall of his long, pale hair as he claimed her. Without obstructions.

Each brush against skin and tug of hair seared through her from her fingertips to her toes. By the time Toren tossed both crowns on the bedside table with a careless clang, her heart raced to the beat of her ragged breaths. And that was before both kings turned to face her, their attention fixed on her.

"Take off your dress," Toren commanded. "And lie back."

With a shiver, Ria shifted on her knees until she could pull the trapped fabric free. Then without hesitation, she jerked the dress over her head and tossed it aside. But what about her underthings? Toren's eyes narrowed at her hesitation, so she decided not to ask. Heartbeat drumming in her ears, she stretched out atop the coverlet.

Only then did the kings finish undressing.

Gods above.

CHAPTER 39

CONNECTIONS

"Remove the rest," Toren commanded, and Mehl was more than happy to comply.

To the sound of his husband's ragged breathing, Mehl ran his hands up Ria's legs, his thumbs curling in to caress her inner thighs. At her shiver, he smiled. But Toren wouldn't be in the mood for slow torment, so Mehl continued upward to loosen the thin string holding her underclothes cinched around her waist.

He wasted no time drawing the delicate fabric down her long limbs before tossing the scrap of cloth aside. Unfortunately, her chemise still covered far too much. Mehl cupped his hands at her hips this time, but when he began another slow sweep up, Toren growled low, and his palm connected lightly with Mehl's ass to prod him on.

Mehl's lips twitched with amusement, but he freed Ria from her chemise without delay. Then he straightened, turning to Toren with a quirked brow. "Well, my lord husband? What is your next command?"

Ria released the tiniest huff of a laugh, but Toren's eyes

narrowed on his face with deliciously deadly intent. "I want us joined."

He almost quipped back "obviously," but then the true meaning behind those words slipped through. A magical linking. Suddenly, Mehl's pulse beat in his ears, a frantic but hopeful drumming. They'd spoken of claiming out in the hallway, but he hadn't imagined Toren would be ready to do it so completely. His very spirit soared at the idea.

Except... "Ria must agree, of course."

Toren's lips took on a wry twist. "I imagine so, as she does the linking."

"Without coercion," Mehl insisted even as he flushed slightly at the hint of a rebuke.

Ria leaned up on her elbows, a frown creasing her brow. "Do I seem like I've been coerced? What's wrong?"

Toren leaned over her. "We want you to join our magics as you almost did before."

The sight of his husband hovering over Ria, caging her between his strong arms, made Mehl tremble and his cock go painfully hard, but at her dismayed gasp, his heart fell. Perhaps he'd been wrong that she was merely insecure. Maybe she didn't want them in such a deep way.

"You're serious?" she whispered.

"We are meant for each other, the three of us," Toren said in a low, intense voice. "Only the gods know what is to come with Ber's threat. I don't want to waste another moment being anything but whole. Together."

Mehl eased closer, stroking his hand along his husband's side as he caught Ria's gaze. "Almost from the moment I saw you, I knew this to be right. We should be one."

Her eyes didn't leave his, but he couldn't read the emotions swirling within them.

His heart didn't dare guess how she would respond.

RIA'S BODY burned and ached for the two men leaning over her, but her mind was left stuttering over their words. *Join us. Meant for each other. We should be one.* Instinctively, she wanted to ask again if they were serious, but not even her poor, insecure heart could doubt their sincerity.

But what did *she* want?

A fierce sweep of love seemed to lighten her body, and her hands lifted almost of their own accord, one cupping each king's face. Yes, she loved them. Body, spirit, heart—all sang in the presence of these men, and it didn't matter how long she'd known them.

For she *knew* them. Toren's fierce nobility and Mehl's steady watchfulness. The scoops and hollows of their deepest dreams and fears, meshing and flowing with hers. Somehow, they each gave something the other lacked—more than one thing, truth be told. In her deepest self, she'd felt the same as they had.

They belonged together.

"Yes," Ria whispered.

Mehl sagged with relief, but that possessive edge glinted in Toren's eyes until she shivered from the stark promise. Toren darted down to nip her lower lip, then shifted to kiss along the side of her neck. Still propped up on her elbows, she had a perfect, tantalizing view of Mehl as he bent to tug her nipple into his mouth.

The twin sensations made her moan—but then Mehl's hand slid across her lower belly. Her breath hitched. But he didn't slide his fingers down to caress her. Instead, he reached up and wrapped his hand around Toren's cock. Heat shot through her at the sight.

Toren's groan rumbled against her neck a moment before

he jerked his head up. "Take Mehl with your mouth," he gasped. "Like last time. But you'll be on your back."

Quick as thought, Mehl propped a pillow behind her head and upper shoulders as Toren kissed his way down her body. Her legs shifted restlessly, and her heart pounded frantically in her chest. Then Mehl cupped her cheek gently and tilted her head up until their eyes met.

"Can you take me this way, love?"

Mehl canted his hips forward, and his hard length bobbed close. Gods, she wanted to take him this way. Turning her head, Ria wrapped her hand around the base of his cock and tugged gently until she could wrap her mouth around the tip.

She could spend her life in some variation of this position —and if the linking worked, she would have the opportunity to do so.

TOREN GLANCED up Ria's body and nearly spent himself at the vision of her mouth wrapped around Mehl. The way Mehl knelt beside her, she was able to cast her eyes Toren's way—a better, more complete bonding than when he'd taken her from behind in the receiving room. He hadn't been able to see her face then.

With a growl, Toren shoved her knees wider apart and licked up her slit, pausing to flick and kiss her nub relentlessly until she cried out around Mehl. Which made Mehl moan and Toren lose all sense of patience and self. Panting, he tested her readiness with one finger, then two. Gods, she was so wet.

Ria lifted her hips and squirmed, her cry more demanding than pleased. Toren shifted forward until he knelt between her spread legs and hooked his arms beneath her knees. His hands cradled her lower back as he raised her hips high. It was a vulnerable position, her body barely touching the bed, but she didn't seem to mind since it kept him out of Mehl's way.

As Mehl's eyes slit open to watch, Toren plunged forward at the same time he jerked Ria's hips closer, claiming her in one stroke.

Her back bowed, and Mehl hissed in pleasure. But for a moment, Toren couldn't move. He was too overcome—with her, Mehl, them. Power surged through him until his vision went blurry with it, and instinctively, he did his best to claw the energy back. To restrain it no matter the cost. His hands shook as he clutched Ria's hips, afraid to move.

Then Mehl grabbed a handful of his hair, tugging until Toren leaned closer. As soon as he did, Mehl claimed his mouth in a fierce kiss. A hint of panic welled up, along with his energy, but Ria reached down and stroked her fingers along his outer thigh in a teasing dance.

Distracting.

Maddening.

Mehl drew back. "Let go, Tor. Just let go."

Ria wiggled beneath him at the same time Mehl released his hair, and Toren let his head drop with a groan. Fortunately —unfortunately?—his vision was clear enough to watch Mehl pump into Ria's mouth with increasing fervor, her cheeks hollowing as she worked him.

With a helpless cry, Toren lost his hold.

He could no longer consider his energy. There was nothing but Ria's sheath gripping him as he took her. Mehl's hand sliding down his arm. Ria's fingers now digging into his thigh. Their cries rose and mingled. Pleasure magnified.

Almost together, they exploded, and in that moment, he felt it—Ria's power grasping at his. This time, he let the power flow, much as he would for a testing, but for once, he allowed himself to be open. Vulnerable. When their thoughts began to merge, he threw the door wide to the darkest parts of himself and invited them to enter.

And in that lull, Mehl and Ria poured in.

~

THIS WAS IT—SHE was surely dead. Maybe Tes was a seer.

Intriguingly, the afterlife weighed Ria down rather more than she'd expected. If she'd been alive, she would have sworn that she couldn't breathe. But what was air compared to this bliss? Maybe the weight atop her was merely there to keep her from floating away.

Then her anchor groaned.

No. Still alive. It seems I'll need air after all.

Smiling softly, she wiggled, and her warm, gorgeous weight rolled away. Toren, who'd fallen atop her in the aftermath. She had instant regret as cool air rushed over her, prickling her skin and making her heart twinge with sudden loneliness. Not that she was alone. Though on his back now, Toren's fingers curled possessively around her thigh, and Mehl smoothed her hair tenderly away from her face.

It was such a wonder to be connected to them so thoroughly that she didn't have to look to see who touched her where. Their energy was hers now, and hers was theirs. Even feeling the link, Ria struggled to believe it. But as far as she knew, this type of joining couldn't be broken without great effort. They were truly hers.

Had she ever had anything in her life that couldn't be snatched away at a whim?

Finally, Ria blinked her eyes open and allowed sensation to set in. Her muscles ached blissfully. Her thighs felt sticky, and the salty tang of Mehl's release still sang on her tongue. The kings had said they would claim her, and she certainly felt taken. Thoroughly possessed.

Mehl leaned over her, a soft smile on his lips but a hint of worry creasing the corners of his eyes. "We weren't too rough, were we?"

"Gods, no," Ria answered on a contented sigh. "That was nearly perfect from start to finish. The only thing better would be you taking me after Toren."

Mehl sighed. "Indeed."

A strange, giddy feeling bubbled over her, a euphoria she'd never experienced before. With a cheeky grin, she patted her belly. "His seed better work fast."

Mehl returned her grin, but abruptly, Toren rolled back over, propping himself on his elbow at her side. He studied her face intently as his palm settled over hers on her stomach. "Does it bother you, then? Waiting like this?"

Had she not caught a hint of his true worry, she might have pinched him. "No more than it does either of you. Less than Mehl, I'd say. But it's only temporary. *And* I was only teasing."

Toren relaxed, the fierceness slipping from his expression. As Mehl slid out of bed, Toren lowered his head to her shoulder and snuggled against her side. Now that they were linked, she could tell on a deeper level that his energy was still heightened, but there was a mellowness to it, too. It didn't surprise her at all when his eyes closed and his breathing evened.

The bed dipped on her other side, and she turned her head to see Mehl kneeling next to her. She frowned at the damp cloth in his hand, but clarity hit with a shiver when he bent to clean the stickiness from between her legs. Echoes of pleasure trembled through her, but it was more than desire this time. His tender care twisted her heart.

Once he disposed of the cloth and returned, Mehl curled up

beside her, too, his arm over Toren's. Peace swept through her, and she let her eyes drift closed. Slowly, her mind floated toward slumber, at ease now that both kings rested against her.

But it felt like only moments before someone knocked on the door, jolting her awake.

"Forgive me, Your Majesties," Feref called. "But High King Toren requested I wake him an hour before his meeting with the leader of the mages."

Mehl groaned against the side of her breast, and Toren muttered a curse into the blankets. Though equally disgruntled to be awake, she couldn't help but smile at the picture he made. At some point, Toren had slid to his stomach, his arm still flung over her waist. His hair tangled around his head and down the strong lines of his back. The delicious, lickable lines of his back.

Another knock. "Your Majesties?"

"A moment, Feref," Toren growled. "Make that several moments."

The chamberlain hesitated. "I will return in ten minutes," he finally called through the door.

Toren turned his head toward her and Mehl until she could make out one disgruntled eye. "Rest time is over, I suppose."

"*I* don't have a meeting," Mehl grumbled.

"True." A wicked smile crossed Toren's lips, but Ria's gaze was drawn to the smooth flexing of his muscles as his hold tightened on her waist. "However, there is much to do for all of us. I announced that Ria's formal presentation and celebration of the breeding contract would occur in two weeks, but now there are more complications to consider."

That ended her distraction like nothing else could. "What do you mean?" she demanded.

Mehl lifted himself to his elbow and smoothed a finger

across her furrowed brow. "Our linking was like a marriage, love."

Oh, no. This was not heading where the sick feeling in her gut suggested. "So?"

Toren's hand slid up her side to her breast. "So we need to make arrangements to make you our queen."

Ria squeezed her eyes closed at the unfairness of it all. For truly, she hadn't had a long enough nap to plan a murder.

CHAPTER 40

FLEDGLING

If the pinched line of Ria's lips or the sharp rise and fall of her breast beneath Toren's hand hadn't warned him of her anger, the echo of her thoughts along their link certainly did. But why? He could see comprehension dawning on Mehl's face, but Toren still couldn't grasp where he'd gone wrong. Why did she grow annoyed at his every attempt to exalt her?

With a resigned sigh, he slid his hand away from her breast and boosted himself up to sit cross-legged at her side. "Go ahead. Shout at me if you wish."

Mehl shot him a warning look, but he ignored it. The confused line forming between Ria's brows held far more interest, for hers was the reaction that mattered in this situation. He and Mehl had asked to join with her—she had agreed. Why would the mention of a formal marriage offend or confuse her? Toren needed to know if she'd misunderstood. He had to know what bothered her so.

Had she decided that their new link wasn't worthwhile after all?

Ria worried a strand of her hair between her fingers, picking absently at one of the tangles their lovemaking had caused. "Well, now I can't shout. Not with you looking at me like that."

He lifted a brow. "Like what?"

"Like you're expecting betrayal," Ria answered at once. "I don't understand it. I wasn't happy about becoming a duchess, so I'm not sure why you thought I'd be happy to be a queen."

Tenderness softened Mehl's face as he peered down at Ria. Clearly, he understood the problem better than Toren did. "Ria," Mehl said gently. "You *are* our queen now. What mere ceremony could compare to our link? Yet others cannot see our joining, so a ceremony is customary."

"In two weeks?" Her lips twisted as she glanced at Toren. "And don't try to claim you won't declare it should be done in place of my presentation, regardless of the short span of time for us to prepare."

He hadn't thought he could grin, but his mouth disagreed. "You aren't wrong."

"Well, stop." A fierceness lit her expression, a deeper strength than he'd previously seen. Even after everything. "For my entire life, I've been told what I should do or be. How to use my magic, which commissions to work on, which designs to reshape. My life was ordered to my father's whim, and to question that order was to feel the bite of pain. Now, you're telling me who I'll be once again."

Horror at the comparison wiped away any hint of amusement—particularly since her words rang with uncomfortable truth. "I would never—"

"Physically hurt me. I know." Ria gripped his forearm in a gentle hold. "But Toren, you have to give me time and space to choose *something*. A few days ago, I was the tailor's daughter.

Do you honestly expect me to sit on the dais as a queen only a handful of days later?"

His heart insisted it be so. He wanted her as included as Mehl so that she never felt a lack. But with their link bolstering her words with mental images, portraits of her fears, the full picture finally solidified. Shame heated his skin and churned in his stomach. She was precious enough to marry, but he'd treated her like any one of his courtiers, ordering her about at his whim. And if he *did* get his way, she would be the one to suffer for it.

"I'm sorry, Ria," he murmured, bending to kiss her brow. "You're right. I've been High King for so long that sometimes I forget how to be a mere man."

She blinked up at him, clearly surprised at his admission. "I...don't think I know what to do with that."

"Accept it for what it is. Both apology and confession," Toren said, his smile wry. "If you wish to remain the royal consort on a formal basis, I'll honor your request, but I consider you my wife every bit as much as I consider Mehl my husband. Provided that is acceptable to you, Mehl?"

His husband's soft laugh warmed the space and dispelled some of the lingering tension. "You know it is. And seeing it is so, we should do our best to grant our wife's wishes. Starting with an official escort to both the royal library and the mage's library. Would you like to do that this afternoon, Ria? After a formal introduction from the both of us, no one will stop you from learning about your magic."

No matter how much Toren wanted her at their side each day, the brightness of her dawning smile made stifling his own desires more than worthwhile.

~

ALTHOUGH MEHL PREFERRED the quiet times when he and Toren helped each other dress, they'd spent too much time talking to Ria for that. While Ria returned to her room with Feref so she could prepare, Mehl and Toren bathed as quickly as possible before allowing a handful of servants to unsnarl hair and pick out clothes. It was foolish, but appearance was no small part of power, at least at court. They could not afford to lose regard.

By the time they rejoined Ria in the corridor, Mehl wanted fiercely to avoid more people—except for Ria and Toren, of course. He couldn't imagine how *she* felt if he, long accustomed to court life, was tired of the constant attention. What had Toren been thinking to simply declare that they would be formally married soon? No matter how much Mehl agreed with the sentiment, he'd realized at once that it was a mistake. She wasn't ready.

Perhaps none of them were.

Barring tragedy, they had centuries to explore their link. Hadn't he and Toren been together for decades before their own wedding? Really, it might have taken that long to plan the elaborate ceremony and the surrounding celebrations. His husband was worried about including Ria, but offering her a lesser wedding would be an insult. Although the possibility of tragedy did loom at the moment, she deserved better than continued haste.

Time would be a far better gift. If Toren hadn't understood that yet, then seeing Ria's stunned awe as they walked through the Grand Library surely clarified things. It was obvious that she'd never had a chance to see it, even though the room was open to all. Her father must have prevented her from studying. The very thought had Mehl's hands clenching into fists.

As soon as they passed through the door to the Mage's Library, Sir Everot, a high-ranking Mage-Archivist, practically leapt from his seat in shock at their entry. And no wonder—

such disturbances weren't common since visitors had to petition for entry in advance.

At least there were some benefits to being royalty.

Sir Everot bowed. "Your Majesties. My lady. It is a pleasure to see you this fine afternoon."

Ah, Everot was a clever one. Even Toren's lips twitched at the question hidden in the man's tone. *What are you doing here?*

"Thank you, Everot. It is a pleasure, indeed," Toren replied. "But we will not disturb your work for long. Sir Everot, it would please me for you to make the acquaintance of Lady Ria, Duchess of Nevial. Ria, Everot is in charge of the Mage's Library."

The archivist inclined his head. "Well met, my lady."

Ria smiled. "Well met."

"Lady Ria is to be given full access to this library," Mehl said, making it clear that both he and Toren were in support of the visit. "Please help her with any information that she requests."

"Ah." Sir Everot blanched, but he drew himself together admirably. "Is she an apprentice to one of the city mages, Your Majesties?"

Mehl caught the echo of Ria's resigned sigh.

As did Toren. "I do hope you are not questioning King Mehl's order. Its polite delivery did not intend to suggest the possibility of debate."

"Of course not," Sir Everot hurried to say. "I meant no insult, Your Majesty. However, some of the texts here could be dangerous without guidance. Unfettered and unsupervised access could prove harmful to Her Grace."

Fear took up sudden residence in Mehl's heart. And he wasn't alone—he sensed varying degrees of uneasiness from both Toren and Ria. What should they do? It was important for her to learn more about her gift, but would she get hurt in the process?

"Did your father provide you any formal training, love?" Toren asked.

Sir Everot's ears perked up at that, though whether it was the question or the endearment, Mehl couldn't guess.

Ria didn't appear to notice. "No," she replied. "What I know I learned from my mother before her death, and those skills were sufficient for my work. Father would never have gone to the expense of more than that. But I...I can't imagine attempting anything dangerous. Altering fabric never seemed particularly risky."

"Altering fabric?" The considering gleam of a scholar sparked in Sir Everot's eyes. "A fascinating use of transfiguration magic. I recommend taking lessons from an experienced mage when possible, but I could pull out some nice, safe student texts on the matter in the meantime. Come, I'll show you the shelves on theory and get you settled at a table with a few."

Ria stared at the archivist with the same wide-eyed horror of a new recruit handed their first weapon. Though Toren frowned with worry, Mehl chuckled. "Why not get started?" Mehl asked, gently nudging her with his elbow.

She bit her lip. "Now?"

"We were going to take her to the royal archives next," Toren reminded him.

Mehl shrugged. "It's nearly time for your meeting, isn't it? I need to consult with Feref on a few matters, myself. If Ria is amenable, we can meet her here when those things are done."

Toren gave a grudging nod, but Ria nibbled on her lip a moment longer. Then she drew herself up with resolve and met Sir Everot's gaze. "Thank you. I would love to."

For the first time in his life, Mehl understood what it meant to watch a previously injured bird spring into flight.

～

BEFORE SHE'D FULLY PROCESSED the change in plans, Ria found herself trailing Sir Everot through the large room, though the space was made almost cozy with all the towering shelves, tables, and scattered chairs. On the distant end, a pair of young men, perhaps adolescents, sat close, their heads tipped together as though whispering secrets. Talking about her entrance with the kings, most likely. No doubt the gossip would hit the village before dinner.

The cost of my new life, I suppose.

Ria caught a hint of movement out of the corner of her eye, then shook her head at the sight of the guard following at a respectful distance. A bodyguard in the library? The kings sometimes had them even in the palace, but with Tes caught, it felt like too much. But knowing Toren, this was yet another cost. Annoying, but not too much to bear.

Sir Everot stopped at one of the tall bookcases and pointed at the center shelf. "Only take books from this shelf or the one below for now," he said, his tone firm but kind.

Ria turned her head to read the titles, and her heart seemed to pick up its beat with each one. Were there truly so many theories on alteration and transfiguration? She stifled the urge to grab them all, but based on the archivist's laugh, the desire must have been obvious.

"Let me select the best starters," he said.

The archivist truly must have known the books well, for it took him only a moment to grab a pair from the row and start toward one of the tables. Ria wanted to skip after him like a child, but she managed to maintain a stately pace. Although no one here knew she was technically married to the kings, that reality was emblazoned on her heart. She had to do her best to act like it.

Once Sir Everot dismissed himself to return to his own work, she lifted the first book—*On the Uses of Alteration*—in her hands and simply held it, savoring. Promises of status and power might impress some, but this...this was better than either. She reminded herself that it was not dignified to squeal, but the battle was hard-won. How could it not be?

She'd finally received the keys to unlock herself.

CHAPTER 41

PROGRESS

"Thank you," Toren said politely to the head of the palace mages. "I appreciate the extra care you are giving this situation. I realize it is no small matter to require such a deep oath of secrecy."

High Mage Erense inclined her head. "Unfortunately, I cannot guarantee I will find a mage willing to take this on without immense compensation. A magical oath consumes energy, so they will have to possess a deep natural ability to bear that on top of the task itself. The higher the power, the higher the price."

If only I could donate some of mine, Toren thought sourly. But it was the rare person who could withstand his power, much less channel it. Ria might someday learn how to use his excess energy through their link, but even if she managed that feat in a few days' time, she was no illusionist. And for this, they needed a powerful illusion, indeed.

"I am willing to pay well, of course," Toren assured the mage. "So long as it is within normal bounds."

"Naturally, Your Majesty," Erense agreed.

The High Mage was an interesting woman, somehow both coldly stern and warmly kind. Because of his own struggles with energy, Toren rarely felt easy around mages, but Erense was one of the better ones. She was too sharp to flatter him and too nice to make him uncomfortable. If anyone could find the best mage for the job, it would be Erense.

He opened his mouth to bid her farewell, but another problem sprang to mind: Ria's lack of training. "One more thing. Are there any mages specializing in alteration magic here in the palace?"

"Hmm." Erense tapped her finger against her lower lip. "Yes, but none at the High Mage level. Most possess the skill as something secondary. Do you have a task that requires a full master of the art?"

Did he? Truth be told, Toren had no idea what level was required for teaching. "I must confess ignorance, I fear. It's for Lady Ria. The duchess is gifted in that skill, but she received no training outside the home. You will have to tell me if any mage here has sufficient ability."

Erense smiled. "That partially depends on the strength of Lady Ria's talent, but guidance up to an intermediate level would not go amiss for anyone who is self or family taught. Shall I make inquiries?"

"That would..."

Toren hesitated. Out of habit, he'd almost agreed without a moment's consideration, but Ria's earlier words haunted him. *Give me time and space to choose something.* Wouldn't he be treating her like a courtier yet again if he made this decision for her? He would give her everything—but only if she wanted it.

"I will speak to Lady Ria about the matter," he finally said. "I cannot say for certain what she will want to pursue, but if she wishes to seek that kind of training, I will send her to you. I trust that you will grant her an audience even if I cannot be present."

The mage's polite smile bloomed into true pleasure, her expression showing no signs of mockery. In an odd sort of way, she seemed almost proud. Was he that dictatorial, then? It seemed he should consider taking more care with everyone.

"Of course, Your Majesty," Erense replied. "I would be pleased to speak to your lady at her convenience, provided I am not in the middle of another task."

Your lady. The slight emphasis on the honorific was both an acknowledgement of Ria's importance and a politely couched inquiry—one easily ignored if he wished.

He didn't wish.

"You have heard that Lady Ria is now the royal consort?" Toren asked. At Erense's nod, he injected a hint of smug haughtiness into his voice. "It is not a temporary position. Treat her as you would a queen."

Ria might not ever be willing to marry them formally, but Toren was undaunted. No matter her title, she would be honored in his kingdom. Any who treated her as lesser would face his wrath. And from the gleam in the mage's eyes, he could tell that the message was perfectly clear to at least one person.

WHEN MEHL RETURNED to the Mage's Library, he found Ria frowning down at a book with intense concentration. He stopped and leaned against the side of a bookcase, content to simply watch her for a moment. She appeared oblivious to the curious glances she received from the pair of young students across the room and the heavier, more considering gaze of Sir Everot. She hadn't even looked up at Mehl's entry.

Her brown hair glimmered with hints of gold beneath the mage lights, and the teal of her dress showcased the warm undertones of her skin. Set against the rich, variegated shades of the wooden table and the jeweled hues of the books' bindings, she looked spectacular. She could have been posing for a portrait. *The Scholar Queen.* Ah, she would be so angry at him for the very suggestion.

Abruptly, she looked up. "I can't concentrate while you're staring at me."

"I hadn't thought you'd noticed me," Mehl replied, crossing the rest of the space between them.

Ria shrugged. "I felt the increase of your energy. Toren will be here soon, too."

Would he? Mehl turned his attention inward and was surprised to find that she was correct. Now that he studied their link, he could detect the shift in Toren's power that indicated movement, but he hadn't noticed without her prompting. Interesting. Was it more apparent to Ria because she'd forged the link or because she was better with magic? Perhaps she'd been analyzing their connection when he'd arrived.

"Were you seeking us out on purpose?" Mehl asked.

A line formed between her brows. "No. Would it be a problem if I had been?"

"Of course not." He leaned against the edge of the table and smiled. "It's only that I hadn't noticed the energy shifting until you said something."

"That's curious. I sense you both clearly, whether I want to or not." Though her words were wry, she returned his smile. "I wonder if it's dependent on our talents or if it's only me. I do tend to be aware of people in general."

The sad reason behind that possibility struck him like a blow. Her father. Those who'd suffered abuse were often sensitive to things that others missed.

"Not that I'm perfect at observing my surroundings," she continued. "Or I wouldn't have been injured in my own bedroom."

Injured? When had she...? Ah, she was surely referring to Tes without mentioning her name. Wise, considering they weren't alone. "You were distracted."

Ria shrugged. "I suppose."

"Well, I'm afraid I'm here to distract you in a different way," Mehl said, attempting to change the subject. Only to chuckle at the glimmer of desire sparking in her eyes. "And not that way, either. The royal archives, remember?"

Gods help him, she actually looked disappointed. He had to admit that he would far rather drag her and/or Toren back to their bedroom himself, but they needed to see this other task done. Although... The royal archives were typically empty since the head archivist was the only other non-royal allowed entry. Mehl could bend Ria over a table and—

He nearly groaned. No, he couldn't. Not and do what he really wanted. If it took months—he wouldn't even consider years—for her to get pregnant, he would lose his mind.

Ria laughed. "Perhaps a *quick* introduction to the archivist would be best."

"Oh, certainly." He narrowed his eyes on her face. "We have a full court dinner soon, after all."

At Ria's groan, he could only grin.

HOURS LATER, Ria plopped down on the stool beside her dressing table and waited for one of the servants to undo the elaborate braids she'd worn to the interminable dinner. Part of her hated that her things were still separate from Mehl's and Toren's, requiring her to change in her old room, but it was also nice to have alone time after the frenzied afternoon and evening.

A maid in an immaculately tailored dress stepped up behind her and began to pull out her hairpins. *Sort of alone,* Ria thought wryly. But if she was to live as the royal consort, she would have to learn to count these moments as such, for she could already tell that true privacy was hard-won for the royal family.

Feref's voice echoed from the outer room as he instructed the other servants to put away her discarded clothing. After all that had transpired, she didn't know what to make of the chamberlain. He was scrupulously polite—almost to a ridiculous degree. Did he fear that Toren might still dismiss him? She couldn't let that happen. The last day had demonstrated Feref's value beyond any doubt.

According to Mehl, Feref had already spoken to Tes about their latest plans and had helped the princess write the letter they would use to explain her presence. No questions or hesitation, only loyalty. He kept track of the kings' every appointment, too, and no small amount of palace business. How often had she heard Toren defer a matter to Feref today alone?

She'd spent most of the dinner observing the chamberlain as he directed the entire meal without the slightest show of effort. He'd done the same thing at the morning court, too. Did the man sleep? She couldn't recall a moment when one of the kings had called for Feref and he'd failed to appear.

That Toren had nearly set the man out on the street on her behalf turned her stomach.

As soon as the maid finished with her hair, Ria gave her a grateful smile and stood. Toren and Mehl would be waiting for her, but she couldn't let her current musings go without speaking to the chamberlain. So she gathered her dressing robe securely over her sleeping gown and strode forth into the sitting room.

Feref inclined his head as she neared, but his gaze never lifted above her chin. "We've put the room back in order for you, Your Grace. Please notify me personally if there is anything you need."

"There is something," Ria said. At his frown, she had to brace herself for his inevitable displeasure. Surely, he hated her. "I need to apologize."

He flinched, his eyes flicking up at that. "Pardon?"

"My arrival nearly cost you your place here," she said. "I'm sorry."

At a single glance from him, the servants cleared out of the room with a quickness. "Lady Ria, that is unnecessary. My own hasty actions nearly brought me to ruin."

"Actions prompted by my foolish acceptance of that poison *before* I entered the palace instead of after I left," Ria insisted.

Surprisingly, a smile lightened the chamberlain's expression. "That is true. However, after learning more about your past, I understand why you did it. In truth, I owe you thanks for defending me before Tor—High King Toren could send me away. He is rarely inclined to shift course on a decision."

He'd almost called Toren by name. Casually. Ria peered at Feref. "You were friends once, weren't you?"

"In our youth, yes," the chamberlain replied. "He is a good man, even if he struggles to believe it. As is King Mehl. If you bring them happiness, then I will be content, Your Grace."

Ria sighed. "You needn't call me that. You know better than most how I came to be here. After all, I am only a merchant."

"Ah." Feref grimaced at the echo of his own insult. "And I am sorry for that slight. I know perfectly well that nobility is not always found in noble families. Certainly not exclusively.

My own behavior shames me. I hope you will forgive me for the insults dealt to you in my attempts to protect the kings."

"Of course." To her surprise, they shared a smile of understanding. Could they become something like friends? "Thank you."

Awkwardness descended for a moment, but then Feref's formal mask slid back into place. Bowing, he swept his arm toward the door. "If it pleases you, Your Grace, I will see you to your room. I'm certain the kings will be most gratified by your presence."

Ria laughed lightly. "I imagine so."

Together, they approached the door, but at the sight of the bolt of fabric propped neatly against a cabinet, her steps slowed. "Oh! I believe I do have another need, Feref. Could you arrange a room for me just outside the family wing for dress fittings? I have orders yet to fill."

The chamberlain's brows rose. "As royal consort, you needn't—"

"I don't care if I'm somehow named empress of the entire continent," Ria interrupted. "I'm not neglecting my former commitments."

"I see." A new respect lit the chamberlain's eyes. "Then I will see it arranged. But if I might make a suggestion?"

"Yes?"

"Don't let Toren hear you joke about becoming an empress." Though Feref grinned, his tone held an earnest note. "He doesn't need any new ideas."

Ria laughed all the way to the kings' bedroom.

CHAPTER 42

TRIALS

Toren had told Ria that she didn't have to be there, but he'd known at once that the words were wasted. She'd marched out of their bedroom to go change clothes, tossing a warning over her shoulder not to start court without her. And so he hadn't, though he'd much rather be picturing her asleep in their bed than keeping an eye on her where she stood near the dais.

She hadn't accepted marriage, at least not yet, but Toren hadn't been willing to yield on one bit of respect. She stood in the place of highest respect amongst the courtiers, so near the throne she could have leaned over to speak to him. She'd been displeased by the inevitable attention that move would receive, but if she wouldn't sit on the dais at his side, he would grant her the next best courtesy.

Unfortunately, he hadn't considered the timing until near the end of court, when the only thing left was delivering final judgments to prisoners. Tes's crime had been formally announced this morning, so they had three days until her punishment was given. But today, Toren would sentence Belak, Ria's father—and he'd situated her in the man's direct sight.

What had he been thinking? Toren let out a low sigh. He hadn't been thinking particularly well after a heated night abed with only scattered sleep, that was what. The last time he could recall being so distracted was around the time he'd married Mehl.

Fitting, if currently inconvenient.

There was only one other judgment to deliver this morning. The second son of a minor lord had brutally assaulted another lord's servant. Intolerable. Without a qualm, Toren stripped the man of any hint of noble title—present or future —and allowed him only three choices: enlist in the guard with no chance of full knighthood, find work in a trade, or leave the country for good.

"But Your Majesty, if my older brother should die after my father—"

"Then your younger sister will become lady in his stead," Toren said coldly. "You are removed from the succession. I will not have your ilk responsible for the lives and livelihoods of so many."

Of all the courtiers, the more seasoned nobles reacted the least. They were aware of his feelings on such matters after witnessing similar punishments during his reign. But Toren made note of the nervous stirring amongst the youngest. If they were uneasy with the concept of true nobility, then they bore watching.

As did the man before him, who grudgingly accepted a place in the guard. Toren exchanged a single glance with Macoe, who nodded in acknowledgment. There was a high probability the former lord would cause trouble, especially at first, but Macoe had managed to reform a few who'd been similarly punished. Time would tell the result.

It didn't take long for the criminal to be hurried away, the next prisoner marched up the aisle in his place. This man, though. Already seething from the previous case, Toren's anger surged to new heights at Belak's unrepentant scowl. At his side, Mehl's breath hissed out, and Ria tossed a panicked glance his way.

Only then did he realize how his energy shrieked against his shields as a result. Pain pulsed between his temples, and his hands clenched around the armrests of his throne. Toren forced himself to take a deep breath. At his husband's mental prodding, he channeled some of the excess through Mehl.

He had to maintain control.

As Belak was shoved unwillingly to his knees, Toren feared it would be hard won.

Maybe she shouldn't have come here—but at the same time, how could she have not?

Nerves tumbled in her stomach and danced to the frantic beat of her heart, all accompanied by the ache of Toren's energy surging through their link. At least he was calming that. But if she glanced down at her father where he'd just been forced to kneel, she didn't know what would happen to her own emotions. Nothing good, for certain, and that might crack Toren's control.

For the moment, she kept her eyes on the twin thrones where the kings sat. Her husbands through the link, they would say, but it didn't feel real yet. The presence of her father only increased that sliver of doubt. Oh, gods, what if he did something to ruin this? Her muscles locked with fear at the thought.

"Your Majesties," Feref intoned across from her. "I bring forth Belak Orindl for judgment."

"State his crime," Mehl said—probably because Toren looked ready to commit murder.

"Belak Orindl stands accused of abuse and negligence of a child, abuse of his adult daughter, enslavement of another citizen, and attempting physical harm of another in the presence of the kings."

Ria's palms grew damp. Those were heavier charges than she'd expected, somehow, yet they were all true. How had she survived? How had she dared concoct a plan to escape? Perhaps she was stronger than she'd ever given herself credit for.

A fierce sense of pride swept through her, enough that she was able to look at her father when he finally spoke.

"The account given by my daughter is pure falsehood, Your Majesties."

Her father appeared...diminished. His face was gaunt, and she caught a hint of a tremor in the hand resting against his side. Then he clenched his hand into a fist, and her heart gave an instinctive thump of panic.

There are guards. There. Are. Guards.

"This is not a trial," Toren bit out. "Both King Mehl and I witnessed the bruises you inflicted upon your daughter, confirmed by the healer who repaired them. With my own eyes, I saw you handle her roughly, and you would have struck her if not for King Mehl. You told us yourself that you were preventing her from leaving your home and shop. It is obvious that you used her talent and magic for your own benefit under threat of harm or death. I should kill you where you stand."

Her father's fist tapped the side of his leg, an impatient

gesture that made her take a step back. At the movement, his head jerked her way, and recognition lit pure fury in his eyes. "You wretched whore. You will pay for this."

Ria's chest squeezed until she could barely take in a breath. Suddenly, the guards didn't matter. If her father managed to get free, he would kill her. She knew that fact down to her very soul. That fear kept her eyes locked on his.

Fabric rustled from the dais, but she couldn't force herself to look at the kings' reactions. In any case, she didn't need to—their link provided enough emotion for a lifetime, so much she couldn't process. Only the sight of the courtiers dropping to their knees behind her father told her that one or more of the kings must have stood.

Then she sensed Mehl's approach. His warm, steady energy wrapped around her even before he reached her, easing some of her fear. As her father attempted to shrug off the guard holding him down by the shoulder, Mehl slipped his arm around her waist. Two bodyguards stepped up beside them with swords drawn.

"You would be wise to remain still and hold your tongue," Mehl said in the same deadly tone he'd used with her father the day they'd met. "For threatening the royal consort, I could kill you right now."

"Consort?" Belak sneered. "I see she has—"

"Silence." Energy throbbed through the room with Toren's sharp command. Ria heard a few gasps from the force of it, but no one dared say a word. "Feref, render him unable to speak."

"That is—"

Her father's voice cut off abruptly, and Ria tore her gaze away from his sudden panic to see Feref lowering his hand, a glow of magic still fading from his fingers. It seemed the chamberlain had other talents useful to the kings. A gasping sound returned her attention to her father, whose hands now gripped this throat as he coughed.

Toren stepped down from the dais. "You can breathe, as all here know. It's a common enough spell to use on unruly criminals. Now. For the harm you have done our wife and have threatened upon her children, who will be *our* children, you will spend the remainder of your life in the dungeon. Your assets have already been forfeited to Ria Orindl, Duchess of Nevial and Royal Consort. We will reconsider your punishment once per century. Know that the final decision will be in Lady Ria's hands. If unexpected harm falls upon her, the same will be visited upon you."

Ria's breath caught. Toren hadn't forced the decision upon her now, when she hadn't had time to process it all, but in a hundred years' time, he would grant her the right to determine her father's fate. It was a stunning show of favor, for any criminal bad enough to be brought before the kings was always and forever judged by them.

The low hum and hiss of whispers flowed inevitably from the crowd, too careful and faint to draw the kings' censure. Neither Toren nor Mehl showed signs of hearing, though surely, they'd anticipated the rumors the announcement would cause. Gods above.

It was nearly as much of a spectacle as a wedding announcement.

MEHL STIFLED A LOW CURSE.

Had Toren intended to effectively announce their marriage, or had it been a slip of the tongue? *For the harm you have done our wife...* Fuck. The declaration was far from a formal state wedding, the kind that would crown Ria queen, but the implications would be perfectly clear—she should be considered such in all but strictest formality.

A quick peek at Ria's face showed fear blended with contemplation as she watched her father being led away. No signs of anger, which meant she hadn't noticed Toren's slip. If accident it had been. Annoyance rose within Mehl until he nearly growled. But he could say or do nothing now.

Toren returned to the dais, his unhappiness palpable. "That is the second case of assault and abuse I have judged this day. See that this does not become a trend, lest the punishments become harsher. Also, I am given to understand that in the latter case, the victim was dismissed by the authorities when she sought aid. I suggest each noble investigate their underlings for any hint of negligence."

With that pointed pronouncement, Toren gestured toward Feref, who announced the end of the morning court. It was an unusual action, considering Mehl wasn't with him on the dais, but he understood why. Toren hadn't wanted Ria to feel unprotected, but he also hadn't broken his promise not to force her onto the dais.

Oh yes, calling Ria wife had been an accident. If it had been otherwise, Toren would have expected both of them to join him. Unfortunately, they would still have to make an awkward and obvious exit. By law and custom, the courtiers wouldn't leave until both kings had departed, nor would they stand with Mehl off the dais.

He could have given them leave to rise, but it would be far quicker to sweep Ria away first. *"Shall we go?"* he sent.

Ria blinked up at him in surprise. *"Y-yes."*

As they slipped around the dais and headed toward the back exit, he smiled. *"Does speaking mind-to-mind with me bother you?"*

"*No,*" she replied at once. "*It's merely that Toren is most likely to do it.*"

The soft tone of her mental voice left him with no doubt—she truly hadn't noticed the slip.

Sudden fear squeezed his heart. Would she sever the link when she did?

CHAPTER 43

FROM THE HEART

Toren's anger burned so hot that he was halfway to his office before he realized he'd forgotten to remove his formal overrobe before exiting the antechamber. Again. So once more, they met startled gazes, curious stares, and excessively long bows and curtsies as they walked. He had to get a handle on himself. Too much turmoil, no matter how minor, would bring his people fear.

A few—quite a few—deep breaths later, he'd regained some semblance of control.

As soon as he entered the office, Toren headed for one of the chairs in the corner. He could drape his overrobe there, and if Feref didn't get by before the scribe arrived, the robe might go unnoted. Even if it didn't, it would at least be out of the way. And unwrinkled, which would please Ria.

He spun to face Mehl and Ria, who'd trailed him in. "I don't suppose one of you would help me with this?"

Usually, Mehl would have offered to do it at once, but he simply stared at Toren instead. Was Mehl angry? His lips made a thin, annoyed line, and his narrowed eyes edged perilously close to a glare. But why? What could Toren have done?

As Ria glanced between them, a frown formed on her brow. "I suppose *I* could. Is there something special that needs to be done? I've seen you remove your overrobe by yourself before, so I'm not sure what's different about this one."

"I didn't care about the state of the clothing in *those* circumstances." Toren couldn't stop a small but wicked smile from taking shape. "Alas, I'll have matters of state after the midday meal that will require court clothing. Less appealing than ravishing the both of you, but necessary nonetheless."

Though Ria flushed, her eyes said it was more desire than embarrassment. "I see."

But while she was helping him remove the heavily embroidered robe without disturbing his crown, Toren kept stealing glances at Mehl. Oh yes, his husband was absolutely upset. The question was...why? The more Toren's anger drained away, the stronger Mehl's appeared to grow.

"What is it?" Toren sent.

Mehl's lips pinched so tight that they nearly disappeared. *"Do you not realize what you've done?"*

Toren froze. *"What do you mean?"*

"Gods above, Tor." As Ria smoothed the robe carefully over the chair, Mehl incinerated him with his gaze. *"In the throne room. You called Ria our wife in front of the entire court."*

What? That couldn't be right. Frantically, he skimmed his memories of his interaction with Ria's father, though the haze of anger made it difficult. Nothing terrible until...until Belak's near-insult. The man had no doubt been about to call her a whore, and that had been the final tap that had shattered Toren's tenuous control.

For the harm you have done our wife...

Toren shivered against the cold filling his heart. What had

he done? He'd promised Ria time, and now he'd stolen it. Intention hardly mattered in the result, even if his words had been technically true. A link like theirs was considered a marriage by law, which was why he'd been nervous about testing her when they'd first met—the full force of his magic could forge such a link if he lost control.

But for royalty, there was another layer to marriage. The title of king or queen wasn't automatically granted upon a linking. It required a formal wedding with a great many contracts signed in the process. As far as Toren could recall, there hadn't been any royal couples who hadn't married legally soon after linking. It was an understood process, and the nobles would have known how to treat Ria based on past protocol.

Referring to her as their wife without any mention of a legal engagement would create its own mini-chaos of etiquette. Everyone would wonder how Ria should be regarded. Some might consider it a slight, and no few would begin to wonder if Toren, Mehl, and Ria had skipped the elaborate ceremony and wed in secret. The nobles would question incessantly. Should they snub Ria since she hadn't earned a place on the dais or treat her as queen to gain favor just in case they *had* married quietly?

Those stares and prolonged bows hadn't been because of the formal robes.

The line between Ria's brows deepened as she turned away from the chair. "You might as well tell me what's wrong, because I can feel it brewing through our connection."

Much as he felt the sick churn of regret.

He took a deep breath. "I hope you'll forgive me, Ria."

If she didn't, he would never forgive himself.

❦

Undefined worry became true fear at Toren's words. What did he mean by that? Oh, gods, did he want to break their link after speaking to her father again? Surely, he must be considering the risk of merging with her bloodline after that.

Ria squeezed her hands together in front of her waist. "It's about what happened in the throne room, isn't it?"

"Yes," Toren said roughly. "But I promise you this was not intentional."

Her heart clenched as tightly as her hands. "I understand. I don't blame you for reconsidering after that. It must be a concern to bring such foul blood into your family line."

"I—" Toren's words cut off, his brows scrunching. "What did you say?"

"You wish to end our contract after my father's display," she said, trying her best to keep her voice steady.

Mehl stepped around Toren as he hurried to her side. "No, Ria. That's not what he meant."

Toren's nostrils flared. "It absolutely is not. My own twin has threatened me for centuries and may have even murdered our mother. I could hardly criticize *your* family."

"I...don't understand, then," Ria said.

And she didn't. Toren and Mehl had protected her back there, and Toren had even given her future control of her father's fate. She could have asked for nothing more of them. Yet the erratic pulsing of Toren's energy and the distress she felt from both of them told her she was missing something.

"Ria..." Toren rubbed the back of his neck in an almost sheepish manner. "When I sentenced your father, I referred to you as our wife."

Her head went light and airy, but she wasn't sure if it was relief or shock to blame. That was all?

Wait. That is a lot.

Numbly, she dropped into the chair beside Toren's overrobe. What did it mean? She'd begged for time to adjust before she considered a marriage. Did calling her wife in front of the court bypass a formal wedding? Oh, gods, did that make her queen?

"You said you would not force me," Ria whispered.

Toren knelt in front of her seat. "I give my word as man and High King that I had no intention of doing such a thing. I told you I think of you as our wife in my heart. I suppose when your father sparked my rage, I spoke from that place rather than my head."

Her eyes itched and her nose burned from the sudden rush of tears she fought not to shed. "What...what is my place, then? What now?"

"The same as we have agreed," Toren answered, his voice firm and sure. "The nobles might have some confusion, but you will remain Royal Consort as long as you wish it. As this is my folly, I will think of a way to fix it. Perhaps an announcement that we have linked will ease the bulk of their curiosity since that is the source of my wording. They can wait until never for word of an official wedding if that is your wish."

Ria stared down into his pained but earnest gaze and sniffled. She should stay angry, but that emotion slipped away like fine silk. She could feel for herself that it was an accident, the mix of his emotions too raw and self-castigating for anything else. Added to that, Mehl's anger and worry pulsed in, and she knew without asking what he thought.

That she would leave them over this.

But why? Because Toren had accepted her into his family so thoroughly he'd forgotten the whole world didn't know it? Tenderness for the brash, forceful man kneeling before her sent a tear tipping from her eye.

Toren's expression crumpled. "Ria..."

"Oh, search our link," she muttered, another tear slipping

out. "So long as you don't try to force me onto that dais, I'll get over it. I'm not sure why I'm crying, but it isn't sorrow."

"I do not wish to bring you unhappiness." He brushed the tear away with his thumb before cupping her cheek. "I'll do my best to make this up to you."

Mehl's hand settled on her nape, and a hint of heat flared within her. "I'll keep that in mind."

If nothing else, it would come in handy later.

Mehl fought the urge to tighten his fingers possessively on Ria's nape like an animal claiming its mate. What was wrong with him? But when Toren looked up, that same stark possessiveness gleamed in his eyes. Suddenly, Mehl understood. The impulse shaking his hand was no small part fear.

They might have lost her.

If there wasn't so much to be done, he had no doubt Toren would have hauled them both to the bedroom for the rest of the day. Mehl longed for the same so devoutly that he could almost taste the tang of Toren on his tongue and the silky slide of Ria beneath his fingertips. Someday, he would bend Ria over the arm of this chair and claim her while she took Toren in her mouth. Wouldn't that be a nice change?

Ria trembled beneath Mehl's hand.

His husband groaned. "Stop with those thoughts, at least for the moment. The scribe will be here any moment, and we can't follow through on the idea, besides."

That much had slipped along the link? Mehl dropped his hand in case it continued, for the echoes of that vision weren't likely to fade anytime soon. "Sorry."

Ria glanced between them, a vulnerable glint returning to her eyes. "In the throne room... When I think back to Toren's words, didn't he say 'children'? Ours? Mehl, does that mean someday…?"

He smiled. "If you are willing, it would be my wish for you to bear my child, too. It's only fair that Toren suffer this same torment when it's my turn."

"Cruel but fitting," Toren said with a growl—the playful kind. "After that, we'll both take you when we wish and see what fate decides."

At Ria's hitched breath, Mehl had the undeniable urge to skip ahead to that glorious future. Of course, then he would miss the birth of their first two children, so that wasn't ideal, either. He would just have to suffer through.

Such a difficult life.

"So," Ria began, then paused to clear her throat. "Um. You said there was a lot to do. Is there anything I can do to speed things up? I would hate for the two of you to work late."

Mehl grinned. "Indeed?"

She made an attempt at an earnest nod. "Oh, yes. It would be tragic."

Toren darted forward to give her a quick kiss before he stood. Mehl's gaze went immediately to the outline of his husband's semi-hard cock, which…probably didn't help his husband gain control. He forced himself to look at Ria instead, but her rapt expression on Toren was no better than his had been. Mehl found himself joining Toren in that uncomfortable state.

"I suspect we should all find duties in entirely different rooms," Mehl said dryly.

Both spouses laughed, but there was heat beneath the humor.

"Ria has her studies or her shop business," Toren said, looking down at their wife. "Which should be your focus, love. Mehl is working with Feref on preparing Tes for her 'punishment,' and in addition to my usual tasks, I'll be meeting with several mages. I've also increased the number of spies and guards in the entire kingdom. The Centoi delegation apparently arrived through a portal fairly near the city, but we still should have had more warning. I want to know sooner if my brother decides to come here after his wife's...death. There was certainly a reason they killed Tes's double and brought her body in on a funeral bier."

That reminder certainly served to cool Mehl's ardor. Although the threat might appear lessened, logic and instinct both told him there was more to come. Toren was right. They might prefer to stay abed, but that would not see them prepared.

As in most things, it was now a waiting game.

CHAPTER 44

PLANS

The next week was the quickest—and the best—of Ria's life. Each afternoon, she worked with Feref on setting up her tailoring workshop, and in the mornings, she either attended court or buried herself in the Mage's Library beneath stacks of glorious books. She far preferred the second, but Toren looked downcast if she missed too many court sessions. He'd claimed that the sight of her standing at the front of the crowd lightened his days.

How could she resist that?

But she had been certain to attend on the day of Tes's sentencing three days after her father's. They'd had Tes wear her servant's guise, the same one from the dining room, and given her a false name. As Toren had sentenced the woman to death for attacking the royal family and stabbing King Mehl, Ria had shivered at the cold, deadly anger in his voice. Tes had to be wondering if she would be executed in truth.

Now, only a week after Ria's father had been thrown back in the dungeon, she stared out the window of her new workshop at the courtyard where tomorrow's "execution" would be carried out. What if something went wrong? Neither Toren nor Mehl appeared to have any doubts about the mages who would help with the task, but it still had her stomach knotted with nerves. She couldn't imagine how Tes felt.

Ria turned at the sound of a knock in time to see Feref enter and bow. "Your Grace, your first client has arrived."

Whatever snobbery had afflicted the man when they first met had disappeared entirely as she'd directed him on how the workshop should be appointed. There wasn't a single hint in his voice or manner that he disapproved of the royal consort performing fittings in a modified guest suite outside the family wing.

"Thank you, Feref," Ria said with a smile.

His lips tilted upward, if only the slightest fraction, before he directed her client into the room. At the sight of Lady Gartren Hesslefyn, however, Ria had to suppress her own instant dislike. The woman was their—her—most demanding customer, and Ria had suffered more than one harsh word from the lady. Even the odd elbow a time or two, although the woman had claimed not to see Ria when she'd swung her arm back.

That wasn't likely to happen again, at least. If it hadn't been before, it was clear now that Toren would not take it easy on anyone who hurt her or Mehl. He wouldn't have someone executed for a stray elbow, but he would happily send them to the dungeon. Ria had a feeling this lady wouldn't be willing to risk that unpleasant fate.

Ria put on her best pretend smile as Lady Gartren halted in front of her, hesitated, then gave a reluctant curtsey. "There's no need for that, Lady Gartren."

A hint of anger flashed in the woman's eyes at Ria's use of her first name, but she forced her own fake-pleasant expression. "Thank you, Your Grace."

The choked sound of the honorific nearly made Ria laugh, but fortunately, she was long accustomed to hiding those kinds of reactions. Especially during work—the wrong sound could prompt her father into a rage. But in this case, Ria wanted Gartren to leave pleased. If she were careful, she might start a trend amongst the noble ladies, but it would take balance to achieve.

She was counting on the cleverest courtiers to boast of having a dress created by the royal consort, in which case Ria's talent might remain in demand. And maybe—just maybe—she could learn to wield a little power from that very thing. Only the favored would receive one of her designs, after all.

"I realize this is an unusual situation," Ria said. "But no matter my current station, I would not have it said that I break my word. I know you're counting on this gown for your engagement ball, so of course you were the first I thought to see."

Lady Gartren relaxed at those simple hints of continued deference, though Ria considered it more politeness than anything. Well, perhaps a bit of her own cleverness, too. The lady was the second daughter of a duke and held no small amount of power at court.

"You have my thanks, then." Lady Gartren glanced around the room with a hint more interest, but aside from a couple of displays, there weren't any dresses out here. Only fabric samples and patterns. "Was I not to try on my gown today?"

Ria gestured toward the door at the back. "Of course you are. There are maids ready to assist you in the other room, and then you'll come out here for me to adjust. I'm afraid I'd have to bring bodyguards if I went back with you myself."

The lady's eyes widened as she noticed the pair of guards stationed by the door. "I see."

It was a perk Ria enjoyed as much as she did the entire self-designed workshop. Once Lady Gartren stood on the platform in the center of the room, Ria began to circle her, tucking, shifting, and reshaping the fabric until it fit the lady to perfection. But each time Gartren's voice turned waspish, her eyes tracked toward the bodyguards, and she snapped her mouth closed. No misplaced elbows, either.

Ah, what a glorious way to work! All design, no abuse.

Gartren had just left the other room after changing back into her day dress when another knock sounded on the door. Though Ria knew exactly who it was, she fixed her best puzzled look on her face and called for the person to enter. Feref, as planned, who bowed and extended a tray with an envelope atop.

"Forgive the interruption, Your Grace," Feref said, no hint of awkwardness in his tone. "This missive was delivered to your former residence with some urgency."

After thanking Feref, Ria lifted the envelope and broke open the seal at once. Lady Gartren's eyes widened, for she'd surely expected Ria to wait until she'd left to read the note. And she would have, had the scene not been planned.

"Oh, my." Ria placed her fingertips against her lips. "I should go speak to Toren and Mehl at once."

Sly curiosity pinched the other woman's smile. "I do hope it isn't bad news, Your Grace."

The bold, probing wretch, Ria grumbled to herself. But it was exactly what she'd expected.

"Yes and no," Ria replied. "It seems my cousin was widowed. Since she's expecting a child, she hopes to stay with my family until she decides how to proceed with her life. I'm afraid I may be her last living relative."

That was almost true, actually—Tes was now family of a sort, and the rest of her relatives might as well be dead. And even Ria's blood family was small and distant enough that she might not even receive word if they all died off.

"Has she heard of your..." Gartren's lips twitched. "Change in station?"

Ria only broadened her smile. "It seems not. If you'll excuse me, I must go discuss the matter with Toren and Mehl. I do need a lady's companion, after all."

Since Ria wasn't choosing that companion from the court ladies, there was a certain amount of insult in the statement, but Lady Gartren showed no sign of offense. No doubt she considered it ignorance on Ria's part. That or a duty beneath her own importance. Who wanted to sit in attendance of the former tailor's daughter?

Hah. A princess-in-hiding, that was who.

MEHL STOOD at the edge of the courtyard, his arms crossed as he studied the low platform being constructed in the center. On the opposite side of the square, four mages leaned close together, gesturing here and there as they consulted. But they all knew the plan. Even though Mehl was not a mage, he was more than happy to stand here and remind them.

This secret mission was the Kings' own order.

Once the platform was complete, three of the mages formed a triangle around it, and the final mage stood in the center. A circle of light flared in a ring in front of the outer three before sweeping up to form a dome around the central mage. This was standard, a shield that blocked sight of the spells used for execution. But that wasn't what the lead mage was weaving today. No, he was building illusions and teleportation spells of such intricate design that the light started growing dim before they finished.

Sir Macoe slipped up beside him as the shield winked out. "Studying magic now?"

Mehl snorted. "You know very well I am not. Are you prepared for tomorrow's proceedings?"

"Yes, Your Majesty," Sir Macoe answered. "More than prepared."

It was a simple exchange. Innocuous. Yet they understood each other perfectly. Sir Macoe already had his trusted guards at the location where Tes would stay until they could present her as Ria's cousin. Despite Tes's innocence, the warrior in him hated having her so close to Ria, but he couldn't deny it was an excellent plan. As was ordering the bodyguards to observe the princess while offering protection.

Oathbinding spell or not, it would be a while before she had Mehl's full trust.

Then Sir Macoe sent him a mental message. *"Remain on your guard. A contingent bearing the royal standard of Centoi alongside that of Prince Ber departed the Centoi palace a few days back. One spy transported back to warn us, but the other still trails them."*

Mehl kept his gaze on the platform even as his mind cataloged each worry. *"Is Ber with them?"*

"Possibly, but the spy didn't get a clear look."

"When do you expect their arrival?" Mehl asked next.

Only he was close enough to hear Sir Macoe's sigh. *"A week and a half. Possibly two. No mages were with them that the spy could see, so if they're attempting a transportation spell, it'll have to be in the next large town a few days' ride away. But since our own mages have been ordered to refuse them transport into our borders, even that wouldn't get them far."*

It was a sad state of affairs when any envoy required such careful tracing. This was the kind of attention usually reserved for an enemy. Although their strained alliance with Centoi hadn't been severed on paper, it was growing increasingly obvious that it would soon end. He shouldn't be surprised. Matters had started heading that direction when the Centoi king had allowed Ber to stay with them.

"I believe I must prepare for dinner," Mehl said aloud. "I'll be sure to tell High King Toren that you're giving admirable attention to your duties."

Namely the stealthy ones.

TOREN HAD JUST RESUMED work after speaking to Ria about the arrival of her so-called cousin—in front of the scribe, of course —when Mehl strode in. He groaned low at yet another interruption, but one look at his husband's face had the sound cutting off. Something was...not wrong, exactly. Important. What pressing news did Mehl bear now?

"Give us a moment, Iyeth," Toren said to his scribe.

"Considering the time, Your Majesty, should I complete my current tasks in preparation for tomorrow?" Iyeth asked as he stood.

A glance at the window revealed a rapidly sinking sun. No wonder the poor man was subtly begging to go home. "That is an excellent idea. Forgive me for losing track of the time."

"It is no matter, Your Majesty."

By the time the scribe gathered his papers and departed, Toren was ready to drum his fingers atop his desk with impatience. But he resisted. Gods knew Iyeth had been patient with him this day despite his scattered thoughts. It would be some time before he established a new routine, which would settle his mind immensely.

As soon as the door clicked shut, he leveled a stare on Mehl. "Tell me."

Mehl huffed in a short, wry laugh. "You know me well. I spoke to Sir Macoe in the courtyard a few moments ago. It seems a new contingent is on its way from Centoi, and your brother is likely with them."

Toren's body went cold. "It is far from time for the challenge. He must have something planned regarding Princess Tes."

"That's also my assumption," Mehl said. "Whatever his plans, I hope they don't counter ours."

Indeed. Keeping Tes safe was more important than ever. If Ber wanted her dead, he would stop at nothing, and if word of their mysterious prisoner had given him pause, that could be the reason for his journey. That or revenge.

Either way, the pretend execution had better be convincing.

CHAPTER 45

EXECUTIONS

The courtyard was the absolute last place Ria wanted to be, but since she was one of the people supposedly wronged by Tes, she hadn't felt she could avoid attending the so-called execution. Maybe she was a little curious, too. Executions were so extremely rare that most of the courtiers had come to see it, either ringing the square or staring from the castle windows. The blend of excitement and uneasiness in the air had her feet itching to move.

A steady drumming began, the beat uncomfortably close to her own pulse. Every whisper and shuffle ceased until there was nothing but the incessant pounding. *Badum. Badum.* Though she was safe—she *knew* she was safe—standing to Toren's left with guards stationed in an arch behind them, her muscles went stiff beneath a wave of fear.

Then Toren's fingers brushed against hers, and the beginnings of panic eased away at the telling sweetness of that touch. It seemed a small thing, but in such a deeply formal situation, he usually stuck stringently to protocol. And as ridiculous as it sounded, even that tender brush of their hands would be noticed and gossiped about amongst the courtiers.

Honestly, those people needed better things to do.

A small, plain door opened in the outer wall, and two guards hauled Tes through. Not that they needed to do so. Once they were through the door, the princess ignored the other guards moving forward to surround her and marched down the path toward the assembled nobles with her head held high. She kept her shoulders pushed back as far as they could be with her wrists bound in front of her, too. No hint of submission in sight.

Ria hid a grimace. Would anyone believe the woman was actually a servant?

Maybe they should have told Tes to slump—or cry. Anything but stare boldly at Toren as the guards drew her to a halt in front of him. Then again...the princess had only their word that she would not be truly executed, and after her betrayal at her husband's hands, she probably wouldn't believe it until she was safe.

This was a true reaction. Gods. As far as Tes was concerned, she was facing her death.

Suddenly, the drumbeats ceased.

"Anmara of the Centoi, you have been found guilty of attempting to assassinate members of the royal family of the Kingdom of Llyalia. By the wish of your own kinsman, you are to be executed here. However, I will grant you a few final words before your sentence is carried out," Toren said coldly.

Tes's chin lifted higher. "I vow unto my very soul that the people in Centoi who abandoned me to this fate will pay for it. Even in death, my spirit will fly free for its revenge."

Ria shivered at those words. Because she felt them, the magic behind those two sentences ringing like a bell to any who could detect magic. Beside her, Toren stiffened, and a couple of the mages surrounding the center platform shifted nervously. Would she, Toren, or Mehl be included in this? But no. Tes had said "in Centoi," not here.

"May your spirit find its peace," Toren replied.

It was a polite statement on the surface, one often granted to the dying. But after Tes's curse? He might as well have wished her good luck on her quest for revenge since that was the only thing that *would* bring her peace. A few hissed whispers reached them, but under the circumstances, they were fewer than Ria was accustomed to hearing in the throne room.

Ria couldn't quite tell if Tes recognized the second meaning to Toren's words, but something shifted in the princess's gaze. Without knowing the woman better, it was impossible to say for certain what. Not that there was time to analyze. The guards directed Tes to turn before marching her toward the center platform.

In short order, Tes was stopped again, this time by a priest, who circled her while chanting prayers and incantations. Did they even share the same religion as Centoi? It didn't exactly matter, since the princess wasn't truly being executed, but Ria couldn't help the pinch of embarrassment at her lack of knowledge.

And Toren thought she would make a good queen? Hah.

The priest finished his prayers and stepped aside, leaving the courtyard in total silence once again—until the drumming resumed. *Badum. Badum. Badum.* The solemn sound reverberated through her entire body and thrummed in her soul.

Two of the guards grabbed Tes by each arm and led her forward, but the princess didn't resist. Instead, she stepped onto the platform the way a true queen would. No quivering, crying, or pleading. Once in the center, she spun on her heel to face Ria, Toren, and Mehl, but the princess stared over their heads as the mages activated the shield around the inlaid spell.

With only a single lift of his hand, Toren ordered the final mage forward. Ria wasn't sure about the others, but this mage had full awareness of his task, an illusion strong enough to fool the entire court. According to Mehl, the man would be paid a full chest of gold if he performed the required spells perfectly.

An entire. Chest. Her father had been a successful tailor, but Ria had still never seen so much gold in her life. It was difficult to even fathom. Yet as the mage's hands lifted and his power roared to life, the amount made more sense. This...this was almost as powerful as Toren's wild magic, but it was controlled.

Meticulously.

After a week of solid study, Ria could identify a couple of alteration-spell components in the magic that circled Tes in darkening swirls, but then the shield the other mages cast strengthened and grew more opaque, both physically and magically. As the spells reached their crescendo, Ria could barely make out the princess's form at all.

Crack.

All at once, the magic inside the shield seemed to collapse in on itself like a trap—a deadly, horrific trap. Silence reigned a heartbeat before a hollow thud. Then the spells winked out, and all Ria could see was Tes's body collapsed on the wood.

Lifeless.

BEFORE TOREN COULD STOP to think, he pulled Ria into his arms, where she pressed her face against his chest. He should have stood firm, but her little, horrified cry had been his undoing. Inside, he cursed, even as he stroked his hand over the tumble of her hair. Hadn't Mehl explained the mechanics of their plan? He was supposed to.

"Ria, be calm," Toren sent into her mind. *"That's not Tes. It's part of the illusion."*

Though she nodded, he felt her shiver.

But only a heartbeat later, she pulled free and took a step back. "Thank you, Your Majesty," she said as she wiped away a tear. "I'm afraid I wasn't prepared to see death so close. It was beyond kind for you to comfort me in the middle of your solemn duties."

He wanted so badly to smile at the deft apology, but he would not ruin her return to formality by doing so. Mehl, on the other hand... He practically vibrated at Toren's other side, no doubt prepared to hurry over to their wife's side.

Ria leaned forward enough to give Mehl a small smile. "And thank you as well, King Mehl, for your obvious concern. Though I am happy to see my attacker gone, it was a shock nonetheless."

The drums resumed, but Toren was close enough to hear his husband's growl. Had they switched places? Toren could readily admit that he was more inclined to such grousing than Mehl, so the change lent an unusual lightness to an already strange event. A lightness that required hiding before anyone noticed his mismatched mood.

Fortunately, the head mage spun and bowed before Mehl could spoil Ria's quick thinking with hasty action. "It is complete, Your Majesties. Your Grace."

"Thank you." Toren nodded toward the final piece in their plan—Vesset. "If the healer will confirm her death for the final record?"

Vesset hurried to comply, though the man knew the truth well enough. Even so, he made a good show of it, spending quite some time running his magic over the body. "No sign of life, Your Majesty."

No surprise there, since the illusion had been cast on an

assemblage of clothing, straw, and clay shaped to resemble a person. Some type of teleportation spell had swapped the decoy with the real Tes.

"Good," Toren said. Then he gestured at Macoe. "See the body properly disposed of. We will begin morning court at half past the hour."

He heard a ripple of shocked murmurs at his blunt statement as he headed up the stairs and back into the palace, and he was sorry for it. There would be a certain wariness for months after this, despite the clear charges of assault and attempted assassination he'd had read in front of the entire court. It was the main reason he'd waited to perform the "execution" that he'd initially planned to do at once. Haste would have only brought more fear.

As High King, his authority might be absolute, but acting cruelly wasn't just wrong—it was a sure way to be assassinated in truth. Death was a sentence given sparingly, and one he often passed up even when their laws allowed it. Though his ancestors had deemed it a possible sentence for striking or, if one were particular, *touching* a member of the royal family, Toren had never counted himself as precious as all that.

His apparent death sentence for their "assassin" would be analyzed at teas and dinners and balls for months. The older nobles would be perfectly aware that he would normally choose imprisonment for such a crime, and many would wonder why he'd executed a citizen of Centoi—partially at the request *of* the Centoi.

He needed to decide whether or not to sever their alliance soon. Doing so would suggest that there had been something worse behind Tes's attack than had been announced, which might settle some of the speculation. But it also risked war. Of course, if Ber was named King Ryenil's heir, war was almost inevitable. The longer he delayed the decision, the longer he would have to prepare.

So often, it was not good to be king.

ALTHOUGH MEHL HAD HEARD from Sir Macoe that Tes was safe, the week that followed her supposed death had made his nerves wind ever tighter. They couldn't risk any unusual activity, so he, Toren, and Ria hadn't seen the princess since she'd been whisked away by that spell. Not that Mehl had reason to doubt her safety. Sir Macoe hadn't appeared to leave the castle, either, but his reports remained regular. A new letter had even arrived from Ria's "cousin."

But he wouldn't rest easy until Tes was settled into the household, hopefully this very evening. According to their spies, Ber was a little over a week away if the good weather held. The longer Tes was part of the household before his arrival, the better. It would give her more time to fade from the courtiers' thoughts—and gossip.

Restless, Mehl sought out Ria while he waited for word from Feref. He didn't dare distract his husband. Toren was in his study, reading over the treaty between their kingdom and Centoi for anything useful. The alliance would surely be severed, but it was important they didn't miss any stipulations that could bring harm to their kingdom if ignored.

Toren was nothing if not scrupulous.

Mehl entered the Mage's Library, his gaze going directly to Ria's usual table. But unlike most other days, Ria wasn't there. Nor was she searching the bookshelves. Mehl frowned. Hadn't he sensed her in this general area? His ability to find her and Toren through the link wasn't as precise as hers, but it wasn't *too* far off.

Fortunately, before he could rile himself into full worry, Sir Everot directed him to the Royal Archives. But why there? She'd been given permission, of course, but Mehl had no idea what she might find there about alteration. Had past monarchs kept records on magic? He had to admit that he hadn't done much exploring in the archives, though he'd had access for over a century. There was simply never enough time.

But Ria would make time.

Smiling at the thought, he strode through the short hallway and entered the archives. The room was lit only by magic, and the dim glow gave the endless shelves a solemn, almost gloomy appearance. There were few tables, since only royals and the highest level archivists were allowed access, so it didn't take long to find Ria.

Ria…slumped across the table.

Mehl broke into a run, reaching her side almost before he could process the scene. Nearly frantic, he bent over her and pressed his fingers against her pulse as he scanned her body for injury. Only to immediately feel foolish—her breathing was slow and steady, proof enough of life. She was…sleeping?

Gods above. He'd thought there'd been a real assassin.

His heartbeat slowed its frantic pace as he noted the way her head was nestled into the crook of her arm. Her mouth was slightly open, a tiny hint of drool in the corner, and he grinned at the sight. At least the book she'd been reading was on the *other* side of her arm.

Poor Ria. They'd all been on edge the last week or two, and none of them had slept well. Considering how often they'd also made love…

A knock sounded on the door, and Ria stirred. Mehl stepped back, just in time to avoid a collision when she jerked upright with startling speed. "What? Who…?"

Ria rubbed her palms against her eyes and then blinked up

at Mehl. If not for yet another knock, he would have kissed her. "Did we keep you up too late last night, Ria?"

"Maybe." She grinned. "But that's not exactly unusual."

Mehl tucked a strand of her hair behind her ear. "We should let you sleep tonight."

"Don't you dare—" A third knock cut across her words. This time, Ria sighed before calling out, "Enter."

The door opened, but the servant stopped just inside the entrance. He held a silver tray with a note on top—a note that trembled like a fallen leaf in the breeze thanks to the man's shaking hands. Mehl smiled. There was something about this room that tended to have that effect, almost as though the kingdom's history had a force all its own. Or maybe it was simply its forbidden nature.

"Pardon me, Your Majesty," the servant said. "I have a message for Her Grace. Feref bid me to bring it in his stead."

Mehl accepted the note and carried it to Ria, anxious to hear what it said. Had Feref and Sir Macoe finalized arrangements for Tes's arrival?

It only took Ria a moment to read. "Well, then. It seems my cousin is almost here. I should head for the receiving room."

Mehl wanted to relax at the words, but he couldn't. Another plan nearly completed—but *nearly* was still too far from *completely*.

CHAPTER 46

INTEGRATIONS

Ria kept her steps measured as she and Mehl headed toward a small receiving room near the throne room. Blessedly, this meeting wasn't formal enough to require the main receiving room where she, Toren, and Mehl had first sealed the breeding contract. She wouldn't be able to look anyone in the eye while standing next to the throne where the kings had claimed her. No, this meeting would take place in more of a sitting area, one favored for generations by royal spouses and consorts for just this purpose.

They arrived before Tes, which Ria supposed was some matter of etiquette. It wasn't something Ria had run across yet in any of the books she'd grabbed in the royal archives, but finding anything there that wasn't too detailed for her needs was nearly impossible. She hardly needed to know the finer points of negotiating a trade deal while being a guest in another kingdom—she needed to know how to survive daily court life.

Ria dropped onto an overstuffed chair and rubbed at her

lower back. The latest text had been so unrepentantly dull that her lack of sleep had caught up with her, and now her back suffered from the way she'd slumped over the table to nap. The book hadn't even been useful, either. She would give the archives one more search before she asked for help. It wasn't as though her lack of knowledge was a secret.

The entire castle was probably waiting for her imminent failure.

Mehl sat in the chair beside hers. "Are you feeling unwell?"

"No," Ria answered automatically, though she wasn't sure it was true. Nerves had her heart pounding and her stomach roiling. "But I suppose I'm anxious to see how my cousin is faring."

She'd almost said "Tes," a habit that could cause a real problem. One slip could ruin all they'd done to protect the princess's identity. Nor could they refer to her as Lora. Instead, the princess had chosen Ryssa as her new name. Though a blend of Lora and Etessa, the name was common enough that it shouldn't arouse suspicion.

A servant entered through a side door and placed a tea tray on the table next to Ria. She tried not to grimace at the elaborate setup with its many cups and plates and spoons. She could pour a basic cup of tea without spilling, of course, but she had a feeling something so simple would have an elaborate series of rules here. The upper classes always came up with such random, pointless things to weed out the likes of her.

Mehl's frown was for her, though, not the tea service. "Do you dislike tea? You're practically glaring at it."

Had she been? "I was merely wondering how complicated it will be to drink it."

"Ah." Comprehension cleared the worry from Mehl's face. "Not as much as you might think, but more than you're probably prepared for. I wouldn't worry over it at the moment, though. Your cousin won't know our court etiquette either, and I hardly care. It's a waste of time as far as I'm concerned."

She should have known he'd understand, since he was a former bodyguard. But of course, her "cousin" probably had more rules of etiquette memorized than Ria and Mehl combined. Tes—Ryssa—wouldn't be able to say anything about it, but she would see every misstep. Why did that bother Ria so much?

The door opened, and two guards swept in ahead of a woman in a plain, black gown—decent quality, but decidedly merchant class. Pale blonde hair had been braided and pinned into a simple knot at the base of her head, and her face was free of cosmetics. But there had to be some illusion at play, for Ria barely recognized the princess as she advanced.

Regardless, Ria leapt to her feet and hurried over to grab the woman's hands. "Oh, Ryssa, I'm so happy you made it safely."

It was no lie. As their hands linked and the princess gave her a tremulous smile, a profound sense of relief swept through Ria. The spells had worked. Tes truly hadn't been executed. Not that she'd thought Toren and Mehl had lied to her. It was simply difficult for her heart to refute the apparent evidence that she'd seen with her own eyes.

"Thank you for hosting me here," Ryssa said softly. Then her gaze slid behind Ria, and she gasped. "Oh! Is this…?"

The princess was skilled at pretending, indeed. Ria did her best to match her, but she feared she fell short. She'd forgotten that Ryssa and Mehl would require introduction. Hastily, she stepped back to provide a clear view between them.

"King Mehl, please allow me to introduce my cousin, Ryssa Moyair."

Ryssa sank into a deep curtsey, but there was a trembling lack of refinement in the motion. As befitted a merchant's wife, Ria supposed. But Mehl showed no lack of politeness as he stepped up beside Ria and inclined his head.

"Please rise, Madame Moyair," Mehl said. "I hope you will accept my condolences for your loss."

Wobbling slightly, Ryssa stood, and Ria almost darted out a hand to offer steadiness. But there was a hard glint in the princess's eyes that suggested the movement had not been weakness. "Thank you, Your Majesty. Please do call me Ryssa. Being referred to as Madame...it hardly feels fitting now, what with my husband..."

Oh, the things the princess could say in that heavy trail of silence. It was masterful, really, the way Ryssa had said nothing but the truth—except for her name—and yet followed their story precisely. No doubt the guards who'd escorted her in would carry the tale of the royal consort's sad, widowed cousin without question.

"You needn't talk about it," Ria assured her. "Your letters were enough to detail your grief."

Ryssa smiled. "Bless you, cousin. I am touched by your kindness."

"I'm afraid I'm hoping you will do *me* a kindness," Ria said. Another partial truth. This hadn't been planned for her benefit, but it might become such all the same. "If you'll sit, I'll explain."

Although the princess nodded, she gave Mehl a shy, uneasy glance as Ria directed her to the chair he'd previously occupied. And wouldn't any commoner be nervous to be seated casually in the same room as the king? The only thing worse would have been Toren's presence, but they'd already planned for him to avoid this particular meeting. Ryssa's acting could only go so far.

Mehl sat across from them, his posture easy and casual. "Consider me here as Ria's...partner. Not as king," he said.

Ryssa's hands trembled in her lap. "Very well."

"Would you like tea?" Ria offered.

"I..." The princess's eyes met hers, silently questioning. *Should I do it?* At Ria's hesitant smile, Ryssa nodded. "Though it is not my place, would you allow me to pour for you? I'm afraid my manners might prove inadequate for this court, but I would like to do so, all the same."

"Please do," Ria said. "I'm certain you'll do beautifully."

Naturally, Ryssa dispensed with the chore with a simple grace, only a slight rattle here and there to imply inexperience. Ria released a slow, silent sigh, conscious of the guards, and tried to relax as the princess handed her a cup. Served by the Jewel of Centoi. What a strange turn her life had taken! But Tes —Ryssa—was kinder than one might expect. She'd understood perfectly how uncomfortable the tea service had made Ria.

She held the cup and saucer the same way the others did, but she couldn't bring herself to drink. Her nervous stomach refused the idea. "Now. As I implied in my letter...what I really need is a lady's companion."

Ryssa froze. "Oh, I am not a lady."

"Nor am I," Ria replied with some amusement. "I am more concerned with the companion part. We may not have seen each other since we were younger, but I know you better than anyone here at court. I merely need a friend. Otherwise, there's no one to speak to besides Toren and Mehl."

The princess pretended to give the matter a great deal of thought, asking questions and discussing logistics until the tea was cold. Of course—easy acceptance would have been odd for a commoner being thrust into the royal court.

Ria should know.

TOREN HAD every intention of protecting Tes. She was family now, and he had given his word. But after three dinners at his table, he had nothing but regret for the way he'd gone about it. As Ryssa, the princess was soft-spoken and pleasant, barely noticeable in her seat to Ria's left. If he hadn't known better, he would believe she *was* a merchant's widow.

Yet she made Ria uncomfortable.

He hadn't expected that since his wife had been enthusiastic about helping Tes. Ria had even made the woman a couple of dresses to augment what Toren had procured. So why, then, did she spend most of dinner picking at her food and tapping her foot underneath the table where the courtiers couldn't see? It had to be the princess.

By the gods, he couldn't tolerate it. *"Should we find another shelter for Tes?"*

Her startled gaze flitted to his face, then away. *"Of course not. Why?"*

"You're not eating, and if you tap your foot any harder, you'll manage to vibrate the stone."

"I will not." Her lips turned down. *"If you must know, I'm nervous. How could I not be? Your brother will be here within the week. What if he figures out the truth about Tes? Ryssa, I mean. We really need to be cautious not to slip when speaking of her."*

So it was only indirectly related to *Ryssa*. Even so, Ria's pallor bothered him. Was she worrying herself sick over it all? Mehl had found her napping in the archives the day the princess had arrived. Despite his own body's protest, he'd ensured she slept better every night since, but she didn't seem much better. She'd almost dozed off at the previous dinner.

"If this is affecting you so poorly—"

"You'd better not threaten to throw Ryssa out," Ria snapped

into his mind, though her annoyed huff was audible enough for Mehl to lift a brow.

"I didn't say I would." Not that he hadn't considered relocating the woman, but that action held too much danger. *"However, I wonder if one of the healers might have a tonic to calm your fears, or at least ease the physical symptoms."*

Ria's hand tightened on her spoon. *"Really, Toren, stop. I'll be fine. Anyway, I eat far better when I'm not stuck in front of the entire court, too. Don't you see the sly looks Ryssa and I receive?"*

Oh, he did, and he made note of each one. Any he missed would be duly cataloged by either Mehl or Feref, no doubt. Toren couldn't force anyone to like Ria, nor would he attempt it. But he could make it clear in a myriad of ways that they would do best to treat his and Mehl's wife with politeness.

Thanks to his temper, their link was no longer a secret. He'd announced it formally the day after his slip of the tongue. With that in mind, the boldness of some of those glances bore greater watching. Did they truly think he and Mehl would sever their link with Ria to marry one of the noble ladies below, the same ladies they'd had plenty of time to consider already?

It would be a foolish thing for the noble houses to hope for, but if not that, there might be something darker at play. Undercurrents of dissent could flow toward treachery, and that wasn't a good thing amidst his brother's threat. He made note to discuss the matter with Mehl and Macoe.

"Do you feel unsafe because of their stares?" Toren asked instead of answering her previous question directly.

Ria's glance swept over the crowd. *"Not exactly, but my stomach still won't untwist itself. I suppose I'll simply have to become accustomed to the attention."*

Ryssa peered at Ria, and the princess's brow lined with a slight frown for a moment. Then she noticed Toren's regard and returned her attention to her plate. Had that been worry—

or calculation? He gave brief consideration to summoning one of the healers to examine Ria's food, but before he could, Ria offered Ryssa a slice of honeyed fruit. The princess accepted without hesitation.

What in the world was wrong with him? Simply to become Ria's companion, the princess had been required to swear multiple, magically binding oaths. She'd done nothing to earn such mistrust. Hadn't she been victimized enough by his brother?

Unfortunately, his unease lingered even after the plates were cleared and they stood to leave. In the flurry of rising courtiers, Mehl leaned close. "What is it?"

"Ria," Toren whispered. "Look at her."

She was speaking softly to Ryssa in a tone too low to hear, but the stark white of her skin stood out well enough. Quickly, he sent a request to the head healer to check every plate and goblet that had been on the table, just in case. If not poison, the food itself could have been off.

It was a good thing he'd refused to allow her to enter and leave the dining hall behind instead of beside them. He kept his eye on her as they turned to begin the procession down. But Ria only made it a few steps toward the end of the table before she faltered. He spun to offer support, but Mehl was faster.

As Mehl caught Ria mid-collapse, Toren's power surged until his eyes ached from the force. Tes flinched, but she hurried to Ria's side without hesitation. Toren halted her with a single, fiery glance.

"What did you do?" he demanded, his voice a bare, pained whisper beneath the sound of the shocked courtiers.

"Nothing!" Tes insisted, shaking her head frantically. "It's probably your fault."

He clamped down on his power with a ruthless mental hand. "Explain."

"Well. Do you think she might be...?" Tes's words trailed off, but her palm cupped the slight bump of her own stomach. "The way she was acting, I wondered..."

Toren's mind went completely blank.

CHAPTER 47

THE EXAM

Mehl had barely managed to catch Ria before she hit the floor, but it was an awkward hold. He scooped her up into a more secure position, one of his arms beneath her knees and the other cradling her back. With her head nestled against his shoulder, the steadiness of her breath along his neck brought him a tiny amount of comfort. She might be ill or injured, but she was alive.

Whatever Toren and the princess had been whispering about appeared to be resolved, for they fell silently into line behind him when he started to move. Had Ryssa blamed Toren? Surely not. His husband would have ordered her to remain behind—or to return to her rooms—had she dared something like that. But had he missed something important? Unfortunately, Mehl had been too intent on steadying Ria to pay much attention.

The sounds of the crowd faded to a low, indistinguishable rumble as they rounded the High Table and advanced toward the doors. The courtiers' shocked murmurs didn't matter. What Mehl noted were the expressions of those he passed, whether surprised, worried—or smug. Especially the smug. Anyone at these tables could be a threat, and if he discovered any here were to blame for Ria's condition, he would run them through himself.

Once out of the dining hall, Mehl hurried toward the nearest sitting room. There were a ridiculous number of them in this section of the palace to allow for smaller, more private gatherings amongst the courtiers, but in this moment, he found himself grateful for the extravagance. It allowed him to find a quiet, comfortable room for Ria away from any prying eyes—and it would be easier to guard.

Mehl halted in the middle of the room, Toren closing the door behind them. A quick scan of the area revealed two sofas that would make a comfortable spot for Ria to rest, but he couldn't bring himself to let her go. In his arms, she was warm and alive, her breath a balm to his nerves.

Then a puff of that breath hit his neck more sharply, and her head rocked against his shoulder. His eyes went straight to her face, only to collide with her confused, worried gaze. "Mehl?"

"Relax, Ria," he answered gently. "You merely fainted."

Her lips twitched. "Merely?"

"You've been under a great deal of stress recently. I'm certain it is only that."

As Toren rushed over to stand on Ria's other side, Mehl could tell that she didn't fully believe his words by the way she continued to stare at him. But then Toren cupped her head in his hand, and she shifted her attention to their husband. It was a timely reaction, for Mehl didn't want to confess the darker worries plaguing him, not until she was stronger.

Could Ber have found another way to strike?

He found himself eyeing Ryssa where she stood by the door, her hands twisting together anxiously. Logic—and a quick probe of her oathbinding spells—told him she was not to blame, but he couldn't help the kernel of doubt. Then she lifted her chin and sent him an angry, forceful frown that imparted its meaning well enough.

Look elsewhere, for it is not me.

Only a few moments passed before the healer rushed in. Ryssa had to close the door behind him, but Vesset was in too much of a hurry to notice. His attention went immediately to Mehl and Ria before scanning the area, much as Mehl had.

"Please lay her down on the sofa, Your Majesty," Vesset said, already heading to the nearest one.

Ria shifted in his hold. "I'm fine now. I can walk, Mehl."

Toren's breath hissed out, though his hand stroked hair from her face with gentle care. "You crumpled in the middle of the dining hall. Your ability to walk is under serious question."

As with so many things, Mehl was in total agreement. So instead of arguing, he simply strode to the sofa where the healer waited and settled Ria gently onto the soft surface. Ryssa was already there, too, sliding a cushion beneath Ria's head before she'd fully reclined. Mehl met the princess's eyes and noted only concern. For all their sakes, he hoped he was right.

"Please move back," Vesset said, all unruffled calm in the face of so much worry. "I would rather not struggle to keep my healing magic from locking on anyone else during the examination."

That prompted their movement as nothing else would. In moments, Mehl joined Toren and Ryssa on the other side of the room. Watching. Waiting.

And desperately praying nothing was terribly wrong.

～

THE GIDDY, joyful haze of healing magic disappeared far too soon for Ria's liking, leaving her with nothing but worry. No matter what she'd told Mehl about being fine, she was perfectly aware that something was wrong. Aside from collapsing after that blow to the head during Tes's attempted "rescue," Ria couldn't recall ever fainting before in her life. Could it be lingering effects from that?

Vesset smiled down at her. "I told you there was the potential for this."

He had? What? When? Ria cast her mind back to anything the healer might have said, but her memory was a total blank. "I don't understand."

"Ah, I see," he said, patting her hand. "I should have considered that you're still dazed, Your Highness. Forgive me. I mentioned before that you had a good chance of conceiving, and that has clearly occurred. You're with child, though it's early yet."

It took a moment for the words to trickle through, but she still couldn't quite process them even after they did. "So quickly? Surely, it hasn't been that long."

"When were your last courses?" Vesset asked gently.

Ria did her best to recall. Before she'd first come to the palace with her father for certain. How many weeks had passed since she'd entered the breeding contract? Three? Maybe four? It all blurred together at this point, but either way, it was long enough that her courses should have come. And she hadn't even noticed.

"I'm not sure," Ria confessed.

The healer's smile didn't falter. "Don't stress yourself over it. How have you been feeling? Any symptoms?"

"Sick to my stomach." And wasn't that the most obvious? Ria blushed. "I should have realized, I suppose. I've been tired and sometimes lightheaded. But with Prince Ber..."

Did the healer know the prince was on his way? She couldn't recall if Toren or Mehl had announced it, or if it was a secret best not shared. But there was no need to elaborate. Concern pinched Vesset's brow at the mention of Ber alone.

"His challenge is cause for fear. That is true," the healer said. "However, for your baby's sake, you must try to remain calm. Perhaps it would be best for you to skip court functions until your pregnancy is more settled?"

Fear speared her heart. "More settled? What does that mean?"

After a brief hesitation, Vesset sighed. "The first three months are the riskiest. It is so for nearly everyone. Your Highness, if you feel the slightest hint of stress, you must summon me at once to help calm you."

Ria found herself glancing at the princess where she stood awkwardly beside Mehl. She couldn't have been much more than a couple of months along when she'd arrived here, not if she and Ber had married right after she found out. She'd been sent here during her absolute most vulnerable time. Gods, but Ria could kill Ber herself for such cruelty.

"Calm," Vesset reminded her.

She took a deep breath through her nose and prayed for steadiness.

"Well, Vesset?" Toren snapped.

The healer turned and bowed. "Congratulations, Your Majesties. Your wife is expecting your first child."

A sense of wonder rushed through Ria at those words, though the healer had already told her. Her hand slid to her flat belly. It was difficult to believe that new life grew inside her, despite having longed for that very thing. But she was almost afraid to look at the kings. What would they feel now that their initial goal was complete? The feelings she received through their link seemed almost...numb?

"Ria," Mehl whispered, the awe in his voice drawing her attention despite her fear. Shock and pleasure lit his face, and the knot of tension inside of her eased.

But then she looked at Toren.

His skin had gone a worrisome shade of white, and his pupils had practically swallowed any color in his eyes. "It seems you were right, Ryssa," he said, almost too softly to hear.

Then he stumbled over to the nearest seat and sank down into it like a man facing his imminent demise. Her heart pounded with renewed fear, and a tiny, worried cry slipped from between her lips. This wasn't good.

Not good at all.

How often had Toren prayed for this very thing? An heir. A guarantee that his kingdom would remain safe from his brother's darkness. But that had been before. When the mother could have been anyone. Even the child itself had been a concept more than a potential person. A means to an end.

But this was their child with *Ria*, not just anyone. The love that rushed through him now was terrifying in its intensity. He'd never fathomed its depths, yet he couldn't seem to share it. Instead, he had himself shielded close. He didn't dare risk overwhelming Ria with this.

Ah, what would their child be like? Would they look like him or favor Ria? Share the burden of his useless power or have her transmutation magic? Oh, gods, what if the same darkness Ber had inherited...? No, no he would not allow it. He wouldn't even think it.

A hand settled on his shoulder, and soothing calm filled him. *"Tor? What is it?"*

"The weight of this..." Toren dropped his head into his hands

and did his best to breathe. *"I never expected to feel this much. Really, this was hardly unplanned. But how will we protect Ria and our child? Another person, Mehl. I would die for them, and we've only just found out."*

Mehl's fingers tapped restlessly against his shoulder. *"Well, you might want to share some of that sentiment with Ria. She looks like she's about to cry, considering your reaction."*

Toren straightened so quickly that his husband had to jerk back to avoid a collision. But he couldn't gather enough words for an apology. His focus was locked on the tear that slipped from the corner of Ria's eye and the way that she gripped her hands together tightly over her stomach. She wouldn't even look at him. Unlike the healer, who glared at him as though he wasn't High King but rather a criminal in need of punishment.

Toren couldn't find fault in that reaction, not after seeing the shattered look on Ria's face. Hastily, he hurried over to kneel beside the sofa. "Forgive me, Ria. I was overcome."

She sniffled. "If you have regrets, it's a little late—"

"No!" he exclaimed, a little sharper than he'd meant to. At her startled glance, he made sure to soften his tone. "No, love, I do not have regrets. I am pleased beyond measure. It was merely a shock."

Her brow lifted, and he sighed with relief at the hint of spirit returning to her demeanor. "Toren. We've spent most of our free time..." Her gaze flicked to Ryssa and then Vesset, and her cheeks went pink. "Well, I can't imagine how you're surprised. In fact, we have an entire contract over it."

"It seems concept and reality are two different things," he muttered. But he dropped a kiss on her lips before she assumed he'd spoken coldly. "I mean that in the best possible way. It's scary to be responsible for another life, and I suppose I never fully realized it until now."

Another tip of Ria's brow. "You're responsible for an entire kingdom full of lives."

"Not every moment and certainly not alone." Toren shuddered at the very thought. "Even so, I may care deeply for my people, but they aren't my heart. You, Mehl, our child…I fear my ability to keep you safe will not be sufficient, especially with my brother near."

Mehl's leg brushed his side as he eased closer. "Between the three of us, we'll manage, Tor. We'll work together to ensure our family is strong."

And wasn't that the trouble? Toren had no clue how to strengthen or guard family. Even risk to Mehl, who was a trained warrior, turned Toren's stomach with fear, because… well, he'd lost every bit of family he'd ever had. Parents, cousins—even his own twin brother. Either dead, distant, or treacherous. What did he know about keeping family close? He'd barely managed with only Mehl.

There was so much risk.

Suddenly, he had to fight the urge to make demands. To insist that Ria marry them legally—and now—so she could gain the protection of being queen. To order Ria into bed for the next several months, a ring of guards protecting her from the slightest harm until their child was safely born. Or perhaps to have her accompany him and Mehl at all times so he would always know she was secure.

He truly might do anything to protect them both.

But he couldn't, and that was possibly the greatest terror of all.

CHAPTER 48

PUNISHMENTS

Despite Ria's protests, Toren carried her back to their bedroom himself. He would not risk her fainting again. And since the healer had suggested that Ria probably wasn't eating enough at the strained court dinners, Toren ordered food to be waiting and an attendant ready to help her with a bath. Then she could finish the evening with a full night's sleep.

To say that they received stunned looks as the High King carried the consort through the halls was an understatement, but Toren refused to acknowledge them—or sate their obvious curiosity. He'd commanded Vesset and Ryssa to silence, too. It would be best not to confirm any rumors about a possible pregnancy or illness until Ber had come and gone. Ria would be in enough danger from his brother's presence without that, too.

Toren strode into their sitting room and settled Ria directly onto a chair at the small, informal dining table. He and Mehl used this spot for the occasional quick meal, but he would have her eat here far more often. He would not rely on the formal court fare to see her nourished, not with her nervousness on top of the rich food.

"You can't insist on carrying me everywhere," Ria grumbled.

"Probably not, but give us a day or two," Mehl said as he dropped onto the nearby sofa. "It's rather alarming to watch a loved one crumple like that."

A slight flush warmed Ria's cheeks, but whether it was from Mehl's endearment or her embarrassment at fainting, Toren didn't know. The door opened before he could ask, and servants streamed in, some with food and others heading toward the door leading to the bathing chamber. He examined the trays as each cover was removed. A hearty but simple bread, broth-rich soup with stomach-settling vegetables, and slices of pale, easy-to-digest meat. Oh, and a sweet pudding, but not an excessively complicated one. Finally, she was presented with two goblets—one with water and the other with juice.

As soon as the servants departed, Ria frowned up at him. "You're going to be insufferable, aren't you? Honestly, Toren. This had better not be the tasteless fare given to the truly ill, or I will contemplate violence. And you know how I hate violence."

He couldn't resist a quick, somewhat wicked grin. "There are other punishments."

"If I'm properly guessing your thoughts, that's more like a reward," she said, rolling her eyes.

But she began to eat, and since she didn't threaten bodily harm, he had to assume the cook had accurately followed his directions to avoid blandness. Satisfied, Toren retreated to the sofa. Mehl lifted his arm, and Toren settled against his warmth with a contented smile. Together, they kept an eye on Ria as she ate. Mehl played with a strand of his hair or danced his fingers along his shoulder, while Toren simply savored the feel of his husband's thigh beneath his hand.

An unexpected but perfect moment of contentment.

Ria glanced over her shoulder and smiled. "That's the happiest I've seen you both in days. Maybe ever."

Toren ran the tip of one finger up Mehl's thigh just to feel him shiver. "There is much to celebrate."

Her gaze locked on his hand. "I can think of better ways to do that."

It was tempting—so, so tempting. But there were dark circles beneath her eyes, and she slumped a little in her seat from exhaustion. She needed a full night's sleep. In truth, they all did. Stress had alternated with passion for far too many weeks now.

"No," Toren said, though he couldn't keep the regret from his tone. "None of us will find our pleasure tonight, unless that pleasure is sleep."

Mehl's leg twitched beneath his hold. "Tor—"

"We cannot afford to run ourselves ragged before Ber arrives." After a moment's hesitation, Toren moved his hand. It would not be a kindness to torment his husband further after that decree. "I'll simply have to make it up to you tomorrow."

His husband groaned, and Ria winced. But neither argued. Still, perhaps it was time for a hasty retreat. He stood so abruptly that Mehl's finger snagged his hair with a sharp twinge. "I'll use the bathing room while you finish eating, Ria. If we go in together..."

They all knew what would happen if they went in together.

～

MEHL WATCHED his husband's retreating form with equal parts bemusement and aggravation. It wasn't that Toren was wrong, exactly. Mehl could see for himself how tired Ria looked, even if she didn't want to admit it. For that matter, he was exhausted, too. There'd been far too many worry-filled days and sleepless—if worthwhile—nights to claim otherwise. But giving that little teasing caress before declaring a sex-free night?

Toren was going to pay for that.

"He can't be serious," Ria muttered.

"Oh, he is," Mehl countered. "Unfortunately."

She dropped her bread, and a look of horror crossed her face as she turned in her seat. "He's not going to do this for the entire pregnancy, is he? I will go mad."

"What, celibacy?" The thought was too horrid to contemplate with his body already so aroused. "I dearly hope not."

Ria shuddered. "As do I."

If it wasn't so frustrating, their husband's excessive worry would be endearing.

While Ria returned to her meal, Mehl contemplated how Toren would act with their first child, and he could only come to one conclusion—mush. If Toren didn't take that poor babe to court sessions at least once to keep them close, Mehl would eat his crown. Tradition be damned. If the High King wanted to hear petitions while holding a baby, he would.

And Toren would.

Though his frustration hadn't entirely faded, he wore a fond smile when his husband rejoined them. Toren quirked a brow, but Mehl didn't explain. Instead, he escorted Ria to the bathing chamber before returning to the sitting room. His husband was still standing beside the abandoned table, his absent gaze resting on the half-empty plates.

If Mehl was lucky, he would have time for a little bit of revenge. "Going to bed?"

Toren's eyes met his. "I suppose I should."

Neither of them moved. His husband wore only a dressing gown, and his long hair fell, still damp, down his back. Casual. Slightly mussed. Just the way Mehl preferred, in truth. As a young bodyguard, it had taken every speck of discipline he'd had not to stare at his High King at times like these—and more, to maintain his guard. But the thought of any injury to Toren had been worse than thwarted desire.

Now, he had no need to hold back.

Mehl crossed to his husband's side. "Shall I tuck you in? I have a bit of time before I can use the bathing chamber."

He heard the shudder in Toren's breath. "Mehl. I was serious about—"

"Oh, I am aware." Just as he knew the smile he gave was thoroughly wicked. "There shouldn't be too much danger to your virtue."

Toren huffed.

Smile widening, Mehl ran his finger along the smooth silk of the dressing robe. Down, down along the ridges of his husband's muscles. "Is this new?"

"Ria made it," Toren said, his voice going clipped.

Perfect.

Mehl let his hand slide lower. He gripped his husband's hip, his thumb caressing the dip of muscle that followed his hip bone. "It feels quite comfortable."

A hiss. "Mehl..."

One last bit of torment. With his free hand, Mehl traced the twin indentation along the other hip where it arrowed straight toward his husband's cock—and he didn't stop. But he only gave one quick, teasing caress down that hardened length before he stepped back with a grin.

"Forgive me, Tor," he said. "I forgot that decree you gave. On the sofa. With your hand sliding up my thigh. I suppose I should go see if it's my turn in the bathing chamber."

Then he strode merrily away to the sound of Toren's harsh curses.

~

RIA HAD FALLEN ASLEEP TUCKED between the kings, but they all must have shifted in the night. As she stirred awake, the edge of her hand met the end of the bed. She was curled on her side, facing away from her husbands, and based on the shadowed room, it was somewhere around dawn. She let her eyes drift closed beneath the heavy weight of her lids.

Only to be awakened fully by a deep moan. Mehl's, if she wasn't mistaken.

"You'll be quiet as I have my revenge," Toren whispered, so low her ears barely caught the sound.

Revenge? What had she missed?

The bed began to shake in an unmistakable rhythm, and instantly, she went hot and wet. Why had she been so foolish as to turn to her side? The view she was missing... Ah, but if she rolled over carefully, they might not notice the movement in the tumult. Aside from her own pleasure, she didn't want to interrupt their moment together.

Beneath the sound of a hissed moan, she slipped silently onto her back, her eyes carefully closed. The rocking didn't stop, but she waited a moment longer before finally cracking her eyelids open and turning her head slightly. And oh, what a reward. Just an arm's stretch beside her, Mehl lay on his back, his legs spread for Toren's taking.

Toren leaned over him, and the muscles on his arms stood out in relief as he braced his hands on each side of their husband's head. Her gaze trailed down Toren's chest to where his hips flexed with each thrust, Mehl's cock trapped between them. Her body went so hot she nearly tossed the bedding away for some slight relief. But no. That would disturb them for sure, and so far, they hadn't noticed she was awake.

Or so she'd thought. Suddenly, Toren's eyes met hers, and the passion there brought a gasp to her lips. Mehl stretched out a hand, his fingers linking with hers, as Toren held her gaze with blatant possession. Then he bent down to kiss Mehl, long and hard. Ah! She burned in place for approximately forever before he finally shuddered and both men cried out in release.

Gods. She was panting nearly as hard as they were.

Toren dropped down between them, but he didn't rest for long. He rolled over, his hand going to her waist. "We didn't mean to wake you."

"I would have been sad indeed to have slept through that," she said between lips gone dry.

Her husband's smile was easy, but his hands were not as he tore away the bedclothes. Hastily but gently, her gown and underclothes followed until she was spread out bare beneath him. Beside her, Mehl wiped his abdomen clean, then propped himself up on one elbow to watch them. Lazily, he reached out to trace a finger over her breast.

Toren kissed his way down her stomach, lingering a moment where their child grew before continuing on. His breath danced across her mound as he met her eyes over the length of her body. "Finally, it will be Mehl's turn to have you. But I'll not deny myself a thorough taste first."

And gods above, did he keep his word.

MEHL HAD ONLY JUST CLEANED the remnants of his release from his chest, but Toren and Ria had him hard again. Unable to fight the need to touch, he knelt beside them to better reach both. He tweaked Ria's nipple, then roamed his hand down, his flesh singing from the softness of her skin. Then the taut muscles of Toren's arm, smooth over hard, as he continued his journey all the way to his husband's ass.

It fired his blood, the way Toren worked Ria with his tongue—patient but greedy. Hungry, but delaying the full feast. Ria squirmed and bucked, and only then did his husband hesitate. Was he worried about hurting her? The healer had said that was not a concern. So Mehl gripped Toren's hair to encourage him to continue. Not restraining—but close.

Only when Ria cried out, crossing the first peak, did Toren push back against his hand. Mehl released him at once and was rewarded with a deep, Ria-and-Toren-flavored kiss. All three of them moaned at the dark heat of that sharing, but it wasn't enough.

Pulling away, Toren rose from the bed. But not to leave. Mehl shivered as his husband studied them both. "Take her," Toren commanded with a growl.

Nearly shaking with the need to claim her, Mehl knelt between Ria's thighs. But he paused to meet her gaze. Was she truly willing? Did she want him? She stared back at him with desire, but her breath still came in sharp pants from Toren's lovemaking. Perhaps he should—

"What is it?" Ria asked, worry dimming her expression.

He brushed a stray hair from her cheek and ran his finger gently along the line of her jaw. "Are you sure?"

Ria canted her hips toward him. "Gods, yes. If you don't hurry, I'll kill you."

"Threatening the king, hmm?" Mehl asked, chuckling with no small amount of relief. "I suppose I'll have to punish you as Toren did me."

Despite the seemingly harsh words, he entered her slowly. Carefully. And in her heat, he found all of them. Their desires blended through their link as Mehl claimed her, and he knew at once that this was what they'd been missing. That final piece that had kept them slightly out of sync.

He couldn't resist caressing her with each thrust. He captured her gasps and sighs with his kisses—at least until Toren lost the remainder of his control. As his husband claimed his lips in a hard kiss, Ria shuddered and cried out beneath him. Then Toren bent to suck her nipple into his mouth, and she screamed.

So perfect. So them. Mehl would never let either of them go.

And as he found his release, it was all of him they both received.

CHAPTER 49

EXCUSES

When Ria woke again, Mehl and Toren were gone. No doubt in the middle of morning court. Stretching, she savored the ache in her body from their earlier lovemaking. She'd wondered before if Toren would grow jealous once Mehl was able to physically claim her. Fortunately, he hadn't—rather the opposite. He'd been aroused enough that he'd taken her, too. She'd drifted back to sleep a happy woman.

Still, it was nice to be alone for a while. Instead of calling for a servant, she padded into the bathing room and soaped herself clean in the shower before sinking into the coolest of the soaking pools. Ah, bliss. It was soothingly warm, but not so hot that she worried about overheating and harming the baby.

The baby. Smiling, she rested her hand on her stomach. How had she been so blessed? Had the midwife boosted her fertility when removing the contraceptive spell? Or maybe the gods were taking pity on not only her, Toren, and Mehl but also their entire kingdom.

At the moment, it absolutely felt that way.

She was drying herself beside the soaking pool when Toren hurried in, his face lined with worry. "Ria! Thank the gods you are well. Once we left court, Feref told me you hadn't awakened, but when you weren't in bed…"

Smiling, she wrapped a drying cloth around her hair. "I wanted a nice soak without anyone hovering."

"And what if you had fallen?" he asked, glaring at the tile floor as though it could attack.

Truth be told, she probably should have considered that, but if she didn't stand firm now, Toren would coddle her to the edge of sanity. "I was careful. I'm sorry I worried you, but if you'd checked our link, you would've known I was fine."

"It's only…" He stepped forward to embrace her, but she held up her hands to stop him. His expression turned to hurt. "Has my concern angered you so greatly?"

Ria shook her head and gestured at his court attire. "That overrobe is embroidered velvet, and I'm still damp. If you want to ruin such fine, expensive fabric, do it out of my view."

Toren glanced down as though to confirm her words. Had the man forgotten what he was wearing? Probably, since he was accustomed to such garb. But fine flowers had been stitched along the hem of the forest green velvet and in decorative swirls along his chest. Depending on the type of thread used, there was a chance it might shrink, puckering the whole design. The servants could remove water stains from the velvet with enough effort, but the stitching—

"Perhaps I should change," Toren said, laughter in his voice.

"Please do," Ria countered primly. "I'll not have Feref angry at me again for causing the servants so much extra work."

Toren sighed with resignation, though his eyes still twinkled. Maybe she should worry about his clothing every time he went on a rant. "Very well. I'd rather wear something simpler at my desk, anyway."

She grabbed her robe from its hook and shrugged into it, then followed him to the dressing room door. "I'll go get dressed, too. And I'll call for servants so that you don't have to worry. I *am* sorry. Next time, I'll at least have someone outside the door in case I need help."

His frown suggested that he was about to argue with such light precautions, but before he could, she gave him a quick kiss and slipped out of the room. If she stuck around, he would have her bundled up in bed before she knew it—without him or Mehl. Then it might become a habit. Sleeping in was one thing, but she had far better things to do for the next nine months than lie in bed by herself.

At the moment? She wanted to finish the clothes she'd secretly been working on—formal outfits for her presentation to the court. Toren had delayed the event because of Tes's execution and the arrival of Ryssa, or Ria wouldn't have had a chance to create anything at all. The presentation would have been a few days ago, in fact. Now she would go before the court in a handful of days.

The kings had wanted to commission clothing to announce the search for a breeding alliance, and now she was creating the outfits with their child growing within her. Ria sighed. After last night, part of her wished she hadn't talked Toren out of a wedding announcement instead. For the world to know she fully belonged to them...

But that was the problem, wasn't it? The world. Her lack of knowledge would cause the kings no small amount of trouble. No matter how she felt, she couldn't allow them to invite that.

～

AT THE CASTLE wall bordering one side of the soldiers' field, Mehl placed the practice sword on the rack and then rolled his shoulders against the satisfying ache. Instead of his usual intensity, he'd felt only enjoyment as he'd gone through the drills, even when he'd sparred with Sir Macoe. He was simply too happy to do anything but revel in training, one of his favorite activities—well, his favorite outside of bed, of course.

Sir Macoe set down his own sword, but he didn't leave. Crossing to an open area beside Mehl, he slipped into stretches designed to keep his muscles limber. Mehl followed suit. An unexpected leg cramp or muscle spasm would only make Toren and Ria worry, and Toren was on edge enough. With his protective instincts roused by Ria's pregnancy, it would be a good idea to avoid catching his eye, at least with anything that would cause concern.

They went through the stretching routine in silence, until the remaining guards either left for the bathhouse or grabbed new weapons and returned to the yard to spar. "They are near the border," the captain murmured as soon as they were alone.

Mehl tensed. "The Centoi?"

"And Prince Ber," Sir Macoe said with a nod. "Are you certain he should be allowed entry? Having been exiled..."

"Though I'm not happy about it, Toren and I both think it's best," Mehl replied, much as he hated the words. "If we don't hear what he has to say openly, he'll only try to slip in through other means."

Sir Macoe lowered his arms and straightened. "I have a count and description of each person in the group, and those have been noted on a daily basis, too. We'll not be caught in another deception like the last."

Mehl rotated his wrists. "Say nothing, but put extra guards on Ria. She's with child."

"There is much speculation to that effect, since she fainted last night," Sir Macoe said. "I take it you're waiting to announce it?"

"Until Ber is gone," Mehl confirmed.

"Probably wise." Sir Macoe eyed a group of approaching warriors. "Back to work for me." The captain cleared his throat. "Thank you for your advice, Your Majesty."

That last was a little louder as the group neared, and Mehl hid a smile as Sir Macoe suddenly bowed, then walked over to the next soldier in need of a sparring session. It was a strange thing, to be at a higher rank than the person he had once trained under, but they'd settled into a respectful relationship, all the same.

But Mehl still couldn't bring himself to drop the honorific and call the captain merely Macoe, as Toren did. Some habits were buried deep, he supposed. Like storing the padding he wore for training and heading to the showers. Most times, he reminded himself to use his own bathing chamber in the palace, but when he wanted a moment alone, he let himself follow routine.

Though once, he would have done none of this alone. Not really. Warriors lived and worked in close quarters, so it was a little unnatural that the others made themselves scarce when he trained. Today, the bathhouse was mostly empty already, but the few who'd been there made short work of cleaning up and hurrying out. He didn't even know their names to bid them farewell.

Such things usually soured his mood, but this time, they only dulled it. Other warriors might avoid him because he was now king, but not Ria. She'd taken him in—body and soul—like a gift, just as Toren did. If two people could care for him so much, then the loneliness he was subjected to during training truly had nothing to do with *him* as a person.

If others couldn't handle his rank, then it was their problem.

~

RIA'S WORKSHOP was connected by a single door to the room where she did measurements and fittings, and she'd never been more grateful for that separation than now. She didn't want any of the court ladies to see these designs and ask for something similar in an attempt to undercut Ria's presentation. And some of those vipers would.

Not all, by any means. Most of the ladies were carefully neutral, and she respected that. Life could be difficult at court even without a newcomer with an uncertain social status to deal with. But there were also several women who had been genuinely friendly. Well, potentially genuine. It could be difficult to tell considering court machinations, but she'd never heard any dire rumors about the women in question during her years of doing fittings for her father. Ria knew more about the people here than they realized thanks to that.

She ran her finger down the soft, silver fabric on the nearest stand. This robe was Mehl's, the cloth chosen to compliment his dark hair. Creating the spells for the embroidery had taken some time, but she was pleased with the effect. Green leaves the same shade as Toren's robe and brown whorls that would complement her dress—if she ever finished it— gave the effect of a forest in the moonlight.

A fine match for Toren's, a deep royal green embroidered with countless silver sparks of light. She'd added more of the earth-brown whorls at the hems of his, too. But what should she do for hers? Ria tilted her head to study the cloth pinned together on the dress stand. She was simply too undecided about the brown to actually stitch it together, much less add embellishment. What had she been thinking? It would go well with her coloring...because it was the same shade as her hair. Unless she wore her hair up, they would blend together terribly.

After a quick knock on the door, Tes—Ryssa—peeked in. "Your companion is here, ready to accompany."

Ria smiled at the cheerful words. "Come in, Ryssa. See what you think."

Understanding Ria's caution, the princess hurried in and closed the door quickly before anyone could see. Though Ria didn't expect any clients, there was always the possibility of a nosy, spying servant tipping off one of the ladies. It would be silliness to risk offending Toren with such an action, but she'd learned never to underestimate the wiles of a bored and/or malicious noble.

Ryssa frowned at Ria's unfinished dress. "Oh, you can't get married in brown."

"Married?" Ria's heart plummeted, and her ever-present nausea surged until she had to close her eyes and breathe through it. "What has Toren done now?"

"Got you with child?" Ryssa asked with amusement. "Linked with you and Mehl? I assumed a wedding would follow. Is that not what these clothes are for?"

Ria sighed with relief. "So Toren didn't make any announcements at court?"

"Not that I'm aware of," the princess answered. "But I wasn't there since you weren't."

"Thank the gods," Ria breathed, finally daring to open her eyes again as her stomach somewhat settled. "I thought you knew something I didn't. These outfits are for my presentation, when the details of the breeding alliance are to be formally read. And before you ask, Toren and Mehl *do* want to marry me, but I refused. Our existing contract will secure our child's future well enough for now."

Ryssa gaped at her. "But why? It's obvious that you care for them."

"That's why," she said, trying to smile at the princess. And probably failing. "A tailor's daughter as queen? I would be a constant source of embarrassment, if not active trouble. I can't do that to them."

The princess took her hand—then gave it a rough shake. "After all I've seen, I absolutely cannot imagine Toren being embarrassed about anything, and Mehl comes from equally humble origins. Your words sound more like an excuse than a reason."

Ria scowled. "Easy for you to say. You are a princess, complete with all the training that entails."

"Yes, training to be the sole monarch after my father's death. Look how that turned out." Ryssa's lips twisted for a moment, but then her expression smoothed. "However, here... Toren and Mehl already have a routine. They would no doubt ease you into any new duties, not hand you the running of the palace and bid you good luck."

There was truth in that. The kings didn't *need* help, and at this point, she was lucky Toren let her walk. Even so... "Court functions already verge on disaster."

"Ria." The sudden intensity on Ryssa's face caught her by surprise. "You could stand in the middle of morning court making gowns, and Toren would stare down anyone who lifted a brow. He'd probably make your designs official court wear. As I said, you are not going to embarrass him. Also...I'm here as your companion. You helped save my life. If you want me to give advice in formal settings or any other, I'm happy to oblige."

"I..."

Ria couldn't think of a single way to express her lingering fears, but Ryssa didn't seem to expect her to. "Think on it," the princess said. "In the meantime, how about gold or cream for your dress? You could add brown, green, and silver embroidery to pull it all together."

It was an excellent idea, one she started to explore as soon as the princess left to inquire about tea. But comparing fabric swatches was far easier than weighing Ryssa's other words against her own fears. *Was* she only making excuses?

Or could she really dare to marry the men she loved?

CHAPTER 50

CONFESSIONS

Toren picked at the salad in front of him, unable to tolerate more than a couple of bites before his stomach threatened rebellion. Ironic, since he'd chided Ria for not eating enough. However, not only was her court presentation tomorrow, but they'd received a formal missive from Ber earlier, delivered at morning court for maximum impact. He'd requested an official meeting in two days.

By rights, Toren could have denied his entry to the kingdom after his exile, but that would have been the wrong choice for several reasons. For one thing, Ber rode under the flag of the kingdom of Centoi, which was still technically an ally, and there was no telling what position he held there after Tes's supposed death. Toren wasn't yet prepared to challenge their treaty. Aside from that, Ber knew the palace's secrets as well as Toren did.

Better to face him in the open than find his knife in the dark.

"Are you unwell, Toren?" Ria asked with concern. "You're not picking up my nausea through our link, are you?"

He startled a little at the question, and chagrin flashed through him. Truthfully, he'd forgotten Ria and Mehl were even at the table. They didn't always share the midday meal, but that was hardly an excuse. This was the smaller, more intimate dining room used for family meals, not some formal banquet hall. Though he sat at the head of the rectangular table, Mehl was in the first seat to his right and Ria to his left.

Not exactly easy to miss.

"Forgive my inattention," Toren said. "I was lost in thought."

Ria's brow wrinkled. "I'm not worried about how much attention you're paying me. You've barely touched your food."

"She's right," Mehl said.

Ah, excellent. Now Mehl was studying him with a concerned frown, too.

Might as well confess.

"My stomach does feel a little uneasy," Toren said, stabbing one of the purple leaves almost rebelliously. "I suppose it's possible I'm picking up on your nausea, Ria, but I suspect it is mostly stress. Not only is your presentation tomorrow, but Ber made a formal request to meet with us in two days. I worry over what he has planned. We still have a few years before he can complete his challenge for the throne, so what is behind all this effort?"

Having been at morning court, Mehl had already known about the missive, but Ria had been too tired to attend. Gods, Toren hated to tell her anything that would cause fear or concern. But what else could he do? She needed to prepare for this as much as they did. In the worst case, she could be a target.

Her hand shook as she lowered her fork, and he found he

couldn't bring himself to eat the leaf he'd speared. "Out of curiosity," Ria said, her voice trailing off on a note of hesitation. "What happens to Prince Ber's challenge if you marry a second time?"

"A second time?" Toren asked, startled. That was an odd response to his news. "Do you think my brother will attempt to harm Mehl? That would not serve his purposes since, yes, I could remarry. That would give me another hundred years."

Mehl's gaze flickered between them, but his emotions were unreadable.

Unlike Ria, whose blush betrayed her embarrassment. "No, no. I didn't mean... I don't even want to consider something happening to Mehl. I was more thinking... If the three of us *do* formally marry at some point, how would that affect the challenge?"

Toren's mouth dropped open. What was she suggesting? That she would marry them to stop Ber? His hand tightened around his fork until it bit into his skin. He wanted *her*, not political expediency. He'd once thought he might be willing to convince her by nearly any means necessary, but apparently, he'd thought wrong. Such a thing had not occurred to him, and he was surprised by how much it hurt.

On top of it all, he couldn't even answer her question.

"I don't know," he replied, more sharply than he'd intended. "I could search through the royal archives for the records about the full law and the spell used to bind it, but I won't. Because I would never marry you for *that*."

"Marry for..." Ria's eyes widened. "Oh, no, I didn't mean it that way. I'm sorry, Toren. I've been contemplating the future, and that question occurred to me in the process. It would never be why I married."

Toren's heart skipped a beat. She'd been seriously considering a future marriage? After her initial reaction, he'd feared she would never be ready. Had he been wrong? Though he wanted to demand she explain, he clenched his teeth together to stop the impulse. She hated when he pressured her, and no matter what, any inquiries from the High King could be considered that, even when he spoke only for himself.

He cast a helpless glance at Mehl, but his husband was already staring at Ria. "Should we ask questions," Mehl said, "Or are you keeping your thoughts and feelings about this close?"

Her blush deepened. "I should have known I couldn't dance around this, and I suppose it isn't fair to do so. Yes, you may ask, but I could simply tell you. I've been trying to decide what to do about marriage. The truth is, I want to be bound to you both more than I could ever have imagined, but I'm struggling with my worry. Ryssa said it would be impossible to embarrass you. But what if she's wrong?"

Toren barely heard anything beyond "I want to be bound to you both." What could be more important than that? Yet he hesitated to say what was in his heart—that he would haul her to the temple right now if his high-handedness wouldn't upset her. It would be easy enough to accomplish. He'd already had his scribes draw up the proper contracts in case she ever changed her mind.

"If I didn't embarrass Toren, then you won't," Mehl said, his brow lifting in Toren's direction.

"Ah. Yes. Or rather, no, you wouldn't." Toren cleared his throat and prayed he could produce a coherent sentence or two. "You could never cause such an emotion in me. Rather, I would happily banish any who dared to mock you."

She gasped. "Toren! You can't simply banish people for something as small as that."

"Mockery of our beloved queen would not be small," he

said. "But perhaps a demotion would do. Any noble that foolish shouldn't be in charge of others, at the least."

As Ria stared at him in shock, Mehl laughed. "I don't know why you're surprised, love. The only thing I find unexpected is that Tor hasn't hurried us both to the temple already."

Toren tapped his finger against his lower lip. It was such an appealing thought. But... "Ria deserves a full royal wedding, complete with all the pomp and celebration she desires. As I said, I am not marrying her for expediency's sake. We may take all the time she wishes."

"I'm not even sure I've agreed," Ria pointed out. "Or that you've truly, officially asked."

With Mehl to his right and Ria to his left, it was easy for him to take both their hands. He glanced at Mehl, who nodded, before turning to Ria. "Will you do us the honor of marrying us in the grand temple in front of all? It would bring my heart joy for the world to see the depth of our full commitment."

"As it would mine," Mehl said. "Will you, Ria?"

She sat so very still, her expression frozen with disbelief. A tear slipped from her eye, and his heart cracked. Had he pressed too soon, after all? The words had felt right, but perhaps he had ruined everything. She pressed her fingers to her lips, and another tear slipped free.

But then she nodded. "Yes. I'm terrified you will regret it, but yes."

Relief loosened his hold on their hands, but it was just as well. Immediately, he rose, a love and joy too profound for words filling him until it was impossible to remain seated. He scooped Ria into his arms so quickly that her chair toppled over, but he merely grinned over at Mehl.

"This calls for a celebration, don't you think?" Toren asked. "Whatever you have planned for the afternoon, cancel it."

Then he carried Ria all the way back to their bedchamber, gawking courtiers be damned.

~

RIA SQUIRMED in her seat and smiled at the secret, delicious ache the movement brought. She'd been well-rewarded for her bravery in accepting the kings' proposal, that was certain. She could only thank the gods for the soaking pool in their bathing chamber, or her muscles might have gone stiff after so much exertion.

Now, she only had an hour to spend in the archives before she would need to get dressed for dinner. Toren and Mehl had both told her she needn't go, but she couldn't avoid court functions forever, especially not after their engagement was announced. It also seemed a poor choice to show weakness only a couple of days before Prince Ber's arrival, even if she would rather be reading.

"*You're* looking satisfied, and *I'm* ready to flee at the first opportunity," Ryssa said, her hands clenched tight atop the table. "I can't believe they let me in here."

Ria patted the top of her hand. "You are family," she said, but she didn't miss the bodyguard's presence beside the door. "The kings trust that my cousin is up to no harm. I'm sure you bring Mehl comfort. He has worried about me being in here alone since the time he found me napping in my seat."

"You fell asleep here?" Ryssa blinked at her, then laughed. "And you didn't realize you were...far too exhausted?"

She understood what the princess wouldn't say with the guard so near. How hadn't Ria realized she might be pregnant? "I suppose I didn't want to slow down enough to listen to my body. There's so much for me to learn. And looking at the time, I'd better get busy learning it."

Tipping her head down, Ryssa pulled out the needlework she'd brought, but before she started working, she moved down another seat. "I do not want to know *any* of the secrets in this room," the princess muttered in explanation.

So that was why she was so nervous. Ria winced. Why hadn't it occurred to her that the princess of Centoi might be uncomfortable in the restricted royal archives of another kingdom? Ria had anticipated that Toren and Mehl might dislike Ryssa's presence here, but she really should have considered the princess's feelings. Learning the wrong thing could put her in an awkward position, indeed. Next time, she would wait until one of the kings could accompany her.

But they were already here, so Ria might as well use her time wisely. She opened the first tome she'd grabbed, a text so old that the pages had slightly yellowed and the ink had started to fade despite all the preservation spells imbued into the book. Toren couldn't remember if the laws made provision for marrying a second person while still wed to the first, but she intended to find out. She would happily forgo a long engagement and fancy wedding if it saved them all—entire kingdom included—some grief.

Really, she could forgo the fancy wedding altogether. Just the thought of that much scrutiny made her feel a little sick.

The reading, on the other hand, made her incredibly bored. It wasn't only the sheer number of laws established when the kingdom had been formed—it was the wording. The text was so lengthy and archaic that she struggled to keep her mind from drifting, and where it wanted to drift right now was straight into sleep.

Her time was nearly up before she muddled through enough pages to reach the laws of succession and how that succession might be challenged. There were more than she'd expected, and there were multiple things that could be used to prevent an unsuitable heir from claiming the throne. But what about for an existing monarch?

She found that a couple of pages further in. Sure enough, the first such law detailed the birthright challenge, which allowed another of royal blood to make a claim if the current monarch hadn't produced an heir a century after marriage. If that spouse was lost before the allotted time, the monarch would have another century after their next marriage. Nothing about concurrent marriages, though.

But what was this note? *For spell component, see RRK, p223.* Ria placed a bookmark between the pages and flipped to the front of the book, hoping to find a definition for RRK. Nothing there—or in the back when she looked. What kind of reference tome didn't give details about what it referenced?

She wanted to slam the book closed, but she couldn't. Not without earning the Head Archivist's wrath. She could only allow herself a frustrated groan loud enough to earn a questioning look from Ryssa. Unless Ria wanted to get an archivist involved, it seemed she would have to ask Toren.

In the meantime, she had to prepare for dinner.

CHAPTER 51

INEVITABLE

Ria frowned over at Toren for what had to be the tenth time since dinner had begun. He was so tense that even the courtiers at the nearest table eyed him uncertainly. Apparently, their afternoon hadn't relaxed him nearly as much as it had her. She wanted to ask him about the research tome, but not if he was already upset about something.

Mehl leaned closer to Toren and spoke low, but his question drifted her way. "Is there something we should be aware of, Tor?"

The High King sighed into his wine glass. "I want to make the announcement tonight, but it's better to wait until Ria's presentation tomorrow."

She lifted a brow. "*The* announcement?"

"Since we're not sweeping you away to the temple," Toren said wryly, "Then an engagement announcement it will have to be."

"But why is it best to wait until tomorrow if you're this worried about it tonight?" she asked.

He sighed again. "I know how much you hate attention. Besides, I'm already worried enough that you'll faint again after dinner without adding additional strain. You *did* eat something beforehand, right?"

His concern for her was what stressed him so? Ria's heart warmed, and a flush of pleasure rushed over her. Still, he needed to calm down. The sentiment was sweet of him, but his tension bothered her more than the attention would. Well, possibly. She didn't exactly relish the stares she was about to receive.

But she would have to get used to them if she were to be queen.

An alarming thought best left untouched right now.

"If you continue to look so unhappy, they'll never believe you're pleased about the engagement when you do give notice," Ria pointed out. "Go ahead and make the announcement when you wish. It might be better, anyway. Tomorrow will be long enough without more piled on, and there will be more time for the nobles to process the news before I have to speak to them."

Toren studied her face. "Are you sure?"

"Yes," Ria insisted. "So stop the angst."

Chuckling softly, Mehl gave her a wink.

"After this course, then," Toren said.

Ria glanced down as a plate of fish was set in front of her. She tried not to wrinkle her nose at the smell that wafted up. There was absolutely no way she would be able to eat this without casting the first two courses back up in front of the entire court, but if she didn't at least try, Toren's renewed ease would disappear once more. Certainly, the nearest nobles would notice if she sat here with an entire dish untouched.

This time, it was Ryssa who leaned close. "Just cut up the

food and bring the fork to your mouth periodically. No one is close enough to see if the tines are empty."

"Except Toren," Ria muttered.

Which brought his immediate attention, of course. "What was that, love?"

Ria started cutting up the fish as she searched for a distraction. Would it upset him again to ask about the research tomes? Ah, well. If it did, it would at least be better than another lecture about food.

"After my latest trip to the archives, I was wondering... what book is RRK?"

Toren sputtered, nearly choking on the sip of wine he'd just taken. He took several more long pulls from the cup to hide his reaction. Or to avoid answering her question, which seemed about as likely.

"Ah, nothing important," he said. When he took a bite of fish, she assumed that would be all—but then he connected mentally. *"What were you reading? RRK stands for* The Rites and Rituals of the Kingdom. *Only I can unlock that one. Literally. Not even Mehl's energy will open the vault that holds it."*

Well, that explained why there'd been no clearer description of the initials in the book she'd read. It was a code intended for the High King to understand and no one else. *"I wanted to see if there was any mention of what would happen to Ber's challenge after we marry."*

His lips pinched tight. *"It doesn't matter, since I'm not marrying you for that."*

"It matters because I want to know," Ria countered. *"I want to wed you both regardless, but if it does change the level of threat for the better, that would be a comfort for all. Do you want to sit around worrying for months if there's no need?"*

"We'll know as soon as the vows are said." Toren's mental voice was suddenly heavy with exhaustion. *"The magic that*

binds our laws is deep and unmistakable. Ah, but most do not realize the weight we carry to rule this land, and me in particular. I am forever the focal point, so it will hit me the hardest."

Everyone in the kingdom learned that many of their laws were sealed with magic, but it was a revelation to hear that they were sealed through the High King to such an extent. How much harder must that be with his intense well of power? It was a terrible burden.

Ria forced a smile to remain on her face, but she lifted the empty fork to her mouth with an annoyed swipe. *"I'm sorry."*

"You realize there was no food on that, right?" Of course Toren hadn't missed that detail. *"As for the other, I'm well accustomed to it. However, if it will ease your heart, I'll let you read the relevant passage in The Rites and Rituals. Just eat."*

She nearly dropped her fork. He would let her read a book so secret that only he could unlock it? Suddenly, it wasn't merely the scent of fish that made her queasy. She could hardly fathom receiving such trust. But she didn't want to make him rescind the offer by saying so.

"The smell is making me sick," Ria said instead. *"Ryssa suggested this to avoid notice by the courtiers."*

Toren gave a slight, if frowning, nod and let the subject drop. Thank goodness. Ria relaxed against the seat for one blissful moment. Soon, she would be the center of attention, so she should enjoy the respite while she could.

A STRANGE FEELING twisted Mehl's gut, and he had the uncomfortable suspicion that it was jealousy. He wanted dearly to deny it. Tried to ignore it, in fact. But the longer Toren's and Ria's mental conversation went on, the deeper the sour feeling bit. Ah, it made no sense. He'd watched the two of them make love that very afternoon and had experienced only desire. Why be jealous now?

But really, he knew.

Mehl had no clue what RRK could be.

There was no doubt Toren was sharing that secret knowledge with Ria. Her eyes had widened with shock at one point, and Toren wore his somber, this-is-important expression. Even more, Mehl could feel their mental conversation because of the link. It was like knowing two people whispered about you behind a column but being unable to hear what they said.

He still hadn't shaken it by the time the course was nearly over. Would it show during the announcement? He was elated that Ria had agreed to marry them, but even so, this new, dark emotion might mar things. He would have to find some way to purge it—and fast.

Toren nudged him under the guise of reaching for his cup. *"Tell me what's wrong."*

He should have known that Toren would be the one to do the purging. *"Fine. I was jealous."*

Mehl caught a flash of Toren's surprise. *"Of Ria and I speaking? A few hours ago, she had my cock in her mouth while you took her from behind, but you're upset that we spoke mentally?"*

"Ah." Jealousy or no, he went semi-hard at the reminder. *"Not exactly. It's only...I don't know what RRK is, and we've been married for nearly a century. Together for longer. How have I not earned enough trust to hear of it?"*

Toren's sudden laugh earned more than one odd glance. *"And you've probably spent less time in the royal archives during that time than Ria has in the last couple of days. Had you ever spent hours pouring over law books and stumbled upon that mention, I would have eased your curiosity, too."*

Was it relief or annoyance at himself that flushed hot through his body? Ria had said it was a book, hadn't she? He should have considered that it was a matter of interest and not trust that had led Toren to share with her first.

"I was being foolish."

"Yes." Toren smiled over the lip of his cup. *"But I imagine jealousy will happen to all of us from time to time. You know it has happened to me. It's inevitable. Also, if you must know, RRK stands for* The Rites and Rituals of the Kingdom. *Only I can unlock its vault, but I haven't had cause to bother for a few centuries now. It details the spells behind our laws, and I'm not a mage to have use of such information. I'll show it to you at the same time as Ria, if you like."*

Mehl shook his head. *"I'll do no better than you with such a book."*

Even though his jealousy had been unreasonable, the information eased the silly emotion all the same. But he supposed Toren was right—such feelings were inevitable. Gods knew he'd felt a similar envy before, though not because of someone they both loved as they did Ria. Whether it was a clingy courtier or merely endless meetings taking Toren's time, the bite was the same.

"We should both stand for the announcement," Toren said. Then he hesitated. *"If you would like, that is."*

Apparently, embarrassment was inevitable, too. *"Of course I would."*

Then together, they told the world of their new happiness.

By the time he woke the next morning, Toren loathed the day he'd announced this presentation. Not because of the event itself. It was more that Ria's anxiety now had him twisted up with worry, not to mention the dregs of Mehl's insecurity the night before. It was true that misunderstandings would happen, but all the same, he hated that he'd inadvertently hurt his husband. He would have to watch closely to ensure that Mehl felt no lack.

Ria rubbed the tip of her nose against Toren's chest. "We should get moving. Today is not the day to be late."

On his other side, Mehl slid his hand across Toren's waist, earning a groan, as he pulled free of their tangled limbs and sat up. "She's right. Gods know Feref is probably pacing the dressing room already, and we've yet to make it to the bathing room."

"What?" Ria bolted upright. "Is it that late?"

Mehl laughed. "No. Feref's that obsessed with a proper presentation. Get ready to have your hair wound around some kind of tiara after last night's announcement. He'll have you dressed like a princess."

"Oh! About that…" Both excitement and nerves danced in her eyes as she nibbled on her lower lip. "I designed us clothes for the presentation, but I was thinking to save them. I know you wanted to commission something new from my father, so I'm not sure if it's a requirement for this type of event. If not… I'm thinking they may work better for our wedding."

Warmth filled Toren at the soft words, his sour mood fading at her thoughtfulness. Tenderly, he brushed a hair off her cheek. "It was more a tradition than a requirement. Whatever you and Mehl desire, I'll be happy to comply."

He glanced at Mehl—thankfully, his husband's demeanor was clear of last night's unhappiness. "I know little about fashion," Mehl said. "I'll yield to Ria's discretion on this."

"Good," she said, a smile brightening her face. "I want more time to work on them, anyway. But please tell me we won't have months of celebrations like you did when you two got married. If we wait too long, I'll have to keep making alterations for my growing waist."

Truly, it was a delightful reason not to delay. "One month. Once Ber leaves again, I'll declare a month of celebration before we wed. Feref may well kill me for the rush, but we'll see it done."

She bent down and kissed him, and Toren weighed the merits of being late, after all.

These days, it was nearly unavoidable.

CHAPTER 52

THE PRESENTATION

Ria stared at her reflection in the mirror with wonder. Could this really be her? She'd never dared to wear this shade of green, pale and only two removed from the deep, vibrant hue the kings alone could wear. It looked lovely with her hair and complexion.

She ran a trembling finger over the warm silver bound high across her brow.

As Mehl had joked, Feref had indeed produced something like a tiara, a circlet in this case. Elaborate braids surrounded it so tightly that only the part over her forehead was visible. Diamonds dangled from the circlet at regular intervals, dancing just above her eyebrows when she shook her head. She wore a matching silver necklace, too, with a larger diamond that nestled just above the valley between her breasts.

There was nothing too elaborate about the thin green fabric of her gown, but she studied the simple lines with a seamstress's eye. The diaphanous swirl of green fell in gentle waves down her body with all the grace and joy of a rolling spring meadow. Lovely, but the cut had been the height of fashion two years ago. Though it was still in style now, it wasn't the latest.

Where in the world could Feref have found it?

Ria spun away from the mirror and crossed into the sitting room where the chamberlain waited. "Feref, I'm curious. Where are you getting my clothes?"

"Ah." His expression turned abashed. "Our seamstress had started a wardrobe for a royal consort before she needed to take leave. When she returns, she will not be pleased with the plundering."

Ria frowned at the pale green fabric. "This isn't a consort's color, though."

"No, it isn't." Feref grinned, a hint of pride in the curve. "I had her prepare a few pieces like this in case Toren was required to form a political marriage as part of the agreement. I'm certain Kleren will be horrified that I've allowed you to wear it without a proper fitting, but it looks fine to me."

Truly, it would have been a nightmare for Toren and Mehl if they'd dismissed Feref. The man was frighteningly prepared.

She smiled at him. "I might have used my alteration magic a touch. When your seamstress returns, she'll have no need for shame."

The door opened, and Mehl poked his head through. "We really will be late if we don't hurry."

Ria's stomach dropped in an abrupt, nausea-surging plunge. She'd been able to bury her worries about the presentation beneath her professional curiosity, but no amount of staring at her new dress would get her through this event. All she could do was conquer her fear as best she was able.

Nodding, Ria waved at Feref and followed Mehl into the hall where Toren waited. Both kings looked spectacular in royal green robes traced with delicate embroidery in silver and gold. Toren wore a gold crown of twined leaves and Mehl a similar crown in silver. The three of them matched, but not perfectly—her gown wasn't as close in design as the kings' robes were. Appropriate, she supposed, since she hadn't married them yet.

Heat flared in Toren's eyes. "I can't wait to see you in full royal colors."

"You certainly can." Ria gave a teasing curtsey. "You're the one who chose a wedding date a month in the future."

She heard a choked sound from Feref behind her. "A month?"

Toren's smile took on a wicked slant. "I have faith in you, Feref. Only pray Ria doesn't tease me into moving it sooner."

From the taunting light that entered Toren's eyes, she suspected she wasn't the only one who heard the chamberlain's whispered curse. "Be kind," she said, trying not to laugh. "Or poor Feref will run away to the countryside and leave us to plan everything ourselves."

"I could be perfectly content on a farm," Feref groused.

Mehl laughed, and the warm sound eased away some of Ria's nerves. Not all, but for the moment, she thought she could keep her breakfast where it belonged. As they'd planned, she situated herself to Toren's left before they started down the corridor. The kings normally entered the throne room from the back door, not the front entrance.

But today, they escorted her. A show of favor, sure, but also one of affection.

Ryssa joined them along the way, trailing behind Ria like a proper attendant. It was an odd thing to have a born princess following her, though Ria was from a merchant family. In all her wildest daydreams of escaping her father, something like this had never entered her mind as a possibility. Reality seemed destined to crash down upon her, taking away everything she was afraid to love.

Better not to think about those fears right now.

When they reached the grand entryway that stretched in front of both throne room and dining room, Ria sidled closer to Toren. Had there ever been so many courtiers packed into the massive space? Probably so, but not any of the times that Ria had attended. Any noble in riding distance must have hurried this way after the previous night's announcement.

Ria stiffened her spine—which was Ryssa's advice, actually. *If one is to stiffen from fear, better to direct that energy into an unyielding posture. The more afraid you are, the taller you should stand.* Ria had to admit that it did make her feel more regal to march beside Toren with her shoulders back and her chin held high. It didn't matter if she fooled anyone else, so long as she fooled herself.

As they approached the throne room doors, the courtiers stepped back from the runner so quickly that one of the ladies tripped on her gown. Mehl's hand darted out to steady her, the motion so fast that their advance was barely slowed. Ria longed to glance over her shoulder to see the lady's reaction at receiving the king's own aid, but she had to settle for the surprised—and mostly pleased—whispers swirling around them.

Warmth filled Ria for Mehl and his constant kindness. Had she not seen him when danger was near, she never would have believed that someone so affable could be such a fierce warrior. But perhaps his easy-going patience had been a boon when he'd been a bodyguard. He'd no doubt stood guard for hours without a sign of complaint.

He'd shown that same patience while waiting for her to fall pregnant, too...and in the slow, steady way he'd taken her body each time since. Toren claimed and Mehl coaxed—yet both were equally relentless. At the thought, a flush of heat swept through her, and she couldn't stop her breathing from speeding up.

She heard a hiss of breath from Toren's direction. *"Unless you want to be presented to the court in a more carnal way, I suggest you divert your thoughts. That type of claiming has not been seen since ancient times."*

Ancient times? Claiming? *Carnal?* Ria darted an alarmed glance his way, but his expression was as stoic as ever. Her heart pounded in her ears. *"What are you threatening?"*

"Nothing, in truth," Toren said, unbending enough to smile slightly. *"Though the first two or three monarchs did bed their spouses in the throne room after the wedding so that all could bear witness. We could always shift the tradition to the presentation, instead."*

Gods above. A public bedding in front of all the courtiers? As they proceeded through the throne room doors, Ria gave serious thought to closing those doors behind them so she could punch the High King in the stomach. Honestly. What was he thinking, saying something like that when she was already so nervous? This was difficult enough without images like that in her head.

"Is that ancient tradition or current *fantasy?"*

He hesitated, and her poor heart fluttered harder. *"It was the former, but the latter holds surprising appeal. Perhaps I like the idea of an audience more than I would have thought. At dinner last night, I had the unexpected urge to spread you on the table for dessert."*

Ria gasped, both from horror and the sudden rush of desire. Though she could think of few things worse than being so exposed in front of the judgmental courtiers, a scene like that in an empty dining room... Bah. Would it be a breach of etiquette to fan herself all the way down the carpet to the dais?

"Toren!" she said with a groan. *"Are you trying to turn my skin permanently red before the courtiers enter?"*

He chuckled softly. *"No, but it's difficult for a person to be nervous when they're both aroused and annoyed. You're welcome, dearest."*

Too bad they were almost to the throne, for she had the sudden, conflicting urge to both smack and kiss Toren for his unusual attempt at help. And the worst part? He wasn't wrong. The burn of desire and annoyance had swept away the bulk of her nerves, leaving her steadier as she halted at the base of the dais.

As Toren continued to his throne, Mehl paused in front of Ria. Smiling, he lifted her hand to his lips. "I could tell by his face that he was teasing you. How are you holding up?"

"I'll make it through." Ria leaned closer. "But we need to talk to him about some of his stranger fantasies."

Mehl's grin flashed wicked. "Oh indeed? Perhaps we should."

Then he joined Toren on the dais, and it was time for her hour of torment to begin.

Courtiers packed the room all the way to the door and spilled out into the entryway. Nevertheless, Toren noted a slight gap around Ria and Ryssa. The nobles working to distance themselves would have no doubt claimed it was out of respect, and for a couple of them, that was probably true. But not all.

"Make note of those who give Ria more worrisome glances and tell me if any of them are among the ones to step forward with a request," Toren said mentally to Mehl.

His husband nodded slightly. *"I'm observing as we speak."*

Feref stepped forward, scroll at the ready, and began the

litany of formal announcements. It was standard fare, the kind of court news Toren already knew, whether through gossip or one of the reports he received. It gave him another few minutes to eye the crowd himself.

There wasn't nearly enough kindness to be found.

Perhaps he should consider dismissing the court for a month or two after the wedding. These noble families had estates to tend, but too many here had apparently forgotten that sacred charge. Oh, they couched their presence in requests, or in seeking marriage alliances, or in introducing their newly-of-age children to kings and court. But Toren knew it was the chase that brought them, and what they hunted was status and power.

"For today's official business," Feref intoned, "We have the presentation of the new Duchess of Nevial."

Toren and Mehl stood, and instantly, the courtiers fell to their knees—save Ria, who curtsied as he'd told her. She would never kneel before him again. Except in pleasure, but he had to lock that thought away at once. He'd already tormented himself enough while distracting her on the way in.

"Come forward, Ria Orindl," Toren said.

He didn't like her pallor as she approached the throne, but there was nothing he could do about it except to keep this brief. She halted at the base of the dais, and after a quick exchange of glances, Toren and Mehl stepped forward until they were at the edge. Time seemed to suspend as the courtiers awaited his words.

"Turn to face the court," Toren commanded, though he wanted to pull Ria close and march out the back door. Instead, he waited until she complied. "I present to you Lady Ria Orindl, Duchess of Nevial and Princess Presumptive of the Kingdom of Llyalia. She is now the betrothed of High King

Toren Eyamiri and King Mehl Eyamiri, Sovereigns of the Kingdom of Llyalia, by oath and contract."

He paused, and some of the hastily stifled sneers he noticed made his energy flare in sudden response. He caught it back with his shields even as he reined in his temper. Oh, yes, it was time for a reckoning with his indolent, self-absorbed nobles.

"None of this is a surprise, since I have already introduced Lady Ria and announced our betrothal last night. But all new nobles deserve an official presentation to court, just as each of your families were given upon attaining your rank." Toren swept a fierce look across the gathered crowd. "I know very well how you regard a merchant joining your ranks, but I would remind you of your own origins."

Mehl released a tiny, satisfied huff beside him, and Toren's tension eased a touch.

"From the moment the first Eyamiri king established this kingdom, all noble houses were chosen based on honor, dedi-cation, and skill. Your own ancestors were warriors, diplomats, and tradespeople who fought free of two wretched empires to build the magic of this place." That reminder earned more than one averted gaze. "As such, snobbery will not be tolerated in this court. I trust you will welcome Lady Ria with the same enthusiasm my ancestors did yours."

Fortunately, Mehl took over, then, for Toren was tempted to deliver a deeper, more scathing history lesson. "It is our great honor that Lady Ria accepted our proposal, though we already have a link born of truest affection. From this day forward, may we all hail Lady Ria Orindl, Duchess of Nevial and Princess Presumptive."

"All hail Lady Ria Orindl," the courtiers intoned, some more enthusiastically than others.

Once Ria had resumed her previous spot, Toren sent her a

slight smile. Her eyes widened in surprise before pleasure slipped in, and that hint of happiness eased his anger and returned his energy level to something far more pleasant. As much as his energy ever was, at any rate.

He and Mehl sat, and court continued in all its monotony. But Toren didn't forget the reactions he'd seen. With Mehl's help, Toren either denied or gave less favor to requests made by those who'd shown Ria dishonor. It wouldn't take long for the courtiers to recognize that he'd meant what he'd said.

Nobility served a purpose, and they would do well to remember it.

CHAPTER 53

THE RECEPTION

As Feref intoned the final few announcements, Mehl studied Ria. She'd held up well enough during the awkwardness of a court presentation, but as the time neared for the reception, signs of strain bracketed her lips and stiffened her posture. His stomach turned. The plan had been to meet her at the reception after his and Toren's usual exit, but that was intolerable. He couldn't leave her to fight her way out of this ravenous crowd alone.

Especially not after Toren's rebuke of the nobles. Though well-deserved, it might heighten tensions rather than ease them. Mehl should know—he'd once borne much the same. Now, even those who hated Ria would hurry forward to show their deference, no matter how fake that respect happened to be. It would be difficult for a newcomer to the court to identify the genuine amidst the dross.

Toren's mind brushed his. *"We'll escort her out."*

Mehl hid a smile. *"Was my worry so obvious, or were you concerned, too?"*

"Both, though you hide your feelings well enough from the others."

Despite the warmth in Toren's mental voice, he held his shielding so tight and his demeanor so reserved that he gave off a definite sense of coldness. Mehl studied him out of the corner of his eye. His husband was worried about something, enough that his energy vibrated with restless urgency beneath the careful shields. Had the nobles upset him so badly?

Mehl didn't have time to ask. The announcements concluded, and as usual, he followed Toren in standing. As the two of them headed toward Ria, the courtiers sank to their knees, and the guards nearest the dais scrambled to adjust to the sudden change in plans. Mehl felt a twinge of sympathy for the frustration hidden in the warriors' brusque movements, though they were too well-trained to show their displeasure on their faces.

He generally tried not to burden his former colleagues, but for Ria, he would do it.

This time, Mehl offered her his arm, and after the slightest hesitation, she took it. Then they strolled from the throne room with their heads held high, Ryssa trailing behind. Stares from the boldest courtiers accompanied them all the way through the doors, but Mehl was accustomed to that. All that mattered was offering support to their wife.

They were nearly to their destination before Ria quirked a brow at him. "I do not recall this being part of the plan."

"Because it wasn't," Mehl replied, unrepentant.

A guard opened the doors to the secondary throne room, and they followed Toren through. This was where they'd first claimed Ria, so it had seemed a fitting place to host the reception. It was yet another sign of their support, too. No others had been allowed to use this room, not since Mehl's presentation after his and Toren's engagement.

At the sight of the wooden thrones at the far end, Mehl found himself doubly glad that they'd escorted Ria instead of slipping over through the back corridors before she and the other nobles arrived. How could he have sat on that throne beside his husband without Ria there to complete them?

Impossible.

"I find this room wouldn't be the same without you in it," he murmured in her ear. "I'll surely never think of it the same way again."

A pink flush colored her cheeks. "Behave."

Beneath the windows, tables had been covered with an abundance of refreshments, though Mehl thought of them more as props. Plates and cups held as polite shields, the food and drink barely consumed in the process. What kind of etiquette demanded such waste? He sighed to himself. At least the untouched food would be given to the neediest in the city after the reception. Leftovers never went into the trash bin here.

Toren had long insisted on such—one of the many reasons Mehl loved him.

Mehl had to release Ria to take his seat. But as soon as he settled into his throne, his cock went hard with the memory of the last time he'd sat in this room. He'd had Ria on his lap at first, his fingers bringing her to—No. *Not the line of thought to follow right now.*

Though she stepped back to stand beside Ryssa, who seemed intent on studying the refreshment tables, Ria's gaze darted to his obvious arousal. Her eyes went wide—then hot. Her lips parted, and he groaned. He could still feel the slick heat of her mouth working him and see the fire lighting Toren's expression as he'd claimed her from behind.

Gods.

Whose idea had it been to have the reception here?

Abruptly, Toren's mind connected with all three of them. *"If Ryssa wasn't here, we'd recreate that scene, but with me and Mehl swapped. Perhaps we'll return here later."*

Both Mehl and Ria groaned—but then all three of them laughed.

This was going to be a long morning.

RIA DID her best to circle the room, but it was a nightmare of politeness. Cushioned knives and hidden barbs—that was what she dodged, for the most part. Thanks to Toren's speech, absolutely no one was willing to be rude to her outright. But it didn't matter. She'd studied quite a few of these people while they were in her father's shop, and she'd overheard rumors about more of them than that.

Ryssa leaned close. "Why are courts everywhere the same?"

"Power, I suppose," Ria answered, shrugging. "Difficult to function like a normal person when the slightest thing could topple your position."

The princess nodded. "Indeed."

Lady Gartren Hesslefyn stepped into Ria's path. The lady dipped into an immediate curtsy, no sign of the hesitation that she'd shown before her dress fitting. Her eyes, though—they held the same cruel slyness they always did. Whatever words were about to pop out of her mouth, they would surely be a lie.

"Oh, Your Highness, it is a pleasure to see you again," Gartren said as soon as she straightened. "You look radiant today. Absolutely *glowing*. I can see why our dear kings are so eager to marry you."

It was at least the fifth pointed reference to the rumors of Ria's pregnancy, if the most subtle one so far. Did the lady expect her to admit to having an expectant mother's glow?

Hah. One thing her previous trade had taught her was how to keep her deepest thoughts and opinions secret around nobles.

"It would be difficult not to be radiant beneath Toren's and Mehl's care," Ria said, smiling softly. "This kingdom doesn't hold two better men."

Lady Gartren's nostrils flared slightly. "Naturally. You are beyond fortunate to have been chosen, Your Highness. Many ladies were hoping to be *beneath* their care."

Ah, the lady hadn't missed the hint of an innuendo. Ria allowed her smile to widen. "That I can understand."

"Well, perhaps all will heed High King Toren's timely admonishment." Gartren's gaze flicked dismissively down Ria's body, and the lady's nose tilted up. "We must earn our nobility, after all. The magics that bind us are not easily altered, so we would all do better to conform."

"It seems so, Lady Gartren," Ria managed to answer, though her thoughts had stuck on a single word—altered.

She'd seen references to the old magics that bound the laws into place, and Toren had told her about the book detailing how. Could that magic be altered? If so, how far? Ber's challenge would be moot if the law no longer applied. Suddenly, she longed for nothing more than the library, where she could pursue the idea sparking inside of her. How much longer would this reception last?

She barely remembered to acknowledge Lady Gartren's farewell before continuing onward. Fortunately, it was time to loop back around, so Ria could at least catch a few glimpses of the kings as a distraction from her racing thoughts. Mehl gave her a slight smile, and she couldn't help it—she went a little soft and warm inside. Then she noticed the quiet, stern stillness gripping Toren as he looked toward the door, and that softness faded.

Ria peeked in the direction of his gaze. Ah, Sir Macoe stood guard on the other side of the entry from Feref, so Toren's attention could be on either. Was there a problem? Had the captain or the chamberlain delivered bad news? *No, not Feref. He appears perfectly calm.* Sir Macoe had an air of tension about him, however.

A tingle of foreboding raced over her skin. Was Ber here? Through her link with the kings, a pulse of Toren's energy shoved a gasp from her lips. If she wasn't mistaken, that power was tinged with helpless rage.

And that scalded her blood with fear.

TOREN HAD to sever his mental connection with Macoe before the man was hurt, for only a handful of words had sparked Toren's anger—and thus his magic—to perilous life. *The convoy is near the city, but Prince Ber has disappeared.* He ground his teeth together before he followed the urge to order everyone out. That would cause panic, and that was the last thing they needed.

Mehl's hand brushed against his. *"What's wrong?"*

With his husband, Toren was free to open a mental link without risk of harm, but even so, Mehl hissed low at the energy that seeped through. *"Word from Macoe. Ber disappeared from the Centoi contingent, though it's nearing the city. He's using the secret tunnels, I imagine."*

"He must know we'll expect that," Mehl replied calmly, channeling away some of the excess energy. Toren took a deep breath as the force of his power eased. *"Shall I go check them with Sir Macoe?"*

Toren's heart skipped a beat. *"No! Above all, Ber knows what hurting you would do to me."*

His gaze caught on Ria, who was doing her best not to stare at him in concern. Between his pulse of energy and her worried glances, a few of the courtiers had started looking his way. Toren kept his expression as cool as possible. He could not afford to lose control. Now, there was another he had to protect—another he would die for. If Ber hurt Ria or the baby she carried...

"You're scaring me," Ria sent.

Toren pressed his nails into his palms, a grounding pinch of pain. Control. He could maintain control. *"Try not to react,"* he cautioned—for her and himself. *"Ber is near the city, but the spies have lost track of him. Still, we need to see the reception through, or there will be a panic."*

She stiffened slightly, but only for a moment. *"I understand."*

Then Ria tipped her head toward Ryssa's and whispered something. The two ladies laughed lightly, the breathy sound difficult to hear over the noise, but it was enough to make the courtiers around them relax. How did she manage it? Toren could hear the hint of strain around the edges of that laugh, yet none of the nobles appeared to notice.

"I had to hide much while living with my father," Ria explained. *"But I don't want to linger on that. I would rather know how much longer we must be here, because I need to go to the library as soon as possible."*

"The library?" That odd comment certainly provided a distraction. *"My brother is near, and you want to read?"*

Exasperation slipped through with her answer. *"I have an idea, but I need to consult the Rites and Rituals book you mentioned. Please. It may come to nothing, or we may be able to stop Ber now."*

She had an idea that might end his brother's threat *now*?

Toren studied the regal line of Ria's jaw as she inclined her head toward a courtier like a born queen. He couldn't imagine what she might have in mind, but he trusted her absolutely. Whatever it was, she believed her plan held promise. But what could she have learned in a single turn around the room?

Possibly nothing—but he would give her the chance to see.

CHAPTER 54

OF THE BLOOD

Mehl longed to toss every single courtier out into the hallway and slam the door shut behind them. Ber could be anywhere, waiting to strike. How could they just sit here? This very room held an entrance to the secret tunnels, and even though Toren had sealed the escape passages with magic, that was no guarantee of safety.

When Toren's energy was heightened, he struggled to wield the spells passed down by the royal family. If he'd made an error, Ber could have gained entry. And that wasn't the only possible weakness. The banished prince had already found a way to manipulate the servants' amulets. What if he had secret knowledge that would allow him to enter the tunnels, too?

Sir Macoe had slipped out to check the passages, and their most trusted bodyguards were quietly sweeping every room in the palace. It didn't help Mehl's restlessness. He shifted in his seat, and the strap binding his knife to his thigh pinched like a rebuke. He wanted to be out *there*, doing his best to protect his family, not watching snide courtiers pretend to be nice to Ria while casting sidelong glances toward the thrones.

But ultimately, leaving to track Ber wouldn't be the wisest choice.

Though he would far rather toss away his overrobe, draw his concealed knife, and join the other guards, an action like that stood a good chance of causing a panic, and panic would only benefit Ber and any spies he might have sent. Far too much harm could be done under the cover of that chaos, when proceeding as normal would allow anything unusual to stand out. Observing the gathered nobles for signs of treachery might be less satisfying, but it would be more practical.

"I know you'd rather join Macoe," Toren sent suddenly. *"But I need to escort Ria to the library after this. Will you accompany us?"*

"The library?" Mehl asked, doing best to hide a frown. "Why?"

He felt more than saw Toren's shrug. *"She has an idea that might help, but she needs to look something up first."*

Mehl couldn't imagine what Ria had in mind, but it must be worthwhile if Toren was considering it. *"Naturally, I'll go with you. As satisfying as it would be to stop Ber before he can get near, I will not leave you unguarded. But what of Ryssa? She shouldn't be alone, either."*

"We'll leave our bodyguards with her outside the library, I suppose." The side of Toren's hand brushed his in the slightest caress. *"At least this reception is nearly over. I know it must pain you in a situation like this."*

Indeed.

Mehl studied everyone who neared Ria, from the courtiers to the servants hurrying by. Unfortunately, it was impossible to tell for certain whether the nobles' insincere smiles and cutting glances hid actual malice or was typical snobbery. Nor did the servants show signs of anything but industriousness, barring the occasional well-hidden exasperation. It could have been any normal court event.

By the time Toren and Mehl stood, indicating the end of the reception, he'd still seen nothing of note. Were they all innocent of spying for Ber? As Toren said a few parting words of thanks, Mehl scanned the nobles' faces once more, but there was nothing to indicate a plot afoot. Any collusion with Ber was thoroughly concealed, if it existed at all.

Toren offered his arm to Ria to escort her out, and in such a close crowd, Mehl slipped behind his husband to follow, Ryssa beside him. From the gasps of the court sticklers, he'd committed a terrible offense. The king exiting a room behind a princess presumptive? Horror of horrors. The most daring would gossip about it for days—but he welcomed that if it would distract them from insulting Ria.

Not that Ber's imminent arrival wouldn't consume most gossip for weeks.

Once they left the secondary throne room, Toren led them in the direction of the library. It didn't take long for the crowd of nobles to thin into small clusters, then fade altogether, until the four of them were alone. Well, as alone as one could be with a pair of bodyguards trailing behind.

Mehl caught Ryssa's eye. "The Centoi emissaries should arrive by evening," he said, keeping his voice low.

Her nostrils flared. "I see."

"It appears they have lost one of their number along the way." Mehl lifted his brows in warning, and subtly, she nodded. Message received. "Regardless of how it happened, there may be trouble if the envoys are upset at the loss. I hope you will stick close to Ria, especially if there is an argument. Court affairs can be distressing for newcomers, and both of you are that."

"Thank you for the warning, Your Majesty," Ryssa said. "I will be extra careful with Her Highness's health and with my own. Of course, in the moment, I'll have to do as my lady commands."

Mehl tipped his head in acknowledgment. "Naturally. But I thought it best that neither of you be surprised."

Although Ryssa fell silent, she wasn't unaffected. Mehl was close enough to detect the telling surge of power as she reinforced her shields, and her expression held an uncanny focus. He almost wished Ber would find her first, for he had a feeling Ryssa would happily gut her treacherous husband before the man had time to recognize who stood in front of him. But no. She would not act so hastily while she was with child.

Once she'd given birth? Then, all bets were off.

As soon as the door to the archives closed behind them, Ria sagged against the edge of the nearest table in relief. A momentary thing, surely, since there was still Ber on the loose. But for a single moment, she allowed herself to savor her triumph. She'd survived both the presentation and reception without making a fool of herself.

Thank the gods.

Then Ria's gaze landed on the door, and unease slipped back in. Ryssa had insisted she was happy to sit on the bench in the corridor, and there were at least three guards out there. But would she really be safe? Her tense demeanor had been worrisome, too. Although the princess wasn't the timid kind, she was vulnerable where the prince was concerned. Was she afraid of what he might do?

"Do you think Ryssa is truly fine out there?" Ria asked.

Mehl nodded. "Angry more than anything, I'd say. As for safety, our bodyguards do know that Ber is missing and that even your companion might be a target. And don't forget that she is cloaked in a glamour."

Ria let out a long breath to release some of her tension and then stood. "You're right. I suppose I'm used to it."

"Wherever he is hiding, I doubt he will break his cover even if he does recognize her," Toren said, his voice vibrating with the force of all the power he withheld. Ria frowned. The longer they delayed, the more his energy would build up. "He is too intent on destroying me."

"Then we should hurry," Ria said.

The High King nodded.

She followed Toren's clipped steps to one of the patches of wall between the bookcases, where he settled his hand beneath a sconce holding a mage-lit globe. His magic pulsed, and Ria flinched at the sharp, sudden snap of it. Even when that pulse had faded, the fine hairs on her arms still prickled from the heightened energy in the room.

Perhaps this had been ill-advised with his control so weak.

A *crack* made her jump, but it wasn't Toren's power. Part of the wall slid out a hair, and Toren dug his fingers into the gap and pulled it out farther. Really, it looked like a long, deep box with a lid made of stone. She expected him to carry the entire thing to the table, but apparently, that wasn't necessary. Somehow, the slab remained suspended without additional support.

"Mehl," Toren said softly. "Could you help me lift the lid? I would normally use magic, but..."

But he might destroy everything in the room.

Mehl apparently didn't need that reminder, for he rushed forward to grab one side of the stone slab. At Toren's signal, they heaved it upward, leaning it back against the wall. Ria peeked over the lip of the wall-turned-box. What kind of container held one of the most important ancient tomes in their kingdom?

A surprisingly nice one, considering the exterior. The finest silk velvet in a shade of deep royal green lined the inside, so soft-looking that Ria's fingers itched to touch. Her father had bought many fine fabrics for nobles, but she'd still never seen something so rich. Did they have a skein of that hidden somewhere? If so, she would surely use it on their wedding outfits, even if it meant a redesign.

"Are you going to look at the *book*?" Toren asked, a hint of humor in his quirked brow.

With a sheepish smile, Ria stepped closer and forced her attention on the ancient tome settled atop the velvet like an offering. Even largely untrained, she could feel the layers of protective magics preserving the book within. Should she lift it free, or did it need to remain inside?

"You'll have to open it within the box," Toren offered before she could ask.

Ria nodded, but she hesitated to lift the plain leather cover. What page did she need? RRK...223. Or was it 232? She nearly sought out the other book again, but she supposed it didn't matter. If the first number was wrong, she need only check the second. She didn't have time to hunt down other texts.

So with trembling fingers, she opened the ancient tome, and as she settled the leather gently against the lining, the sumptuous velvet brushed against her skin. Ria shivered—but she couldn't linger on the sensation. Instead, she had to focus on turning the thin, age-worn pages until she reached the one she thought she needed.

Page 223.

Upon the failure of the first crown prince to sire an heir upon his estranged wife in the two hundred years before his untimely death, I, the first king of the Eyamiri line, do set forth this rite as completed in my seven-hundred-and-twenty-eighth year. Through my own vast store of power, the first queen and our daughter, the next ruler of this kingdom, have merged into law each stipulation regarding succession. Only the magic of our blood can alter the deep oaths binding us all, and as such, a proper heir must be ensured.

Ria stared down at the text. What was this? It was mere description, not a rite or ritual as such. *How* had the queen and their daughter merged this into their laws? Would a trained mage understand something she was missing? If Ria hoped to use her alteration magic to change the law allowing Ber's challenge, she had to have a better understanding than this. Gods, she prayed the next paragraph would give more details.

And it did—sort of.

This law was made for family, and so it has been bound by such. Instead of a team of mages, only my wife, daughter, and youngest son stood within my Circle. To repeat our exact methods would be impossible, but shields and incantations mattered far less than intent. At least one to guard and one to focus my power, those were the only things required. All else was a boon to lessen the burden.

There it ended. So...what? Toren was the High King, and he obviously held a great deal of power. Mehl could guard. But the one to focus? Technically, it could be her. But directing energy took many forms. Ria could turn an influx of energy to alteration, but other mages might focus it into a countless variety of spells. What if this needed some other type besides hers?

Her shoulders slumped. "Do you understand this any better, Toren?"

His warmth offered comfort as he leaned over her shoulder, but his annoyed huff brought rather the opposite feeling. "Oh, I understand this perfectly. My ancestor didn't want this changed. Ever. That's why he only involved family and didn't provide more detail."

"What did he mean by the magic of your blood?" Ria asked.

Toren wrapped his arm around her waist, his hand cupping her belly tenderly. "Only those of close descent can wield many of the spells integral to the kingdom. That's why our first child had to be mine. I don't think we've had anyone both strong and skilled enough to change or add to the magically bound laws in several generations, though. Mostly, we maintain the connection and enforce the existing laws. Even the royal seal I use is linked."

Ria wanted to growl with frustration. Toren was strong enough, but he couldn't wield his vast power. She and Mehl could channel and disperse it, but neither of them was a skilled mage. How could they hope to make the first change to the kingdom's laws in generations?

And *should* they?

For if the Eyamiri line was the vital underpinning, perhaps the requirement wasn't quite so unreasonable, after all.

CHAPTER 55

A POINTED MESSAGE

Toren stared at Ria as she paced circles around their private sitting room. After changing out of their formal wear, they'd retreated here, even allowing Ryssa entry so she wouldn't be alone. It was a rare event that outsiders were allowed into such a personal space—the last time was when Ria and her father had come to fit them for new clothes.

Now, Ria threatened to wear a track in their floor.

On the sofa beside Toren, Mehl shifted restlessly. "What is it?"

Ria might not have told him why she wanted to go to the library, but Toren had a good idea after reading the passage she'd sought. "I'd wondered if the laws could be altered with my magic," Ria said, confirming his suspicions. "But at this point, I have more questions than answers. I'm not sure the law *should* be changed or even if I'm capable of doing it if so."

Toren frowned. "You think the Right of Challenge is just?"

"Not exactly." Ria halted in the center of the room, her hands on her hips. "But it's clearly important not to let the

Eyamiri bloodline die out. I...I'm surprised you were so casual about producing an heir."

A spark of anger had his spine snapping tight. "I was not. However, I took the throne young since my mother was murdered well before she would have died naturally, and I do have a couple of cousins who would suffice. I saw no reason to rush a breeding alliance, hoping instead that Mehl and I might naturally find someone suitable without pressure."

Ria flinched, her expression turning pained. He didn't need Mehl's fingers pinching his thigh to realize the mistake in his words. They'd found *her* because of that pressure. Blast it. Before she could say a word, Toren leapt to his feet and strode to her side.

"Ria. That might have been my intention, but I am *not* sorry for how things turned out," Toren insisted. "In this, my brother has done Mehl and I a favor, for our lives would not be so complete without you."

Her eyes softened, though the hurt lingered. "I feel the same. But the way you said that..."

"I know." He tucked a loose tendril of hair behind her ear. "I'm sorry."

Ria shook her head. "There's no need to apologize, really. You've shown me time and again how you really feel. But between pregnancy and stress, my emotions are askew, and I'd built up so much hope about changing the law, too."

"I'm sorry," he said gently.

"It's not your fault." Despite the softness of her words, a scowl darkened her face. "If only the first king had given the stipulations more thought. *Why* not allow you to appoint a suitable heir, if nothing else? An actual challenge is so silly when there are other choices."

"Yes, it is," Toren agreed.

But he was as bound to obey as any other ruler before him.

Abruptly, Macoe's mind brushed against his. *"Your Majesty, the Centoi contingent has reached the palace and requested an audience."*

"Any sign of Ber?"

"None," the captain replied.

"Arrange the meeting with Feref. We'll return to the throne room."

Toren disconnected the link before he allowed himself a single sigh. "Time to greet the envoy. Princess Tes, are you sure you wish to accompany Ria for this?"

Though she startled slightly at the use of her real name, the princess nodded. "My disguise should hold, and we won't be the center of attention since we aren't on the dais. Provided you're allowing in courtiers? The two of us standing beside the dais in an otherwise-empty room wouldn't be particularly stealthy."

He would rather the meeting be closed, but it wouldn't be the best choice—and not only for how exposed it would leave Ria and Ryssa. Secrecy would only stir the rumors more. "Some will be allowed, yes."

The princess stood, her mouth firming into a resolved line. "Let's get this over with. Then we'll only have to worry about Ber."

Unfortunately, that was likely to be the worst part.

MEHL STUDIED the Centoi contingent with a critical eye, but there was nothing overt he could criticize. This was a more typical group than the one that had brought Tes with her fake wedding invitation—no herald and no high-status noble in sight. In fact, if not for the spies Sir Macoe had sent, Mehl wouldn't have guessed that Prince Ber had accompanied them. There wasn't nearly enough flash for the prince's usual style.

What was going on?

At Toren's gesture, the head of the group approached the dais. Mehl examined the man as he knelt. He wore the well-made but simple clothes typical of a diplomat and had the posture of a low-ranking noble or possibly a second son of a higher house. There was no sign of mockery or derision in the lines of his body or the tilt of his head. No haughty scorn hidden in the twitch of his mouth. Essentially, he was the opposite of Lord Aony.

"Welcome," Toren said in a tone that was not, in fact, welcoming. "I am curious to hear what has prompted another visit from the Centoi."

The visitor kept his gaze on the base of the dais. "I, Sir Owein of Centoi, bring greetings from King Ryenil Breren the Mighty, Sovereign of the Kingdom of Centoi to High King Toren Eyamiri and King Mehl Eyamiri, Sovereigns of the Kingdom of Llyalia. In light of recent events, His Majesty the King wished to deliver an official response concerning the death of his daughter."

Mehl tensed at those words. It wasn't entirely unexpected that the king would do so, but he'd thought a missive more likely. Much business was conducted that way, for then it would be in writing. A verbal response quickly fell into rumor with no way to substantiate fact.

"We will hear his words," Toren said.

Sir Owein nodded, but he didn't look up. "King Ryenil the Mighty sends his thanks to the Sovereigns of Llyalia for their aid in returning the body of Princess Lora after her foolish plan went awry. Be assured that His Majesty was unaware of her intentions, otherwise he would not have sent messengers in search of her. It grieves the king to consider the worry caused by news of her supposed abduction, followed by her death on your land. He is certain that Your Majesties would have offered adequate guards to the Jewel of Centoi had he known of her presence."

What? Mehl stared at the top of the man's head as though it would bring his message clarity. For surely, King Ryenil wasn't blithely dismissing the death of the daughter he'd guarded so closely. He'd named her their kingdom's jewel, for gods' sake. Yet he would offer no censure for her loss at the hands of bandits?

Maybe he had been part of the plan all along.

"The Kingdom of Centoi wishes to maintain our strong alliance with the Kingdom of Llyalia," Sir Owein continued. "This may, of course, be strained by the fact that our only remaining heir is Princess Lora's bereaved husband, Prince Ber Eyamari. Please know that the prince is committed to maintaining peace between our kingdoms. So it is declared by King Ryenil the Mighty."

Did King Ryenil expect Toren to merely shrug at Ber becoming the Centoi king? Ah, but probably not. There was no doubt a deeper reason for this farce. Now, the courtiers who'd heard his message would be more likely to believe that the Centoi sought peace. It could give Ryenil some leverage if Toren decided to end the alliance.

"Thank you, Sir Owein," Toren said, his voice cold and dispassionate. "My chamberlain, Feref, will see you and your attendants situated in a guest room while I compose a formal reply. If the hour grows too late, you are welcome to stay for the night."

The envoy inclined his head. "Your kindness is greatly appreciated, Your Majesty."

Mehl half-expected Ber to rush in while Sir Owein and the rest of the group took their leave, but even after the throne room was clear of the Centoi, there was no sign of the man. Why? What was he waiting for? Did the prince intend for someone in his party to cause trouble during their stay? Possibly search for information?

"I wanted them under close watch," Toren sent.

Wise—but also a risk.

Mehl already hated their very presence.

RIA HAD SUSPECTED that something was wrong at the Centoi palace, but after hearing the king's callous words, she was certain. The man had essentially said that his daughter had deserved her fate. He sounded more worried about the alliance than the unexpected death of his child. But worse? Unless he was lying, the king had actually believed the body of Ryssa's guard had been the princess.

He couldn't recognize his own daughter.

Would the princess be upset? As the envoys filed out, Ria cast a sidelong glance at Ryssa, but the princess's expression was carefully blank. Bored, almost. Her hands were folded serenely at her waist, and when she caught Ria looking, Ryssa smiled.

"Shall we go rest, dearest cousin?" the princess asked softly. "I would suggest luncheon, but I doubt I could eat after all the food at your reception. Unless you're hungry?"

Ria should have been, since they'd barely touched anything while mingling with the nobles, but this meeting had soured her stomach. Probably Ryssa's, too. "A rest sounds nice. I don't think I could sleep, though. Would you like to join me in my sitting room for embroidery?"

"Whatever you wish, Your Highness," Ryssa said.

Ah, she'd forgotten that the other woman was supposed to

be her lady's companion, not simply a friend. That meant she would have to follow along with whatever Ria planned. Some might consider that position an honor, but in truth, it sounded terrible. With a cruel lady, the companion would surely be miserable.

She would have to get the princess's true opinion once they'd left court.

Toren and Mehl stood, and the gathered nobles sank to their knees. Even Ryssa. But as the princess had instructed, Ria curtsied instead. Apparently, even the kings' betrothed couldn't simply stand there and watch them leave, but the same amount of deference wasn't required. Nor were guests required to give such deep obeisance, though that varied based on rank. Had Ryssa's identity been known, she could have gotten away with a curtsy, too.

There was far too much to learn. And if Ria was ignorant of such basic court traditions and rules, why had she thought she should mess with one of the kingdom's fundamental laws? Abandoning that idea would clearly be for the best.

As soon as the kings had gone, Ria and Ryssa linked arms and slipped through the crowd as quietly as they could. Fortunately, there were far fewer courtiers present for this, only those few who'd been lingering close enough to hear of the envoy's arrival. She and Ryssa only had to pause once to exchange pleasantries before they made it away from the nobles.

But Ria waited until they had entered her sitting room to speak openly. "You don't *really* have to stay for embroidery. I'm sure you must be upset, and it's not as though you're a true lady's maid in the traditional sense."

"Oh, but I am." Ryssa dropped onto her usual seat and grabbed her embroidery basket from the side table. But instead of opening the lid, her fingers squeezed tight around the rim until Ria worried the thin wood would snap. "Until I find a way to reclaim my kingdom, I have nothing but that. It has long been clear that my father is too far gone in his bitterness to care about anyone. I'm sure he cried tears of joy over my body, though others would count them as sorrow."

Ria frowned. "According to Toren, the king doted on you."

"Because he treated me like his jewel?" Ryssa snorted. "That name wasn't a kindness. It was a reminder. I was to be nothing but what he shaped me, a valuable bauble to be affixed to my future husband's crown. He did his best to control every moment of my life. But at my supposed death, he gained the only thing he really wanted. Someone besides me as his heir."

The matter-of-fact tone brought a lump to Ria's throat. Maybe there was a little bitterness to the princess's words, but simple acceptance outweighed it more than it should. But Ria understood better than many would. She'd suffered at her own father's hand, and she'd struggled for years not to let it define her.

"What are you going to do?" Ria asked.

A hard glint entered the princess's eyes. "Right now? I'm going to sit here as your companion, take out my embroidery, and stab the only thing I can: Ber's face on this youthful folly of a tapestry. And hope one or both of the kings kill him while he's here."

Ria blinked. "*That's* why you expended magic to retrieve your needlework?"

"A pregnant woman needs to have some form of catharsis when she can't stab the useless, treacherous, lying piece-of-slime father of her baby," Ryssa snapped.

Perhaps it was...best not to argue. Ria sat and pulled out her own embroidery, a bit of trim for her dress. But it was difficult to keep her attention on her own work as the princess threaded her needle with blood-red string and began to jab and tug until wound-like lines scarred the delicately embroidered face already on the fabric.

Whatever Ber had planned, it had better not involve his estranged wife—for his own sake, anyway. If not for the child the princess carried, Ria would have slipped her a knife and then cheered her on.

Instead, she and Ryssa could only sit there and wait.

CHAPTER 56

UNINVITED

Toren had been at his desk for hours, and he still hadn't decided what to write. He'd drafted a few replies to Ryenil's message, of course, but none of them had been right. What did one say after such a callous missive? The memory of the Centoi king's casual dismissal of his daughter's death sparked Toren's energy to dangerous levels each time he ran through the scenario again.

At this point, even the bodyguards stationed beside the door looked alarmed at his heightened power.

With a deep breath in and then out, Toren put a lock on the latest surge of energy. He needed to think rationally about this. If his emotions were in charge, he would send a note formally severing their alliance with Centoi, along with a private letter of rebuke. Unfortunately, that might not serve their people best. There was significant trade between the two, so a hasty break would cause chaos and hardship to those who didn't deserve it.

Toren's mother might have been the High Queen, but it had been his father who'd taught him about the common people. King Nemin had hailed from a modest and minor noble house, and as such, his perspective had been quite different. Each time he'd taken Toren to see his grandparents on their estate in the west, they'd traveled quietly, and Nemin had made a point of stopping in a variety of average villages. Eventually, they'd explored the other regions the same way at Toren's request.

He was very aware that the people who would be most affected weren't merely columns on a report.

Though Toren did his best to keep poverty at a minimum, no small number of families might be left destitute from a major disruption. Like ore. Being more mountainous, Centoi traded a great deal of it, and blacksmiths in nearly every village in Llyalia replied upon a steady supply. Not to mention the farmers who sent grain to Centoi—or flax to the weavers, who sold much of their linen to, of course, Centoi. And that was only a small sample of industries that would be harmed.

They *did* trade with other kingdoms, but it would take time to account for such a shift in volume. New agreements would need to be formed. New routes created and set. So no matter how much Toren wanted to tell King Ryenil to take a leap from his highest tower, he couldn't. At least not yet. No amount of anger or pride would be worth so much suffering.

He would take his time easing free of these ties.

The door opened, and Mehl strode through, his expression a storm of frustration. "No sign," he said as he halted on the other side of the desk.

Toren sighed. "I would love to believe he had no intention of entering the palace at all, but I'm not that much of a fool. If I had to guess, I would say he's waiting for dinner or for morning court tomorrow. Ber always has loved to make a grand entrance."

"Should we have Ria and Ryssa eat in their rooms?" Mehl asked, frowning.

He nearly snapped out a harsh *yes* at the question. Ria and their child should be safe, far from Ber's machinations. But the words caught in Toren's throat. Not only would Ria hate it, but there was no guarantee it would really be safer. If Ber predicted that move, he might go after her in her rooms the way Tes had.

"No," Toren decided. "Whatever happens, we'll face it together."

Abandoning the blank page on his desk, Toren stood.

It was time to prepare for dinner.

ALTHOUGH THERE'D BEEN no sign of Ber, Mehl couldn't shake the uneasy feeling humming through his blood as he sat down beside Toren at the table. Ria took her seat on Toren's other side, Ryssa beside her, and the nobles began to file in to claim their usual places. It was a familiar routine, but nothing felt normal this night. Not when he had to examine every single person in the room for signs of treachery.

The reason for Mehl's turmoil appeared in the open door as soon as the last noble sat. There was a brief swell of sound as hissed exclamations and startled whispers swept around the room, but in the subsequent silence, Ber strode through, Sir Macoe at his side. Fury stiffened Mehl's spine. Had the captain found a way to betray them despite his oaths? The man gripped the hilt of his sword, but was it in protection or in threat?

Toren settled his hand on Mehl's forearm. *"I told Macoe to bring him in if he showed himself. I want this finished."*

Relief eased his anger, but it barely touched the tension zinging through Mehl like a blast of his husband's energy. He hadn't seen the treacherous prince since well before wedding Toren and becoming king, but the sly smirk on Ber's face was much the same. Before, the prince had sent his challenge for the throne in a letter. What would he do now that he was here?

With the courtiers so silent, Ber's footsteps cracked loudly against the marble as he marched toward the dais. His long, dark hair whipped around his royal green cloak as he marched between the rows of long tables on his way to the High Table. As he passed, the nobles did their best to duck forward, lest they make contact with so much as a strand of his hair.

If he had an ally, it wasn't readily apparent.

Naturally, Ber had dressed as a prince who *hadn't* been exiled—beneath his cloak, he wore a tunic and pants in a lighter shade of royal green. He'd even donned a thin circlet over his brow as though he still had the right. Mehl's hands clenched into fists at the slight, but Toren gave his arm a warning squeeze.

Not that Mehl was deceived into thinking Toren was unaffected. His husband was moments away from losing grasp on his energy. Out of reflex, Mehl opened a link and let some of the power pass through him, but Toren surprised him by holding some of it back. Was he planning to blast his brother before the terms of the inheritance challenge were met?

When Ber finally came to a halt a couple of paces from the dais, he sketched a mocking bow. Then he straightened without leave to do so, his gaze direct on Toren. Mehl thought he heard a soft gasp from Ria, and he could guess why. Toren and Ber weren't identical, but they looked very similar. Except where Toren was light, his brother was dark—hair, eyes, disposition. If the gods had designed the perfect foil, it would be Ber.

Perhaps they had.

"You are bold to break the terms of your exile," Toren said, his voice cold enough to preserve their dinner for the next generation. "And bolder still to abandon the Centoi contingent with which you entered our borders. I could have ordered you executed for your temerity at any time."

Ber's smile held derision, but his eyes were unreadable. "Showing care for me, brother? I am honored."

"You know it is not care."

"Very well. I do know." The prince inclined his head. "As for why I didn't accompany the Centoi...this has nothing to do with them. I did not want our business to be confused with theirs."

Toren barked out a laugh. "You're now Ryenil's heir. I believe they are inextricably entwined at this point. What you do affects the Centoi."

The muscle in Ber's jaw twitched. Was it annoyance? Anger? Mehl couldn't fathom that the prince actually cared what happened to anyone in Centoi. He'd long ago shown that he thought of no one but himself.

"They certainly *will* be entwined if I win our challenge." Ber's smirk returned. "Why do you think I have come?"

Toren's hand twitched atop his arm, but Mehl detected no hint of upset on his husband's face. "A good question, since you're supposed to be grieving your tragically lost wife," Toren said sharply.

There were enough indrawn breaths from the courtiers that Mehl couldn't tell if Ryssa had been among them. He didn't dare look at her, lest she draw Ber's notice. She'd reinforced her glamour, but there was no guarantee he wouldn't guess her true identity.

Above all, she needed to remain silent—and that would be understandably difficult to do.

RIA WAS AFRAID TO BREATHE, much less move, but beneath the table, she gripped Ryssa's wrist in a gentle but firm hold. A reminder, really. Whatever that wretched prince planned to say, it would be difficult for the princess to avoid a counter. How could anyone expect her to be quiet in the face of the man who'd betrayed her so completely?

"Oh, I am grieving," Ber said to Toren. "But she did get what she deserved."

The muscles in Ryssa's arm tightened beneath Ria's hand, but the princess didn't make a sound. A feat worthy of a commemorative statue, surely. Though Toren could appear unfeeling at times, his brother's blank expression as he'd delivered that judgment was a lesson in casual cruelty. The words had cut Ria's heart deep—and they hadn't even been directed at her. How much worse to be the woman in question?

From the delay in Toren's response, he must have been shocked, too.

"That's cold, even for you," the High King finally snapped.

"She wanted to see what manner of man you are, and she succeeded," the prince said. "I could not have described your character so well with mere words. My wife had to experience it for herself."

If Ria hadn't been studying Prince Ber so closely, she would have missed it—the slight flick of his eyes toward Ryssa with those final words. But wait. No. She had to be mistaken. Gods, she *prayed* she was mistaken. If the prince had seen through their ruse, the princess's life would be in danger for sure.

Then again, if Ber did know that his wife was alive in their court, then his statement made no sense. He'd sent her here to experience Toren's supposed ruthlessness, not his kindness, so Ber wouldn't have considered her survival a success. Perhaps he'd been distracted by movement, either from Ryssa or a servant behind her.

Or it was a struggle for him to meet his brother's gaze.

"You know perfectly well that I would not mistreat a member of my family." Toren straightened in his seat. "Had the princess identified herself to me at once, I would have welcomed her despite your crimes. She needn't have camped outside the city."

"She should have been safe." Ber *tsked*. "Alas, for bandits. Really, Toren, I'm worried for our people if you allow such criminals to run rampant across the kingdom."

Such an unusual, almost calm, discussion for supposed enemies.

Ria glanced between the brothers. The conversation lacked...something. A certain fire. It was as though their hearts weren't in it, yet they spoke as though they hated one another. Was it because of Toren's mixed feelings for his twin or because Ria was unfamiliar with Ber's mannerisms?

Either way, a sense of wrongness niggled at the back of her mind.

"Curious, those bandits," Toren said. "We've found no sign of any others in our subsequent sweeps of the area. Your wife was an unlucky woman, it seems. No matter what you think of me, you must concede that I would have guarded her better here."

Once again, something flickered in Ber's eyes, and Ria saw it for certain this time—the prince looked toward Ryssa. Easily dismissed the first time but suspicious the second, particularly with the timing. Ria's heart dropped. If Ber didn't know, he suspected.

"My perfect, perfect brother," the prince drawled. "Of that, I have no doubt."

Ria's breath caught. What did it mean? It was possible Ber had come to confirm that Toren had killed his wife and child. But if the prince had discovered that his plan had failed, there was no anger evident in his demeanor. Only disdain and cool reserve. He must intend to strike later.

"What do you want, Ber?" Toren demanded. "Why are you here?"

Ber's sly smile returned. "Rumors accompanied the body of my dearest Lora. I wanted to confirm them."

At the name Lora, a tremble shook down Ryssa's arm. Ria finally dared a quick glance, but the princess's face held no sign of turmoil. Her expression was serene—almost bored. But Ria knew how much the princess hated that name. For him to call her Lora... It was yet another sign of his lack of regard—and possibly a hint about his poor intentions.

Toren leaned forward, and the brothers' gazes locked in a silent war. "Do tell, Ber. It is clear that you want to."

Though he didn't look away, the prince's grin widened.

"I heard that you'd entered a breeding alliance," Ber said. "I thought I should see if there's another woman who needs to be saved."

One little statement, and Ria's blood ran cold.

CHAPTER 57

ULTIMATUM

Stark fear froze Toren to his seat for a single heartbeat before rage pulsed his energy to new heights. Ria flinched, and Mehl's breath hissed in. Beyond the High Table, the nobles seated nearest shuddered from the force, and Ber's eyes blazed with satisfaction. Toren scrabbled for his shields, barely managing to harden them before he exploded half the dining hall. That would be the kind of disaster his brother wanted.

"You will not threaten our wife," Toren snarled.

Ber's eyebrows rose slightly. "Wife?"

Toren should have felt bad about the slip—Ria had been angry when he'd uttered something similar at court—but dark pleasure filled him to say the words aloud. "Lady Ria has agreed to wed Mehl and I formally, but we have already formed a link. She is our wife. Still, I hope you'll understand why you aren't invited to the official wedding. All things considered."

He expected his brother's anger, but what he received was another sly smile. Toren's gut clenched. He'd seen that same look far too many times. From the day his magic tutor had called his power ungovernable to the moment he'd exiled his brother after their mother's suspicious death, every difficult or terrible time in his life had been greeted by Ber's enigmatic smirk. Now, it no doubt heralded trouble.

"Then I should deliver my terms for the inheritance challenge now, lest I mar the happy event," his brother said. There it was. Except…was it Toren's imagination, or did Ber's grin dim? Ah, not likely. "As my own blessed union was irrevocably ruined, I can hardly imagine dealing the same blow to my brother. I trust you're prepared to listen?"

Did he have a choice? Toren's fists clenched. If this was a trap, it was one he couldn't avoid. Not with the inheritance law. "State your terms. Then leave."

Ber's laugh sliced uncomfortably through the dining hall. "Not in front of others. This is for you to hear alone. Unless you'd like to force the issue? By tradition, I *could* demand to live in the palace until the inheritance challenge is complete."

"You're suggesting you meet alone? No," Mehl snapped, half-rising before Toren gripped his arm once more.

Grudgingly, his husband dropped back into his seat.

Toren caught his breath against a surge of power. Although he'd wanted to store as much energy as possible in case he needed to use it against his brother, Toren had to concede another tendril to Mehl's channeling. It was either that or incinerate them all in a surge of fear and rage. For the threat was undeniable—if he didn't agree to a private meeting, Ber would insist on remaining, and that would place Ria and Ryssa under constant threat of harm.

And if Ber learned that Ria was already pregnant…

"I'm afraid this matter is for those of Eyamiri blood," Ber said. "Though if you'd prefer I stay, Mehl, I suppose you can have the room beside yours prepared, since my status as prince wasn't revoked with my exile."

A terrible oversight, that. Even so, Toren gave Mehl's arm a warning squeeze. "No. We will settle this today."

It went against Toren's every instinct, yet he couldn't refuse. For the sake of all, he had to get his brother far, far from the palace.

If Mehl had thought he hated the stifling expectations of his current role before, it was nothing to the helpless anger he felt at royal convention now. For the second time in a single day, he had to resist the urge to spring from his seat and draw his blade. Not that this situation would have been any better when he'd been a mere bodyguard. He would have had even *less* authority to react then.

"I am king, and thus privy to the rules of the inheritance challenge," Mehl bit out.

Ber's smile didn't waver. "Not this one. In any case, don't you have others to guard?"

The prince's gaze shifted to Ria and Ryssa—a telling motion. It was the third time Ber had looked toward Ryssa, and the mention of "others" implied he expected Mehl to guard both women. But why would the king be protective of a simple companion in a situation like this? Either Ber knew Ryssa's identity, or he had somehow discerned that Ria was pregnant.

"*We have to get him out of here,*" Toren sent, his mental voice tight with strain.

Unfortunately, that was true. "It is not acceptable for the High King to be so unprotected."

"Fine." Ber shrugged. "Macoe may remain at a distance."

It was too easy a concession. And why Sir Macoe? Mehl's fingernails dug furrows into the tablecloth. As king, it was perfectly logical that he accompany Toren, not the captain of the guard. Ber had to be planning some trickery, and he would use his brother's lingering—if deeply buried—affection to do it. There was no other reason for him to isolate Toren.

"Macoe, escort Prince Ber to my private receiving room. I will join you when dinner has concluded," Toren announced, his voice taking on that implacable authority that meant it would be a waste to argue. "Our meal should not be disrupted for such a minor inconvenience."

Though the prince hadn't been here in centuries, he inclined his head, spun on his heel, and strolled from the room like a guest well-acquainted with the High King's own receiving room. Not a sound could be heard except the clack of boots-on-stone and the rustle of the prince's clothes. Even when Ber and Sir Macoe disappeared through the door, no one made a single noise.

Toren lifted his glass. "Ignore my brother. There is no reason for his unseemly behavior to disturb our dinner."

Then somehow, Toren picked up his fork and began to eat.

Every bite Ria took rolled down her throat like a rock, jagged and unyielding. She couldn't have managed more than a few nibbles, but her stomach was too full of anxiety to fit much food, anyway. How was Toren eating as though it was any other dinner? Ryssa, too. If Ria hadn't been close enough to see the strain in their demeanor, she would have thought both of them entirely unfeeling.

When Toren tipped back his head for a sip of wine, Ria exchanged a frustrated glance with Mehl. Like her, he was mostly pretending to eat, though he appeared to consume more than she could. Was he also nervous? Surely, a warrior would handle the tension better than the average person.

"I'm unsettled, too," Mehl whispered into her mind. *"Although in this case, I don't want to be sluggish. It's best to eat lightly if there's an imminent threat of battle."*

Bile crept up the back of her throat. *"Do you think it will come to that?"*

Mehl let out a low curse that had Toren eyeing him. *"I should not have said that. I didn't mean to make you more afraid."*

"You didn't answer my question."

"Fine," Mehl said, ignoring their husband's intense stare. *"I don't know for sure, but it's a possibility. Not so much against Toren, though. If Ber hurts him, he forfeits his right to inherit as part of the challenge."*

Really? If Prince Ber couldn't attack, then...? Ria frowned down at the roast she should have been eating. *"In that case, why are you so worried about this meeting?"*

"Because Prince Ber is not someone you should underestimate."

A difficult truth—one she couldn't deny.

They didn't linger once the meal was complete. Almost as one, all four of them stood, and though they began the long walk to the door in silence, murmurs flowed around them by the time they exited. To Ria's ears, most of the voices sounded concerned. Toren might have stemmed actual panic by continuing the meal, but the fear was far from gone.

Part of Ria hoped that Toren led all of them to his receiving room despite Ber's insistence on meeting alone, but he headed straight for his office, instead. Her steps slowed just over the threshold. Four bodyguards ringed the room, and the healer stood from his seat and bowed at the sight of them. Why was Vesset here? Did Toren anticipate an injury?

As soon as the door closed behind them, Mehl rounded on their husband. "He's going to try to manipulate you any way he can."

"I am well aware," Toren replied. "But I must go, anyway."

Though she'd been quiet since Ber's arrival, Ryssa stepped forward. "I should leave the palace. He'll have less to threaten you with if I'm not here. I...I think he might have recognized me."

That was a terrible idea, one Ria couldn't countenance. But before she could do more than slip up to Ryssa's side, Toren shook his head. "You will stay. Wandering the streets where anyone could find you is hardly safer than being protected here by my guards."

"Then give me a weapon," the princess insisted.

With the flick of his fingers, Toren summoned one of the bodyguards, who pulled one of the knives from his belt and handed it over without comment. The man hadn't even resumed his position before Ryssa had the blade secured in her boot. Ria could sympathize with her concern—her own knife was strapped to her thigh beneath her dress.

"I must go," Toren said. Then he looked over his shoulder. "Vesset. Ensure the health of my wife and our child as well as Lady Ryssa in this tense time."

Surprise flitted across one of the guards' faces, but it was quickly masked. Even so, all four snapped to greater attention as Toren's words hit. Though there were rumors of her pregnancy, there'd been no confirmation until now. That the guards were tasked with protecting not only the king and new princess but also the heir to the throne hadn't gone unnoticed.

Toren kissed a scowling Mehl before easing over to do the same with Ria. But she couldn't let him leave with a single, quick kiss. She wrapped her arms around his waist so tightly that he let out a surprised *oomph*, and for a moment, she settled her face in the vee of his shoulder and took in his warmth. His scent.

Unfortunately, though, she couldn't linger. So she forced

her hold to loosen and slipped back enough to accept his kiss. "Come back quickly," Ria whispered. "And without a scratch."

Toren cupped her cheek. "I'll do my best. Don't let Mehl do anything foolish, hmm?"

Ria laughed softly, but the low sound cut off when Toren slipped from her hold to march toward the door.

Gods, let him be safe.

ALL THE WAY to his sitting room, Toren seethed. His brother had caused him grief time and again—he was accustomed to it. But the fear and worry Ber had evoked in Ria and Mehl? That was one step too far. They didn't deserve the suffering his horrid brother could bring. It was past time for that to end.

This meeting was dangerous for so many reasons. Not only would Toren be practically alone with the man who most wanted him dead, but he wouldn't have a way to channel the energy building in him with every step. He was a barely banked fire surrounded by tinder, and the slightest nudge could set everything aflame. But he couldn't allow his brother to hurt his family any longer.

As promised, Macoe stood just inside the door, ready to protect. Mehl might not understand why the captain had been permitted, but Toren did. Macoe was blood-bound to the Eyamiri family with oaths so absolute that to break them would bring instant death. It was a harsh requirement, but necessary—the royal family needed at least one person they could entrust with the kingdom's deepest secrets.

Mehl could be given the same confidence, of course. But Ber had set the rules of this meeting, and it was clear he would not trust the king with whatever he wanted to say. Even with the captain's blood oaths, Ber gave Macoe a dark, annoyed look as the man closed the door behind Toren.

"There isn't an unknown portion of the law, and the challenge you sent was accurate and complete," Toren said before he reached his brother's side. "You're wasting both our time."

That slow, sly smile spread across Ber's face. "You're correct. Didn't it occur to you that I lied to get this meeting?"

Halting just out of reach, Toren took a deep breath against twin surges of anger and energy. "Of course it did. Lying is all you know how to do."

Abruptly, Ber's grin dropped. "More than you know, Tor."

Was that...sadness in the depths of his brother's eyes? Uneasiness tangled with the thread of anger in Toren's heart, and he peered more closely at Ber. Did his brother have regrets? Or—no. As Mehl had warned, Ber only sought to manipulate. He would pretend any emotion if it helped him reach his goal.

"Just tell me what you want," Toren snapped.

No smirk this time. Instead, Ber inclined his head. "I'm here to tell you the truth."

CHAPTER 58

CLAIMS

Did Ber actually think Toren would believe that he was here for honesty's sake? Toren stared at his brother's earnest expression. Theoretically convincing, but such a demeanor was easy to feign. Especially for Ber.

"Truth," Toren scoffed. "A fascinating concept to discuss with someone so poorly acquainted with it."

Ber's dark eyes pinned him. "And you're not as acquainted with it as you think."

What was this? First, his brother had hinted that Toren didn't know the extent of his lies, and now Ber claimed that Toren wasn't aware of the truth, either. It was just the kind of enigmatic conundrum that his brother loved to present—or cause.

"Which do I not know, then?" Toren asked, scowling.

After casting another annoyed glance at Macoe, Ber headed toward a grouping of chairs on the farthest end of the room. He dropped into one and then stared at Toren expectantly. Wretched traitor. Ber ruled this conversation, and he knew it.

But Toren wouldn't show his annoyance. He strode over to claim the seat across from his brother with an ease he didn't feel.

"The answer to that question is...both," Ber said in a low, solemn voice.

Gods, he hated his brother's games. "What are you trying to claim?"

"It's no simple *claim*." Ber leaned forward, his hands gripping the armrests. "Some of the things you believe to be true are not. Similarly, you've taken things I've said in the past to be lies when they weren't. An example? You think I'm your enemy, but that honor goes to your supposed ally, King Ryenil."

Toren stared at his twin. Was he trying to sow discord between the two kingdoms? The relationship was already strained after recent events, but Ber had manufactured no small part of those. "Do you really expect me to believe that?"

"No, but you need to. If you want to save both our families, it's vital," Ber insisted. "I am not your enemy. I never have been."

Of all the things his brother could have said, this made the least sense. Not his enemy? Hundreds of years of history stood in direct counter. "You jest. You've hated me from the moment you first understood the differences in our magic. Mother sent you away because of your jealousy."

"No." Ber's nostrils flared. "She sent me to the Centoi after the second time Ryenil tried to have you killed."

What was Ber talking about? Toren had dodged a couple of attempts on his life over the centuries, but that was typical for any leader. Even the most beloved person in the world would be hated by someone, and as the kingdom's primary ruler, it was inevitable that he'd be a target at times. But as a child? He had no memory of such a thing.

"See? Truths you do not know." A hint of Ber's smile

returned. "Listen, Toren. I *was* jealous of you when we were children. How could I not be? You have immense power, and I have practically none. But then I grew obsessed with figuring out why. Do you recall how much time I spent in the library?"

Toren could see it clearly—Ber tucked behind a stack of books in the archives, his gaze intense on yet another tome. Toren had thought their inclination to study had been one of the few things they had in common, but he'd never stopped to consider his brother's motivation. Except, of course, to wonder if Ber hoped to somehow become High King.

"I do remember," Toren conceded.

"What I discovered was this." Ber's eyes narrowed. "Any time the deep laws ruling our kingdom have been changed, it has been by a monarch with unusual amounts of energy, which meant your rule could be pivotal. Unfortunately, I wasn't the only one to figure out how important you might become. The head cook caught the first assassin slipping poison in your food. I caught the second trying to sneak into your chamber and alerted the guard."

"Impossible," Toren said out of reflex. "I would have heard the commotion from the second attempt, if nothing else."

But it was possible. There was a reason the royal family had bodyguards, after all.

Ber shrugged. "They never made it to your bedroom door. When I checked on you, you were sound asleep."

Shock blanked his thoughts for several moments, but the numb emptiness was all too short. Years of disappointment and hurt surged within, the pain so strong his fingernails dug into his palms. *How dare Ber pretend he'd watched out for me!* Everyone knew how much Ber hated him. It had long been one of the kingdom's juiciest bits of gossip.

Toren's heart pounded like the energy drumming against

his shields. He had to calm himself, or that power would flare out of control. He sucked in a breath, then released it in an even stream. These lies were no more than he'd expected. Too bad acceptance hadn't made the reality easier.

"I can think of no motivation for Ryenil to do such a thing," Toren finally said.

"King Ryenil requested a betrothal between you and his daughter, but Mother denied all such requests until you were old enough to consent," Ber said, no sign of his usual mockery in his tone. "She believed he'd decided to eliminate you because of your power if he couldn't link the families through marriage. So she asked if I would foster there as a distraction even though we hadn't quite reached adolescence, and I agreed. All this time, I have been a spy."

Despite all his anger and doubt, each word picked at Toren's mind, chipping away at the walls he'd built against his brother. *No. He lies.* "You've forever loved to gloat at my misfortune, and you've mocked me more times than I can count. You sent your wife here to be murdered so you could claim the Centoi throne. I—"

"You're wrong." A dark, nearly vicious expression crossed Ber's face, and his fingers went white around the armrests. "Whatever you end up believing about me, be certain about this. When I said I sent Tes here to discover the type of man you are, I wasn't lying. I knew you would protect her and our child as soon as you discovered the truth. Keep her here, hidden. From her horrid father. From me. From everyone. Nothing else matters so long as she and the baby are safe."

Once again, Toren could only stare at his brother. In all their years of life, he'd never seen such protectiveness from Ber. Never. Could his brother feign such a fierce demeanor? The glint in his eyes that suggested he'd kill anyone who laid a finger on Tes? It was beyond Toren's every experience with his twin.

And for the first time in ages, he truly didn't know what to believe.

~

MEHL PACED the perimeter of Toren's office like a sentinel patrolling the parapets. This was intolerable. Even at a distance, he was linked enough with his husband to feel echoes of his emotions—shock, anger, uncertainty. But worst of all? Toren was wavering. Whatever foolish tale his brother was spinning, Toren wanted to believe.

And badly.

The door opened, and a servant passed a basket to one of the bodyguards. Although Mehl knew what it should be—the princess's embroidery—he stopped the guard to claim the basket for himself. He'd been tasked with keeping everyone safe, and it was a duty he would not shirk. So he lifted the lid and searched for anything amiss.

He spotted quite a few skeins of thread, a packet of needles, a tiny pair of scissors, and a surprising assortment of folded cloth. However, the works-in-progress bundled near the top were what gave him pause. Was that...a gaping wound sewn across her betraying husband's chest? Had she seriously embroidered a detailed image of Prince Ber just to depict in fabric how she wanted to kill him?

Ryssa snatched the basket from his hands. "It's the only way I can stab him at the moment," she muttered before marching back to her seat.

As Mehl tapped his fingers against the knife hidden beneath his robe, he couldn't help but contemplate how long it took to learn embroidery. For surely, he could see the value in stabbing something sharp into Ber's visage. Repeatedly and with vigor.

It seemed to be the only way the princess could tolerate the situation. Though she began to jab her needle into the fabric with a scowl on her face, a little of the tension eased from her shoulders. Mehl had to admire her fortitude. At this point, she had the most right to make Ber suffer.

"I can't stand this," Ria cried, jerking to her feet. "I can feel his turmoil."

Mehl hurried to her side, but at a soft word from the healer, Ria closed her eyes and breathed deep. Though she settled a bit, Mehl gathered her into his arms. "I know, love. I can, too."

Gods, but he longed to charge out of the room after their husband. Too bad he couldn't. At this point, the best he could do was keep the rest of their family safe and trust in Toren's good sense.

SOMETIMES, hope was a miserable thing, a fact Toren had learned at the hands of the very man sitting across from him. How often had some small kindness prompted that fickle light to spark in Toren's heart, only to have a new cruelty extinguish it? All his life, he'd heard how twins should be close. The best of friends. But that had been forever impossible with his own.

He couldn't betray Princess Tes by misplacing his trust now.

"I don't know what you mean," Toren said. "The princess's body was delivered to the Centoi court some time ago. Do you have another wife you'd like me to protect?"

This time, it was *Ber* who studied *him*. Toren braced himself for insistence—or for probing questions—but his brother gave a sharp nod. "No," Ber said. "I'll only have Tes until the day she kills me. I'm sure she has at least three plots in mind already."

That assessment rang so true that doubt rejoined hope in causing Toren turmoil, but there were some risks he could not take. He was not a young man free of responsibilities—he was High King, husband, and father-to-be. A situation like this took infinite care and thought.

"Once again," Toren said, "Tell me why you devised this meeting. I know there's a greater reason."

Sighing, Ber swept his hand through his long, dark hair. "Fine. King Ryenil planned to have Tes killed as soon as our child was born. Then once I'd successfully challenged you, he would raise the child while I reigned here. I'm sure you can see what happens then, right? He'd have me murdered, and his bloodline would end up with both kingdoms, my child his little puppet."

The claim sent a new wave of rage through Toren, and his shields shuddered beneath the surge of his energy. He had to breathe. In and out. Right now, calm control was the only tool he had. There was no punishment he could deliver and no control he could take. Not at the moment.

It could be a lie, he reminded himself.

But of all the things his brother had said, Toren suspected this was truth. He'd already noted that something was terribly wrong in the Centoi court, and the king's callous message about his daughter's death had only confirmed it. Such a sick plot matched everything he'd learned about King Ryenil.

The question was whether or not Ber was in collusion.

Toren struggled to unclench his teeth enough to speak. "Knowing this, you still challenged me?"

"For your own safety. Besides, you *need* an heir." Ber leaned back in his seat. Then forward again. Why was he so agitated? "Preferably more than one. I infiltrated the Centoi court a little too well, Tor. I should have stayed away from Tes, not fallen... I should have left her alone. The things I learned after gaining Ryenil's trust haunt my sleep. But I can't leave Centoi. As long as I'm the next in line to your throne, he'll try to get you out of the way. He considers my exile an inconvenient formality. As we wait out the terms of the challenge, you're safe from assassins. You have no idea—"

Ber's mouth snapped closed, and the horror that twisted his expression in that moment made Toren's stomach roil. But he couldn't relent. "This is too much trust to expect, Ber."

His brother nodded. "Then I'll deliver my terms and leave. They are simple enough. Use your power to alter the inheritance laws. I don't care how, so long as I'm removed from succession. Do that, and the challenge will naturally end. But don't announce it. Only an Eyamiri will know, and our cousins are too far-flung to notice."

"You want me to pretend the challenge is still active?" Toren asked.

"Through the birth of my child," Ber answered at once. "And yours, if you produce one. By then, perhaps I'll see to Ryenil's downfall. Whatever you do, though, trust no one who isn't blood-oathed to loyalty. Even the servants bear watching."

As a hint of his brother's fierce protectiveness returned, Toren couldn't stop staring. Who was this man he'd thought he knew? "I don't understand you."

"You never have." Ber stood, turning his intense gaze on Toren. "Don't tell Tes what I've revealed to you. Not yet. If the gods favor me, I'll have everything settled before she learns the truth."

"It will be easy enough not to tell her." Toren smiled, though he felt too conflicted for amusement. "Since I'm afraid I have no talent for conversing with the dead."

Ber's laugh rang out. "Well, then, this may be the last time we speak. Be well, brother."

What did he mean by that? Before Toren could cobble together a question or even a response, his twin spun on his heel and strode out the door.

CHAPTER 59

SPECULATION

Toren leapt to his feet and rushed after his brother. He refused to allow Ber to have the final word, especially with so much business still between them. Yet again, his twin thought to disappear.

Not this time.

"Your Majesty, are you sure—"

Ignoring Macoe, Toren swung the door open and instinctively turned left, toward the palace entrance. Sure enough, his brother strode down the corridor with quick, clipped strides. Toren almost had to run to catch up, but he managed to snag his brother's arm and pull him back around while they were out of hearing distance of the nearest guards.

Ber's glance flicked over Toren's shoulder at Macoe's approach. The captain was closer than he'd been in the receiving room, but Ber would simply have to accept it. Something he must have realized, for although his glare cut back to Toren, he didn't complain.

"Was there something left unsaid, Your Majesty?" Ber drawled, jerking his arm free of Toren's hold.

"A great deal, but little that we have time to address," Toren replied. "Where are you going?"

His twin shrugged. "Where I please."

Toren lifted a brow at the change in his brother's demeanor. *This* was the angry, sullen, flippant brother he knew. How could he shift so wholly in mere moments? "You're *not* disappearing again, not with the Centoi contingent awaiting my reply in the morning. I'm sure you'll travel back with them, so you should remain with them until the morrow."

"I do not wish to stay here," Ber argued. "Tell me your message, and I will deliver it to the king myself."

Toren shook his head. "I will not have my words misconstrued."

Abruptly, Ber's mind connected to his—for the first time in centuries. *"I will tell him that you are unhappy with both Princess Lora's actions and my status as heir but that you are committed to maintaining the alliance."*

"No. You may not speak for me," Toren managed to answer.

But only because he didn't have to use his voice. The lump in his throat burned with the fire of a million things unsaid. Of a connection so easy and pure that it never should have been abandoned. Toren's fists clenched in reflex.

That link between twins...here it was, as easy to maintain as it had been during childhood. But they were both more shielded now. Toren could only catch glimpses of his brother's inner turmoil, and he was forced to guard himself tightly for so many reasons. His energy throbbed to be set free, the secrets he held pounding at his mind.

Despite their bond, there could be no reconciliation. Not with so much standing between them.

"Your control has improved, Tor," his brother sent.

"It has had to," Toren countered. *"You will wait with the*

Centoi contingent for my written message tomorrow morning, or I will consider all your claims this day to be lies."

Shock passed across their connection as Ber scowled. *"It is torment to be here, where so many consider me a villain. But I will concede, provided you give me your oath not to discuss with anyone except your husband, your wife, and Macoe what I have said this day. No one else is to know until I permit otherwise."*

Toren's stomach turned at the thought of keeping this from Tes. He wanted to rail at his brother, to describe in detail how much pain the princess had suffered over his betrayal, but he couldn't. Not without betraying her himself. Yet if he could be certain of one thing, it was that letting Ber disappear now could end in disaster later.

"On my word as High King, I promise that for one year's time, I will disclose the details of our discussion only to my spouses or to Macoe, provided you remain in your assigned room until you leave with the Centoi messengers tomorrow."

Ber flicked his hand out in a gesture of denial. *"One year isn't long enough."*

"If you weren't lying to me, then I dare not risk my family by leaving Ryenil to fester for longer. He may grow weary of waiting out the terms of your challenge."

Whatever else, it was clear that Ber *had* told the truth about his hatred of staying here. His face twisted with the kind of pain one might expect during torture, but after a moment, he closed their mental link and nodded.

"Fine," Ber said aloud. "Macoe, escort me to the diplomats' suite and have Feref prepare me a room. It seems a more welcoming inn is not in my future."

This time, when his brother turned to leave, Toren didn't stop him.

~

HOW LONG COULD a meeting between enemies take? Ria cast an envious look at Ryssa's embroidery. Why hadn't she thought to request something to occupy her hands? It didn't have to be a project quite so bloody-minded as the princess's current design featuring a severely wounded Ber.

Just...something.

Mehl had resumed his pacing. Ria considered joining him, but her body cried its exhaustion already. Had she ever been so tired? Maybe the time her father had accepted too many orders for ballgowns before the season's most prestigious event, forcing her to work for a week on a few hours of scattered sleep. But that was a maybe. Between her pregnancy, the stress of her presentation in the morning, and the turmoil of Ber's arrival in the evening, she was spent.

"I hope His Majesty returns soon," Vesset said, concern ringing in his voice. "Both of you ladies should rest. Pregnancy is hard on the body, as is stress, so you should be careful to get plenty of sleep."

Ryssa cut her gaze toward the healer. "I am content to remain for as long as my lady needs. I have enough energy for my embroidery yet."

If Vesset had any thoughts about the princess's current project, he wisely kept them to himself. "Her Highness wouldn't wish for you to exhaust yourself, I'm sure."

It took a moment for Ria to realize that "Her Highness" referred to her rather than Ryssa, and by then, the healer was looking at her oddly. Almost with chastisement, but it was clear he wouldn't dare that. Heat crept into her cheeks.

"Of course I wouldn't," Ria said. "You needn't stay with me if you're tired."

Before the princess could answer, the door swung open, admitting Toren. But not Sir Macoe. A single bodyguard trailed the High King, instead. "Tor!" Mehl exclaimed, pivoting mid-step to hurry toward their husband.

Silently, Ria stood, her gaze locked on Toren's face. As Mehl tugged their husband into a hug, she studied his expression. Tired, worried, confused...all easy to spot. But there was something about his eyes. A shuttered quality she'd never seen while he was with Mehl. Was the news bad? Ah, but she shouldn't forget that they weren't alone. He would no doubt tell them what had happened once he'd dismissed the guards.

Though she approached more slowly than Mehl, Ria reached them before Toren stepped free of their husband's embrace. As soon as Toren eased back, concern wrinkled his brow, and his gaze swept down Ria's body before returning to her face.

"You're well?" he asked, drawing her into his arms next.

She relaxed against his familiar warmth, and the knot of tension in her gut unwound at the feel of him. "Yes. I've been worried, but a little worry won't get me *that* overwrought."

"I know you're not easily overcome, or you would not have survived to find us," Toren murmured. "But I was concerned all the same."

She couldn't stop herself from kissing his cheek.

"Where's Sir Macoe?" Mehl asked over her shoulder.

"Escorting Ber to the diplomats' quarters and ensuring he remains there," Toren replied, finally releasing her. She expected him to order the guards out so they could speak more freely, but he frowned down at her, instead. "You and Ryssa should rest. I must compose a reply to King Ryenil before I consider bed, so why don't you let Mehl escort you to your rooms? We can discuss my useless meeting with Ber upon the morrow. It was no matter."

Ria blinked at him. He'd been gone for over an hour having

a private meeting with his greatest enemy, and it was *no matter?* "I—"

"Seriously?" Mehl demanded at the same time.

"Yes, seriously," Toren said, lifting a brow at Mehl. "Would I jest about such a thing? Tonight, my brother is under careful guard. I would like everyone to take advantage of that and get an easy night's sleep."

Before either she or Mehl could argue, Toren linked their minds. *"What was said in that meeting can only be shared with you two. Not even Tes. See her to her room, and we'll discuss it once I rejoin you in our chamber."*

Though Mehl made a grumbly sound low in his throat, Ria nodded. Not because she wasn't curious—but because she was. Toren sounded resolved, so the easiest way to find out what was going on would be quick, efficient compliance. With that in mind, she let her shoulders sag and her head droop, though she'd fought hard not to let her exhaustion show until now.

"That sounds lovely, now that I know you're unharmed," Ria said.

His frown swiveled her way, alarm crossing his face. "I didn't realize you were so tired. Vesset could have used his magic to help you nap."

"I couldn't bear to sleep while Toren was in danger." Ria gave his arm a comforting squeeze. "But I would have told you had it been much longer."

With a *snap* that drew everyone's eye, Ryssa secured the lid of her sewing basket and then stood. The princess was no fool, and based on her tight expression, she'd no doubt realized that Toren wouldn't discuss the meeting around her. But why? Had he learned something terrible?

What didn't he want the princess to know?

"I confess I *am* tired," Ryssa said. "Shall we?"

It was a quiet, awkward walk to the princess's chamber.

❧

Part of Mehl longed to pace their sitting room the way he had Toren's office, but his restlessness was overridden by the feel of Ria snuggled against his side. He half-reclined on the sofa, Ria stretched out beside him. She'd nestled her head against his collarbone, and he'd draped his arm around her shoulders to hold her close. Though her breathing had slowed as if she'd fallen asleep, her fingers rubbed absent patterns across his chest.

"How long does it take to write 'shove off' in formal decree form?" Ria mumbled.

Despite himself, a smile curved his lips. "Ridiculously long, it seems. Although I doubt that's what he'll say. Severing the alliance suddenly would be a disaster for our people."

"What do you think he'll do?"

"Come up with some politely coded way to *warn* King Ryenil that he *will* be told to shove off if he doesn't straighten up." Mehl curled his arm beneath hers so he could settle his hand against her belly. "I hope Toren teaches that skill to our children, for it is not one I possess."

Ria chuckled. "Nor I."

They fell silent. Waiting. Just waiting. He half-expected her to bring up Toren's meeting with Ber, but she seemed more inclined to rest than to speculate. If that was what she needed, Mehl wasn't going to interfere. It had been a cursedly long day, and *he* wasn't even growing another life.

When Toren finally entered, though, Ria sat up, her elbow forcing a gasp from Mehl's lungs. "I thought you were asleep," he said.

"Only dozing." Her eyes were heavy-lidded, and her hair

tangled down her back. But her focus was sharp on their husband. "I have to hear what happened."

Mehl rested his hand on her waist as he stared up at Toren. "We're in accord there."

Their husband dropped into the seat closest to the sofa and scrubbed his hand across his face. "You won't like it, but not for the reason you might expect."

"What, then?" Mehl asked, bracing himself.

"Ber claims it's Ryenil who wants me dead," Toren replied. "And that he sent Tes here because he knew we would hide her. He said he went to the Centoi court as a spy for mother and issued the challenge because he learned Ryenil wanted to have me assassinated if I wouldn't marry his daughter."

Helpless anger bloomed in Mehl's chest like fire. He'd known the prince would try to sway Toren with some sympathetic tale or manipulative claim. This sounded like both. Gods curse that traitor. No wonder Toren had radiated doubt.

"Why not ask Tes?" Ria shifted, and a strand of her hair caressed Mehl's hand. "Wouldn't she at least know if her father had tried to form a betrothal between her and you?"

Toren tipped his head against the back of the chair. "I *can't* ask. For his cooperation tonight, I've given my oath to tell only you two, at least for the next year. He wants to keep her ignorant of his intentions, good or ill."

More doubt.

"Is there any question his intentions are ill?" Mehl ground out.

His husband sighed. "I know what you're going to say, but...I'm not sure anymore. He said he expects her to kill him for what he's done, but he wants her and their child safe, regardless. If you'd seen the look in his eyes..."

A sudden worry chilled Mehl's blood. "Gods. You didn't confirm that she's here, did you?"

Toren lifted his head to glare. "Of course not. Yes, I want to believe my brother, but have some faith in me. If what he claims is true, he'll have much to atone for. And even if he manages atonement, I'm not sure I'd ever fully trust him again. However, I can no more dismiss the possibility that he's telling the truth than I can the likelihood that he lies. Ryenil *has* been acting strange, and I cannot afford to ignore him if he's a threat."

A solid point. Mehl let his eyes slip closed and tried to tamp down his anger. He'd spent more centuries than he wanted to contemplate watching Ber lead Toren around by his softer emotions, but in this case, Toren was right. Mehl couldn't allow anger to cloud his judgment, either.

Which meant he might have to give the traitor a chance.

CHAPTER 60

THE GIFT

Ria could feel the tension and anger radiating off Mehl, but her worry was all for Toren. His weariness seemed to weigh him down like a jewel-encrusted cloak as he slumped against the back of his seat. And who could blame him? Family was complicated at the best of times, and his relationship with his brother could never be called anything resembling *best*.

"Did he actually have new terms to deliver?" she asked.

She expected Toren to shake his head no, but he nodded instead. "Aside from hiding all of this from the princess, he wants me to use my magic to change the inheritance laws. He wasn't specific as to how they should be changed, so long as it renders him unable to inherit."

Mehl straightened, jostling her a little as he swung his leg from the couch. "That makes no sense. What could he possibly stand to gain?"

Though Ria wondered the same, she hesitated to ask another question. She should have thought better of her last one, for the lines of exhaustion on Toren's face had only grown.

All of this could be discussed after a solid night's rest. Not that *Mehl* appeared likely to sleep. Their husband's turmoil had him in an uproar.

"According to Ber, Ryenil wants him to take the throne of Llyalia from me with the ultimate goal of combining the kingdoms." Toren sighed, a heavy, pained sound. "Apparently, if Tes wasn't 'dead' to the king, he would have murdered her after the child was born and raised the baby himself while Ber ruled here. Then after a few decades, Ryenil would have Ber assassinated and place the now-grown child on the throne of Llyalia instead. A puppet ruler, essentially."

In reflex, Ria crossed her arms over her stomach to protect the child within. "That's awful."

"But is it true?" Mehl asked. Despite the anger in his voice, he rubbed her back in gentle, comforting circles. "That sounds extreme. Surely, our spies would have detected some sign of this?"

"I suppose it depends on how effective he's been at hiding it."

Ria's heart twisted at Toren's flat, tired tone. *I can't take it anymore.* Before Mehl could ask yet another question, she hurried over to their husband and slipped into his lap. Toren enfolded her in his embrace as her arms curled around his neck, and as she nestled her face against his neck, she felt him drop a kiss against her hair.

She'd meant to comfort him, but the peace that filled her at the gesture suggested she'd needed a bit of comfort herself. Though Toren could be fierce and sometimes even chaotic, there was a timeless steadiness to him, unending like the pulse pounding beneath her lips. She couldn't resist soaking it up.

His hand slid slowly up her back, and her body went warm and soft at the caress. Without thought, she kissed the soft, tempting skin at the base of his neck, and he shivered. Against the side of her leg, she felt his cock harden, but the sigh ruffling her hair suggested that exhaustion held him in a greater grip than desire.

"I'm not sure you really mean that," she quipped, shifting her leg to rub against his hard length.

Toren's chuckle sounded dry to her ears. "I'm not sure, either."

Mehl's eyes narrowed. "What are you talking about?"

"Whether I want to take you both to bed for sex or to sleep," Toren muttered.

At the choked, growly sound of frustration Mehl released, Ria lifted her head to look at him. Her brow wrinkled in confusion. Mehl's lips were white from how tight he pinched them, and his hands were gripped into fists atop his legs. Who was he upset at? Ber? Toren?

Her stomach dropped. Was it her?

"I don't understand how you can consider either sex *or* sleep," Mehl gritted out. "Your brother remains a threat."

Not me.

Her fear for herself faded, but as she felt the way Toren sagged beneath their husband's harsh words, her worry for him increased. She glared at Mehl. Couldn't he see the hurt he'd caused? "I know you're feeling protective, but why are you so angry? It isn't Toren's fault."

Mehl leapt to his feet. "It's not that I'm angry *at* him. It's only..."

"That he's afraid," Toren murmured, his somber voice a low rumble beside her ear. "Afraid that I am falling victim to my brother's manipulation again by letting the subject go. But Mehl, that is not the case. We're all exhausted. Especially Ria, who carries our child. More than that, though...I *hurt*. Heart and soul. Have you considered that no matter the truth about my brother, my family is broken? So. Broken. Maybe I'm a fool for trying to form a new one with both of you when I don't even know if my own twin is secret ally or mortal enemy."

Ria's heart crumpled—as did the anger on Mehl's face. Poor Toren. Burying her head against his neck once more, she held him close and tried her best to send him some of her strength. Her love. She heard Mehl's footsteps approach, and his heat warmed her back as he leaned down to kiss Toren.

"I'm sorry, love. I should have thought," Mehl whispered. "Let's go to bed, and we'll show you how much we belong."

At Toren's nod, Mehl helped Ria to her feet, and together, they practically stumbled to the bedroom—but not in a rush of passion. This was the slow, slurred walk of exhaustion and uncertainty. A weariness of the soul. By the time they reached the bed, Ria nearly fell atop the covers fully dressed.

But no.

Almost numbly, she stripped off her dress as the kings removed their own clothes. Yet when she finally slipped beneath the sheets beside Toren, she knew she couldn't rest. Like Mehl, she longed to show their husband how much he meant to her. She tucked herself against his back, her arm curling around his chest as Mehl wrapped his arm around them both, and grazed her lips along Toren's spine.

Quiet and tender—that was how they made love. For Ria, it was touch—a caress here or a soft kiss there. For more than anything, Toren needed reassurance, and mostly from Mehl after all that anger. So she smiled against Toren's back as Mehl kissed his way down their husband's chest. When Mehl pushed him to his back, Ria was the one who danced her fingers teasingly along Toren's parted thighs before Mehl claimed him.

It wasn't their usual heated frenzy—but she drifted off to sleep in sated contentment anyway.

Despite a night spent curled around either Ria or Toren, conflicting emotions still simmered deep in Mehl's gut as he sat upon his throne. Yes, he had faith in Toren, but he also knew his husband's weakness—an understandable one, in truth. Though Mehl didn't have a twin, he did have a sister, and it would take a great deal for him to believe she'd betrayed him. The very thought brought him pain—as Ber's betrayal did Toren. How could it not affect his husband's perception of his twin?

While Mehl hadn't lied last night when he'd said he wasn't mad at Toren, the deep well of anger inside him was very real. But this fury was all for Ber, who'd hurt Mehl's beloved time and time again. Ultimately, it didn't matter if the prince turned out to be an ally. He would never forgive Ber for the wounds he'd inflicted on Toren.

It was inexcusable.

Morning court was a cesspool of nosy courtiers and opportunistic lordlings, all hoping for a sight of the disgraced Prince Ber. Those with scheduled petitions probably considered themselves lucky, for they had a perfect view of the Centoi contingent, including Ber, currently marching up the royal green runner. The nobles held their composure well enough, since most had been at dinner, but the pair of merchants awaiting their turn gaped openly from their spots in line.

Thanks to them, the tale of this meeting would spread throughout the city well before the midday meal. Mehl sighed. At least the rumors might be a little more accurate.

Ber halted at the base of the dais and bowed with his usual hint of mockery. Not a thing about his demeanor suggested he was an ally, not as he'd claimed to Toren. When directed to rise, the prince did so with a careless grin, and he waved his servant to his side without regard to protocol.

"I bid welcome to the emissaries of King Ryenil of Centoi," Toren said, his voice almost bored as he flicked his fingers toward Feref. "Since you have far to travel, I will not keep you. Feref will give you my written reply to carry to King Ryenil. Please do so with my regards."

Ber accepted the offered scroll with a smirk. The servant at his side lifted his hand as though to take the scroll from the prince—or so Mehl had assumed. Instead, the man held his cupped hand higher, revealing a tiny box tucked against his palm. Mehl tensed like the guards standing on each side of the dais. The spells imbued on the doors were designed to detect all magical artifacts, but mistakes were always possible.

"On behalf of King Ryenil, I present this gift to your esteemed husband, King Mehl," Prince Ber said. "I'm afraid it was forgotten during yesterday's...tensions. Unfortunately, the king does not have an equivalent offering for your betrothed, as the news of that happy event had not yet reached him. I'm certain he'll send an appropriate gift in celebration."

Everything about that little box heightened Mehl's suspicions, but Toren merely inclined his head. "Please thank King Ryenil for his thoughtfulness. If you'll give the box to Feref, he'll deliver it to Mehl's private rooms for later appreciation."

After a magical examination, of course. Everyone in the room understood that. But even with that additional precaution, Mehl wouldn't open it when anyone else was present. He eyed the box as Feref accepted it from the servant before returning to his usual place near the dais. Did the thing even open? It was too tiny to discern details from here.

Toren dismissed the Centoi contingent with a surprising lack of fanfare, and Ber behaved well enough that it might have been a normal state visit. But Mehl studied the prince's every move. Not even the swish of his cloak went unnoticed as Ber marched back down the runner with the emissaries.

At the door to the throne room, Sir Macoe stood guard, and Mehl exchanged a knowing glance with him. *Follow until Ber is out of the palace.* Without so much as a nod, the captain spun on his heel and trailed after the departing group, a new guard slipping into his place so seamlessly that most wouldn't even notice.

Mehl barely paid attention to the other petitions, his thoughts instead on the little box Feref quietly passed to one of the court mages for examination. It wasn't unusual for visiting dignitaries to offer gifts to the High King's spouse, but it was typically something sent by the husband or wife of that nation's monarch. Otherwise, gifts were offered to the royal family as a whole.

But it wasn't a strict rule. There would be no real breach in etiquette for King Ryenil to offer a gift to another monarch's spouse, though Mehl had a feeling the king hadn't been involved at all. This had Ber's touch, and that meant that the box was probably dangerous.

When Toren stood, Mehl followed out of reflex, and he barely remembered retreating from the throne room to the small antechamber where Feref helped them remove their elaborate overrobes. But as soon as he'd stripped down to his tunic and pants, Mehl pinned the chamberlain with his gaze.

"Where did you have it taken?"

"In consult with a healer, the mage carried it to your private study for examination," Feref replied. "I thought it better to have it there than a room shared with High King Toren or Princess Ria."

Mehl nodded. "Thank you."

Lips twisting in annoyance, Toren lifted a brow. "You're not thinking to exclude me, I hope."

"Thinking to?" Mehl braced himself for his husband's displeasure, but it couldn't be helped. "No, I have already decided most firmly to exclude you. Above all, you must be safe, and if there's misfortune hidden in that box, I'll not have you be the one to find it."

"Mehl—"

"Give me this, Tor," Mehl insisted. "I stayed behind while you met with Ber. Trust me with this."

Toren's frown deepened, and his energy pulsed. But he inclined his head. "Fine. So long as both mage and healer are present as safeguard."

"Done." Before Toren could think better of it, Mehl dropped a kiss on his husband's lips and headed for the door.

It was time to find out what Ber had left behind.

CHAPTER 61

WARNING

Mehl frequented his own study far less than he did Toren's. Although he used the room to review the accounts and sometimes to interview new staff, he left the finer details of household management to Feref. In fact, Mehl had barely changed the decorations after becoming king, and so the tiny, rectangular box sat atop the same low table chosen by Toren's father a millennium or so before.

On the other side of the table, one of the court mages, Islil, waited beside a healer named Mery. Both women were reliable and seemingly trustworthy, but Mehl was still surprised to see them. He'd expected Toren to summon the highest-ranking in the land out of an over-abundance of caution.

He gave a quick, absent greeting as he stopped beside the table to study his unexpected gift. The box appeared to be made from a rich, deep brown wood, but gold scrollwork and inlaid pearl covered much of it. What was the purpose of such a thing? It would hold very little gold or jewelry. Possibly tea or perfume?

Though in this case, poison seemed more likely.

Mehl met the healer's gaze. "Did you detect any harmful substances?"

"I did not, Your Majesty," Mery replied.

Islil shook her head before he could ask. "No harmful spells, either, King Mehl. A surprise, coming from…"

"Prince Ber," he finished for her, then waved away her sputtered apology. "You needn't hold your tongue about him around me. You're unlikely to say anything I haven't thought."

"He is still a prince of Eyamiri blood." The mage's cheeks flushed red. "I'm sure if High King Toren heard me disparage his brother, I would be scolded. Thus, I must beg Your Majesty's grace in forgetting the slip."

Truly, he was the last one she should worry about in such a situation, but he wasn't going to make her more uncomfortable by arguing the matter. "Of course. As for the box, did you note whether it opens?"

"There is a small button," the healer said, answering for Islil. "Shall I press it?"

Once again, Mehl nearly argued—he could press a button himself—but he had a feeling Toren had ordered these two not to let him do anything remotely risky. So instead, he merely nodded. His pride would only delay matters, not help them.

After the mage cast a shield around the box, Mery touched a tiny pearl on one corner. With a soft snick, a blade shorter than the length of his thumb shot free, and the healer let out a low yelp of surprise. But it only took her a heartbeat or two to regain her composure before she lowered her hand to just above the blade so she could scan with her magic.

While she and Islil did their work, Mehl knelt down for a closer visual examination. It was an odd object to hold a knife, especially such a small one. Unless the wielder stabbed a major artery, it wouldn't do the kind of damage a healer couldn't repair. The blade didn't even look particularly sharp. It could perhaps slit a throat or gut a person, given enough force and determination, but a regular dagger would do a better job of either.

If Ber had meant to send this as a threat, it was an odd one.

"I'm still detecting no hint of magic," Islil said. "Beyond the spell maintaining the integrity of the blade over time, that is."

"There's no poison, either." Mery straightened. "In fact, I can't find a trace of *any* kind of poison, herb, or potion ever being used on this. Even the inner lining wasn't made with suspicious dyes. It's a strange device, but it doesn't appear to be dangerous. Blade notwithstanding."

As soon as the mage's shield faded, Mehl picked the knife up, though both women looked worried that he'd touched it. He made a mental note to tell Toren not to scold them. They were in an awkward position, being ordered by one king to protect the other. But Mehl couldn't delay his investigation because of that. He would learn no more without physically examining the device.

The fancy box made a terrible hilt for a hand his size. If this was truly meant to be a weapon, it had likely been designed for someone with a slighter frame, but even then, it would be difficult for the wielder to get enough leverage for an effective blow. Maybe he was thinking too much like a warrior? For all he knew, it had been designed to open missives.

"It appears to be nothing more than a gift, after all," Mehl said. "But I am grateful for your care in examining it. Thank you. You may go."

After the briefest hesitation, the two bowed and then left. Only then did he drop onto the soft, aged cushions of the nearest chair so he could take a closer look. Ber wouldn't have given this to him for nothing. It was simply impossible that... Wait, was the lining poking out the tiniest bit at the base of the blade?

It took a few jabs with the tip of his dagger and a great deal of tugging, but eventually, he worked a piece the size of his fingernail free. And on it? The edge of a letter. There was writing on the cloth. After finding that, care warred with impatience as Mehl fought to free the lining without damaging it. The thin silk had been wound around something inside that box—probably the mechanism that held and released the blade.

He was ready to throw the whole thing against the wall by the time he freed the cloth and smoothed it across the low table in front of him. The silk was nearly the length of his forearm, and nearly every bit of the gold-colored fabric was covered in bold writing. With his name scrawled along the top, the message was no doubt a new one.

Mehl—

Keep your mistrust of me. It is well-deserved. However, as I know your diligence in protecting my brother, I cannot neglect to warn you of any known threats. Firstly, Ryenil has planted six spies amongst the royal servants over the course of the last decade. I could not determine whether all six still remain, but I will list their names and last-known positions at the end, along with the three noble families involved in Ryenil's plans. I am uncertain how many from each house bear knowledge of the plot—that is for you to investigate.

Second, and of greatest concern... The assassin responsible for my mother's death was never found. This person was placed in the palace before I was born, I believe, and Ryenil has never admitted to their presence. However, the vial of poison I discovered is a type he prefers. I found it wedged beneath a saucer on the tea tray, suggesting the involvement of a servant. Toren would hear no words I spoke in defense, but had he investigated more thoroughly, he would have discovered that I never touched the stopper on that vial.

Not that it matters. Search for a similar poison amongst the long-standing servants, and my family might find true closure. At the least, guard Tes and our child. Ryenil must not know she lives, and placing her so visibly as your new bride's companion is a risk I do not like. If she or my child are harmed, I will kill you myself.

And if Toren hesitates to use his energy to change our laws, find a way to force him. We must remove every fleck of Ryenil's power.

Prince Berrett Eyamiri, Loyal Son of the Blood

Mehl read the bold message four times before he made it to the list of names, but he found he could barely register the shock of those. Instead, his eyes were drawn time and again to one key claim: *"he would have discovered that I never touched the stopper on that vial."* For as Mehl thought back to the day of the queen's murder, he could recall little about the vial in question. He'd been too intent on protecting Toren from any possible threat.

Had anyone checked for fingerprints on the stopper? Magical resonance? Ber didn't have much magic, but he did have some. If the vial had been sealed with a spell, he would have needed to use his own energy to deactivate it. But surely, Toren would have considered that. Wouldn't he?

Great. Now I'm afflicted with this doubt, too.

Scowling, Mehl wrapped the silk around the end of his dagger and slipped the whole thing into its sheath, concealing the note until he could show it to Toren. He couldn't bear to trust his husband's twin, but he couldn't dismiss these claims, either. As much as it galled him to admit, Toren was right—there was something fierce in the way Ber spoke, both of King Ryenil and of Tes.

He'd written *"Ryenil must not know she lives"* with such bold, harsh strokes that had he used paper, it would have shredded beneath his pen. It simply didn't match with everything else Mehl knew of the prince. He'd never shown care for another.

Never.

Gods above. What if everything Ber said was true?

CONCENTRATING on work was nearly impossible, but Toren gave it a valiant effort. Unfortunately, he only managed to make it through one trade proposal from the southern Empire of Moiwa before setting down his pen to massage his temples in frustration. How could he be expected to compose a reasonable reply while waiting to hear what had happened with the box?

At least Ria and Ryssa had remained upstairs, out of Ber's view, and would be occupied with a dress fitting for some time. Toren checked regularly with Macoe to learn of his twin's progress in exiting the city, but of course, making it through the curious crowds was taking a while. Until the Centoi contingent, including Ber, were well beyond the city, it wouldn't be safe.

If then.

When Mehl strode through the door, Toren leapt to his feet, and his energy surged against his shields in response. His husband channeled the excess away without comment. But as Mehl reached the other side of the desk, his hand wrapped around the hilt of the knife tucked in his belt, and alarm threatened Toren's control over his magic once more. Was there some new danger?

"Mehl? What is it?"

His husband froze. "Ah, sorry. I didn't mean to startle you. I hid something in the sheath."

Toren turned his frown to the dagger Mehl drew. Had the blade turned gold, or—no, that was fabric wrapped around the metal. A sinking sense of dread soured his stomach, though there was nothing about the cloth to inspire it. It could be anything, really.

But he knew it wasn't just anything.

"Ber left a message," Mehl said as he unfurled the scrap of gold.

Once Mehl had smoothed the fabric across the desk, it took Toren a moment to look. But he couldn't deny reality, no matter how much pain it brought. Bracing his hand against the surface of the desk, he bent to read his brother's latest claims. Nothing too unexpected, until—

Toren dropped into his seat with a thud. His mother's murder. How had he been in a room with Ber and neglected to interrogate him about that? Yes, there'd been much to discuss, but the lapse still hurt him down to his soul. It was one of the major rifts between them and was the very reason for his twin's exile.

But why did Ber believe there'd been no investigation? Only the results of that had seen him banished instead of executed.

Toren had found Ber holding the vial—that was truth. But as his brother said in the note, there'd been no proof that he'd ever opened it. The healers hadn't found so much as a drop of poison on his skin or clothes, and the magical seal on the stopper had held no trace of his energy. Even so, Ber was tricky and often cruel, and there'd been a definite possibility that he'd been involved somehow. Toren hadn't been willing to risk him remaining in the palace after that.

A search of the palace hadn't revealed a better suspect, so as time had passed, suspicion of Ber had solidified into certainty. But if Toren had been wrong about that, then a spy might still linger among them. Would they try poison again? It didn't seem likely with the inheritance challenge active, so they at least had some time to investigate.

Starting with the servants and nobles listed on Ber's note. Though it could all be a lie, Toren wouldn't chance it. A quick mental message to Feref would see the servants investigated, but the noble houses would require a great deal of care. As would the guard. Ber might not have listed any among those ranks, but Macoe would need to do a thorough check, regardless.

Tapping his finger against the desk, Toren contemplated the three noble houses at the bottom of the list. Ogewn, Hesslefyn, and Poberie. Of those, only the House of Hesslefyn held any real power, being the current head of one of Llyalia's ten ducal seats. But he wasn't surprised. He'd already been watching Lady Gartren because of the sly, snide way she looked at Ria when she thought no one noticed. According to Feref, the lady had also been rude when exiting from a dress fitting, and—

Toren's blood ran cold. "Mehl. Do you know who Ria is fitting in her workshop today?"

"No. Why...?" Mehl's voice trailed off in confusion, but he followed Toren's conclusion quickly enough—Ria could be with a traitor from one of those houses. His hand went to the hilt of the dagger he'd just sheathed. "But I suspect I should find out."

As must I.

Toren folded up the incriminating message from Ber and locked it into a drawer before he rounded the desk. No one else should see that note. He would have no spy giving warning to any on the list.

And if any hurt Ria?

It didn't bear consideration.

CHAPTER 62

TEA TIME

Ria lowered herself into her seat with a happy sigh. "Lady Elah is the most pleasant of my customers, don't you think?"

"Oh, yes," Ryssa agreed, a smile on her face for the first time since Ber's visit. "House Maqessi must be solid allies of the Eyamiri family, for Lady Elah appeared genuinely concerned with making you feel welcome. I recommend encouraging any overtures she might make toward friendship."

Ria shook her head. How long did one have to be a royal princess to gain that kind of confidence? "I don't know how you can be so sure of her."

"Oh, I'm not entirely certain of her, of course." Ryssa shrugged. "But over time, you'll see that people have... patterns, I suppose. The way she gushed over her dress and emphasized how happy she'll be to wear one of the new princess's designs to the ball suggests she's eager for you to know that she's an ally. It could be a show, but I didn't notice any of the sharp edges the sly type tends to hide beneath their smiles."

That matched Ria's impression. Not only that, but she'd never heard Lady Elah gossiping about other people even when Ria had been a nameless seamstress working in the shop. The noble woman had always come with either her lady's companion or one of her close friends, and discussions had invariably shifted to happy topics. Their favorite trends of the season, recent pleasant outings, or their kindest suitors, for instance.

But Ber's arrival had introduced a new element of doubt into Ria's heart. Who could tell who told the truth at this point? She sighed. She was in no way prepared for this kind of intrigue. "I'm not sure I can trust my impressions of others," Ria confessed.

Ryssa's smile dropped as her gaze slid down. "Perhaps I am not the best to ask. After all, I slept with and then married the worst liar of all."

There was such a wealth of pain and self-doubt in the princess's tone that Ria nearly broke and told her of Ber's claims. For if he *was* telling the truth, then Ryssa hadn't been wrong in her belief in him at all—and based on Ria's own observations, she had a feeling that was the case. But saying so would betray Toren's trust in her discretion, and there was a solid chance the princess wouldn't believe her, besides.

Especially since Ber's motives made no sense. Why allow his wife to believe he was evil when she was clever enough to be part of the plan? Ria didn't understand. Unfortunately, the princess couldn't help her figure it out, since Ria refused to put Toren in a difficult position.

All she could offer was an attempt at comfort. "Even a villain can feel. Perhaps he did have some affection for you, no matter what. Why else would he send you away to die instead of killing you himself?"

"To avoid all suspicion, I imagine." Ryssa sighed. "Listen, I know he must have said something to High King Toren to try to exonerate himself. Ber is good at spinning tales, as I well know. You needn't feel bad about asking me to leave if the three of you need to discuss his claims, because I no longer want to hear them. I have no interest in his actions."

"It doesn't bother you that he's now the heir?" Ria asked. "Aren't you curious what your father is doing, choosing him?"

"My father is the most wretched man imaginable." The princess gripped her skirts in her hands as though suppressing a surge of pure violence. "Siding with Ber is no surprise. I can't even describe how hard I've worked to find solid proof of my father's evil, for if I had that, I would challenge him for the throne at once. That, or greet him with a knife in the dark."

Ria's mouth dropped open at those harshly spoken words. It wasn't that she couldn't sympathize—she had a terrible father of her own. But the princess's cold, certain resolve sent shivers down her spine. This. This was why Ber might have wanted his pregnant wife away from Centoi at any cost. If the princess learned how far the king had gone in his attempts to take over Llyalia, she would act without considering the possible ramifications.

When Ryssa did find out, she was going to be furious.

No wonder Ber expected her to kill him.

"Are you...thinking to go back someday?" Ria ventured.

"Absolutely." Ryssa's hand settled on her belly. "I realize I have no right to ask this, considering how I treated you when we first met, but I would beg a boon of you."

Well, that sounds ominous.

Ria braced herself. "What is it?"

"Once I've healed from giving birth, I plan to ask King Mehl to help me train," the princess said, meeting Ria's eyes. "And when I'm ready, I'm going back to free my people from these cruel tyrants. Will you guard my child when I go? Hopefully only until I've succeeded, but...possibly forever. I want them to be raised safely, and by someone with honor."

Ria's stomach lurched from the grief that swept through her at the sad request. She had only started to imagine what her own child would be like, while Ryssa had to contemplate leaving hers behind. And not for some frivolous reason, either. Thousands of people counted on the royal family of Centoi to be earnest, fair, and honorable rulers. No matter what else the princess wanted, she would not abandon her duty to them.

Ria nearly deflected by saying she would have to speak to Toren, but it would be a waste of time. He'd already claimed Ryssa as family. And considering all she'd recently learned about the Eyamiri bloodline, she knew there was no way he would cast out a child of direct blood, no matter the circumstances.

Above all, neither he nor Mehl were capable of such cruelty. Even if Ria didn't accept the responsibility, they absolutely would.

"I give you my word," Ria said softly.

Just then, a knock sounded on the door, and at her call, Feref entered the sitting room, a maid trailing behind with a tea tray. "Forgive the intrusion, Your Highness," he said. "Since you have another appointment near the lunch hour, I thought you might appreciate refreshments now."

"Oh, thank you." Ria smiled. "Though it's only for a brief repair to a torn seam."

Feref sketched a bow. "Nevertheless, I would not have either of you famished."

It amazed her sometimes how kind Feref had become after their initial difficulties. Recently, he'd started to attend to her with nearly the same dedication he showed Toren, though she supposed it was partly because she carried Toren's heir. Not that she was going to complain even if that was the cause. Such favor from the palace's chamberlain made life far more pleasant.

The tray had only just been set up when Vesset arrived. As the healer strode through the room, Feref frowned. "Is all well? I thought you were with King Mehl."

Vesset shrugged. "I had work to catch up on, so I sent Mery."

"Ah." The chamberlain nodded. "Did you get your message composed in time, then? I suppose it was quite lengthy."

A curious flush rose up the healer's neck and settled into blotches on his cheeks. "Since my son has refused to answer normal letters, yes. Surely, he will not ignore a missive delivered by a noble envoy."

A noble envoy? Was he talking about one of the Centoi?

"Does your son live in Centoi?" Ryssa asked.

At the princess's tight tone, Ria peered at her curiously. It wasn't that unusual to have family in one of the surrounding kingdoms, was it? Though Vesset smiled at the princess, there was a touch of sadness there—or maybe regret—that also gave Ria pause. There was clearly a subtext to this that she was missing.

Vesset nodded. "He is a healer in the king's court. Well, still an apprentice, really. He wanted to earn his way without my influence."

"Wait, the king's court?" Feref's eyes narrowed. "Hasn't he been a full healer in one of the outlying villages for several centuries?"

"According to his last letter, he became an apprentice to the royal healer to expand his training." Pride should have filled Vesset's expression, but Ria would almost swear it was worry. "I thought I told you."

The chamberlain shook his head. "You must have forgotten to do so."

Then the door swung open, and the rush of Toren's energy swept in before he and Mehl strode through. "Interesting," Toren drawled, his tone colder than she'd ever heard it when he was speaking to one of his inner circle. "I cannot recall hearing that fact, myself."

Although the color fled from the healer's face, his smile remained. "I'm not certain I mentioned it, Your Majesty. I wouldn't expect such minor details about my family to be important to you, after all."

Ria barely registered the ringing sound of a blade being drawn before Mehl was standing in front of the healer, his knife at the man's neck. Her pulse leaping in her ears, she wrapped her arms across her stomach out of instinct. But when Feref stepped in front of her, she gasped. Was something so wrong that the chamberlain had to protect her?

What in the world was going on?

MEHL DUG the blade into the side of the healer's neck just shy of breaking the skin. Enough pressure, and the man would likely bleed out before he could think to heal himself. But even if Vesset *did* act quickly enough to clot the flow with his power, the distraction would allow Mehl plenty of time to inflict other wounds.

All of which the healer knew.

"Your Majesty?" the man whispered.

"It's you." Out of the corner of his eye, Mehl spotted the tea tray situated on the table between the two women. "Tell me neither of you drank that."

Ria blinked at him in confusion, but Ryssa's gaze was sharp as she shook her head. But then, she would understand better than most what it might mean for the healer's son to be in her father's court. Especially without mentioning the matter to Toren.

"Feref brought us this before his arrival," Ryssa said. "But I've yet to pour."

At that, Feref paled, his hands lifting in surrender. "I'm not involved in any dark deeds. If you like, I'll drink the entire pot of tea myself."

Despite how terribly the chamberlain had acted upon Ria's arrival, Mehl was fairly certain he was telling the truth. Yet the queen had been murdered by someone close enough to her to slip poison into her drink. None of them could afford to trust too much, not in a situation like this.

Apparently, Toren agreed. "Pour and drink from both cups."

Feref flinched, hurt flickering for a moment in his gaze. But after a quick bow, he moved slowly and carefully toward the table. With measured motions, he lifted the teapot and filled both cups—then without hesitation, he downed them both.

The healer shifted on his feet, and Mehl pressed the blade a touch deeper. "Move again and you die."

Vesset froze, a line of sweat the only movement as it rolled down his brow.

"What's going on?" Ria asked.

"My father always uses the people you love most against you," Ryssa said softly. "If the healer's son is in the Centoi court, he's compromised."

Ria gasped. "But Feref and the tea...?"

"Poison was slipped into my mother's tea." Anger and

sadness rang in Toren's tone, but Mehl didn't dare turn away to comfort him. "I'm sorry, Feref. Though I believe in your loyalty, I had to be sure."

Mehl's gaze locked on Vesset's, and the weight of grief he found was answer enough. Even so, he had to ask. "I don't suppose you're able to prove yours?"

"Not...in a way that matters." The healer squeezed his eyes closed. "Go ahead and kill me."

Despite the information they needed to glean from the man, Mehl almost did.

"Bind him," Toren ordered, and one of the guards stepped forward to comply.

But Mehl kept his knife firmly in place even as Vesset's arms were jerked behind his back. Only when the magic-suppressing cuffs were locked around the healer's wrists did Mehl step back, but his control was hard-won. His muscles *burned* with the desire to rend. To stab and stab. What kind of healer would act in such a way?

The guard pulled a pair of vials from Vesset's pocket. "What should I do with these, Your Majesties?"

Had he burned before? Pure rage scalded Mehl's insides at the sight of those vials—one of them suspiciously similar to the one found near the queen. Then a blast of energy pounded through the room, this time strong enough to make the teacups rattle.

Clearly, Toren had also noticed.

"I didn't want to do it," Vesset whispered. "Had orders not arrived with the envoy..."

The floor trembled beneath their feet. "You may thank the gods that Macoe is almost here," Toren gritted out. "For if he doesn't see you secured in the dungeon in the next few moments, you'll be dying a slow, painful death. You'll write out a full, complete confession, or you'll die horribly anyway."

"But my son..."

Mehl gaped at the man for his gall, but Toren gave a nod. "I will see what I can do."

Though Toren's energy practically crackled through the room, Mehl was too angry to attempt to channel it, and when Ria stood as though to move closer, he shook his head in warning. If Toren hurt her or their child because of his fury, it would be a tragedy for them all. Apparently, she understood. Her shoulders slumped, but she remained by her seat.

Vesset had barely been hauled from the room before Feref paled again. "Toren, you have to send someone after the Centoi contingent," he said in a rush, his usual formality gone. "Vesset was sending a message to his son, or so he claimed. But..."

Icy fear chilled Mehl's blood.

The healer knew nearly everything. That Ria carried Toren's child. That Tes was here, alive and healthy. That she had been given permanent shelter.

Everything, in fact, that King Ryenil didn't need to know.

CHAPTER 63
QUESTIONING

For a moment, Toren's mind went blank, but rage boiled in his gut like his restless magic, waiting impatiently to overcome his control. Vesset had been the one to betray his family. *Vesset.* The man he'd trusted to care for Ria and their unborn child.

Mehl's fingers wrapped firmly around his wrist. "Take deep breaths, love."

Awareness returned with a sharp snap, clarifying the others to his view. Ria, Ryssa, and Feref had all moved to the far edge of the room to escape the wild pulse of his energy. Telling, since Ria had long ago stopped hesitating to step in. Even Mehl bore signs of strain in the pinched corners of his mouth.

Toren did as his husband suggested and focused his intent on merely breathing. Little by little, he pulled his energy back into himself as Mehl channeled some of it away. But that only helped somewhat. If he were to genuinely consider altering the inheritance laws, now would be an excellent time. He probably had enough raging power to create an entirely new kingdom.

Unfortunately, there was something else he needed to do first. "Feref's right. We must stop the Centoi."

There was one way Toren could do that with minimal disruption, and it would use some of this energy besides. Except...it would require the one thing he hadn't believed he still possessed—trust in his brother. As twins, they could reach each other over great distances with enough power, but Toren hadn't attempted to do so since he'd been rebuffed for such a thing during their youth. Until yesterday, he and his brother hadn't spoken telepathically at any distance for centuries.

Ber had shown that their ease of connection was still there, though, when he'd connected with Toren despite the shields he'd formed against telepathy. With that being the case, he was sure the distance would matter no more now than when they'd been children. But just because he *could* warn his brother didn't mean he *should*. Doing so would require at least some belief in Ber's claims. What did it mean that he was already contemplating how to do it?

Gods above. Maybe he *did* believe his brother.

"Toren..." Mehl began.

"I must confer mentally with Macoe," Toren said, though his gaze flicked toward Ryssa. From his husband's scowl, it seemed he'd understood the hint—Toren wasn't speaking to the captain. "Give me a moment."

Once again, Toren took a deep breath, but it was impossible to remain calm. Even that morning, he wouldn't have believed himself capable of doing this. But with this final betrayal by Vesset, his brother's claims seemed more likely to be true. Key among them? Ryenil as enemy. Even Ryssa had calmly said her father was willing to use people.

Besides, if Ber was intending another betrayal, then he would learn of Vesset's letter to the king once it was received. Warning him now would only reveal the information a week or two sooner—a risk while the Centoi were still in Llyalia, but a risk that could be managed. However, if Ber *was* on their side, then Ryenil would never learn their secrets at all.

Toren closed his eyes, sucked in another breath, and then sought the link he'd tried to ignore since childhood. A bond formed in the womb, and one not easily severed. Energy, a fragment of his vast store, streamed away in an invisible line, reinforcing their connection across the distance. As soon as he made mental contact, he caught a moment of profound shock before his brother's emotions shuttered.

The link snapped firm. *"Toren? Did something happen to Tes?"*

Such a simple question, but it tore something in him with its pain-filled honesty. That was *not* the demand of someone who wanted his wife dead, yet Toren still didn't dare to admit to her presence. *"No one here has been hurt,"* he offered instead. *"Not yet. But we found a traitor. Vesset sent a letter with someone in your party, and although I haven't had time to learn all it contained, I presume it will reveal many facts that neither of us want the Centoi king to know."*

"Who?" Ber snapped, his mental voice cold and deadly. *"Who received the letter?"*

"I don't know. Vesset is being hauled to the dungeon as we speak, but I will soon question him further. However, with time being crucial..."

There was the briefest hesitation before Ber spoke again. *"I can't believe you told me."*

"Nor can I," Toren admitted. *"But if you were to betray me either now or after reaching Ryenil, the results would be the same. It seemed prudent to gamble on your truth."*

"I see." Was there hurt in those tight words? *"It will serve you well. I'll find a way to destroy the message without drawing Ryenil's ire. You may not trust me, but I'll ensure both of our*

growing families remain safe. As always. Just...for all our sakes, change the inheritance laws."

Abruptly, the connection cut off.

But not before Toren caught the edge of his brother's tumultuous emotions.

IT WAS JUST AS WELL that Sir Macoe had arrived quickly to haul Vesset to the dungeon, for Mehl wanted to strangle the traitor with his bare hands. Not just for the betrayal itself, although that was bad enough, but also for what he'd forced Toren to do. That little bit of opening up to his brother would likely bring disaster when Ber disappointed him yet again. Mehl recited a litany of curses at the thought. Just when Toren had finally cut his brother off completely, all of this happened.

"That should be a bit more settled," Toren said, no hint of emotion in his voice. "Now, there is business we must consider. In the throne room."

Ria approached, Ryssa trailing hesitantly behind. "I have another appointment. It's a short one, though."

"Shall we have a little visit with Vesset?" Mehl asked before his husband's frown could form into a denial.

Toren hesitated, his gaze sweeping the room. "Although I wish to interrogate him, I am not sure that I wish to delay this."

"Oh," Ria said.

Seeing the way her shoulders slumped, Mehl decided to intervene. Yes, they needed to see if they could do something about the inheritance challenge, but it could wait long enough for their wife to complete her business. He wasn't certain he could focus without forcing the truth out of the healer himself.

"The more knowledge we have of any plots, the better,"

Mehl argued. "Feref and Macoe can escort Ria to the throne room for safety's sake after seeing Ryssa to her room."

The princess was wise enough to give ready assent, and after only a moment, Toren relented. After kissing Ria goodbye, he and Toren left as quickly as they dared without causing concern. But they didn't head directly toward the dungeons. First, they went first to their bedroom to change into simpler clothes. He had a feeling that his husband wanted this trip to the dungeon to be a quiet one.

A hunch that proved correct. Instead of marching through the main corridors, he and Toren stuck to lesser-used hallways, even slipping down one of the staircases used by the palace guards instead of going near the formal receiving rooms. Though a few onlookers no doubt spotted them, Mehl kept up a carefully light conversation about plans for their coming wedding.

Truly a waste, for he wouldn't remember a word of it.

Unlike Princess Tes, Vesset had been imprisoned two levels down, the nicest available for non-nobles. Few of the cells were used on any level these days, but this floor traditionally held diplomats, merchants, priests, and other high-ranking commoners. Ria's father was on the far end, in fact, but as with Vesset, it wasn't a courtesy. These cells were sealed with solid doors—and magic—preventing communication with anyone.

Mehl entered the room ahead of Toren. Although his husband tried to step up beside him, Mehl kept his body angled just in front as Vesset stood up from his bedroll. The healer's shoulders drooped, and grief lined his downturned face. He remained silent, not even bothering to plead.

"Tell me," Toren commanded.

To Mehl's surprise, Vesset nodded. "I will do so. Freely, if you meant what you said about helping my son."

Mehl sucked in a breath. "You would dare—"

"Wait, love," his husband interrupted, gripping his shoulder before he could charge forward. "Vesset. Did my mother know your son worked in King Ryenil's court?"

The healer's jaw clenched. "She did not. In fact, he didn't enter the court until near the end of her reign."

Gods. How did Toren listen to something like that? *Near the end of her reign.* As though the queen had died of natural causes. As though she hadn't been murdered, probably by the healer himself. But Toren's gaze held no emotion as he peered at Vesset.

"Does he serve Ryenil willingly?" Toren asked.

"I don't know," the healer replied, his nostrils flaring. "I can hardly ask him without risking his life. However, King Ryenil's threats have been clear enough. If I don't do what he asks, my son will be disposed of."

"My spies might be able to carry him to safety, but I will not intercede if he returns to Ryenil's court of his own accord," Toren said. Mehl stared at his husband incredulously at those words. Why was he being so generous to a traitor? "However, he will not be welcome in this kingdom, and you will likely be executed for high treason."

Not *entirely* generous, at least.

In Vesset's gaze, Mehl saw only tired acceptance. "I deserve it. Upon King Ryenil's order, I poisoned the queen and left the vial for Prince Ber to discover. The king wanted your brother exiled in the hopes he would return to Centoi."

Oh, how easily he confessed! Mehl's hands clenched as he fought the urge to strangle the rest from the man. Words gasped out in pain would be just as useful—but they weren't always as true. He needed to remember his training. As he'd been taught, not only was torture cruel, but it often prompted false confessions.

"How long have you been planning to kill my wife and

unborn child?" Toren asked, a pulse of energy accompanying the question.

The healer's chains rattled as he stepped forward, clenching his hands together tightly. "I wanted no part in harming her. That I swear. I'd hoped your discretion would prevent him from learning about her, but rumors must have followed Lord Aony back to the capital. Believe it or not, I am loyal to you, High King, and Lady Ria is kind and lovely. I...I carried the poisons as ordered. One would have caused a miscarriage, and the other would kill if that didn't work. But I don't think I could have used them."

Those words snapped Mehl's temper like a flimsy practice sword in full combat. Before he realized it, he had Vesset pinned against the wall, his hand wrapped around the healer's throat. Not enough to choke, though. Glaring, he tightened his fingers in warning.

"I should kill you where you stand," Mehl snarled.

Vesset nodded. "Yes, you should. I have betrayed every oath I've ever sworn for my boy, but I've always accepted the consequences of that."

"You were surely no paragon before," Mehl said, and the healer flinched. "Or King Ryenil wouldn't have chosen your family, would he?"

Beneath his hand, the traitor's throat bobbed. "My youth was not well-spent."

Perhaps Mehl should have asked more about that, but he found he didn't care. There was a misspent youth, and then there was murder. One did not have to lead to the other. "How long have you been working with the king?"

"Since our queen rejected a betrothal between then-prince Toren and Princess Lora," Vesset answered at once. "He believed Toren would be easier to manipulate. I'd heard little from him since the inheritance challenge began, but recent events have clearly spooked him."

"I should kill you, but I won't. I have another plan in mind." Mehl glanced back at Toren, who nodded. "You'll continue writing your letters while we find a way to extricate your son, but you'll provide the information you're given."

He expected the healer to ask whether his sentence would be lighter, but Vesset agreed without a single question. Mehl was content to let him wonder. Gods knew it was what the traitor deserved for all the years he'd left Toren to wonder about his mother.

But once again, Toren proved more merciful. "At some point, you will be executed for murdering the queen. Your cooperation will only delay the inevitable."

Mehl released the healer, who dropped onto his bedroll with a gasping cough. The chains clanked loudly as the man rubbed at his neck. "I am aware. If nothing else, perhaps it will earn me some mercy from the gods."

Though his anger had hardly been assuaged, Mehl spun away and marched toward the door, pausing only for Toren to do the same. There was no peace in knowing. Not really.

Far too much had happened for that.

CHAPTER 64

PATTERNS

Unable to settle, Ria circled the nearly empty throne room, only Sir Macoe there to watch from his place beside the door. She was too accustomed to crowds here, for the way her footsteps echoed in the silence spiked her anxiety to new heights. Why did it feel so wrong without the shush of fabric and hiss of whispers from the crush of courtiers, most struggling to hide their boredom? Or perhaps it was the absence of the kings, their presence a force even without Toren's energy surging.

When the back entrance opened and Toren and Mehl strode in, Ria hurried over. But their expressions had her drawing to a halt when she was only halfway across the room. Pure fury pinched strain lines into Mehl's face, and Toren appeared cold and closed off. Their meeting with Vesset must have been a tough one.

"What did he say?" Ria asked softly.

"He murdered my mother and had orders to kill our child and possibly you," Toren bit out. "He claims it was to save his son, but it hardly matters. He could have come to me or even my mother to solve this centuries ago. He didn't."

Fear prickled her skin. "I never would have guessed that he wanted to hurt me."

"Vesset insists that he didn't *want* to follow King Ryenil's orders," Mehl said, some of the anger on his face morphing into concern as his gaze swept over her. "But he will be punished the same way, regardless. You needn't worry in that regard."

"What...what are you going to do with him?" she couldn't help but ask.

Even if she wasn't sure she wanted to know.

"He'll be executed eventually. I'd intended to have him provide false information to King Ryenil for a while, but the more I think about it, the more I doubt the wisdom of the plan." Mehl rubbed the back of his neck, though it didn't seem to ease his visible tension. "Despite the number of spies we have working in the background, it will take time to capture all the Centoi informants, so word of Vesset's capture might be wending its way to the king already. And we absolutely can't let the healer roam free to maintain appearances, not with the amount of harm he could do with his ability."

"Indeed." Shivering, Ria rubbed her arms. Vesset could have stopped her heart with a thought, especially during her last examination. "It's unnerving. I've never had anyone want me dead. My father needed me for his work, so even when he beat me, I didn't fear that. Do you think...will there be other attempts I should look out for?"

Toren's nostrils flared, and he ran his fingers through his hair with a sharp tug. "Unfortunately, yes. Accept no food or drink from anyone unless it has been thoroughly tested, although even that will be difficult to trust after Vesset's betrayal. I suppose I'll have to find a healer or two willing to swear the deep oaths like Macoe."

"My sister would likely do so," Sir Macoe offered suddenly. "She's skilled enough that Vesset would sometimes send her in his stead, yet she's not malleable enough to be chosen as one of his favored apprentices."

"Remind me later to investigate those apprentices," Toren muttered, scowling.

Ria had a feeling the healer's guild would soon be in a bit of upheaval.

Mehl nodded at Toren, but the look he turned on Sir Macoe was thoughtful. "Ah, Mery is your sister, correct? I wasn't thinking about it earlier, but that's who Vesset sent to examine the box while *he* apparently committed treason."

By the dart of pained alarm on the captain's face, Ria couldn't help but hope that the woman was innocent of wrongdoing. Mehl's tone *had* sounded more curious than concerned, but Sir Macoe obviously worried for his sister. Surely there weren't many healers involved in Vesset's plot? Toren and Mehl would have been assassinated long ago if that were the case, healers being experts on ways for people to die.

"Yes, Mery is my sister," Sir Macoe answered. His expression softened. "Though she is younger by several centuries, we've grown closer since she accepted an assignment in the palace. She's bright, cheerful, and talented, but I assure you she's stubborn in her ideals and loyal, too. She has often complained to me that the top healers tend to snub her because she refuses to become a participant in their machinations."

Ria frowned in thought. What did he mean by that? Maybe she'd been wrong to dismiss the other healers as innocent if they were known for their scheming.

Apparently, the captain noticed her concern. "Your Highness, I didn't mean to imply that the healers are connected to Vesset's treachery," he rushed to assure her. "No matter the vocation, there's always intrigue amongst those who seek greater status or an increase in power. My sister's focus is on healing, though, not moving up the ranks."

Toren slipped his arm around Ria's waist, the sudden contact startling her—then soothing. "Summon Mery, then," he said, his voice a low rumble beside her ear. "Both of you may wait outside the doors until one of us calls for you."

Brows drawing down, Sir Macoe hesitated, clearly loath to leave his post.

Mehl stepped up to Toren's other side. "I am here to keep guard, and six elite bodyguards are shielding the royal entrance behind the thrones. Your presence on this side of the doors will hardly make a difference."

A muscle in the captain's cheek twitched, but he bowed. "Very well."

Once Sir Macoe exited, Ria cast an uncertain glance at Toren, then Mehl. What now? She already knew that Toren wanted to work on changing the inheritance law, but unless he'd discovered something he'd yet to share, he still didn't know how it was done. None of them did. Were they supposed to experiment with something so important?

Toren spun her to face him, sweeping her up to claim her mouth for an unexpected kiss. For a moment, she let herself sink into him. Let herself enjoy the merging. He tasted of hope and despair, love and fear. Or so she imagined. Maybe it was in the tight way his fingers gripped her waist or the way his lips clung to hers when their mouths parted.

Maybe it was the frenetic pulse of his energy around them even when she leaned back in his arms. "I'm sorry," she said.

His brow furrowed. "For what?"

"Nothing I did," she quickly replied. "But it grieves me that you've gone through so much. You're a good king who does not deserve this. You continue to look after your people faithfully, though many would have abused such a store of power when facing so many challenges."

Smiling down at her, he brushed a stray hair from her cheek. "Somehow, you and Mehl both have more faith in me than I do. It's impossible to be certain what is right. How can I be sure I won't abuse that power still?"

"Because we know you," Mehl said, pressing himself against their husband's back. His hand slipped around Toren's waist. It came to rest between Toren and Ria, but not to separate. Mehl's knuckle rubbed a gentle circle against Ria's stomach, and he smiled at her over Toren's shoulder. "And because the three of us will work together in this. We'll provide balance."

Wordlessly, Ria nodded.

"Provided we can determine what to do," Toren grumbled, though his tone was softer with it.

"I have faith that we will," Mehl replied.

Mehl eased away from them a little reluctantly, but he didn't hesitate to move once he was free. She and Toren both watched as their husband took measured paces around the massive throne room. This time, it was no restless ambling born of frustration or worry. This was an examination. But what was he looking for? The description of the original spell hadn't given a location, much less any kind of identifying details.

Finally, Mehl came to a halt between the thrones. The tip of his boot tapped against the stone, but from her vantage point, Ria couldn't tell if there was anything special about the dais.

All of the floor, dais included, had been exquisitely designed, with smooth stone shot through with the occasional sunburst in a slightly darker shade of gray. It was so subtle that she'd never noticed the details amongst the milling courtiers.

Toren kept his hand at her lower back as they joined Mehl, who still studied the floor. The warmth of Toren's fingers brought some comfort amidst the uncertainty, but her knees trembled as she stepped up onto the dais. *This spot is too sacred for the likes of me,* her doubt tried to insist.

She shoved the insidious whisper down. Right now, there was far more to worry about than her doubt.

As soon as Toren glanced down at the sunburst inlaid in the floor of the dais between the two thrones, it hit him—the oathing ceremonies. This was where he would stand for those, but the location *itself* wasn't important. It was the link. The laws and magic that governed Llyalia might technically be fixed to the land, yet at the same time, they weren't. A High King or High Queen of Eyamiri blood could disconnect that energy from the land and hold it inside themselves in the event their people needed to flee.

The deepest of the oathing ceremonies required the participant to shed their blood atop the Bloodstone Crown, the kingdom's oldest artifact—now only used for coronations and oaths. The gold circlet held a red jewel said to be created from the first king's blood. Many thought that part to be a myth, but Toren knew otherwise. During each ceremony he'd performed, he'd joined with the power of that stone to accept the oath, and it resonated with the same energy as both the kingdom's magic and his family's blood.

But the crown, though powerful, was mostly a symbol.

With his connection to Llyalia, Toren could spill his own blood for the other person to drip theirs upon, and if he willed it, the result would be the same. Which meant it didn't matter where he and his spouses stood at all. Wherever they were, if he linked the three of them into the kingdom's magic, they should in theory be able to alter it.

It wouldn't be easy. Although he'd used many spells connected to Llyalia, like the official seal he placed on contracts and missives, he'd never attempted to change one of the underpinning laws before. Though he supposed that part would be up to Ria with her alteration magic, if she could figure out how. Against her lower back, his fingers tingled pleasantly from the contact, but it was also a reminder of what he could lose.

Gods, it was almost too much to ask, especially since he was only the power source.

"Any ideas?" Mehl asked, shaking Toren from his thoughts.

He shoved the fear to the back of his mind. If they wanted to end their current threat, it had to be done. None of them would be safe until Ryenil's paths to power were removed.

"I believe I've figured out how to link us in, provided the two of you don't mind shedding a few drops of blood," Toren said. "It should be similar to an oathing ceremony, but without the pain involved."

Ria shifted away from him slightly. "Pain?"

"The deeper the oath, the more wrenching it is for body, mind, and spirit. Most do not undergo the full ceremony, though. Macoe did so to become captain, so for him, it is soul deep. If he betrays Llyalia or the Eyamiri, he will cease to exist."

The choked sound Ria released had him rubbing her low back in comforting circles. "Then what in the world will I have to suffer to officially become queen?"

"Nothing," Toren assured her. "That is a joining made

before the gods and is thus weighed and measured by them. You'll become one of the Eyamiri that oaths are given *to*."

She didn't look convinced, but she didn't press the issue—of marriage, at least. "What about for this? I'm not worried about the blood so much. Pain, though…"

"I can make no promises, but I don't believe it will hurt us. In fact, I will cease the link if there's a hint that it will." His gaze flicked down to her belly, then back up. "You must tell me if you feel ill in any way. We'll stop, and I'll call in Mery."

Mehl frowned at him over Ria's shoulder. "She hasn't made her oath."

Although Toren would have preferred that Mery had, the more stringent ceremony would require her to rest for a day or two afterward. But everything inside him said they needed to act today. Now. Until they flushed every possible spy from the palace, they were all at risk. If the law wasn't altered and another assassination attempt succeeded, then Ryenil could still find a way to take over. That threat had to be ended no matter what.

"We'll just have to trust Macoe's judgment," Toren said.

He lowered his arm from Ria's waist, but she grabbed his wrist before he could move to the center of the dais. "Wait," she said, fear tainting her tone. "Aren't we going to talk about what we're doing first? How am I altering things?"

"I don't know." Toren grabbed one of the knives from Mehl's belt. "I need to see the shape of the law while we're connected into the fullness of it. I'm not sure if it would be easier to erase the inheritance challenge entirely or to change the way it's done. But we'll be able to speak mentally during the process. If you're still willing?"

Ria shivered at the question, but she nodded. As she lifted the side of her skirt to grab the dagger strapped to her thigh, Toren turned to Mehl. One side of his husband's mouth lifted as he unsheathed his other knife. If he had misgivings, they weren't obvious.

"Shall we begin?" Toren asked, waiting for them to tip their heads in agreement.

Then he drew the blade across his forearm and let the blood plop red onto the center of the dull gray sunburst.

CHAPTER 65

RESONANCE

With the knife pressed against her forearm, Ria met Toren's eyes. She had to ask, no matter how much her throat tightened with dread. She didn't want to think about what would happen if she couldn't do this, but she would never forgive herself if her silence brought disaster.

"Do you truly think the connection won't hurt our child?" Ria swallowed hard. "If this is similar to the oathing ceremony, I fear what this linking might do."

Gentleness and love blended with resolve in his gaze. "Our babe is of Eyamiri blood, so it shouldn't cause harm. I've always found the deep magics of our kingdom to be comforting, even when my control is threatened. But I meant my earlier words. Do not hesitate to bring an end to this if you feel any discomfort at all."

Instinct told her he was correct, but it was a risk. Yet what choice did they have? Finding a way to remove Ber from succession was paramount, though not perfect. Until knowledge of the change was widespread, there would still be danger, but even if the worst happened to her personally, Llyalia wouldn't fall to dark deception. It was time she trusted that she was here in this moment for a reason, and that reason wasn't only in her womb.

Ria sliced the blade across her flesh and hissed at the pain that shrieked through her nerves. Carefully, she held her arm over the sunburst and let her blood drip atop Toren's. There wasn't much, not in comparison to the amount of pain the wound caused, but she'd always hated this type of injury the most. She could work for hours under the dull, constant ache of a battering. Sharp pain was much harder to block.

After a few drops, Ria pulled her arm back and studied the wound. Thinner than she'd feared, and already scabbing up nicely. Still, Toren frowned at the scratch before turning his displeasure to Mehl as he added his blood. Despite everything, she smiled. Their injuries seemed to bother Toren more than his own did.

Mehl didn't sheath his knife. "Try not to draw me in so deeply that I can't maintain guard."

"I'll do my best," Toren said. "But I suspect you should guard against more than the physical. Don't let us go too deep."

Their husband merely nodded.

Toren took her hand in his, and when he closed his eyes, she followed suit. She didn't want to stare down at the splattered blood, for it only reminded her of the burning pain in her forearm. No distractions. Hadn't she learned the trick of ignoring those beneath her father's brutal hand? He had broken her skin more than once with one of his blows and then commanded her to work.

As then, Ria acknowledged the pain before pushing it to a distant corner of her mind. The burning ache was like an impatient client, shifting and huffing over to the side while she helped someone else. It would be waiting for her when she was done, but wait it must. The job at hand took precedence.

Abruptly, the link Toren was forming through their blood snapped to life, and Ria sucked in her breath at the secret realm unfolding before her. Invisible to the naked eye, but so real—and vast. How powerful must the first royal family have been to have created something like this? It would require nothing less than the overflowing energy Toren forever battled against, and no doubt more than one working.

His mind nudged hers. *"Follow me. I'll search for the magical base for the laws in question."*

Astounding. It was all she could think as they ebbed and flowed through spells and energy woven by a master hand, only Mehl their steady anchor. She couldn't begin to understand how Toren found his way through the madness. They slipped through the flow faster than she could process what any of it was.

If it were left to her, they would be hopelessly lost.

Finally, Toren seemed to find what he was looking for, and the jumble of magic clarified more fully to her inner sight. Though she wasn't physically enmeshed with the spells, Ria had to resist the urge to stretch out her hand to touch the glowing lines of power. But how could she tell what any of them meant?

"Look through me," Toren sent.

She merged more fully with him, letting go of herself a little to see what he did. Then she gasped. Words-but-not were threaded through those lines of power, and she had the sense that touching one would send the connected law straight into her mind. Was that what had to be altered, then? The content of those word-thoughts?

Mehl's voice stirred through their minds. *"What does it mean?"*

"Can you not read it through me?" Toren asked.

"No," Mehl replied.

Ria huffed. *"Not quite. I'd have to connect to the thread."*

Toren went quiet for a moment. *"This is important. The inheritance laws underpin much, and the challenge is woven through too tightly to remove. We'll have to alter it. And that...that will rest with you, Ria."*

A wave of trepidation nearly pulled her from the link, but the warm, silent support of her husbands kept her firm. There was no turning back now. Hadn't she always wanted to move her alteration beyond fabric? This was the ultimate chance, if only she could manage it.

"But what should I change?"

She felt the stillness of his contemplation before he spoke. *"The High King or High Queen must create an official line of succession. A proclamation. Written, sealed, and kept in a special vault until their death. When properly bound into the kingdom's magic, the proclamation is inviolate."*

"The heir would be secret?" Mehl asked, worry in his tone.

"Only if the monarch wishes," Toren answered. *"After all that's happened with Ber, I'll certainly not reveal which of my cousins I'll choose to inherit in the unfortunate event I outlive all of my own children."*

The change would be a solid solution, but something bothered Ria about it all the same. Maybe it was the potential for abuse. What if someone on the list turned out to be treacherous? Of course, it was impossible to guard against that fully, but if a likely candidate decided to take their chances with an assassination, what then?

"There is much that can be bound into the proclamation," Toren assured her.

But as she prepared for the greatest alteration of her life, the worry refused to be shuffled to the corner of her mind.

As a bodyguard, Mehl had learned how to split his focus, observing the world around him for any threat despite anything else requiring his concentration. That skill served him well now—though it wasn't easy. Not long had passed, but his head throbbed already from having his physical eyes open to search for danger while his inner eye followed his spouses along the endless tapestry of fathomless magic.

Mehl could perform a few spells, but this…this was far beyond him. He could barely tell that the fragment Toren studied contained something that might be words. Maybe a message? He didn't bother to find out. He was content to trust his husband's report on the matter, and there was an understanding in Ria's thoughts that suggested she saw more than Mehl could, too. They would handle the magic part.

His concern was whether they would do so safely.

As such, Mehl kept his mental view on his spouses as they set to work. If not for the worry forming a lump in his throat, he might have been fascinated. He'd never had a chance to observe something like this. While he watched, Toren's link to Ria strengthened a moment before he connected directly into the thread of magic—but then Ria touched the line of power herself.

Mehl's hand tightened around the hilt of his knife in reflex. What was she doing? He studied her, mentally and physically, for any sign of distress, but to his surprise, he found none. Whatever strength the kingdom's magic held, it bore no danger for their wife. At least not yet. Toren began to channel a little of his magic to her without any sign of a qualm.

Regardless, Mehl couldn't relax. Though their magic appeared to work well together, he couldn't shake the feeling that trouble loomed just out of reach. He split his attention again, but only long enough to check with their bodyguards and then Sir Macoe. All was well, though the captain still waited for his sister to arrive after completing a healing.

His stomach lurched. Why hadn't they waited until the healer was present?

But though his instincts grumbled a protest, Mehl didn't interrupt Toren and Ria. Yes, he would watch. If disaster threatened, he would simply have to mitigate it.

LITTLE BY LITTLE, Toren released his power into Ria, but each bit he gave was a battle. Yes, she could withstand his magic. She'd channeled his energy before, even since falling pregnant. But to this level? His power squirmed and strained against his hold as though sensing its ultimate purpose waiting on the other side of his link with Ria.

His blood practically vibrated, a sort of resonance with the magic of Llyalia—and his Eyamiri ancestors. He could almost hear their whispers, urging him to let go. To see their kingdom changed by their new queen's hand. Yes, Ria was always meant to be theirs, but not just for his and Mehl's sake.

For everyone's.

"*Toren,*" Ria snapped suddenly into his mind. "*I can't alter anything if you won't give me your energy. This won't respond to my magic at all.*"

It wouldn't? He tucked that curious fact aside and took a deep breath, reaching a mental hand to Mehl for steadiness. Then slowly, he began to pry open the shields he'd fought so long to maintain. But he didn't open all of them. Gods help him, not all. If he harmed her by releasing too much...

"*I will stop you if it comes to that,*" Mehl whispered.

And with that assurance, Toren let go.

Seeing the shape of what she was supposed to change without the ability to do so? It was torment. Like the light of false hope flickering in the shadows, only to disappear before one neared it. She was so close she could almost breathe the shape of the words formed into that thread, but they would react to nothing that wasn't meshed with Toren's power.

When his guard finally eased and true magic poured in, she sighed in relief. Finally. Prepared as she was, the force of Toren's power didn't strain her mind, though this time, she didn't channel it away into the ground. Instead, she poured it into her own pool of magic, letting their energy merge.

Hours could have passed as she began to rework the thread —coaxing, shifting, changing. Her words had to be shaped and molded with care, their intent and meaning reinforced time and again. Silently, she prompted Toren as needed and listened to his direction in return. *Connect the proclamation here. The seal for the vault must be linked in there.* Every detail she could imagine, she formed into that space.

Faithfully, she kept to Toren's given law.

Except in one thing.

There would be no hidden assassins lingering on those lists. Before taking the throne, the next in line would be tested against this thread, and any who had purposely harmed a previous monarch would be stricken from the list. Marked a traitor, punishable by death. If they refused to submit to the test, they would not be able to rule at all.

Through their link, she felt Toren startle at the addition, but he didn't refute it.

Good.

She was nearly done forming the change. Now she had to lock it in, fully replacing the inheritance challenge in the process. This was where the bulk of the energy would be required—and where her own doubts hovered. Could she really control this? It was here, perfect to her sight. Ready for that last bit of alteration. But was she strong enough?

"You must," Toren sent, his mental voice trembling with strain. *"I'm not sure I can fight my shields back into place until you've redirected some of this power. Just..."*

No time to think—not with his energy ready to consume them.

Quickly but carefully, Ria merged and shifted, blended and wove. *It must be a perfect fit, indistinguishable from the original.* But such a thing took more magic than she'd ever handled. Before long, she began to pull at Toren's energy more than simply receive.

Was she hurting him? Gods, she'd better not be—

"Keep going," he gasped aloud.

So distant, that voice, but she had no choice but to heed it.

There was no stopping now, not even when a sharp thud reverberated through the room.

As the spell finally locked into place, she barely heard Mehl's curse.

CHAPTER 66

DISCRETION

Another thump landed against the main doors, and it took all of Mehl's discipline not to dart forward. No matter what, he couldn't. He had to protect Toren and Ria. Even without this possible new threat, they worried him enough. Both were frighteningly pale, and Toren was wavering a little on his feet. If they weren't nearly finished with the spell, Mehl would have jerked them free of the magic.

Instead, he reached telepathically for Sir Macoe—but all he found was silence.

The ring of Mehl's sword echoed through the empty room as he pulled it free. If someone had managed to kill the captain, they were in serious danger. And here he stood, unable to help. Mehl ground his teeth together as he angled his body so he could see both the door and his spouses. He would at least be prepared if someone broke through.

After sending a mental command to the bodyguards at the back entrance to be vigilant, he did a tentative probe with his magic, though his head throbbed harder from yet another split in his attention. Resolutely, he breathed through it. Four people were on the other side of those doors—Sir Macoe, Mery, and two whose energy signatures Mehl didn't recognize. The strangers' energies tangled close with the captain's in either camaraderie or combat.

The latter, no doubt.

Abruptly, a sort of click echoed through Mehl's skull, and the blood-link with Toren and Ria collapsed. Heart pounding, he watched the two slump against one another like two trees damaged in a storm. Gods. Should he help them? He couldn't forget the danger beyond the doors, and rushing to offer physical support could be a deadly distraction.

Yet another loud thump reverberated through the room, followed quickly by a second. Ria spun around, nearly causing Toren to topple. Though pale, she seemed strong enough to stand steadily. But Toren trembled where he stood, his face gaunt and his limbs visibly shaking. Bile scorched Mehl's throat at his inability to help steady his husband. Only when Toren managed to drop onto his throne did Mehl manage to feel a semblance of comfort.

Still, his hand tightened on the hilt of his sword.

"I didn't know I could be so empty," Toren whispered. Then he cleared his throat. "What's happening out there? I'm not sure I have the energy to contact Macoe."

"It wouldn't do you any good to try," Mehl said. "I received only silence when I made the attempt."

Ria gasped. "Surely, he's not dead?"

"Could be other things," Toren said, his words slightly slurred. "Head wound. Mental blast. Could even be too busy. Mehl, go check."

Toren was ordering him into danger? *He must be worn to the bone.* "I can't leave the two of you like this," Mehl argued.

"Call two bodyguards in." Toren tipped his head toward the other throne. "Sit there, Ria."

"You want me to sit on the official thr—"

Thud.

She snapped her mouth closed and gave a quick, alarmed glance at the door. Then she lowered herself tentatively onto Mehl's throne. It was an odd, grim sight, but not because he felt territorial about his seat. Blood coated the hem of her butter-yellow dress, and smears of it streaked across the floor between the sunburst and the throne. She must not have watched her step when she'd spun toward the door.

He sent a mental call to Feref to come help with cleanup.

As soon as the bodyguards secured the secondary entrance behind them, Mehl charged forward. If the captain needed help, he would provide it. His thoughts clarified, his focus resolving on one thing—ending the threat on the other side of those doors.

Another scan with his magic revealed that Sir Macoe and the strangers were on the ground, and the blur of Mery's energy appeared to be atop one of them. Helping or harming? Could the captain have been wrong about his sister? Mehl gritted his teeth. If *two* healers were involved in this plot, they had deeper problems than any of them had realized.

Mehl eased slowly through the doors, his gaze flicking over the scene. On the far edges of the grand entryway, soldiers kept any lingering courtiers at bay while Sir Macoe tussled with a servant in front of the throne room doors. Mery straddled a second man's back—a mage by the design of his robes—with one hand pressed between his shoulder blades and another at his neck. Tossing her hair back, she turned her head Mehl's way.

"Your Majesty! Good, you're finally here." When the mage began to squirm, Mery bounced on his back and then bent her head toward his ear. "Stop it, Rencis. I promise you I can stop your heart before your spell hits. You hurt my brother, so I'll happily do it, too."

What was going on here?

Sir Macoe appeared to be winning his battle with a flurry of well-placed jabs, so Mehl lowered the tip of his sword to the base of the mage's skull. Any remaining hint of motion ceased at that. Only honor kept Mehl from digging the blade deep despite the man's acquiescence. He would *not* become as horrible as his enemies.

He pinned Mery with his gaze. "Explain."

"Col said he wanted to walk with me from the healer's quarters since he was helping with dinner preparations, but just as we approached, Rencis here joined us." She glared down at the mage in question. "Without warning, they attacked my brother. A mental blast. Though in pain, Mac managed a punch against Rencis, and I filled in the gap when he took on Col."

Just as she finished, Sir Macoe—Mac?—finished his own battle with a fierce punch to his attacker's face. Swiping a trickle of blood from his forehead, the captain straddled Col and twisted his attacker's arms behind his back. Then he took a rope from his pouch and tied it around the servant's wrists with deft, tight knots.

Mehl scanned the other warriors circling the room, but none moved forward. There weren't *that* many nobles to keep away. "Why aren't the others helping?"

"I don't need it at this point," the captain snapped, clearly forgetting Mehl's current rank in the turmoil. "Better to keep the courtiers away, especially since one of them could be involved in the attack. Took you long enough to heed my kicks on the door and come out, though."

Those thuds had been a signal? The captain must believe him to be inept for failing to respond. Heat crept up the back of

Mehl's neck, but he couldn't reveal why he'd been delayed without disclosing one of the kingdom's secrets. Not even to save himself embarrassment.

"I'll leave that to High King Toren to fully explain, if he so wishes," Mehl replied. "I can only say that my duty as king comes before all else."

It was all the reminder necessary, though he regretted it before the polite mask had finished slipping over the captain's face. "Of course, Your Majesty. Please forgive my lapse."

Mehl wrinkled his nose in distaste, but he could hardly complain. "Forget it. These two need to be hauled to the dungeon, and I must escort Toren and Ria back to our rooms. Do you need immediate healing?"

"A quick repair of my mental channels, perhaps." Sir Macoe shoved himself to his feet and pulled a thin chain from his pouch. Magic-blocking bindings. "Let me tie this one up, and then I'll see to it. Mery, would you mind...?"

The healer shifted her body to allow her brother to secure the mage's arms. "Of course I don't. Unless His Majesty needs me right away."

It was tempting to order her to the throne room immediately so she could check on Toren and Ria, but that wouldn't be best in the long run. They needed to be able to communicate telepathically with Sir Macoe. So instead of following his heart, Mehl forced himself to obey logic.

Protection took many forms, after all.

EMPTINESS WAS both bliss and torment, for although Toren gloried in those precious moments without the relentless push of energy, his gut clenched in fear that his power would never return. Would he forever be emptied as the cost of such a great change? How would he maintain the kingdom if he couldn't use the royal family's unique spells? He might be able to draw up enough power to seal a proclamation or two, but that was it.

"Are you okay, Toren?" Ria asked, the worry in her tone drawing his gaze. His wife stared at him, her pale brow furrowed. "I...Maybe I pulled too much."

He tried to offer a reassuring smile, but her concern didn't seem to ease. "No. It was needed, and I gave freely. I'll be fine." He hoped. "I should be asking how you fare."

"Tired but well," she said.

Toren skimmed his gaze down her body to reassure himself. Aside from being too pale, she appeared—was that blood on the bottom of her dress? He levered himself fully upright, though his muscles screamed at the movement. If she'd started bleeding...but no. Based on the smears on the floor, she'd tracked it over from their mingled blood on the sunburst.

He slumped in relief.

"Toren?" Her frown had only deepened. "What is it?"

He shook his head and leaned back against the throne. "Nothing. I'm not thinking clearly, that's all."

Though he could feel her gaze on his face, Toren closed his eyes, leaning his hand against his palm. Had he ever sat so casually in this room? He couldn't recall it, even when he'd been a child eager to play at being king. Had his mother known he'd played here when court wasn't in session? Probably, but she'd never said a word.

As the silence lengthened, Toren's energy slowly began to return. The trickle was too slight to notice at first, but by the time Feref made it through the bodyguards outside the royal entrance, Toren's muscles had ceased their aching, and his thoughts had grown clearer. When he straightened in his seat this time, it was with far less effort.

Feref slipped around the throne and gave a short bow. "King Mehl summoned me, Your Majesty. What can I do?"

"You know how to clean up the remnants of an oathing ceremony." Toren said, gesturing toward the space between the thrones. "That's no doubt what Mehl was thinking."

Feref took the scene in with a glance. "Likely, I'd say. What about Princess Ria's dress? I am uncertain how the spell works on fabric."

Gasping, Ria examined the bottom of her dress. "Oh, no! I'll do it, Feref. This is not a forgiving color, not if one hopes to maintain the vibrancy. But I know several spells for removing blood from cloth, and I'm skilled at using them."

With a father like hers, of course she was. Toren had to bite back an angry growl.

The main doors opened before anyone could respond, and Mehl strode in, a young healer trailing just behind. Toren trailed his gaze behind them to the entry hall, where Macoe directed a handful of guards in removing two men, both bound. So there *had* been an attack.

At least Toren finally had enough energy to care. "What happened?"

"A servant and a mage tried to kill Sir Macoe to gain entry, but they were foiled by the captain and his sister," Mehl explained, sheathing his sword as he reached the dais. "Motive unknown, but Sir Macoe will do his utmost to find out once they've been removed to the dungeon."

They'd truly attacked the captain? Toren chuckled low. "I'm sure he will."

Mehl moved past Feref, stopping only when he reached Toren's side. But the healer, Mery, dropped to her knees at the base of the dais. Then waited. Gods, he had to summon enough energy to be kingly, didn't he? Of everyone here, she was the only one who'd never seen him otherwise.

Stiffening his spine, Toren stared down at her. "Healer Mery, sister to Sir Macoe, we thank you for your assistance during the attack. I trust you are unharmed?"

She surprised him by meeting his gaze. Apparently, there was more spark to her than he would have guessed. "Yes, Your Majesty, thank you."

"Please stand," Toren said. "And since you'll be acting as my main healer, I invite you to reduce your formality accordingly. Consult with Feref if you need guidance."

Mery jerked shakily to her feet. "Your...your main..."

Toren smiled. "If you are willing to accept an oath similar to your brother's and if your skill proves sufficient, then yes. Also provided you accept, of course."

"I would be honored, Your Majesty," Mery said in a rush. Then she grimaced. "But there are senior healers who might be more suitable. Your health is more important to me than an elevation in status."

Exactly why she's perfect.

"I require a healer who is both talented and discreet." Toren rose—and surprisingly didn't waver. Mery shifted as though about to drop to her knees again, but after a glance at Feref, she remained standing. Good. "If you are willing, then you may begin proving your talent now. If not, I would hear your suggestions for another candidate."

She didn't rush to answer, and he didn't force a response. Fortunately, after a moment, she curtsied slightly and nodded. "I would like to accept, Your Majesty."

"Then accompany us to our rooms," Toren ordered. "And we will speak more privately."

Feref muttered a few words and waved his hand toward the blood, which disappeared with the faintest pop. The healer watched with wide, curious eyes, but she was wise enough not to ask questions. Yes, she would do well, at least if she could heal as well as Macoe claimed.

Toren approached Ria, intent on pulling her into his arms despite his lingering weakness, but she seemed to read his intent. Standing, she laughed. "I can walk, Tor."

But it was Mehl who scooped her up. "Well, pretend like you can't. I have an idea."

Curious. Toren's brows rose, but like Mery, he was wise enough not to ask aloud. Still, he had a feeling they would have quite the mental conversation on the way back to their rooms.

CHAPTER 67

COMFORT

Ria's face burned with equal parts anger and embarrassment. What was Mehl thinking? He hadn't even had the kindness to carry her through the back entrance. No, he'd strode straight through the main doors and past the gawking courtiers who were only held back by a few guards. He'd said he had an idea, but what idea could be worth this humiliation?

"*Look unwell,*" Mehl said into her mind.

She wanted to yell at him, but that would only create another spectacle. Instead, she buried her face against his chest and closed her eyes so she didn't have to witness the endless stares. "*You'd better have a good reason for this,*" she sent.

Mehl linked Toren in before he replied. "*The blood on the bottom of your dress gave me an idea. If we claim that Vesset managed to slip you a potion, it would solve two problems at once. We'll have a reason for his arrest that doesn't include the Centoi, and if King Ryenil believes you've lost the babe, perhaps that will stall more attempts like Vesset's.*"

More attempts? Would she have to worry about her every drink and meal until the baby was born? Ria shuddered at the thought. But... *"I'm not sure I can claim something so terrible. Just thinking about it makes me want to cry."*

"Then you should cry," Toren said. *"That would be only natural in such a situation."*

Nausea shoved up her throat until she thought she would be sick right there. How could they be so casual about pretending to lose their child? Especially Toren, who'd had his hopes pinned on an heir for so long? It shined a new light on what it must mean to live at the palace if such painful subterfuge was normal. Perhaps she shouldn't have accepted the engagement, not if it meant she would have to tell such excruciating lies.

"This is not *normal,"* Toren said, the edge of panic in his mental voice softening her anger. *"And if you truly do not wish to do this, we will not."*

Did she? The idea of denying her child's existence bothered her on a deep, almost panic-inducing level. If something really did go wrong and she'd said that... Ria shuddered again. No, she couldn't. But there was merit in the plan, too.

If Prince Ber was telling the truth, he needed time to defeat King Ryenil from within Centoi. Toren and Mehl might flush out any remaining traitors here, but more could slip in at any time until King Ryenil was stopped. He might focus on other methods, though, if he believed Ria wasn't pregnant.

She peeked at the crowd. Already, there were whispers and subtle gestures toward her bloodied gown. Did she actually have to lie to anyone about her pregnancy, or could she allow rumor to work for her for once? How often had she heard an innocent comment by a lady in her shop become something else later, returning twisted on the lips of a different woman?

That was how gossip flourished, after all.

"I don't want to outright say anything," Ria offered, *"But allowing rumors to speak for us would be fine. Maybe if I stuck close to my rooms for a couple of weeks? Everyone would draw their own conclusions at my absence. And I certainly wouldn't mind eating in private while I'm still suffering from so much nausea."*

Mehl nodded ever-so-slightly, his chin rubbing against her hair. Then he directed his attention toward Toren. "Do you think these two were associates of Vesset? It doesn't seem like a coincidence that they would attack when we were about to bring the healer in for judgment," he said aloud.

Her brow furrowed at the odd statement before she processed what he must be doing—providing a reason for both why they'd been in the throne room and why the intruders had tried to force their way in. Even the way the low pitch of Mehl's voice managed to carry to the nearest courtiers seemed to be intentional. They would likely believe they had overheard something they shouldn't have.

"I imagine so," Toren replied, his voice only a touch softer. "Macoe will have the truth of it to us by tomorrow, if not this evening. That Vesset would harbor such ill-will over losing his bid to lead the healer's guild… Well, we shall see if that was his motive. I can't imagine what else would prompt such treachery."

The whispers definitely intensified after that, but it wasn't long before Mehl turned down another, quieter hallway. She didn't lift her head, though. There were still plenty of footsteps, and even if the bulk of them were only from the new healer and a few bodyguards, Ria still felt exposed. Such scrutiny was not pleasant, not while she was being carried through the palace like a child.

Only the tingle of energy from the strong shields on the

door told Ria when they entered the kings' rooms. *Hah. At least I won't have to worry about eating in here,* she thought with amusement. The shields' ability to detect poison was what had brought her to this point in the first place. If she'd known what that moment would mean, would she have still brought the dye containing her own poison?

Toren brushed his hand along her hair in a quick caress as he slipped around them, and Ria smiled. *Yes. Yes, I would.*

Although there were no more crowds to see, Mehl lowered her gently onto the sofa and knelt in front of her. "Are you certain you feel well after so much spellwork?"

Ria shot a startled glance around the room at his mention of magic, but only Mery had followed them in. Apparently, the kings had meant what they'd said about giving the healer a chance to prove herself, or Mehl wouldn't have mentioned the spell they'd done at all. Still, it would be best to remain circumspect until she knew for sure.

Before the worried frown could fully form on his brow, Ria nodded. "If there was any harm to me or the baby, I haven't felt the effects," she said.

Mery gasped. "Oh, the rumors *are* true." Then the healer pressed her fingers against her lips with a wince. "Which I should not have blurted out so casually. Forgive me, Your Majesties. Your Highness."

Ria's eyes met Mehl's, and humor flickered between them. They'd both been a similar status as the healer, so they would be the last to be offended. Yet before either of them could wave off the so-called irreverence, Toren spoke up from his small desk in the corner.

"I realize Feref isn't here to provide guidance, but do recall that I allow less formality when in private," he said, his tone neutral. "And as Ria and Mehl are less inclined toward ceremony, you hardly need worry you'll be sent to the dungeon for a casual observation."

Mery pressed her trembling hands together in front of her waist. "Of course, Your Majesty. I will do my best to adapt quickly."

The poor woman. Toren was doing his best to make Mery comfortable, and she was doing her best to *be* comfortable— yet both were failing spectacularly. Ria understood, though. There was simply an air about Toren, a dauntless authority he wasn't aware he exuded. Absolutely no one would be at ease around him after only an hour.

"Mery," Mehl said. "Would you examine Ria, please? She is indeed pregnant, and we have just completed a complicated bit of magic involving a blood link. None of which, I might add, you are allowed to discuss with anyone. Not even with your brother, regardless of whether he learns the whole of it. Such secrets must not be overheard."

Despite her obvious nerves, Mery dipped into a slight curtsey. "I give my word that I will tell no one. And it would be my pleasure to help Princess Ria."

Ria found that she couldn't be nervous around the young woman, not even after Vesset's betrayal. With Mehl watching closely, his hand placed "casually" on the hilt of his dagger, Ria closed her eyes and let the healer do her work.

Silently, Mehl stood, easing back to give the healer room to work. Best he could tell, Mery did nothing untoward. Her energy remained steady, and Ria relaxed against the back of the sofa with no sign of concern. But he couldn't seem to lower his vigilance, not even with the trust he was beginning to develop for the healer.

"*She hasn't taken the deep oaths yet, but I believe her to be as loyal as Macoe,*" Toren whispered into his mind. "*Do you still bear a great deal of doubt?*"

Mehl released a soft sigh. "*Not really, but it is difficult to let go of the fear I felt when I couldn't rush forward to stop the attack. I'm not certain I've ever been so torn. But what else could I have done? If my attention had slipped any further and the magic had grown to be too much, all of you could have been lost.*"

"Perhaps you should take Ria to the bathing room for a relaxing soak," his husband suggested. "I'll be writing out the line of succession as soon as Feref gets here with what I need."

Mehl whipped around to glare at Toren. "*You're sending* me to relax? *You need an examination, too. And rest. If I'd been able, I would have carried you along with Ria.*"

"*Did you forget that there was an attack less than an hour ago?*" Despite the snap beneath the question, Toren leaned back against his chair and rubbed at his eyes. "*What happens if I am killed before creating that crucial document, Mehl? It must be sealed into law immediately. That is unavoidable. But in the meantime, it would bring me great comfort if you would see to Ria and yourself when I cannot.*"

No matter how much Mehl wanted to argue, he couldn't. None of them knew what would happen if Toren died without writing down the line of succession. Yet again, his husband would wear himself down for the kingdom, and none of the ungrateful wretches would know it.

Toren's lips twitched. "*A fascinating way to think about your own subjects.*"

"*I didn't mean everyone,*" Mehl said. "*Only the ones who* are *ungrateful wretches.*"

"*If you say so.*" His husband smiled, and a teasing look entered his eyes. "*I'll allow Mery time to examine me if you'll do as I ask. That's almost as good as relaxing, right?*"

It wasn't at all, but it was the best Mehl was going to get. *"Fine."*

A rustle of fabric drew his attention to the two women. The healer straightened with a decidedly relieved expression, and Ria still appeared calm and unharmed. Good news, then?

"All is well," Mery said. "I healed the scratch on Her Highness's arm and checked on the babe. It is early yet, so I was surprised by the child's vitality. Whatever magic you did certainly caused no harm."

Though relief eased some of Mehl's tension, it was Toren who sagged in his seat as though his muscles had lost all strength. "Thank the gods," his husband said. "To help the kingdom, Ria channeled a great deal of my energy. I've been immensely concerned ever since."

"Is that why your energy seems low, Your Majesty?" Mery asked politely. "I would be happy to assist you with rejuvenation."

"If you'll heal Mehl's arm, then certainly." Toren turned a pointed—and self-satisfied—look Mehl's way. "He's promised to go rest with Ria after that."

How did his husband always get his way with such ease? Shaking his head in bemusement, Mehl held his arm out without arguing, though the cut was minor enough that he wouldn't have bothered to see a healer for it. But there was no point in remaining injured with Mery standing right there. In moments, the gash was gone, and he was able to help Ria to her feet without a hint of pain.

"Let's go wash off this dried blood," he murmured by her ear.

Ria frowned. "But Toren—"

"Has crucial work to do before he can join us," he interrupted just as Feref strode through the door with a stack of papers. Mehl switched to telepathy to finish the rest. *"The line of succession, remember? He's all but ordered us to go relax while he writes that part out."*

Although her frown didn't ease, she nodded, and together they retreated to the dressing room to remove their stained clothes. While he unpinned the braids securing his crown, Ria used a quick spell to remove the blood from her dress. Then she just stood there—completely naked—and stared at the cheerful yellow fabric.

Mehl slipped up behind her and wrapped his arms around her waist, her presence soothing and inflaming him in equal measure. "Was there something the healer didn't tell us? Are you not feeling well?"

She rested her head back against his chest. "She told you truly. But I'm weary. Not exactly physically, I think. I'm...not sure how to describe it."

"Ah. I believe I understand." Softly, Mehl pressed a kiss to the side of her neck, and at the feel of his lips against her skin, his cock went semi-hard. *Not now. Focus.* "Mental exhaustion is common in times of great stress and prolonged worry, both of which we've had lately."

Ria let out a little chuckle-huff. "Are you a healer now?"

"No, a warrior." Mehl had to resist the sudden urge to run his tongue up her neck, but he couldn't stop himself from nuzzling against the vee of her shoulder. "It's a common problem in sustained wars, so it's something we're trained to recognize. Once the conflict is over, it's crucial to dispel the tension."

"Is that so?" She wiggled against him. "Is that why Toren suggested we bathe?"

Had there been an insinuation in the way her tongue curved around the word "bathe?" Mehl groaned as he went completely hard. He'd had no thoughts beyond cleansing, but her words combined with the feel of her nestled warm and soft against him...

This time, her laugh was full—and teasing. "Come on, Mehl. After we shower ourselves clean, you can show me how to relieve tension. Maybe Toren will be able to join us before we're done."

Adjusting himself, Mehl followed her to the bathing chamber with a decidedly awkward step.

CHAPTER 68

INTERLUDE

Ria stepped out of the spray of water and admired the sight of Mehl tipping his head back to rinse the soap from his hair. Suds rolled down the corded muscles of his arms and caressed the hard lines of his chest all the way down to his semi-erect cock. Probably down his legs, too, but her gaze didn't make it that far.

Her dedication was rewarded when he hardened fully.

"Ria," Mehl groaned. "If you keep staring at me like that, we won't make it to the soaking pool."

Did they need to? Her hot, sensitive skin prickled with desire, and the ache between her thighs built into longing. But he simply stood there, staring down at her through slitted eyes. If he didn't touch her soon, she would go mad. Unless she acted first, of course. Before he realized her intent, she wrapped her hand around his cock, stroking from base to tip.

Then she let him go.

His breath hissed out. "Ria…"

"We're both clean now. You promised me relief for my

tension after we bathed, didn't you?" She slid her arms around his neck and rubbed her body against his. "It seems I'm really tense. Should I go find my own ease?"

Only that, and he capitulated.

"Far be it for me to neglect you," he murmured, gathering her into his arms.

Her skin tingled and burned as Mehl caressed his way down her back, pausing to cup her bottom before he bent slightly to grip her thighs. Then suddenly, he boosted her up, and she was more than happy to wrap her legs around his waist. At the feel of his hard length settling against her folds, she whimpered.

He chuckled against the side of her neck. "Are you sure you have the energy to do this? You'll have to ride me in this position, love. I'll not brace you against the stone wall for fear I'd hurt you."

Although his words sounded doubtful, one of his hands slid from her bottom and up the crease of her thigh. Mehl shifted his cock slightly, and his finger brushed alongside her clit. Sudden pleasure seared her blood, forcing a yelp from her lips. With a wicked little chuckle, Mehl stroked her in earnest, his finger sliding over her nub as though he'd been born for the task.

Her arms went taut around his shoulders, and her vision hazed over. As the first wave crashed over her, she couldn't hold back a scream. But it wasn't enough. Nearly frantic, she pushed her hips back against his hold, but she couldn't manage the leverage to get him inside her. "I need..."

He lifted her until his cock was lined up at her entrance. "Are you sure you—"

She impaled herself on his length, cutting off his words. *So good.* Her head fell back as she worked herself down, her body yielding bit by bit to his. It was shocking, the way he felt so perfect. He and Toren...each king had their own place in her body and heart. Unique but the same. Now that she could have them both, she truly knew.

Mehl kissed his way down her neck and then ran his tongue around her sensitive nipple. "I love the taste of you."

Ria dug her fingers into his hair and claimed his lips with hers. Then she moved, savoring the feel of him. His length inside her. His hands gentle and supportive where he held her. His body hot and hard against her. And she took him as she pleased. Fast. Slow. Fast again. Until finally, they cried out together, Mehl's hands trembling around her thighs as he spilled within her. Her body went lax against his.

"I love you," she whispered against his chest.

Mehl twitched beneath her, and her heart slammed with the fear that she'd said something wrong. But he kissed the sensitive spot beneath her ear. "I love you, too, Ria."

"And me?"

At the sound of Toren's voice, Ria glanced over her shoulder, and her breath caught at the sight of him. Strong, gorgeous—and just that little bit vulnerable. "Of course I love you," she said, the warmth in her heart spilling out until she melted with it. "I love you both equally. Always."

"Good," Toren said, his tension visibly easing. He stepped close, and his chest at her back sparked her desire again despite how sated she'd just felt. "Since I'd hoped to share my own love with you."

"Sex isn't love," she gasped as Mehl stirred within her again.

"That wasn't what I meant," Toren replied. "But it can be a satisfying way to show the emotion."

When Mehl pulled out, she whimpered at the emptiness, but she didn't have to bear it for long. As Mehl claimed her breast with his hot mouth, Toren slipped into her from behind. Ria shivered from the intense, almost overwhelming, pleasure of being cherished between them, but this time, she was happy to give up control.

And her kings absolutely made it worth her while.

SOMEWHERE BELOW THEM, the courtiers were gathered in the dining room, pretending to enjoy the nightly meal, but Toren was perfectly happy to be in bed rather than among them. Their absence at the High Table would have the rumors flying, of course. But with Mehl curled against his back and Ria nestled against his front, what did he care? He'd been through too much to leave such perfection as this.

Thankfully, it hadn't taken long to write out the line of succession, including the order of the cousins who might take his place if his child—or children—didn't outlive him. Though he hadn't had any hope of disqualifying Ber, he'd long contemplated that very thing, so the list had been easy. The slowest part had been the rules regarding the passing of power, particularly in verifying the honesty of the next-in-line, but he'd left room to amend that part of the document later.

Better to have something adequate now than to have nothing at all.

As his reward for completing the task quickly, he'd been lucky enough to reach the bathing chamber just as Ria and Mehl reached their climaxes. Gods, what a beautiful sight. How had he managed to find two nearly perfect mates? In his entire life, he couldn't have done anything spectacular enough to warrant it.

"Does your mind never cease?" Mehl muttered against his shoulder.

Toren smiled against Ria's hair. "When I'm sleeping. Usually."

"If you're not yet exhausted, we could—"

A knock interrupted the words. Toren merely glared at the door, but Mehl tensed behind him. *"What is it?"* Toren sent his husband.

"Shouldn't Feref be supervising dinner?"

An excellent point—even in their absence, the chamberlain ensured court dinners ran smoothly. Could Mery have returned, then? Toren did a quick mental probe and found that it was indeed Feref standing outside the bedroom door. Sighing, he disentangled himself from his spouses and sat up. Feref couldn't see him, but if there was a problem, Toren would rather confront it upright.

"What is it?" he sent the chamberlain. *"You are not normally here at this hour."*

Worry tinged Feref's reply. *"You and King Mehl will need quick preparation, for you'll want to go downstairs at once. Sir Macoe wishes to make a few arrests before the courtiers finish their meals."*

Toren shoved his hair out of his face, but unfortunately, visual clarity did not bring mental understanding. *"The captain of the guard intends to arrest nobles, yet he went to you instead of me or Mehl? If I didn't believe in both of your loyalty..."*

"He, ah...tried to reach you telepathically earlier, but you did not respond to the mental nudge," Feref explained. *"It seems he completed his interrogation of the latest prisoners earlier than he'd anticipated."*

Wincing, Toren tried to recall if he'd detected Macoe's attempt at contact, but no, he'd noticed nothing. Not only had he been occupied with more pleasurable pursuits, his magical senses were a little blunted while his energy was still renewing. Ah, well. It was unfortunate, but hardly a catastrophe. He gestured at Mehl to follow him as he stood.

"It seems Macoe has discovered something," Toren said. "Ria, if we are to allow rumors to flow as they will, you should rest here. But it isn't my intention to exclude you from important matters. I'll happily abandon that plan if you wish to accompany us."

She rolled into the spot where he'd just been and curled the blanket around herself. "No. I would rather remain here, especially since the rumors are to our benefit."

Toren nodded, and Mehl leaned over to kiss her brow. She wiggled a little, burrowing more deeply into the covers. Toren smiled. Her eyes were already half-slitted with exhaustion, and he couldn't help but watch for one precious moment as she let herself drift off. Then the two of them quietly left their wife to sleep. They had gods-knew-what to prepare for, and it would take Feref's particular magic to get them ready to appear downstairs in time.

There were already several servants waiting in the dressing room. Resigning himself to discomfort, Toren allowed Feref and the servants to spring into action. As soon as a formal robe was dropped over his head, the worst of it started, three servants descending upon him to twist and pull his hair into braids. But he'd long ago learned to block out the twinges of pain.

Nor did he pay attention to the rest of the clothing and accessories the chamberlain selected, not even the crown being affixed to his head. Instead, he connected mentally with Macoe. *"Forgive me, Captain. My magic was consumed during our spell, and I needed rest to recover it. I didn't sense your attempt at communication."*

Better not to mention what form his "rest" had taken.

"Feref thought that might be the case," Macoe replied. *"The*

servant, Col, broke first, but Rencis made his own confession soon after. Both claim to have been hired by Duke Hesslefyn, Col through Miss Kleren Ogewn and Rencis through Lord Eorge Poberie."

Toren's brows rose in surprise. That a sitting duke was implicated in treason should have been the most shocking, but Toren struggled to move beyond Kleren. As House Ogewn was quite small and held little power, two of their four daughters had sought work in the most prestigious positions they could find. The eldest as a governess for the Poberie family at their estate near the Centoi border—and Kleren here in the palace as the royal seamstress.

Kleren had taken leave three months prior, presumably to visit with that same sister. *Near Centoi.* Though there was a chance that both Col and Rencis had thought to take advantage of her departure to implicate her in this crime, Toren suspected that was not the case. For one thing, the two families had both been listed on Ber's note—as had Col. Only Rencis was a surprise in that regard.

"Your Majesty?" Macoe sent.

"Sorry. I was debating the matter." Toren tapped his fingers against the smooth fabric of his robe. *"I've seen Lord Eorge around the palace, but Kleren is not here. Is there another Ogewn present at dinner?"*

"Baron Ogewn himself."

Toren smiled. *"Good. Mehl and I will join you shortly. Be prepared to arrest Duke Hesslefyn and Lord Eorge. Put them on the second level of the dungeon. Baron Ogewn and any other members of these three families present at dinner will be detained in the Guest Towers while we investigate their possible involvement. All others from these three houses who are currently outside the palace are ordered to remain under house arrest until their names are cleared. The servants on my brother's list should also be detained."*

"Very well, Your Majesty."

As Feref held out a long, green overrobe, Toren closed the connection with Macoe and then stood. The time for watching was over. Confining these families in the Guest Towers, well-known for housing nobles who were under suspicion of treason, would make a pointed statement that would ripple across the kingdom.

There would be no more reprieve.

CHAPTER 69

A Dinner to Remember

Though they'd yet to reach the dining room doors, Mehl knew by the lull in sound that dessert was being served. It was always like this near the end of the meal, when the best of the gossip had been dispensed and the weight of prolonged formality began to chafe. Inevitably, the already quiet courtiers would fall nearly silent as the servants swept away the previous course while others brought the final plates.

Tonight, a grim-faced Sir Macoe stood in front of the doors, two guards at his back and others waiting along the wall. "Your Majesties," Sir Macoe said softly. "Shall we?"

Toren gave a tight nod. "Absolutely."

Mehl settled his hand on the jeweled hilt of the dagger at his belt—more ostentatious than he preferred but less notice-able at formal events. After the earlier attack, not even Feref had protested the inclusion of a weapon. Mehl refused to waste time taking out a concealed knife if more trouble occurred.

"I'm prepared," Mehl said.

Sir Macoe nodded. Then snapping to attention, he pivoted on his heel and gave the order to advance. The two closest guards opened the heavy double doors, and the other warriors marched in after. Unlike usual, the captain entered in front of Toren and Mehl, only stepping out of the way once the guards were in place.

After a brief hush, the room erupted into sound. Startled cries punctuated the scrape and squeal of wood-on-marble as several of the nobles jerked to their feet. No one seemed certain what to do, since the monarchs never entered the dining room last. *Never.* As he and Toren strode up the central runner, some of the courtiers fumbled to their knees near their chairs. Others lowered their heads toward their plates, one poor man smashing his nose into the creamy dessert.

Total chaos.

Near the dais holding the High Table, Mehl spotted Duke Hesslefyn at the head of one of the closest tables, as befitted his rank. He kept his head carefully bowed, and in profile, his expression seemed properly neutral. Ah, but his posture was so tense that a servant could balance a plate on his shoulder, and his hands were fisted in his lap. The duke must suspect that he was in trouble.

Mehl and Toren stepped onto the dais, but they didn't circle the table to take their seats. Instead, they spun to face the nobles, who froze into their awkward positions as though they'd been enchanted into statues. *Someone should paint this unprecedented scene,* Mehl thought irreverently before he forced his attention back to the task at hand. He needed to keep an eye on the families of the accused.

"Resume your seats if you're not there already," Toren snapped, and the bite to his tone had the kneeling courtiers scurrying to obey. "And for the sake of the gods, get your faces out of your food."

The nobles lifted their heads, a few subtly wiping away traces of cream. Not the Hesslefyn family, of course. They straightened gracefully, and the expressions they turned toward the High Table were a lesson in noble politeness. Mehl noted the duke's continued tension, but the other members of their House appeared at ease.

As was Baron Ogewn, though his youngest daughter had her napkin clenched in her fist. One table down, Lord Eorge sat pale and frozen beside his mother, Countess Poberie. Mehl suspected that neither parent knew of their children's perfidy, yet they would suffer all the same. What had Duke Hesslefyn —and ultimately King Ryenil—promised to turn these young nobles to treason? Even money and power were useless when stability failed.

"A grievous plot has been uncovered this day," Toren began coldly, and for the first time since they'd done the inheritance spell, Mehl sensed a pulse of power from him. "The healer Vesset was caught with foul poisons, ones that have wrought much harm. Some of you witnessed the foiled attack outside the throne room before the healer's initial trial was to be held."

Tension froze the room so thoroughly that not even whispers broke out at that.

"A servant and a mage were apprehended and have identified their co-conspirators in their treason." At Toren's words, guards began to march down the row of tables, drawing gasps and flinches. Somewhat normal, even amongst the innocent. "Everyone in this room has sworn their loyalty to Llyalia and to the Eyamiri blood that rules it. Even so, some of you have betrayed your vows and chosen the path of treachery."

Not even fear could stop the whispers at that, and as the guards passed, some of the nobles let out little whimpers. But there was a difference in the body language of a person afraid of being falsely accused and a true traitor who well knew their own crimes. Such as Duke Hesslefyn's stone-tight posture and wide eyes. Or the tears slipping silently down Miss Ogewn's unnaturally pale cheeks.

Or Lord Eorge's shaking hand, which knocked over his wine glass rather than gripped it.

As if in slow motion, Countess Poberie turned an aghast look from the wine pooling red across the tablecloth to her son's face, and horror crept across her expression just as two guards came to a halt behind his seat. "What have you done?" she cried.

Lord Eorge merely shook his head.

When two more guards halted behind Baron Ogwen and his daughter, the baron startled. "Ah, you must be mistaken. I..."

At the sight of his daughter's face, his mouth snapped shut.

But it was the circle of guards who halted at attention behind and around Duke Hesslefyn that returned the room to deathly silence. Mehl watched his family the most carefully, for any insight he could gain about the powerful House would be of benefit. And of the seven, not counting the duke, two exhibited the nervous tension of the guilty—Lord Welen, first-born son and heir, and Lady Lene, the duchess.

To Mehl's surprise, Lady Gartren bore the same expression of shock as her other siblings. He'd expected her involvement based on her nasty attitude toward Ria, but unless she hid it well, that didn't appear to be the case. Indeed, as the entire court watched, fury flashed in her eyes, and she glared at her parents.

"There must be a misunderstanding," she said tightly. "For my father would not allow our noble House to be blighted by such a terrible stain."

"This latest insult was one too many," Lady Lene blurted out. "To pass you and your sister over for some common—"

The duchess pressed her lips together before she could finish that thought, but it was too late. Mehl's anger surged at the insult she'd been about to deliver. Still, he kept it in check.

Toren, however…

Mehl sent a quick prayer of thanks that his husband's energy levels hadn't fully recovered, because if it had, the fury-driven wave of power would have caused true harm.

"You dare to speak so of my wife?" Toren's glare shot across the room like an ice-tipped arrow. "She is a hard-working and loyal citizen of this kingdom, more worthy than those of you who fail to do your jobs in the name of chasing glory. Tell me, what great harm has the royal House dealt to you, Duchess? We've enacted no harsh taxes and demanded no tribute. There are many daughters here whom we did not wed, and that is no slight. If you've chosen treason, it is for one reason alone. Power. And you haven't even realized that it would eat you if you gained it."

There was a starkness to those final words that twisted Mehl's heart, but he knew it wouldn't make an impact on most of the courtiers seated below. In truth, even he wouldn't have understood before he'd become king. The crowns and elaborate clothes, the deference and ceremony—all were a velvet-lined trap, as cleverly devised as the puzzle box he'd received from Ber.

Those who most wanted in would be caught the hardest.

As Toren scanned the nobles sitting so still in their seats, he struggled to control the anger currently making a shaky mess of his insides. He'd spent several centuries watching over these people, guiding and ruling in equal measure, and he'd trained to do so for many centuries before that. But until this moment, he'd never been so tempted to turn around and walk away.

What was the value in serving faithfully, giving up much of his autonomy and freedom to protect those who would betray him? He would have met a sooner but clearer end as a tyrant who'd done whatever he wished. In such a case, he would have understood the nobles' actions, even. But turning traitor for power's sake alone...the pain of it cut deeper than he'd expected.

Ah, but you did *do what you wished,* his inner voice chided him.

Toren released a sigh only Mehl would hear. No matter where his anger carried him in the moment, he couldn't deny that he *had* done exactly what he'd wanted—and that was to care for his people. It wasn't his fault that these few nobles were easily corrupted, and he wouldn't wish to mimic a single one of them in their perfidy. Though betrayal was inevitable, it didn't have to change him.

Yet he couldn't show mercy for those who were truly guilty, not and maintain order. "Duke Hesslefyn and Lord Eorge Poberie are to be arrested immediately, and Baron Ogwen and his family are to be confined in the most stringent Guest Tower. Any member of these Houses currently present are to be held in the lesser Guest Towers, and all others will be under immediate house arrest wherever they may be."

Toren waited patiently for the gasps, cries, and exclamations to die down before he continued. "All of them will be questioned beneath a High Mage's most stringent truth spell. As I will not paint an entire family guilty for the actions of a few, the innocent will be granted their freedom and allowed to resume their places in society. Those truly responsible will be brought before the court for final judgment within the week. I suspect more than one execution will follow."

This time?

Silence.

Only for a moment, of course. Duke Hesslefyn leaped to his feet, half-spinning before the tip of a sword pressed against his neck. "I object to this unreasonable decree, Your Majesty," the duke shouted, the effect somewhat lessened since he couldn't turn his head to meet Toren's eyes.

"Unreasonable?" Toren asked smoothly. "Both of the men who attempted to force their way into the throne room claim to be hired by you to kill me. Would a reasonable person let you go in light of such an accusation?"

"Why would a duke of the realm do such a thing?" Hesslefyn's eyes flicked toward the duchess. "My *wife* might have been upset about paltry concerns like weddings, but *I* would never care enough about that for treason. And to pay a servant or a low-class mage like Rencis is beneath my station as—"

"I never said the mage's name," Toren interrupted.

Duke Hesslefyn sputtered, his face leaching of all color. But before he could gather himself enough for another useless lie, a new voice cut over the whispers. "He paid me the money owed Col!" Miss Ogwen cried. "But I was only handling matters for Kleren while she was away. I didn't know what it was for until I saw the attack. Your Majesties, I beg your mercy, especially for my father. You needn't lock him up, because he knows nothing of this. Even I thought this was a matter between lovers. Col might have seen Kleren leaving the sitting room with the duke that day, and—"

"Lovers?" Lady Lene shrieked. "You mean I committed treason for a man who isn't even *faithful?*"

Good gods above. Toren's fingers itched from the urge to pinch his nose. Or rub his temples. Instead, he had to ignore the carefully averted gazes of more than one guilty looking lady and focus on maintaining order.

"Thank you for your confession, Lady Lene." Toren's smile held nothing resembling humor. "And Miss Ogwen. Unfortunately for House Ogwen, mercy only goes so far in the face of such heavy crimes. Your family must all be subjected to the truth spell. However, if your father is as innocent as you say, he will be free to resume his current place. Your case is more complicated, but it will be heard fairly."

At the prompting of the guards, the members of all three houses stood. A white-lipped Countess Poberie watched in silence as her son was bound in chains, and she offered no protest or defense as she was directed to join the others heading to the Guest Towers. Toren found her reaction curious, since she'd presumably hired the eldest Ogwen daughter as a governess. Was Eorge responsible for the plot, or was the Earl involved, too?

Soon enough, they would find out.

CHAPTER 70

CEREMONIES

Two weeks. Two weeks of truth spells and trials and turmoil. If Mehl could have pummeled someone, he would have, but that kind of conduct would be unbecoming of a king. Or so Toren had reminded him just before they'd entered the throne room for this final bit of ceremony. Still, the desire to punch something—or someone—remained. The surge of pain from Toren with each charge intoned by Feref caused Mehl's nails to dig ever harder into his palms.

He was beginning to regret not recommending execution for the lot of them.

Aside from Kleren Ogwen, the only nobles to have dealings with King Ryenil were the duke and his heir, Welen. It seemed that the king had promised Lord Hesslefyn gold, land, and a title in Centoi—in addition to his current holdings—for helping the exiled prince Ber claim the throne. Although Hesslefyn had paid Lord Eorge Poberie to carry out many of his underhanded dealings, the young lord hadn't known the reasons behind his actions. Eorge had been motivated mostly by greed.

The duchess and her eldest daughter had participated out of spite—and with different goals. They'd hoped to get rid of Ria and convince Toren to marry the daughter. Only if that hadn't worked would they have welcomed Ber, though their hopes of joining the royal family must have been temporarily dashed by the announcement of his marriage to Tes. Mehl didn't want to think about their happiness at the princess's supposed death.

The actions of all four merged neatly enough to create a connection between them and Vesset—who actually *didn't* work with Duke Hesslefyn. Vesset's collusion with Ryenil went back much further, before the death of High Queen Ileshe. In fact, the duke hadn't been involved whatsoever in her murder. Lord Hesslefyn hadn't even known why he'd been ordered to intercede if Vesset was captured, but complying with the Centoi king's command had inadvertently solidified a link with the healer—in rumors, at least.

And so the whispers circled the court.

House Hesslefyn sought a path to gain the throne, by marriage or force. They plotted for years and were even prepared to invite Prince Ber to return if it increased their power. And they tried to get rid of Ria and any possible heir. Vesset was caught attempting to poison Ria, wasn't he? The duke sent assassins after Toren, Mehl, and Ria to hide his crimes. Terrible family, resorting to treason. What were they thinking?

No wonder the innocent members of House Hesslefyn had fled the palace as soon as they'd been freed from the Guest Tower.

The only information sealed away—magically, in fact—was King Ryenil's involvement. That would come out when they were ready to confront the Centoi king. In the meantime, they needed to deliver the formal sentences for those they could. Mehl suppressed a shudder. They'd discussed the benefits and ramifications of each possible punishment for longer than he wanted to remember.

As Feref read the last of the charges, Mehl stole a glance at Toren, who stared impassively at the accused kneeling at the base of the dais. But his husband was in no way inured to the proceedings. With their link, he could feel Toren's pain like his own heartbeat. His husband might never admit the emotional cost of these plots, but Mehl wouldn't forget.

"I am deeply grieved by all that has been uncovered in this court," Toren announced. "By the very oaths you took in service to your titles, you should all be executed for plotting treason against your rightful king." Inevitably, murmurs sped through the room at that. "However, I cannot countenance so much death."

Mehl wanted nothing more than to take his husband's hand, but he couldn't.

"Firstly, Baron Ogwen's youngest daughter, Elrie, may keep her noble status but will remain under house arrest for one year, longer if deemed necessary. Duke and Duchess Hesslefyn, their two children, Lord Eorge Poberie, and Miss Kleren Ogwen are all stripped of any titles or claims to nobility, now and forevermore."

The former duke dared to scowl up at Toren. "You're removing my House from its rightful place?"

Toren's breath hissed out.

"We are not," Mehl said before his husband did something he would regret—like crush the man under a wave of energy. "Lady Gartren will become Duchess Hesslefyn, although all vassal Houses will be removed from her control until the House reestablishes its honor. If it ever manages such a feat."

It pained Mehl to grant such a rank to the lady who'd been rude to Ria, but in a way, it was its own penalty. Decades would likely pass before Lady Gartren dared return to court, and for decades—if not centuries—after that, she would be subjected to the kinds of whispers and stares she'd once perpetuated. If nothing else, perhaps she would learn humility.

"In addition to the punishment already delivered, I decree this," Toren said, his voice whipping across the throne room with a definite bite. "The former Duke Hesslefyn is sentenced to die for commanding the attempted murder of the High King, King Mehl, and Princess Ria. Since the rest of his family were unaware of such dark intentions, they will be spared such a final fate. The former duchess and their two guilty children, along with Eorge Poberie and Kleren Ogwen, will be imprisoned in the dungeon for fifty years and then exiled permanently from Llyalia. The healer, Vesset, will be imprisoned for the remainder of his life for following such inexcusable orders."

A few heartbeats' silence was broken by a gasp, then a growing stream of whispers. Only Mehl and Ria knew how Toren had agonized over the decision to order the duke's execution, especially since Vesset's had to wait until the full truth was revealed about King Ryenil. But no matter who Hesslefyn worked for, he had willingly ordered an assassination attempt.

No rank could be allowed to shield him from that.

"This is not a day for celebration." Toren stood, Mehl following a breath later. His husband waited while the nobles sank to their knees. "I truly am grieved, for myself and for Llyalia. However, my hope is that such pointless treachery will be swept away to herald a time of greater prosperity and happiness for all. In fact, I bid you all return to your holdings to ensure stability in the wake of such shocking events. Court will be suspended for two weeks at a minimum."

Mehl gestured at Sir Macoe, who ordered the guards to remove the prisoners—the former duke with some force. Then without a word, he and Toren exited the throne room, whispers swelling behind them like a wave. But from the tone of them, Mehl suspected all would be well soon enough.. The courtiers' energy would shift to the coming power struggle, many seeking to claim the influence lost by House Hesslefyn.

In other words, business as usual.

Weary to his soul, Toren dropped onto the sofa in their sitting room and tipped his head back, closing his eyes. What kind of king was he? What legacy would he leave? Surely not a good one. History would depict him as brutal at the rate he was going, and that would only get worse when he was able to try and execute Vesset for his mother's murder.

The sofa jostled beneath him, and a warm weight curled against his side. "Ria."

"I'm sorry I couldn't be there with you," she said softly.

Toren nestled his head against hers. "I'm not. It was a terrible affair."

"Your judgment was a fair one, love," she insisted, her arm curling around his waist. "I'm still surprised you went so easy on the duchess. Mehl said she confessed to treason at dinner."

"She did," Mehl said, apparently finished changing out of his formal robes. "Everyone at court knows you could have had the lot of them executed for plotting against you. The laws explicitly allow that."

True, yet it stung all the same.

"When will the sentence be carried out?" Ria asked.

"Within the week," Toren answered, opening his eyes. Mehl stood over them with a concerned frown. "We were supposed to have our wedding a week after that, but now..."

"There has been no time to plan, and it's not a great time,

besides," Ria finished. She turned her head until she could kiss his cheek. "So we'll delay it. In a couple of months, it'll be obvious that I'm with child, but we knew our deception couldn't last forever. I would definitely rather alter my dress than try to have a celebration a few days after an execution."

Toren sighed, but this time with relief. She'd been concerned about waiting too long for their wedding because of her pregnancy, so he'd worried that she would be upset. Of course, *he* wasn't precisely happy about the delay itself. He wanted her by their side always and in all ways. Without question. But they deserved a wedding unmarred by such ugliness. It would be far better to clear away as much of the darkness as they could before starting anew with their fully united lives.

So wait they would.

Two months later

Ria smoothed the cream fabric over her growing waist and smiled in contentment. At first, she'd been worried about the delay in their wedding, but now, it felt perfect. She'd had time to settle into the palace, and she'd learned a great deal about protocol during quiet afternoons with Ryssa. But best of all? For the first time, it would be obvious to everyone that Ria carried Toren's heir.

She was tired of hiding behind the careful cut of her dresses, and all three of them had agreed that they could no longer continue the farce. If they'd failed to oust any of King Ryenil's spies, the wedding would be confirmation that the Eyamiri line would continue. But neither Mehl nor Toren thought even a remaining spy would dare to be so bold as to accost her at this point. The court was on high alert, and the constant power struggle taking place would ensure that anyone acting suspicious would be exposed just to earn Toren's favor.

"Are you ready?" Ryssa asked from behind her.

Smiling, Ria turned. "Yes. Are you sure you wish to walk all that way with me?"

Almost three months further along, the princess was already large with child. But a rare smile crossed her face as she nodded. "I would see you happily wed, my friend."

"Even though you're not particularly fond of my spouses?"

Ryssa sighed. "They are good men. I merely can't stop worrying over what happened with Ber. There was something off about it all, and I'm well aware there are secrets you're all keeping regarding the matter. Well-intentioned, I suspect, but it bothers me nonetheless."

"I'm sorry." Ria gripped her friend's hands. "I can only say that none of us are happy about the situation with Prince Ber. We regard you as family. *All* of us do."

The smile settled more fully onto Ryssa's face. "Thank you. Truly. Now, I believe we have a long trek ahead. I realize that a *forest* temple requires going outside, but it would've been nice if the early Eyamiri royals had created an indoor wedding chapel, too."

Ria laughed. "I can't disagree."

Despite her growing size and the gawking nobles bowing most of the way, Ria ended up enjoying the walk, especially once they reached the gardens. There, Toren and Mehl waited beside the temple path, courtiers lining the broad, cobblestone trail like colorful flowers. She left Ryssa's side and stepped between the kings, whose eyes gleamed with happiness as they all linked arms. Then the three of them continued the long walk to the beautiful temple made of living trees and stone.

It was somehow more and less intimate than the carriage

ride they'd taken through the streets that morning so they could acknowledge the people's joy. True, fervent joy, best she could tell. Though Toren had feared that ordering an execution would mar his reputation, his overall fairness in confirming who was guilty had done the opposite. The common citizens in particular were pleased, for even a powerful duke hadn't been spared because of his rank.

The courtiers, of course, were more wary than pleased, but most genuinely liked Toren—or at least approved of how he ruled. As such, the glances toward her belly and subsequent whispers had a satisfied air to them. Not that Ria fooled herself into thinking the approval was for her, though none of the courtiers would be foolish enough to express their dislike openly.

Finally, she, Toren, and Mehl passed through the grand archway and into the temple, where only priestesses waited. The ancient trees here circled a broad clearing, and arching stone columns stretched upward like fingers between the trunks. They met overhead, a silver chain descending from the central point to hold a globe that glowed like a star.

For a moment of purest vanity, all Ria could think was how perfect they fit in this space. Mehl in silver, Toren in royal green, and her in cream, all embroidered with vines, leaves, and stars—they could have been born to walk into this sacred place together. Yet none of them would have been here now if she hadn't spontaneously accepted that little packet of dye.

A miracle, that.

Ria couldn't remember a single word she said during the ceremony. The reverence in Mehl's touch as he took her hand? The contented joy in Toren's eyes as he brushed a kiss across her lips? Those were the things worth remembering—though she wouldn't have said so to the priestesses. But if the gods had brought her and the kings together, They would surely understand.

Love was what mattered most, after all.

Thank you so much for reading The Fae Kings' Bargain. I hope you've enjoyed getting to know Ria, Toren, and Mehl.

Want to continue with The Fae Queen's Revenge before it's released in ebook format? You can read Tes's and Ber's story now on Kindle Vella. They are currently lighting up Season 2 of the Vella serial, releasing each Friday.

ABOUT THE AUTHOR

Willow McCain is the alter ego of USA TODAY Bestselling author Bethany Adams, author of The Return of the Elves series. As Willow, she writes steamy fantasy romance serials full of love, drama, and heat. Don't want to wait for the e-book sequel? Head over to Kindle Vella to read the latest season as she writes it.

- facebook.com/authorwillowmccain
- patreon.com/bethanyadams
- bookbub.com/authors/willow-mccain
- amazon.com/Willow-Mccain/e/B0BKTHBKQ6

ALSO BY WILLOW MCCAIN

AS WILLOW MCCAIN

The Blood of Eyamiri, Seasons 1 and 2 (Kindle Vella Serial)

The Fae Kings' Bargain

AS BETHANY ADAMS

The Return of the Elves Series

The Mage's Curse (Currently in Realm of Darkness)

www.ingramcontent.com/pod-product-compliance
Lightning Source LLC
Chambersburg PA
CBHW060936190726
48286CB00005B/1298